ON THE FERRY TO Skye

J.A. FORDE

Also by J.A. Forde

The Love Along the Way Series

On a Flight to Sydney
On the Slopes of Tahoe
On the Ferry to Skye

Standalone Stories

Afterglow ~ a short story in the Heartstrings & Haunts Anthology

Author's Note

My writing contains mature themes and explicit language and is therefore intended for audiences 18+. On the Ferry to Skye is a fade-to-black romance with implied sexual intimacy; however, no explicit scenes are depicted on the page. This story deals with several issues that could be potentially triggering, such as teenage pregnancy, terminal illness of a grandparent, and death of a grandparent. Your mental health is paramount, so please protect your peace and well-being if these are themes you are sensitive to.

This book is in part a love letter to the Scottish Highlands, a place that holds a special place in my heart. I hope that I have conveyed that love on these pages and have represented Scotland and its people in a way that showcases how beautiful and incredible this country is. Cluaran may not be a real town on the Isle of Skye, but I hope you will feel at home there. It is also my hope that those who do call Scotland home will feel that I represented them and their country with care and respect in these pages.

Happy reading!

To the man who's written me a box full of love letters over the years, this one's for you.

SCOTS & GAELIC TERMS

Lass – a young woman or girl

Lad – a young man or boy

Aye – yes

Wellies – Wellington boots, rain boots

Shinty – a traditional Scottish sport that closely resembles field hockey

Bonny – pretty or beautiful

Dram – a serving of whisky

M'eudail (may-dall) – my dear, my darling

Mo nighean (moh nee-uhn) – my girl, my lass, my daughter

Mo chridhe (moh chree-uh) – my heart

Tha thu bòidheach (ha oo boy-och) – you are beautiful

Mo leannan (moh len-ann) – my sweetheart

Tha gaol agam ort (ha g-ill ack-am orsht) – I love you

Slàinte (slanj-a) – cheers

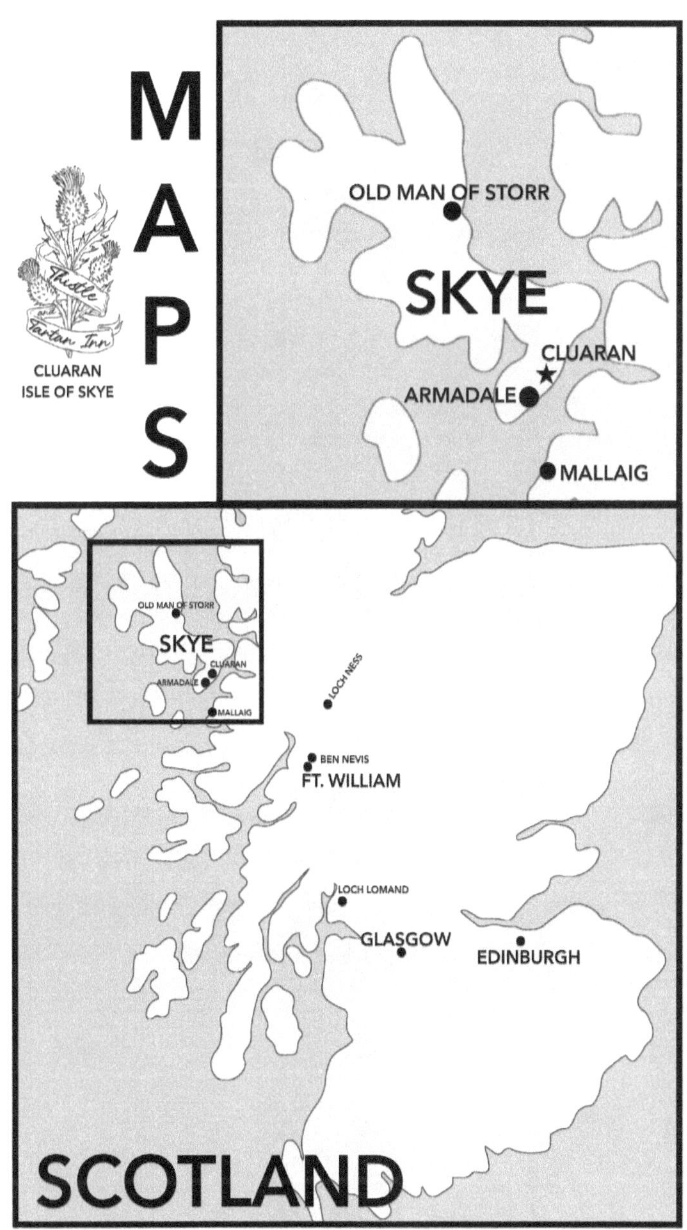

MAPS
Thistle and Tartan Inn
CLUARAN
ISLE OF SKYE
OLD MAN OF STORR
SKYE
CLUARAN
ARMADALE
MALLAIG
OLD MAN OF STORR
SKYE
CLUARAN
ARMADALE
MALLAIG
LOCH NESS
BEN NEVIS
FT. WILLIAM
LOCH LOMAND
GLASGOW
EDINBURGH
SCOTLAND

PROLOGUE

JAMIE — TEN YEARS AGO

Her grandparents told me not to bother looking for her. That she'd moved on from our summers on the Isle of Skye. That I'm better off without her. That they are too.

But they wouldn't tell me why. They wouldn't tell me *anything*.

What am I supposed to do? Spend my final summer on Skye without her? Pretend last summer didn't happen? Pretend I haven't spent this entire year regretting the way I left things? Never speak to her again?

No. I can't do any of those things.

Even if our years-long friendship is damaged beyond repair, the last time I saw her cannot be the *last* time. I refuse to accept that. I can't allow the shame of what I said to haunt me forever. I have to at least attempt to set this right. Even if it won't matter—even if nothing changes—at least I'll have tried.

I make a conscious effort to look right before left, then step off the curb to cross the street. The Green Gables Pub looms ahead of me with its whitewashed stone upper floors standing out against the luscious green of the street level. It's her parents' pub. The one named after her mum's favorite story—the same story that inspired *her* name. It's also in Glasgow, a five-hour drive from Skye.

It was the first place I thought of to begin my search, but now that I'm here, I'm not entirely sure what to do. Should I go in and hope she just happens to be here? Do I ask for her parents? Will they know why she hasn't talked to me in a year? If so, I wouldn't be surprised if they tell me to leave before I get the chance to see her.

I scrub my sweaty palms down the sides of my thighs, the denim abrasive and rough against my skin, and suck in a deep breath. On my exhale, I wrap my hand around the brass handle of the ornate green door and pull it open. I've never been here before, but she spent years sharing stories of finishing homework in her dad's office and making shortcrust pastry with her mum in the kitchen.

And it's exactly like I imagined.

Music surrounds me in a wave along with the rich aroma of hearty food, making my mouth water. There's something about the smell of a Scottish pub that can't be recreated anywhere else. It smells like home—as it should, considering I practically grew up in one for fourteen years. Well, not in the pub exactly, but the inn it's attached to.

I bypass the empty hostess stand, moving farther into the dim-lit space. A haggard looking barkeep runs a rag over polished mahogany and offers me a wry smile from behind his beard. I could get myself a pint, considering I'm eighteen, but with one goal in mind, I won't be able to enjoy the experience of buying my first legal beer without first getting some answers.

Awkwardness prickles against my skin as I turn on the spot like a top. I know what I'm looking for, but I almost don't expect to find it. I feel like a buoy lost at sea—by definition, I'm where I should be, but I'm untethered and adrift.

The overhead music fades with a crackle of static and the screech of a microphone's feedback, drawing my attention to the stage in the back. To a man sitting on a stool with his guitar. On cue, the patrons of the pub shift, pulled toward the stage and the promise of live music, and a table in the corner appears...

And she's there.

She's *right* there.

Her blonde hair, falling in waves around her shoulders. Brown eyes that I can picture in detail, even if I can't make them out through the gloom. They're rich and warm, inviting and deep. How many times have I looked into those eyes and understood exactly what she was thinking? How many staring contests have I forfeited, just to call best out of three and do it again? How many times did I happily lose myself in them?

What I wouldn't give to be back in my grandparents' old campervan, tartan blanket spread beneath us, rain falling heavy on the roof, the golden flecks in her irises as warm as her skin against mine.

God, I can't believe it. *She's right there.*

Her head falls back on a laugh and my chest constricts. I wish I could hear it. It's a sound I took for granted, and I haven't forgiven myself for that. Not yet... Maybe not ever.

The rest of the table is obscured, so it's only her I see.

But hasn't it *always* been her? Or at least it should've been, but I was just too oblivious and cavalier to see it.

I take a step, and then another, my shoes sticking to the concrete floor. The crowd shifts again, and instead of seeing more of her, I see a guy. Was he the one who made her laugh?

Envy coats my throat, its viscous texture so real I force myself to swallow hard.

It used to be me who made her laugh like that.

When her grandparents said she'd moved on, had they meant she was seeing someone? It would track that he'd be the reason she didn't come back to Skye for one last summer like we'd promised each other. But could this also explain why she hasn't returned a single attempt of mine to contact her?

The musician starts to play and the raucous noise creates more movement in the sea of people, obscuring the corner table completely. Only when it parts a moment later do I see the whole picture for the first time, and it stops me in my tracks.

Somewhere in that moment, the world shifts. I'm sure no one else feels it, but I do. Because the girl I'm in love with—my best friend, my favorite adventure partner—is settling a tiny baby in her arms. And the guy who just made her laugh? He leans over and presses a kiss first to the baby's head and then to hers.

And the smile she gives him? That used to be mine.

Heat climbs up my neck and the smell that moments ago reminded me of home threatens to turn my stomach. All I can think about is getting out of here before she sees me—before she ever knows I was here.

She did move on, just like her grandparents said, and in the most permanent of ways.

As for me being better off without her... I guess only time will tell.

Because right now, I'm not sure I'll ever be able to come back to Scotland knowing she's here, and it's my fault I never really had a chance to have her.

CHAPTER ONE

JAMIE - NOW

The moment the plane's wheels touched the tarmac in Glasgow, a strange mix of anxiety and something like coming home crashed together in my chest.

Ten years.

I haven't been in this country, touched its rich soil and breathed its crisp, damp air, in *ten years*.

I told myself I would come back someday, after enough time had passed. Yet a decade has come and gone, and I never did. Until now.

The sharp ache that pulsed in my chest the day I left—watching the sprawling city, lush mountains, and River Clyde fade away—was echoed today as I watched that same view come back into focus from my window seat.

I didn't think my first time back would be like this, or that I'd be riddled with guilt and a sense of foreboding. If I'm honest with myself, I didn't think of it at all.

But I'm here now, and my numb indifference to this place is thawing as the countryside blurs past my driver's-side window. My heart is being eviscerated too, knowing there's no one to blame but myself if I don't make it in time—if I don't get to say goodbye to him.

I increase the pressure on the gas pedal and push the engine to drive faster. The hospital in Fort William feels too far even with the Land Rover I rented at the airport. It may as well still be oceans away at this rate.

I'm conscious of the fact Gran might never forgive me if I don't make it. That she might not forgive me even if I do. She's never held it against me that I left and didn't come back, but now?

Now, I'm not so sure.

I pull away from those thoughts and let my brain fully seat itself in the drive. It's been ten years since I drove on the left side of the road, and I don't need to add to Gran's load by turning into oncoming traffic.

Since I moved to the States at fourteen, I learned to drive "the American way" and only ever drove here in the summers when I came back to visit... and then not at all.

I feel a kinship in this moment with Breck, my best friend Rory's boyfriend. He's from Australia, and when he visited the States this past winter, he had to figure this out too. I definitely didn't give him enough credit.

The thought of Rory draws my hand to the screen on the dash. Her name sits just below my dad's. I called him when I landed, promising an update after I see Gran and Grandad. I know that his inability to jump on a plane with me is weighing on him. God, I hope I can give him good news.

I tap my finger on her contact, welcoming the distraction.

"This is Rory, please leave a message and I'll get back to you as soon as I can. Have a great day." Her voice rings through the cab of the car, followed by a resounding BEEEEP. I tap the red end button and attempt to calculate the time difference between Scotland and Nevada, but I don't have the brain power to get it right.

I'll text her from the hospital and tell her to call me when she lands.

I should be there right now, waiting at the airport for her to arrive from Australia. I should be there to hear all about her trip—about how she got the guy and how Breck is moving to Tahoe as soon as he can get his and his daughter Willow's visas in order. But as fate would have it, as she boarded her plane for home, I boarded a plane for Scotland with no idea when I'll be going back.

I run a hand through my hair and glance at myself in the rearview mirror. I'm an absolute mess. The auburn strands stick up at odd angles, as opposed to the neatly gelled swoop I usually have them in. My beard is unruly, feeling thicker against my fingers. That might be a good thing though, considering it's a bit cooler here than back home. Of course, that depends on the day; Lake Tahoe can be as finicky with its weather as Scotland.

I put my contacts in at the airport, so I can't even hide the dark circles under my eyes or the way they stand out against my pale freckled cheeks. I look exhausted. I *am* exhausted.

I've never been very good at sleeping on airplanes, and with the constant fear that I wouldn't make it to the hospital in time, I was on edge through every moment of my flight.

I tap my fingers on the steering wheel and turn onto the bridge over Loch Leven. *Twenty minutes.* I speed over the bridge, the water rushing beneath me and the stretch of land on either side passing by in a shock of green. I can't enjoy any of it. Not yet. Not until I see him.

I finally swing into the car park outside the hospital and thank my lucky stars I didn't hit a lick of traffic. I grab my messenger bag from the seat next to me and nearly rip the door off its hinges in my haste.

I sprint for the entrance and the door slides open, revealing a woman sitting at a desk just inside.

My frantic expression catches her attention. "Sir? Are you alright? Can I help you find someone?"

My gaze swings around the room, but I don't see a map or directory. "I'm here for Angus Murray," I rush out. "My gran said they were in room 1235, but I don't know which way that is." What's left of my Scottish accent tends to creep out in moments of panic, but with the way she's eyeing me, I don't think she's clocked that I'm from here.

The woman shifts some paperwork and checks a chart printed with names and room numbers. The system seems archaic. I shift on my feet and look around again, as if Gran will pop out and lead the way.

"Aye, that's right. You'll want to take this first left and then a right. Head down that hall, and toward the end you'll find the room on the left-hand side."

"Thank you," I say over my shoulder as I bolt away without a second glance.

Left. Right. The sound of my feet slapping against the tiles echoes in the quiet space. Down the hall. 1235 on the left.

Murray is written on a small board beside the door. I made it. I'm here. I drag my damp palms down the legs of my pants, then knock lightly as I push open the door. I don't make it more than a foot inside before a grey-haired pixie of a woman engulfs me, trapping my arms firmly at my sides.

Gran.

Everything in me softens. Relaxes in her presence. Clicks into place.

"*Jameson.*" She breathes my full name against my chest. She's always been tiny, but she feels smaller than ever as I let her hold me.

"Gran," I say, and my voice nearly breaks on the word. All the emotion and strain and unknowns combine like a tidal wave held at bay by a dam that just broke. There's nothing left to hold it back as they slam into me. My breath shudders out and she pulls back to look at me, studying me as the first tear I've cried in years rolls down my cheek.

She swipes it away with the gentleness of a matriarch who's seen it all and then some. "I've missed you, lad."

"I've missed you too. Is... is he... did I make it?" I peer around the corner of the room and lose the battle with my composure. Grandad's chest rises and falls in sleep, and my neck cranes back in relief. Another tear—and then another—streaks down my face. It's only now that I register the soft beeping of the monitors, the tell-tale signs that he's alright. He's still here with us.

"Now now, m'eudail. Come sit down. We should talk."

The soft smile on her lips bolsters my spirits, as does the use of her favorite endearment for me. *My darling*. Maybe it's not as bad as they thought. Maybe it's not as bad as *I* thought.

I have no idea what to do, but she does. She always has. So, I let her lead me to the couch on the other side of the room.

We're barely seated when she speaks, and the words cut through me like a knife. "He's dying, Jameson."

The terror I experienced at the reception desk swells again. "Are they sure?" I croak, clutching my chest as the pain from that blow lances through me.

"Yes, my boy, they're sure. It's his heart. He has some time, but not a lot." Her eyes glisten behind her glasses but her voice is firm, steady. Nothing like my own.

"How much time?" I can't look at her. I want to, but the guilt of not being here is a presence I can't ignore. I should have kept in better touch, continued to visit, made more of an effort.

"Months. A year at most, and that's if we're very lucky," she says, and I finally lift my head, but she isn't looking at me. Her eyes are on Grandad, and there's a wistfulness in her voice that breaks my heart and heals it all at once. "He and I have already been so very lucky, maybe we will be given a wee bit more."

They have been lucky. They've had an incredible life together; they deserve as much time as they can get.

"What can I do?" I ask, at a loss.

She brings her gaze back to me, full of resolve, and lifts a hand to my cheek. "You can stay."

"Stay?" My voice warbles. In Scotland? For how long? The questions run rampant in the moment it takes for her to continue.

She nods, shoulders back and chin lifted in determination. "He was going to ask you himself, but I figured I'd beat him to it. That way, when he wakes up, you can just tell him yes." Her confidence is almost enough to make me speak the word on the spot. "He's missed you. I've missed you. You've been gone too long, and we want you here."

Never one to beat around the bush, my Gran.

I pinch the bridge of my nose, staving off the fresh deluge of guilt. "But I can't just stay. I have a life in Tahoe, work—"

"You can write from anywhere, Jameson, so don't give me that," she scolds, and I feel like a boy again. She's not wrong, and being between contracts with my publisher means I'm even less tied to my work than usual. Add in the burnout I've been battling and...

"I can, you're right, but—"

"Listen, I know you have a life back in America. I'm not denying that. But you had a life here once too. This was your home... Still is. We think it's time you came home. At least for a little while. Your Grandad wants you here. Isn't that enough?"

Her bright green eyes—nearly identical to mine—plead with me to listen to her. My heart wrenches open and the place inside it where

I'd hidden my love for this country, for our home on Skye, pours free.

"I can't stay forever. You know that," I say, and she nods. "But I can figure out a way to make it work—at least for a while."

"Your grandad would love that. I would too." She wraps me in another hug, her size once again no match for the fierceness of her embrace. It rings with everything we've left unsaid and serves as a reminder of the distance I put between us. "Welcome home, Jameson."

I lean into the railing and inhale the scent of the sea, relishing the shifting of my hair as it blows in the breeze. The sun shines on the lush trees and hills of the island in the distance.

Skye.

The memories bombard me in a torrent: this ferry, that island, the inn, my home, *her*. I wish I could say the ten years I've been gone have healed old wounds, but it's clear that isn't the case.

I drag my gaze away from the shoreline, drawing nearer with each passing minute, and look at where my hands grip the bar, my knuckles white.

I need a distraction—and my phone vibrating against my leg presents me with exactly that.

"Hey, Mum."

"Jamie." She sighs, and with that one word, I breathe a little easier. "How are you holding up?"

Finding time for a call yesterday wasn't feasible between talking with the doctors and fighting off the jet lag. But I've needed this call. I'm guessing they have too.

"Alright, I guess." Even to my own ears, I sound tired. "How's Dad?"

"He hates that he can't be there."

"I really do," Dad says, and I can picture him squishing in next to Mum to get near the phone.

"It's not like you could've known Grandad would have a heart attack the same day you had your knee replaced." Talk about the world's shittiest timing.

"I know," he says, sighing deeply. "How is he? Did you have a chance to talk to the doctors?"

"You know him; he's sick of being in the hospital, but he can't resist joking with the nurses and driving Gran crazy." I turn away from the view of Skye and lean back against the rail, crossing my ankles in front of me. "But the doctors are honestly shocked this was his first heart attack."

Mum inhales abruptly and I hear them shifting, and then it's just Dad's voice on the line.

"Sorry, she needs a minute," he says. Angus might be my dad's father, but he's been as good as a parent to Mum too. "The prognosis is really only a few months?" he asks. The sadness in his voice is something I've rarely heard.

"They said it could be as little as a few months, but that it's hard to tell how long his heart will hold out. If he steps back from work at the pub, eats something besides red meat, and takes his meds, it could be longer. Maybe a year?"

I lower my chin toward my chest and slide my thumb and pointer finger up under my glasses to squeeze the bridge of my nose.

"He won't like being told he can't cook," Dad supplies.

"He actually already has a chef lined up to take his place. I guess he's been talking about stepping back for a while."

"Well, that's news to me. But we haven't been over there in a year. Maybe they saw the signs and just didn't tell us?"

I shrug, even though he can't see me. "I'm going to stay a while, I think."

"How long is a while?"

"Not sure. I figure I can cover some of his tasks at the inn, maybe help with the transition a bit. I've—" I break off, running my tongue over my teeth to hold back my emotions. "I've missed too much time with them, you know? I don't want to miss any of what's left."

"Don't beat yourself up, Jamie. You're there now, and I'm sure it means everything to them that you're staying."

Dad's never been a particularly emotional man, but he tends to know exactly what I need to hear.

I rotate back to the view and rake a hand through my hair. "I'm on the ferry to Skye now. They won't release Grandad for a few more days, so Gran asked me to go up and check on things."

"Does it look the way you remember?" he asks.

"It does. And it feels the same too. Like coming home."

CHAPTER TWO

AVONLEA - NOW

I drum my fingers on the steering wheel and follow the slow line of cars off the ferry. It's been a year since I set foot here, and that was only to settle my grandparents' estate. Before that...

Well, I'd gone a whole decade.

Now though—now I'm here indefinitely.

And it isn't where I thought I'd ever move to. At least not until recently. Not until I received an offer I couldn't refuse.

But the anxiety making itself known in my pulse has nothing to do with my love for this place. There's nowhere on earth as beautiful as the Isle of Skye, in my humble opinion. No. It has everything to do with the memories—the shame and pain tied to this town are what's kept me from wanting to come back.

I drive down the narrow roads, away from the Armadale Ferry Terminal, toward the town I called home for eight summers. Toward Cluaran, and the Thistle & Tartan Inn.

During those summers, Aileen and Angus Murray were like a second set of grandparents to me. No, they were better, because my grandparents were...

I shake the thoughts of them away. They won't help me settle in here. It's enough that I'll be working next door to their old farm, bombarded by the memories of that place every day.

I'm doing this for Angus, I remind myself. Dying or not, he wouldn't have asked me to drop everything ahead of schedule without good reason.

But I'm doing this for me too. Living in the city has lost its appeal. It's busy. It's noisy. It's dirty and crowded. Being in Glasgow was the best thing for me and Lennox these past ten years, but I have to believe this change will do us good.

I scrunch my nose against the sting of tears. Leaving my son behind for two months to finish the school year is grating on me. I know it's what's best. I know he'll be fine with Mum and Dad. And I know that making him transfer mid-year would've thrown him further off-balance, especially since he's already struggling. But I feel like I'm missing a limb being this far from him.

Angus said I could take whatever time I need to see him on weekends, and my parents are planning a visit to Skye next month, but it's hard. I miss my boy even now, and it's only been five hours since I kissed him goodbye outside his school.

My heart rate picks up as the quaint town of Cluaran appears ahead of me.

When Angus called me two weeks ago and asked me to move up the timeline of our arrangement, I almost backed out completely. I wasn't ready yet. But I couldn't do that. Not when I learned he'd had a heart attack. That his heart is failing him, that staying on as head chef of the T&T Pub is no longer an option. His words about wanting to keep the legacy of his kitchen in the family had my eyes overflowing with tears.

Family. The Murrays were family. *Are* family...

And now Angus is dying, and the unfairness of that makes me want to scream.

The Thistle & Tartan Inn fills my windshield. Its white stone walls stand out against the green of the trees and hills behind it, and beyond it is the farm. The farm where I spent my summers. The one I haven't set foot on since I was seventeen. Not even when I came here last year to finalize its sale. I met with the solicitor in the inn, unwilling to revisit that part of my life. Especially with Lennox in tow.

Little did I know that day would set all of this in motion. Seeing Angus. Seeing Aileen. Remembering the part of myself that loved this place. Loved them. Having them meet Lennox and embrace him with that same love, easily and openly. They healed something in me that day.

I step out of my car and my shoulders fall away from their position close to my ears as the smell of the nearby loch registers as the scent of home. The wooden door before me is adorned with a brass thistle, wrapped in Murray tartan. The deep greens and blues are struck through by a vibrant red, creating a plaid pattern I know by heart. Almost as well as I know my own Stewart family tartan.

The heavy metal handle compresses under my fingers and the door opens silently. Someone must've recently oiled the hinges. I lift my chin and take in the entry. Wood paneling, rock floors, cozy couches, and a fire in the hearth warming the space. A wistful smile tilts my lips when I find it still looks the same as it did last year—and every summer of my childhood.

Distracted, I catch my foot on the coat rack and the bloody thing pitches forward. I barely catch it—and myself—before I go sprawling across the floor.

The racket draws the attention of the man behind the reception counter, and his head snaps up. "Christ, are you okay?"

I nearly let the rack drop to the floor in my shock.

You know when you're watching a movie dubbed in another language and you see the actor, *know* what they're supposed to sound like, but the voice doesn't match with the words coming out of their mouth?

That is my current predicament.

Because that mouth belongs to Jameson Murray, *my Jamie*, but the voice is wrong—too grown-up, his accent less pronounced from his years overseas.

My brain fights to understand. What is he doing here?

I snap my mouth shut, but it's the only movement my body is capable of making as I stand and stare.

His rich auburn hair is styled to perfection—as opposed to the tousled red mess I remember from our youth—and he has a beard. A beard? The Jamie I knew would never. But I don't know this man. I don't know him at all.

His green eyes are round behind wire-rimmed glasses, mouth pulled taut in a firm line, and the paper in his hand is crumpled beyond usability.

"What are you doing here?" we say at the same time, and I almost laugh, but the lump rising in my throat stops it. I pull my lips between my teeth and wait for him to say something, blinking too rapidly, afraid that if I look away, he'll vanish like a mirage.

He doesn't, and I start to fidget on my feet. The uncomfortable silence stretches between us and I'm suddenly very aware of how cramped this reception area is.

And that's when Aileen walks in.

"Oh good. You're here. You remember Jameson, of course." She nods, as if this is the most normal situation on the planet. As if my world didn't just flip on its axis. "Avonlea, dear, where are your bags?"

I look at Aileen, then back to Jamie, then back to her. I attempt to clear my throat, but it gets stuck, a cracking sound of discomfort the only thing that escapes.

"Bags?" Jamie says, and I flinch at the roughness of his tone.

"Yes, bags, Jameson. Will you help Avonlea bring them in?"

I shake my head and words spill from me without the slightest ability to filter them. "No. No! I can get them. In fact, maybe I should stay someplace else. I'll just go."

Aileen reaches for my arm just as Angus lumbers around the corner, leaning heavily on a cane.

"Nonsense, lass. Get over here and give this old man a hug," Angus says, and tears spring unbidden from my eyes. He looks frailer than I've ever seen him—thinner, tired, a larger-than-life man made small by illness and age—and my heart breaks.

I wrap my arms around him, but it's not until I catch Jamie's gaze on us that the tears spill over. Of course he'd come home now, for Angus—just like I did—and dammit if I don't wish I could be glad he did. But I can't. Because this just made everything about my being here all the more complicated.

I can only hope he won't be staying long. He has a whole life in the States. One I've only glimpsed through the lens of the internet—not that I'd ever tell him that. Maybe I can just avoid him while he's here. He'll be gone before... well, he'll be gone before this has to get complicated.

I bury my face in Angus's shoulder and breathe him in. He smells the same, like spicy aftershave and herbs from the kitchen. He pats my back before gently pushing me away to look me in the eye.

"Those tears best not be for me, lass. Goodness, I ain't dead yet."

I suck in a breath, but he chuckles good-naturedly. I guess he's at the joke-making stage of his diagnosis. I am not, and the shattered look of heartache on Jamie's face tells me he isn't either.

"Jameson," Angus says over his shoulder, pulling me into his side to face his grandson. I avert my gaze. "Would you check Avonlea into room four. She'll have it indefinitely until she finds herself a place in town." He looks down at me with a nod.

That is what we discussed, but it feels impossible that I could stay at the inn now that Jamie's staying here.

If that isn't incentive enough to find my own place ASAP, I don't know what is.

Jamie nods, lips tight and eyes narrowed, then looks down at the computer.

"So, where are those bags?" Angus asks.

"In my car. I don't have much with me right now. I'll bring up the rest of our stuff once I find us a place." I notice how Jamie's shoulders stiffen but try to ignore it. "Thank you for letting me stay here until I do."

"That's what family does." Angus presses a kiss to my cheek and lets me go. "Once you get settled in your room, come down to the kitchen and I'll introduce you to the staff. Of course, you might remember a few of them." He winks at me and slowly walks toward the back of the inn, a slight limp in his step.

Aileen has wandered over to chat with guests in the parlor, leaving just Jamie and me. Alone.

The same tension from before crackles between us. I can't find words for him right now. I can't find words for myself... for this situation. So, I turn on my heel and walk out to my car, wondering how on earth I'm supposed to look him in the eye when I return.

The man who was my first love.

The man who was my first everything.

The man who first broke my heart.

The man whose eyes I look into every night when I kiss my son to sleep.

CHAPTER THREE

AVONLEA – EIGHTEEN YEARS AGO

I'm hiding in the hedgerow.

Actually, I'm hiding *behind* the hedgerow—its itchy twigs scratching at my arms—as I try to see through to the other side. To the inn next door to my grandparents' farm, where the boy with the red hair is running around in the garden.

This is my first time spending the summer in Cluaran, but I didn't think I'd be this nervous. Excited, sure, but not feeling like there's a whole flight of butterflies gathering in my belly. I've always spent summer holidays at camp or with family friends while Mum and Dad ran the pub. When they had time off, I'd skip camp and we'd go on adventures around Glasgow or to other parts of Scotland—sometimes down to England.

This year though, they thought it might be fun for me to spend a summer on the farm where Mum grew up. I'm not sure about it. Grannie and Papa aren't the most *fun* people. At least the farm seems okay—I guess.

I spot the boy again—a boy my age—as he flies through a muddy puddle in a pair of Wellingtons. That *does* look fun.

I'm not sure why I'm hiding except that I don't know him. I don't know anyone here, or what the rules are. Mum and Dad are still inside talking over the details for the next six weeks and they told me to play in the garden.

But I'd rather play in *his* garden...

When I lose sight of the boy through the small hole in the hedge, I sneak around it, hoping to find him again. Before I can blink, I come nose to nose with him. I squeak in surprise, stumbling backward, and land flat on my backside in the mud.

"Sorry," he says. "I didn't mean to scare you." His face crumples, eyebrows drawing down behind round glasses. His cheeks have turned the same shade of red as his hair.

"You didn't," I say firmly, but he totally did. And now my shorts are ruined. *Mum is going to kill me.*

He extends his hand and I slide mine into it, letting him pull me up. Up close, he's taller than I expected. I thought he was my age, but maybe he's older?

"I'm Jamie." The color on his cheeks darkens as he grins down at me. "Did you just move in? Are you going to be living here now? How old are you? Do you want to come play?"

The nervous and apologetic boy from a minute ago is gone, replaced by this energetic one bursting with questions. I giggle and he stops, eyeing me again.

Does he think I'm laughing *at* him?

"I'm ten. I'm here for the summer and staying with my grandparents." I nod toward the farmhouse behind me.

"I'm ten too! You'll be here all summer? Right next door?" His voice rises with excitement and his green eyes shine.

I nod again. "I guess so. Do you live there?" I point at the inn.

I never thought of people actually *living* at the inns I've stayed at, but maybe they do.

It's his turn to nod emphatically. "My grandparents own it. But we don't live *in* the inn. We live in the cottage behind it."

"What about your parents?"

"They live here too, but they work at the distillery in town. So now that school's out, I have the run of this place." He straightens his shoulders and stands a little taller, projecting his voice like he means business. "What's your name?"

"Avonlea," I say, and attempt to dust the grass and mud off my shorts. I guess white shorts weren't the best choice to wear to the farm. But they're cute and matched my trainers—and the bow in my hair. "But you can call me Avi... if you want."

I've always wanted a nickname, and in this new town I can be whoever I want to be. Today that's Avi.

"Okay! So, can I show you something?" He throws a thumb over his shoulder, and my eyes follow it to the inn's garden. It's filled with moss-covered trees and wildflowers and little pathways that sprawl out around the front of the property. It's really pretty. Definitely more groomed than my grandparents' front garden.

I bite my lip and look back toward the house. I should ask Mum, but they're still inside. I won't be *very* far away. I'm sure it'll be fine.

"Okay." I offer him a smile, and he flashes me one in return before reaching for my hand again and pulling me along behind him.

CHAPTER FOUR

JAMIE - EIGHTEEN YEARS AGO

I lead Avonlea—Avi—through the garden, trying to avoid the puddles. I feel bad that I scared her and that she ruined her shorts, so I'm doing my best to keep the same from happening to her white trainers.

But I mean... *white* trainers? On Skye?

Nah, this girl needs wellies.

"Where'd you come from?" I ask, not able to hold in my questions any longer. Our school has less than eighty kids, so a new kid in town is a big deal. When I saw her peeking through the hedge, I had to investigate. And she'll be right next door, all summer!

"Glasgow." She tugs on her hand but I hold on. I want to show her my favorite part of the garden and I won't stop until we get there.

"Cool. Do you like it there? Living in the city?"

I've only been to the city once, so I really don't know anything about it. I've always lived on Skye—same little village, same people.

"It's pretty cool. My mum and dad own a pub there."

I nod and we slip under an archway that leads to my favorite place. *Finally*. It's a secluded garden around the side of the inn—just off the kitchen—and there's a tire swing in the middle. My grandad can see me from the kitchen window when he's in there cooking.

Sometimes, especially during the summer when the inn is busy and they don't want me underfoot, I come out here to read... or write. That's my new favorite hobby—at least when I don't have permission to go exploring.

After the rain we had last night, there's a big mud puddle underneath the swing. Not that it'll hold me back though.

I let go of Avi's hand and run for the tire. The splat of my boots in the mud is drowned out by my excited *whoop!* when I leap up onto the tire and grab the ropes overhead. The swing twists and I can see Avi's shocked face turn to delight as she begins to laugh.

"Come on then," I say, cocking my head, wondering if she'll join me.

"I can't do that!" she says, but the smile she's trying to hide by chewing on her lip tells me she really wants to.

"I mean... you could." I hop down off the tire with another splat.

She looks down at her shoes, already showing smaller specks of mud, then to her shorts and legs that have streaks of mud on them. The skin around her eyes crinkles and she smiles big—so big all her teeth show. Then, without warning, she lets out an excited squeal and makes a break for the tire. Her blonde hair flies out behind her like a yellow flag in the wind, the white ribbon of her bow catching the sunlight.

She looks right at me when she stomps both feet in the mud before launching herself at the tire. But she's not as tall as I am and misjudges the distance, only just getting her knees onto it before grabbing the ropes to keep herself from falling. There's mud splashed up her calves now, but she howls with laughter, her little wheezing breaths breaking through. As the tire rotates on the ropes, I walk closer until we come face-to-face again.

"I think I've ruined my shoes, but that was fun."

"You need some of these." I lift my foot and shake it at her.

"I have wellies," she says, wrinkling her nose. She has small freckles there. They're a lot like mine.

"Can I join you?"

She nods, and I climb onto the tire across from her.

I stand and pull on the ropes to make it swing back and forth. She looks unsure for a second before carefully standing on the opposite side.

Her loud laughs mingle with mine as we take turns pulling to really get the swing going.

She shifts her foot and the mud slicked underneath makes her lose her balance and fall. She lands on her butt on the tire, then slips off backward into the puddle below. The loss of her weight makes the tire flip up and I go tumbling onto the muddy ground too, my palms burning as they slide down the ropes. The tire sways above us lightly, like it didn't just violently eject us both.

I'm breathing heavily when I meet her eye, then look down to where her mouth is open in a shocked little O. Her face is streaked with mud and her blonde hair is going to need a triple wash. I'm sure I don't look much better, and the only thing I can think to do is laugh. It takes her a second of stunned silence before she joins me, but when she does, she can't stop. Her howls shake her body and we just sit there, covered in mud while we clutch our stomachs.

When we eventually catch our breath, one thought is louder than all the rest: I like her.

Avonlea. *Avi*.

Yeah, I think we're going to be best friends.

CHAPTER FIVE

JAMIE - NOW

My hands move on autopilot as I type her name into the reservation system.

Avonlea—I pause, unsure if her last name is still Stewart. I would assume not, based on the last time I saw her, but there it is on the screen. *Avonlea Stewart.* So she didn't change her name? That doesn't mean anything. Many women don't these days.

Avonlea. Avi.

My Avi.

She's not mine. She never really was. But fuck if that wasn't what my brain supplied the moment I caught sight of her grappling with the coat rack.

What is she doing here?

That appears to be a question for my grandad because he sure as hell knew she was coming. Gran did too.

Traitors.

Though I can't really blame them, considering I never explained what happened between us. I just left and never came back. That cowardice sours my stomach because I know it meant missing out on all these years of seeing them—of seeing Grandad—and now the time we have left is so short. Too short.

But why the fuck is *she* here?

I scrawl her name across a note—seeing it there in my handwriting makes my heart ache—and leave her key on the desk. Then I head for the kitchen where I know the old man is hiding.

The door swings open with a cry of rusty hinges, and I drop my head back with a small sigh. I guess this'll be the next one I attack with WD-40. I continue through, passing the staff stationed around the stainless-steel countertop, then make my way over to where Grandad sits at a desk in the corner. It's where he's been spending his days since we brought him home from the hospital last week. He's not supposed to be cooking, so he's been overseeing things from the sidelines—much to his dismay.

"Ah, Jameson," he says, and a wide smile lifts his cheeks. "Did you get our girl all checked in?"

Our girl. God, why does he have to call her that?

"Grandad..." I say with a hint of reproach. "What is she doing here?"

"She's here as my replacement. I asked her to come and take over the kitchen."

He—*What*? His replacement?

That can only mean she followed in her mother's footsteps and became a chef like she always wanted. I pretend not to file that information away and instead ask, "Why do you need her when you have Hamish?" with a harsher tone than I intended. At his narrowed eyes, I puff out a breath, trying to rein it in. This isn't his fault. He doesn't know what seeing her here is doing to me.

"Hamish, lads." He addresses the kitchen staff who are hard at work preparing for dinner service, though his eyes never stray from mine. "Can we have a moment?"

They all nod and file out the back door, probably for a smoke.

"Listen, Jameson," he says, steepling his fingers in front of his face. Why does he always have to use my full name? I feel like I'm in trouble. "Hamish is great, but he's a sous chef—a damn fine one—and that's all he wants to be. He's filled in these past few weeks, but I need someone I can trust to take this on full time. To be *me* when I'm gone."

His bluntness is like a red-hot poker down my throat. He and my gran have come to terms with his future far quicker than I have. I don't think I ever will.

He continues, pointing his finger toward the front of the inn. "That girl is family. She always has been. And with this being a family business, I want her here."

Well, shit, those words hurt too. Because he's right; she is family. Or she was.

But now? Is she really family *now*? Doesn't she have her own?

"You couldn't have warned me?" I'm grasping at straws, desperate for a solution that doesn't involve *her*, here. "You know, when you asked me to stay, you could have at least told me your plan to hire her."

"Is there a reason I shouldn't have hired her?" He lifts a brow at me in question.

I don't have an answer to that, so I just shake my head.

"And that decision was made long before any of this heart failure business. I just brought things forward a bit." His gaze softens on me. "You used to be friends. I know it's been a long time, but maybe you can be again."

He looks... hopeful? As if it could be that easy. As if watching her live here with the family she built after she moved on and forgot about me will be no big deal.

"Yeah, maybe." I nod and turn to leave, only to find Avi herself standing in the doorway.

Her lips are pressed into a firm line and she's tied her long blonde waves into a ponytail so they cascade down her back. Her jeans are tucked into duck boots and the lightweight long-sleeve top she's wearing clings to her body. She has more curves now than she did the last time we were here.

I felt so mature back then, at seventeen, but we were practically kids.

Kids who didn't know a thing about love or relationships, playing at being adults. And look how that turned out.

I clear my throat and stride past her without a single word because I still don't know what I'm supposed to say.

I'm sorry?

Why didn't you come back?

Why couldn't we have stayed friends?

Why didn't you tell me you'd moved on?

Where's your family? The guy you moved on with? Your *child*?

But I don't say any of those things. I just walk away—the way *I* did our last summer together... the way *she* did when she wouldn't let me apologize and disappeared from my life.

CHAPTER SIX

AVONLEA - NOW

I don't know what I expected in seeing Jamie. And how could I, when I wasn't prepared for this reunion?

The sheepish look on Angus's face as Jamie leaves the kitchen should feel vindicating, but I'm too exhausted for anything besides dread.

"You have some explaining to do, sir," I chastise, but it lacks any real heat. What is it people say? *You laugh to keep from crying*? Yeah, that's about where I am right now. Because even if there's nothing this man could do that I wouldn't forgive, he has not only thrust me into an awkward situation, but a potentially life-changing one.

"Who, me?" he says innocently before pushing to his feet. It's clearly an effort and he uses his cane to support most of his weight. "Come here, lass. Let me get a proper look at you."

I step closer, rolling my eyes. Goodness, he's such a mother hen.

"You look good. You're good, aren't you?" He places one firm hand against my cheek and I smile at his concern. "And Lennox, he's with your parents?"

"I thought it was best to let him finish the school year while I get settled. It's only two months." How many times will I tell myself this before I finally believe it? "Now, back to why you didn't tell me Jamie was visiting."

Angus darts his eyes away, looking every bit like I caught him with his hand in the biscuit tin. "He's not," he states.

"Excuse me... Care to repeat that? Because I'm pretty sure the man I just watched walk out of here"—I point toward the door—"was your grandson, Jameson Liam Murray? I thought it was your heart having problems, not your head." I try to joke—that instinct feels easier than the alternative—and it appears to land with Angus because he barks out a laugh. It's infectious, pulling a matching one from me, and it feels good to laugh with this man who has been a mentor, a grandfather, a friend.

He settles himself back behind his desk, dabbing at the corners of his eyes, and indicates for me to sit across from him.

"Oh, my head is just fine, girl. Goodness, you still have sass." He chuckles again. "I meant that Jamie's not *visiting*. He's staying for the time being. To help out around here. To help when I..." He trails off.

This is the first time I've seen a flicker of sadness in his features, and I wish we could go back to the jovialness of a moment ago. Underneath his casual facade, he's hurting more than he's letting on. But as his words sink in—*all* his words—I feel my stomach flip.

"He's *staying*... here?" I whisper.

"Aye. He is."

"For how long?"

"I've just about got him convinced to stay the year. Though if Aileen has anything to say about it, I'm sure she'll push for longer."

The year?

I swallow thickly. There will be no avoiding him for a year, and there definitely won't be any *hiding* anything either... It won't be possible.

"You knew this," I question, "when you asked me to move up here early?"

"Aye."

Of course he did. Meddlesome old man.

"But... why didn't you tell me?" My voice rises to an uncomfortably high octave.

"Would you have come if I did?" he asks gently. Too gently.

I send him a glare because, no, I probably wouldn't have. I would have chickened out, no matter how much I want this job. Because even though we talked about the possibility of Jamie someday, *maybe*, coming back to Scotland for a visit, it never occurred to me that it would happen so soon. That I would have to confront the mess of it all the moment I walked in the door.

"I want you here, Avonlea." Angus's voice is as tender as his hand wrapping around mine. "I want Lennox here. I told you as much when I offered you this job. But I want Jamie here too. I want my family with me..." The words he leaves unspoken contain multitudes.

When I meet his grey eyes, I find a look that mimics the one from last year when I brought Lennox into this very inn for lunch...

The one that told me he *knew*. It was a few weeks later, when he called and offered me a job, that I told him everything. Aside from my parents, he and Aileen are the only ones who know the truth, and they promised me they would respect my wishes. And as far as I know, they have. But now...

"I know the position this puts you in, Avonlea." He raises an eyebrow at me, and I press my lips into a firm line. "I just hope you'll stay. I need you here. And we will follow your lead where Jamie is concerned, but—"

Before he can finish, the back door bangs open and a group of men walk in, tousled hair wet from the rain that started just after I arrived.

"Ah, perfect timing." Angus stands again and pulls me over to the large kitchen island, my hand still in his. "Let me introduce you to your staff."

My staff. This is *my* restaurant. That's what I was promised in return for this move. The T&T Pub is mine. I'm officially a head chef. Of my very own restaurant. It's what I've always wanted, what I've dreamt of since I was a little girl watching my parents run the Gables, watching Angus here, in this kitchen.

"Been a long time, lass," Hamish says. I almost can't believe he's still here after all this time. He's been Angus's sous chef for as long as I can remember.

As my brain attempts to focus on committing the names and faces of the other men around me to memory, my heart feels miles away from this kitchen.

It's pulling me toward the front desk and the man who was once a boy I loved with my whole heart. It's also tugging me toward the city, where another boy, who now owns that heart, is going through his day—without a thought for the fact that his father is closer than he's been his entire life.

CHAPTER SEVEN

JAMIE - NOW

Why would she agree to this?

That question runs rampant in my mind—while I check guests in, while I make small talk with old Mrs. Baird and her pompous son when they come in for an early dinner, while I continue to ignore calls and texts from my agent back home. Brent's a problem for another day.

Because today's problem arrived in the form of a woman I never thought I'd see again. God, she's even more beautiful now than when we were teenagers—back when I thought she was "hot," because using words like *beautiful, gorgeous,* and *fucking sexy* never crossed my mind as a seventeen-year-old kid. But they're crossing my mind now and, god dammit, I can't deny that she's all of those things.

But why is she here?

A pointless question, because I know the answer. It's the same reason I'm here. Because Grandad asked her to be. And because he offered her the restaurant.

I still remember how she'd watch him in the kitchen, a hunger for knowledge in her eyes. She didn't fall far from the tree in that respect—as far as I know, her parents still own the Green Gables Pub in Glasgow. This is what she always said she wanted.

So why didn't she just stay to take over for her mum when she eventually retires? The Gables is *her* family business, why does she want mine?

Not that it's *mine*; I don't have a stake in the inn... but it's the principle of the matter. This family is mine, even if I abandoned it once. I'm here now, shouldn't that be enough?

Grandad hiring *her* presents me with the reminder of what I don't have, what I lost, and what I've been running from for ten years. A future I once saw for myself. A future I've avoided even thinking of since.

"Earth to Jameson." Gran's voice drags me from my reverie.

I blink rapidly until her emerald-green eyes come into focus before me. The ones she gave me, to go with Dad's fair skin and freckles and Mum's fiery red hair from her Irish side.

"Sorry, what?" I ask, still dazed from where my thoughts had drifted.

"Dinner?" She tilts her head and assesses me.

I'm sure my hair is wrecked from running my hands through it repeatedly over the past few hours. I do it again now, with the purpose of settling it into some semblance of style.

"Right, dinner. Is Grandad joining us?" I ask, pulling off my glasses and polishing them against my shirt.

She nods. "And Avonlea, of course."

"Of course," I murmur as I slide the frames back up the bridge of my nose, grateful for the excuse to avoid her gaze. They'd never let Avi—*Avonlea* eat alone on her first night in town.

"Come on." Gran extends her elbow, waiting for me to escort her to the dining room.

I almost protest, tell her there's no one to cover the front desk, but at that very moment, Bonnie walks in, her pressed white shirt tucked immaculately into her blue slacks. She's the inn's night manager and a godsend for Gran... just not for me right now.

"Evenin', Aileen, Jamie. Going in for dinner?" she asks, her accent wrapping around each word.

After only two weeks of being immersed in Scottish brogues, my own accent is already much more pronounced, but it has nothing on Bonnie's.

"Aye. Thank you." Gran nods toward the desk and I have no choice but to step out and take her arm.

"Come get me if you need anything," I add over my shoulder. Maybe she'll give me an excuse to leave dinner early. Based on the appraising look I catch—the same one she's scanned me with every day since I arrived—I'm sure she'd be more than willing.

Gran smacks my arm. "She'll be just fine, Jameson." The look she shoots Bonnie says she's not to interrupt us, and any hope I had of a rescue goes up in flames. "She's been here far longer than you have."

The sting on my arm is nothing to the sting left behind by her words. I know she only meant that Bonnie has been working here for years. But those years are lost time I'll never get back, and no one knows it more than me.

The dining room is lit by iron chandeliers, but the wood and rock that make up the walls absorb most of the light, creating an intimate atmosphere. The wooden tables and hand-carved chairs are rustic and casual, but the candles that are set out for dinner service give off just the right amount of romantic flair. No matter the season, the Thistle & Tartan has always attracted a mix of tourists, locals out for dinner with friends or family, and couples looking to evade prying eyes—which is to say: town gossip.

We find Grandad and Avi sitting at the corner booth reserved for family, and there's a twist in my heart. Gran slides in, sandwiching her between them, and I go for the seat on the outside, leaving as much space as possible.

"Here, Jameson," Grandad says. "I want to sit next to my bride." His eyes are brimming with love for my grandmother as he pushes to his feet.

My personal life may not reflect it, but I'm a hopeless romantic at heart—it's rather impossible not to be when you move around in the publishing world—and yet, I've never found a love that inspires me the way my grandparents' has. The fact that he still calls her his bride after all these years is something truly beautiful.

Unfortunately for me though, this means I'll be sitting beside Avi.

An awkward silence falls over the table as we settle and I attempt to put as much space between her body and mine. I've just reached for my water when Gran speaks up.

"I hope Angus didn't put you to work this afternoon." She shoots him a knowing look.

"Aye well, that's what I'm here for, isn't it?" Avi laughs, and I'm struck dumb by the sound.

God, I've missed it. I never thought I'd hear it again, and it's both a symphony to my ears and an assault to my senses. I have subconsciously compared the laugh of every woman I've been with to hers, and they never measure up. Never.

"Yes, but Hamish had everything under control for tonight," Gran continues. "I hope you at least had time to call and check in with Lennox and your parents."

Lennox? The name swims around my brain along with the vague image of the man from the pub.

"I did," Avi says, shifting in her seat.

When her leg brushes mine, I pull away so fast I bang my knee under the table, drawing everyone's attention. "Sorry," I mumble, dabbing at where my water sloshed over.

"It sounds like Mum and Dad are already spoiling him rotten. Only grandparents can get away with ice cream before dinner."

Everyone chuckles. Except me. I shake my head in confusion.

"Lennox is...?" I ask the table at large.

Avi's throat bobs on a swallow, color slowly leeching from her face as her wide eyes bounce between my grandparents and then to me. "My... He's my son."

I obviously knew she had a child, but hearing her say it—*my son*—only reignites the hurt I rarely let myself tap into anymore.

Letting my curiosity get the better of me, even when I should leave well enough alone, my next words rush out before I can fully form them. "Ah, and he's staying with your parents? Why not with your husband?" I drop my gaze to her left hand... her *bare* left hand. No ring.

My head snaps up. The familiarity of her deep brown eyes, with their flecks of gold mixed in, has *me* swallowing hard this time.

"I'm not married. It's just me and Lennox," she says, her voice a little shaky, and there's confusion across her brow and in her eyes, like she can't imagine why I'd ask such a thing. Even Gran and Grandad appear confused. But none of them know I've seen her with Lennox's father before, so maybe the question does seem overly invasive.

She doesn't clarify further. Of course she wouldn't. She's not about to spill her entire relationship history at the dinner table with her new employers and her ex–best friend, or whatever it is we ended off as. I didn't imagine it though—her with that guy in the pub. But I can't exactly ask her where he is now, can I? It's not my business, and I don't care.

I don't.

"Oh," I say.

Really, Jamie? That's the best you can muster?

"Well, I for one am excited to see him again," Grandad says, breaking the tension. "And your parents too. It's been too long,"

"You've met him? When?" I ask, my tone sharp with surprise. Will the hits of today ever end? Maybe I just need to go up to bed and this whole nightmare of a day will turn out to be just that. A nightmare.

"Last year, when Avonlea came up to settle her grandparents' estate. She and Lennox stopped in for lunch. He's a good lad." Grandad's eyes sparkle with mischief in a way only his can.

"Thank you," Avi says. "I think so too."

I want to ask more about him, but it will only take me back to that last summer—the summer I came back to Skye for her, and she wasn't here.

CHAPTER EIGHT

AVONLEA – NOW

I climb the ladder to the roof—a place I haven't been in years but could navigate with my eyes closed. A place that might be able to hold all the feelings I'm having about being back in Cluaran… with Jamie.

Who's Lennox? he'd asked, and I'd nearly choked. To hear Lennox's name on Jamie's lips was a shock I wasn't prepared for, and I'm not sure I covered it well.

This whole situation is a mess.

I need to think, to breathe, and I can't do that inside the inn.

It's dark now, but the light of the full moon makes it so I can somewhat see as I clamber up the last rung. Only I'm brought up short by a figure already sitting against the chimney.

"You shouldn't be up here," Jamie says, his icy tone freezing me in my tracks.

"I'm sorry. I didn't know you were up here. I'll just—"

"Why are you here?" he asks, and there's so little of the boy I remember in his voice. His accent has dulled from years spent in the States, and the harshness of it affects me more than it probably should.

"I needed some air." I shrug, though I'm not sure he can see it. "Thought maybe I'd find it up here... maybe some perspective too."

He snorts a derisive laugh. "Well, I haven't found any, so I doubt you will either. And that's not what I meant. What are you doing *here*, Avonlea? In Cluaran."

It cuts to the quick that I'm "Avonlea" to him now. I guess the days of me being *his Avi* are well and truly behind us. Of course they are. They have to be. We aren't the same people we were back then.

"I came for Angus. Just like you." My eyes adjust to the low light and I can see him better now as he scrubs a hand across his bearded chin. "I didn't know you'd be here, Jamie."

"Yeah? And, what? If you'd known, you wouldn't have come?" he bites, and I shake off the instinct to flinch, locking my shoulders instead. He has no idea how right he is. I probably wouldn't have, but not just for my sake... for his too, and for Lennox's.

"And what, you're saying *you* would've come if you'd known I was going to be here?" I snap, my nerves too raw to keep my tongue in check.

"He's *my* fucking Grandad, Avonlea." His words hit like a whip crack. "I've already missed out on enough time with him because of you. So, yeah, I still would've come, but you don't need to be here. I do."

That stings. A lot. It also makes zero sense.

"I never stopped you coming back to Scotland." My hands shake and my voice trembles with the anger I have leashed just under the surface. "You were the one who wanted to stay in America. Don't put your choices on me, Jameson."

He throws his hands in the air and shouts, "Forget it. I'm not doing this with you. I'm not here for *you*."

"Noted. And just so we're clear, I'm not here for you either. If Angus didn't want me here, I'd leave. But he does. And *I* don't walk away from the people who actually want me."

He rears back like I slapped him. Without another word I'm back on the ladder and my feet hit the grass without even registering the climb down. That wasn't the perspective I was looking for, but I got it just the same.

He doesn't want anything to do with me... which would be fine, if he wasn't going to be here for a year.

A year. I still don't know what to do with the news Angus shared earlier.

How can he leave his life behind so easily? If he hadn't wanted that life more than he wanted me, we might not be in this situation.

And how dare he blame me for going so long without seeing his grandparents? *Fucking prick.* He has no right to even be mad in the first place. He's the one who walked away. He's the one who didn't want *me*, at least not the way I wanted him.

I squeeze my eyes shut and lean against the inn's cool stone exterior. *What the hell am I supposed to do now?*

I could ignore him for the next two months... but that won't do me any good once Lennox arrives. He may be a miniature replica of me in almost every way, but it was his eyes that made Angus ask the question in the first place, seeing as he once fell in love with those same eyes. Aileen's eyes.

Even if they aren't enough to have Jamie questioning who Lennox's father is, can I really keep this from him? Keep this from Lennox? What right do I have to ask Angus and Aileen to keep this secret now that the circumstances have changed?

"Fuck," I mutter under my breath. I'm more confused than I was when I came out here.

What am I going to do?

CHAPTER NINE

JAMIE - SEVENTEEN YEARS AGO

If Gran catches me up here again, she's going to throttle me.

The light wind glides across my face and I grip the chimney with my fingertips. I'm not sure exactly how many times she and Mum have told me to stay off the roof, but it's probably more than I can count. And I'm eleven, so I can pretty much count as high as I could possibly want.

I watch the road through town with eagle eyes.

Avi is coming today. I heard Mrs. Campbell, her grannie, telling my Gran this morning. I've barely been able to sit still since.

Last summer was ages ago, and it went by too fast. After Avi's parents and grandparents found us laughing in the garden, covered in mud, there was no chance of keeping us apart.

Is she as excited for the next six weeks as I am?

We spent last summer running wild... well, as wild as we could get away with. We learned the hard way that the Campbells wouldn't stand for any shenanigans. The first time we traipsed into their kitchen in our filthy, soaked socks, Avi ended up doing chores all weekend. We got sneakier after that.

We'd steal away with carrots to feed Fergus, their highland cow, or pick flowers for Avi to weave into a crown for her hair, only to end up at the inn for tea. And Gran never seemed to mind throwing Avi's clothes in the wash when we wound up covered in mud *again*. Avi would borrow one of her fluffy robes and we'd play board games or have staring contests in the parlor until her clothes were dry, then she'd go home with her grandparents none the wiser.

I hope we can get their permission to venture further into the village this summer. We're eleven after all and much more responsible than last year.

A gust of wind knocks me into the chimney and I tighten my grip.

But there it is. Avi's parents' car is halfway through the roundabout down the end of the street and I'm about to start jumping when I remember I'm on the roof.

Right, time to get down.

I sit and scoot to the edge where the ladder is and hesitate. This is my least favorite part, and why I usually listen to my grandparents when they tell me not to come up here, especially when it's about to rain.

On cue, a clap of thunder sounds and the grey clouds in the distance darken. I flip onto my stomach and shimmy backward over the ladder, reaching with my toes until I feel the metal rung under them.

My relief is short-lived though, because at about a third of the way down, I meet my grandmother's disappointed eyes through the kitchen window.

I probably shouldn't have set the ladder right next to it, but it's the lowest point on the roof. I was trying to be safe...

Her eyes pin me from behind horn-rimmed glasses and I feel my cheeks heat. I hop down the last two steps, breaking our eye contact, only to be brought up short by Grandad. His arms are crossed over his barrel of a chest, stance wide, but there's a cheeky grin around his lips.

"Jameson..." He says my full name, like he always does, and drags it out in a warning. He glances behind me to where Gran still stands in the window. They're doing that thing where they communicate without saying a single word. At the subtle shake of his head, I straighten my spine, ready for whatever he might say.

But he doesn't speak. Instead, wrapping one of his big arms around my shoulders, he pulls me into his side and steers us away from the ladder and the windowsill. "Next time, son, would you ask me to hold the ladder?"

I spin my whole body to look at him, and the grin from before has become a full-blown smile that makes his cheeks puff up and his eyes squish together at the edges.

"What? I'm not in trouble?" I squeak, not sure I heard him right.

"Not unless you do it again without telling me." He arches a brow and tries for a stern look, but he's never been very good at those. Gran's is better—though she doesn't use it with me much either.

"And you won't tell Mum and Dad?" I swallow. My parents aren't super strict, but they wouldn't be happy to hear I was on the roof. Not after they spent last night lecturing me about their expectations for this summer break if I'm going to be allowed to "run free."

Grandad chuckles and shakes his head again. "Nah. It can be our secret. Well, ours and your gran's. You better give her an extra hug tonight or she might tell." He taps the end of his nose and winks.

"Deal," I say. I can't believe my luck.

"Watching for Avonlea, were ye?" he asks, a twinkle in his grey eyes.

"Oh aye! She's here!" I pull out from under his arm and run for the break in the hedgerow between our two properties. I slip through, his laughter following me, and turn in time to catch his small wave.

The hedge is thicker than it was last summer. I'll offer to trim it for Gran in apology for sneaking onto the roof today—that should make her happy. I pop through right as Avi jumps out of the car and into the light drizzle.

She's wearing a pair of dark denim shorts and a light blue T-shirt. This time, she's got her wellies on. I'm pretty sure her parents threw away both the trainers and shorts from that muddy first day last summer.

She yells "Jamie!" when she sees me and splashes through three puddles, leaving her shins streaked with murky water. When she crashes into me for a hug, the clouds finally yawn open, and we fall into fits of laughter as we get pelted by the rain. But I can barely feel it.

Avi is the only girl I've ever hugged. I mean, I hug Gran and Mum, but the girls I'm friends with from school aren't really interested in hugs. I'm not really interested in hugging them either.

But I like this hug with Avi, and despite the coolness of the rain, I feel warm all over.

CHAPTER TEN

JAMIE - NOW

The past week has been nothing short of torture.

Watching Avi walk around like she belongs is a new type of agony. Because she did once. We always belonged here—together. That's a big part of why I never came back: I knew it wouldn't feel the same without her.

So why did I think it would feel the same now?

I avoid the kitchen at all costs, unless I'm desperate for caffeine or food—which seems to be all the time. But I'm *not* trying to see her.

I'm not.

After our tiff on the roof the night she arrived, I'm unsure how to proceed. She has no idea how her choices affected my own, but she's right; it *was* my choice to stay away from Scotland, to allow the pain of losing her to taint this place for me. I regret that now more than anything, and it's not fair of me to expect her to understand.

I pull my glasses off the bridge of my nose and squeeze. There's a tension headache building behind my eyes from staring at my computer screen for too long, oscillating between thoughts of Avi and the email staring me in the face. The one to my agent, telling him I want to take a sabbatical. Telling him I won't be pursuing another contract with my publisher for the foreseeable future. He's going to flip when he reads it, and I don't really want to deal with his feelings right now. I can hardly get a hold of my own.

The last seven years since I signed with Brent have been a lot. I've loved them, and I'm grateful for him and my publisher for taking a chance on a college kid with a manuscript and a dream. They changed my life. But now my contract is up—the series that made me a best-selling author is complete—and I'm not sure where to go from here.

I want to write, but the words aren't flowing.

I've had writer's block before, but this is different. It's like inspiration evaporates the minute I reach for it.

The book I sent Brent months ago is sitting in my inbox, filled with his revisions. But I can't bring myself to open it. It's not the right story. I knew it when I wrote it, and I know it now.

I just wish I could figure out what the right story is.

The short story I wrote last winter about Skye came easily, like my subconscious knew I needed to get back here.

But that one is just for me...

I have wondered whether my next book is hiding in these heather-covered hills and glassy lochs. But I'm wary of trying to fit

Scotland into some sort of mold for a contract, even if my agent is breathing down my neck. It's too wild... too free. And that's exactly what I need to be right now.

Wild. Free.

I repeat the words my Grandad said to me years ago when I started my first real story. *If you write it with your heart, you'll never go astray.* My heart needs this—time to focus on my family and to write for myself again.

I pull air into my lungs and gather my courage, then I hit the mousepad and send the email that could destroy my career. With the time difference, I should have a few hours before the floodgates of communication open. But no matter what Brent says, I won't change my mind.

I don't want to be so focused on work that I miss out on what led me out here.

On that note, I close my laptop and notice that the parlor has emptied out around me. We're at about half-capacity at the moment, with ten rooms currently occupied, so I assume most of the guests must be out enjoying the sun before the rain arrives later, as it has every afternoon the past few weeks.

My stomach grumbles so I head for the kitchen in search of Grandad—not Avi—and a snack.

Lunch service starts in an hour so the kitchen is a torrent of movement, with Grandad overseeing it all from his setup in the corner. Good, he's staying off his feet like the doctors instructed. He has more color today and the bags under his eyes are less pronounced, which hopefully means he got a good night's sleep.

"Jameson," he says with a smile when I walk in. He stands from his desk when I reach him to give me a back-clapping hug. We didn't hug this much in my first eighteen years of life, but I've realized how precious each one is and take every opportunity to make sure he knows I'm here and I love him.

I have so much to make up for.

He sits back down, eyes moving over the kitchen with the precision of a seasoned professional. He's allowed to supervise if needed, but he's not allowed to run the show. I'm sure it's driving him absolutely crazy. But that's why Avi's here.

I follow the path of his eyes and take in everyone who's here... and note everyone who isn't.

Anytime I'm in the kitchen, it's always Avi's hair—or the apron tied around her shapely waist—that lassoes my attention. But that perky blonde ponytail is notably absent today.

"Where's Avonlea?" I ask as nonchalantly as I can.

Since she's been back, I've yet to call her Avi outside my head. It feels too intimate, like it's a nickname that belongs to a different Jamie—one from a different time.

Grandad's eyes narrow on me but his lips twitch like he's hiding a smile.

"She wasn't feeling well this morning, so I told her to take the day off. Hamish has everything under control and I can step in a little if need be."

I purse my lips. So much for him taking it easy. "You know you aren't supposed to be cooking."

"It's one day, Jameson, it won't kill me." He pats my arm and I bite my lip to keep from saying *actually, it very well* could *kill you.*

He's an adult, and if he says he feels well enough to help, I'm not going to be the one to stop him.

"Did she say what was wrong? Does she need the doctor?" I ask, hating that I care. I shouldn't care. But I do.

We have a silent conversation, like the ones he shares with Gran, where he's communicating *I'm not sure it's any of your business*, and I'm countering with *Just tell me, old man*.

His lip twitches again. "Aileen said it was cramps."

Ahh... Now I see why he wasn't sure if he should tell me. Well, periods have never made me squeamish—I have Mum, Gran, and the fact that my best friend back home is a woman to thank for that—and this isn't even my first rodeo where Avi is concerned.

"You got any of your famous chocolate biscuits around?" I ask him, and that ghost of a smile grows into a full-blown grin.

"Aye. I think I do."

Five minutes later, I'm headed upstairs to room four with a plate of biscuits and a heating pad on a tray. The note with my swooping *J* initial is unnecessary. I'm not even sure why I wrote it.

I stop outside her door and stare at it for too long.

What do I do now? Knock and personally hand this to her...? What on earth would she think?

In the end, I set the tray on the floor, grab the note and crumple it in my fist, then quickly knock before hightailing it to the stairs. I've just rounded the corner and pressed myself against the wall when I hear her door open.

My ears ring as I picture her face and wish I would have stayed to see it. But I didn't do it for me. I did it for her. Even though it's not my job to take care of her, part of me will always wish it were.

CHAPTER ELEVEN

Avonlea - Sixteen Years Ago

"Avi?" Jamie's voice carries across the hedgerow to where I'm sitting with my back against a tree, arms pulled tight around my stomach. I quickly swipe at the tears on my cheeks, and then I *run*. "Avonlea?"

I slip into the barn and out of sight. He'll want to know why I'm crying, and there's no way I can tell him. He may be my closest friend in Cluaran, but he's still a twelve-year-old boy. I don't want him to laugh at me like the boys at school would.

But Jamie's never been like the boys at school, not with me.

I sink down beside a hay bale, the rough straw prickling my arm, and more tears slip free.

I wish Mum were here. She said she'd come get me when I called, but I didn't want to be dramatic. Making her drive five hours because I got my period for the first time felt dramatic… Still, I never imagined it happening here, with only Grannie to ask for help.

I breathe and tell myself it'll be fine. A few days, a week tops, and then I can pretend this never happened. Until next month, I guess. A little sob escapes me at the thought and I squeeze my arms tighter around my middle. It hurts, but it's nothing to how embarrassed I was when Grannie told Papa that she needed to run into town to get me pads. He went white as a sheet, and then bright red. I'm pretty sure I did too.

I've been hiding out ever since she got back.

But now…

"Avi?"

I must've missed the creak of the barn door because Jamie's looking down at me and there's nowhere else to hide. I lift my head from where I was resting it against the wall and look into the prettiest green eyes I've ever seen. Even in the gloom of the barn, the large chunks of light filtering in through the old roof make them shine.

But I don't want to see him right now.

More like, I don't want *him* to see *me*.

"What's wrong?" His voice is soft and cautious… nervous. "Are you mad at me?"

I shake my head and dash the tears away. "No, I…" I don't know what to say. God, the embarrassment that burns hot under my skin at just the *thought* of telling him is enough to make my eyes fill again. So, I pull my knees in toward my chest, wrap my arms around them, look at my shoes, and say, "Just leave me alone."

Not once in three summers have I asked him to leave me alone. We're practically joined at the hip for the entire six weeks I'm here.

"What did I do, Avi?" There's hurt in his voice, and that only makes the salty tears fall harder.

I can't look at him. I'm too embarrassed, too ashamed, too afraid of what he'll think if I tell him.

He backs away with slow steps that scrape across the cool stone floor.

I've never kept secrets from him, never had to. We've never so much as bickered over anything. He's my best friend—not just on Skye, but in general. Even with all my friends at home, I like Jamie Murray the best.

I lift my head and watch him walk away, shoulders slumped. He's almost to the door when I shout after him. "Wait." His eyes are sad when he turns back around. "I'm sorry. You didn't... It's not..." I blow out a big breath and the words fall out in a rush before I can stop them. "I started my period, okay?"

And then I bury my face in my hands.

This is it for our friendship. Boys don't want to talk about this stuff. They don't want to know about it or think about it. And here I am blurting it out while sitting in a crying heap on the ground.

But he doesn't run away. To my shock, Jamie sinks down next to me until his side is pressed against mine, warm in the damp chill of the barn.

"Why'd you hide from me?" he asks.

I shrug and he knocks his shoulder against mine, coaxing me to finally lift my head from my hands. His eyes are curious, but there's hurt there too.

"I didn't want to talk about it. With anyone, but especially not with you."

"Why?" A line appears between his eyebrows.

I scoff and rub my face against my sleeve, relieved when it doesn't come away snotty. "You're a boy."

"Aye, and you're a lass. Did you tell your grannie?" he asks, like we're talking about the weather and not my period.

My cheeks flame and I nod. "Yeah, and she told my papa." I shudder at the memory. "Maybe I should have Mum come get me. She said she would. I just—"

"You can't go home now. We still have three more weeks of break. You don't really want to go, do you?" he asks, looking distraught at the idea of me leaving early.

I shake my head and lean slightly into his shoulder, but a twinge of pain in my stomach makes me wince away.

"Does it hurt?" Jamie asks, and I nod, pressing my palm over the dull ache.

I'm too mortified to say anything. To my surprise, his warm hand covers my free one where it sits on my lap and he laces his fingers between mine. We've never held hands before... but I think I like it. I think I like it a lot.

"You know," he says, "my mum has a heating pad she uses sometimes. Maybe you could try that."

I lift my head with a snap and our gazes collide.

"What?" he says, taking in my whole face.

"I just... This really doesn't weird you out?" I duck my chin again, but he follows the motion so I can't hide from him.

"No. Why? It's just part of being a girl, right? At least that's what Mum says. Gran too. So, you want to try that heating pad?"

And just like that, starting my period doesn't feel as scary. I nod and give him the first smile I've worn all day. He stands and brushes the hay from his pants then extends his hand. I slip mine into it, getting more used to the feel of holding his, and with a gentle tug, he pulls me from the ground.

"I bet Gran will even give you some of Grandad's chocolate biscuits if you want them. My mum always says they make her feel better."

The bright sunlight is blinding as we walk out of the barn, but it illuminates his smile as he leads me across the garden, through the hedge, and into the warm kitchen of the T&T for tea and biscuits.

I got really lucky with Jameson Murray. I hope we can be friends forever.

CHAPTER TWELVE

JAMIE - FIFTEEN YEARS AGO

I peek out the kitchen window and see Avi sitting in the old tire swing. Well, sitting isn't quite the right word. She's lying across the tire, head hanging off one end with her long blonde hair trailing down toward the ground while her legs dangle off the other. They move just enough to keep the swing rocking gently and her hair swaying back and forth.

I grew four inches this year, giving me a different view through this window than I used to have. I see Avi a bit differently too.

She's always been Avi, my friend who visits in the summer. Avi who isn't afraid to get muddy, to be reckless, to go on an adventure. And she's still that Avi... but she's also more than that.

It's not like I didn't realize she was a lass or anything. Especially after last summer when she started her period. Mum was so proud of me for the way I handled her telling me—that I didn't embarrass her—that she got me a new leather-bound journal to write in with my initials engraved in the front. But this year I've started noticing girls more... and Avi the most.

She grew this year too, and in ways I was surprised by. Her T-shirts fit differently—so do her shorts—and I really like it. I keep having to tell myself not to look, but sometimes, like right now, it's hard not to.

And it's not just me who's paying attention. We've walked into the village to hang out with my school friends a few times and I see the way the other lads check her out. She doesn't seem to notice or take note of any of them, but I always end up wanting to hit my best mates. I like it better when it's just me and Avi. These summers are for us.

"Jameson?" Mum's voice comes from behind me.

She's still taller than me, but Dad says I'll pass her up in a few years with the way I'm growing. We have the same shade of flaming red hair, but hers is wilder than mine... except when I first wake up in the morning.

Her smile is warm when she asks, "Is Avonlea out there?"

I nod, feeling my cheeks heat against the rims of my glasses.

She leans around me and takes in the same sight I didn't want to pull my eyes away from. "She's a bonny lass, isn't she?" she asks, mischief glinting in her hazel eyes.

I groan. "Mum, stop." I give her a little push with my shoulder to get her away from the window.

She chuckles, tipping my chin up with her finger, and I'm reminded why it's impossible to stay annoyed with her. "I was just saying..."

I turn away when she bounces her eyebrows at me, feeling embarrassment flood my entire body.

"Angus is about to get started on the bread for dinner, why don't you go ask her if she wants to come in and help him?" I can hear the smile in her voice.

"Aye, okay," I say, glad for an excuse to get away from this conversation.

The back door creaks when I open it and Avi's eyes fly open. Her gaze lands on me, and even though she's hanging upside down, she smiles. Mum's not wrong, she is bonny. Even if I'm not supposed to think that because she's my best friend... it's still true.

"Hello," she says, continuing to sway back and forth. There's a book on her stomach, held between her hands, like she had every intention of reading but decided not to.

"Hi." My voice breaks on the word and I glance down. I really wish it would stop doing that. Mum and Dad said it will soon, and then my voice will be completely different. Lower. Growing up is weird. "Do you wanna come in and bake bread with Grandad?"

She sits up fast and dismounts the tire with more grace than I've ever displayed. "Aye!" she shouts.

I've never had that kind of excitement for working in the kitchen, but with her mum being a chef, I guess it makes sense. This summer she's really taken to working with Grandad in ours. He calls her his little duckling because she trails after him to all the different workstations. She loves it, especially when the inn has a busy service and there's plenty to do.

"What are you going to do while we bake?" she asks, pushing past me into the kitchen and rolling her long sleeves up her arms to wash her hands.

I shrug. "Watch, I guess. I have my notebook," I say, setting it on the desk and rubbing my fingers over my initials. "Maybe I'll write you a story to read next time you're hanging in the swing."

She looks over her shoulder, hair catching in her eyelashes, and hits me with a smile that brings that heat back to my cheeks. "What kind of story?"

"I don't know... What kind of story do you want?"

"A love story," she says, her eyes softening. "Like in the fairytales."

I grimace. That is not what I had in mind.

She laughs. "Okay fine, write me whatever you want. I'll read it."

"Okay," I agree, relieved I don't have to write her some silly love story.

"What are we reading?" Grandad asks, stepping inside and reaching for his apron.

"Jamie's going to write me a story." Avi's brown eyes are bright and she sounds as excited as she did about cooking.

I wonder if I made a terrible mistake here. She loves to read, at least as much as I do. What if I let her down? What if the story is horrible?

I bite my lip, and Grandad must see my hesitation. "You know if you write it with your heart, you'll never go astray." He winks at me, and I wish I understood what he meant by that. "Well, Avonlea, let's get started then."

Over the next hour, they focus on the dough for the bread before turning their attention to the sticky toffee pudding for tonight's dessert. The smell of butter and sugar caramelizing is heavenly and I can't wait to sneak a piece later... Not that I'll have to be too sneaky. Mum almost always lets me have dessert so long as my chores are done, and it's summer, so I don't even have homework to finish first.

While they've been working—him showing her each step of his process while the other kitchen staff flit around them—I've been poring over the notebook in front of me.

I don't write a love story. What do I know about love? Adventure, on the other hand... *That* I know about, and I decide to write a story about the adventures of Jamie and Avi. But these are adventures we haven't had a chance to have yet, ones I'd love to share with her someday—each summer until we get to them all. Because I think I'd like to spend summers with Avi for the rest of my life.

I wonder if she wants to spend all her summers with me too.

CHAPTER THIRTEEN

Avonlea - Now

"Hey, Mum," I say after tapping my right earbud to answer her call.

"Hello, dear, how are you? I'm not interrupting you in the kitchen, am I?" she asks, and I smile. As a chef herself, she should know I'm always in the kitchen.

"I've got my earbuds in, and I'm in between tasks actually. What's up?"

"I know you've had your hands full getting settled, but we haven't talked much and I want to hear how things are going."

She sounds worried. Probably because she knows better than anyone else the reason for my trepidation at coming back to Cluaran. I've also been avoiding her because I don't know how to tell her Jamie is here. I've talked with Lennox every night and each conversation is both a balm to my soul and a tugging on my heartstrings. I've had to restrain myself from getting in my car and driving home on multiple occasions.

"How are Aileen and Angus? He holding up okay?" she asks, and I shake my head to refocus.

"Yeah, he's doing pretty well. More good days than bad days at this point. And he's mostly following doctors' orders and letting me do all the cooking."

I think about Sunday when my period hit with the force of a battering ram to my uterus and I could barely get out of bed. Dragging myself out of it for cookies and a heating pad was worth it, though. I know it could've been Aileen—she knew why I wasn't coming down to cook—but it wasn't. It was Jamie, and it felt like catching a glimpse of the boy I used to know.

"Avonlea?" Mum asks.

"Yeah, sorry. I'm just distracted."

"See, I knew you were busy. I just want to make sure you're holding up. I know you have a lot of memories there and it can't be easy. I—"

"He's here, Mum," I blurt, cutting her off.

"Who's there?" Her confusion is palpable even through the phone.

"Jamie," I whisper, my face screwing up as I say it. "He's here."

"Wait, what?" Mum shouts into the phone and I startle, but she's in my earbud so there's no escape. "When did he get there?"

"He's been here the whole time," I say, bracing for her reaction.

"And you're just now telling me? Avonlea, you've been there for a week and a half. I—"

"I know. I didn't know what to say. I don't really know what to think myself."

"How long will he be there? Are you okay? What about—" She bombards me with enough rapid-fire questions to make my head spin.

"Mum, stop. This is why I didn't tell you." I glance around, glad the rest of the staff is on a break. "I don't know what to do. He's going to be here for a while, and Lennox arrives in six weeks."

She sighs and I can picture her pressing her hand to her forehead and then squeezing her temples. "You're going to have to tell him."

"How? How do I do that?" My voice rises and I feel the ever-present panic start to bubble beneath the surface. "We're barely speaking as it is. It's all such a mess. I should have known he'd come home, should have at least considered the possibility, and now we're both here... And Lennox is moving up here and I-I don't know what to do."

"Breathe, sweetheart. Are you sure you should stay?" The gentle way she forms the question brings me a modicum of calm. Her voice has always done that for me, it's why I usually tell her everything. If anyone can help me problem-solve, it's her.

"I can't leave now. Angus needs me here, and I love it, Mum. I've always wanted my own kitchen, and this one feels like home. It feels like yours did, but it's also mine, you know? I don't want to give that up, but..."

"If you're set on staying, you *will* have to tell him. And Lennox too. You should've—"

I cut her off before she can go down a road we've traveled more than enough times. "Please don't start. I had my reasons, and you know that."

"I'm sorry. You're right, and it was your decision to make. I just—" She blows out another breath. "I wish I could make this easier for you, but I don't think there's going to be an easy answer now, sweetie."

"There was no easy answer then either," I say, dejected.

"You're right. There wasn't. Maybe your dad and I should hold off on bringing Lennox up until you've had a chance to tell him. The worst possible scenario is Jamie figuring it out on his own."

I squeeze my eyes shut and exhale heavily. "Aye... Aye, you're right. I'll take a long weekend to come see Lennox in a couple of weeks. It doesn't make sense to bring him up before I have a place sorted for us anyway."

"How's the house hunt going?" she asks, and I'm glad for the change of subject.

"Eh, fine, I guess. I've put in a few applications..."

"I thought you were planning to buy?"

"I was, but everything feels too precarious right now. I think a lease makes more sense... you know?" I keep thinking of the worst-case scenario—where this all implodes, everyone gets hurt, and staying here will no longer be an option.

"Mm. That does make sense. Well, if you need help with anything, you call me, okay? No more secrets, please. We haven't had secrets since you were seventeen."

I chuckle at the irony. "Yeah, true. I'm sorry. I wasn't sure how to tell you."

"That's understandable, but I'm glad you did. You'll call Lennox this evening?"

"Aye, as always. He's doing okay, right?" My heart clenches, I miss him so much.

"He's doing great. He misses you, of course, and I think he's excited for the move."

"Is he still having trouble with the kids at school?"

"It's been better this week, or at least he seems better."

That helps ease my worries. The fact that Lennox is having issues with these kids only made our move more appealing, but I'm glad things seem to be improving. Especially since I can't be in Glasgow to try to fix it. Not that I was having much luck while I was back there.

"Good. I'll call him later. Love you, Mum."

"Love you too, Avonlea."

Music fills my earbuds when the call ends, resuming the playlist I had on before. I turn around to look for my phone and find Jamie instead, sitting at his grandfather's desk in the corner, watching me over steepled fingers.

I jump and my frightened squeak bounces off the walls of the kitchen. "Holy shit! How long have you been sitting there?" My mind races over the conversation I just had. What did he hear? I don't think I said anything that would give away my secret, but hell, I know he wasn't there a few minutes ago.

"I just sat down. Sorry I scared you."

It's the most words we've exchanged since that night on the roof.

"What're you doing in here?" I ask, breathless and clutching a hand over the heart that nearly jumped out of my chest.

"I was looking for Grandad." He leans back casually in the chair, his broad shoulders spanning the entire width and his damn shirt stretching across his chest when he presses his forearms into the armrests. Why is this man still so appealing?

I force my gaze to meet his and cross my arms. "And when you didn't find him, you figured you'd eavesdrop on my phone call?"

"That wasn't my intention, Avonlea." The irritated fire that was there during our last conversation is gone now.

I hate the way he's still calling me Avonlea and not Avi, though I don't know why. I definitely should *not* care.

"Well, next time, just announce yourself or something," I say, trying to bring my own reactions down a notch.

"I was going to ask if he needs anything from town, but I guess I'll ask you instead. Do *you* need anything?"

I restrain myself from laughing maniacally and saying *Aside from a miracle that will make it so I don't have to tell you that you have a son and that I hid him from you for ten years, nope!*

Ugh, that's not helpful.

"Avonlea?" he asks, an eyebrow raised.

Oh right, I'm supposed to respond when asked a question. "What? Sorry."

"Do you need anything from town?" His eyes glitter behind his glasses and I'm reminded again of the boy I knew, before he started wearing contacts more often than not. I've noticed that he wears his glasses most of the time now, and I wonder why that is. I wonder *a lot* of things about this man.

"I think we're pretty well covered here." I look anywhere but at him. "Thank you."

"You're welcome," he says, moving to leave.

I blush and duck my head. "Thank you for Sunday too." I'd been wanting to bring it up for days, but this is the first time we've been alone.

"You're welcome, Avi," he says quietly, and my nickname on his lips knocks a shiver down my spine.

I snap my head up.

His hand is pressed to the door and I note how his shirt hugs every muscle of his back, and god, his ass in those jeans... He really grew up well, and that is not something I should be noticing.

Without a look back, he pushes through the door, and all the air in my lungs follows him out in a rush.

CHAPTER FOURTEEN

JAMIE - NOW

As I expected, Brent's response was less than enthusiastic. The barrage of communication over the last five days has been overwhelming to say the least. He by no means believes I should be taking a sabbatical right now. His words exactly? *You'll be throwing away everything you've worked for by turning your back on another deal with Fog City Book Group.*

But I'm exhausted from the grind of the past six years, and I just want a break. I need to find my love of storytelling again, need for it to feel like it used to—less like a job and more like a passion.

I dig around in my side table, looking for the notebook I threw in on a whim while panic packing for this trip. It's the notebook my mum gave me, the leather worn and cracking, and it's filled with tales of my youth—of Avi's youth. The stories of our summers together.

Folded into the back is a printed copy of the short story I wrote last winter. One centered around the adventures I'd planned for me and Avi in our final summer together, the ones I'd wanted to go on with her but that never happened—because she wasn't here.

It was cathartic to write them as if they had, but it also hurt like hell to realize they'd never be real. That story would always be fiction—something I made up to fill the void of missed opportunities.

I scootch back against my pillows and flip through the notebook, watching my handwriting become more and more precise. Taking in the way my writing grew and changed. Seeing how I played around with different styles throughout the years.

I wonder what the teenage version of me would say if I told him what his future looked like—that he'd be a bestselling adventure-fiction writer at twenty-eight with three published books to his name.

It's hard to regret the past when I know each choice and decision led to that success. Moving to the States with my parents. Deciding to stay there for college, where I met my mentor—a man who sculpted me and helped hone my writing so I'd have a book to query my agent with. But at the end of the day, no matter how much I love my life and my career, I can acknowledge that it came at a great cost.

And I'm not willing to continue to sacrifice everything else for that goal. No matter how mad that makes Brent.

I'm here to reconnect with my roots, my family... That is the new goal.

Now I have to decide how Avi being here fits into that...

We can't go back to the way things were between us—I know that—but I'm done existing in this standoff with her.

If I gleaned anything from her conversation with her mum the other day, it was her concern about bringing Lennox up here with the way things are. I don't want her to keep him away because I'm being an ass.

It's been ten years, it's probably time I let go of all the hurt associated with that time. I owe it to myself to try.

With that as my motivation, I head downstairs only to glimpse Avi walking down the garden path in the direction of the street. Acting on a whim, I go after her and let my long legs consume the space between us until I'm close enough to call out.

"Avi!" I shout, letting her nickname slip from between my lips for the second time. Withholding it was my way of keeping my walls up, but it was only hurting me, and maybe her too.

She spins on her heel, blonde hair flying around her face. The wariness behind her eyes tells me she's preparing for the inevitable fight. But I'm not interested in fighting with her. Not today. Not anymore.

I don't know what I want where she's concerned, but an end to this animosity would be a good start.

"Where you headed?" I ask, stopping just inside her personal space. This is the closest we've been since everything broke between us, but I feel that same rippling current of energy. It's like our bodies recognize each other—as if the last time they were this close was yesterday and not eleven years ago.

Her gaze searches mine and I wonder if she feels it too. "Into the village," she says, and tilts her head in the direction of Cluaran's small high street.

"Can I walk with you?" I ask, my feet already moving and forcing her to fall into step beside me.

"I guess so," she says under her breath, and the sass behind it almost makes me smile. The girl I knew is still in there somewhere.

The gravel underneath our shoes is the only sound between us for several moments. I miss the days where we could say anything to each other, where we didn't have these pregnant pauses filled with doubt.

I unconsciously move a step closer until my shoulder brushes hers—pulled to her in the same way I always have been—but she sidesteps away.

"Look—" I say.

"Jamie—" she says at the same time. We both pause, and the smallest smile tilts her lips before she traps them between her teeth.

I capitalize on her silence and continue. "I'm sorry for how I've acted since you arrived. I was surprised to see you, and after everything... well, I guess I don't know how to be around you anymore, Avi."

"And you think I do?" she snaps, a fire burning in her eyes before she squeezes them shut and shakes her head. "I'm sorry," she breathes. "Clearly I'm not sure how to feel about this situation either."

She keeps her eyes down and kicks at a piece of gravel with the toe of her boot, an outward tell of her inner frustration.

"I don't expect things to go back to the way they were before, but we're both here and not going anywhere anytime soon." I swipe a hand through my hair, feeling unsure of my next words. "Maybe we can try to be friends? Or at least not enemies?"

She lifts her head, her deep brown eyes finding my green ones. "I've never thought of you as my enemy, Jamie."

She could've fooled me, but I don't say that. I'm trying to apologize and need to remember that just because I'm ready to say I'm sorry doesn't mean she is. I may believe I deserve those words from her, but I have to be okay with never getting them.

"I'm sorry. For the way things ended between us. I didn't think—"

"Please, don't." She stops and squeezes her eyes shut like she's in pain. "I—Jamie, I—"

There's something imploring in her gaze when she opens her eyes, and it bores into me like she wants to tell me something but can't find a way to do it.

I wonder if the little game we used to play might help her get the words out. "Truth?" I ask with an encouraging smile.

Her reaction is nothing like I expect. Her eyes go wide and she sucks in a sharp breath, stepping back from me and stumbling off the curb and into the street.

I reach for her on instinct, grabbing her by the upper arms and pulling her into me as a car horn blares. The small sedan whizzes by, Gaelic expletives flying from the elderly gentleman behind the wheel.

"Fuck. Avi, are you okay?" My words puff out against her hair and her chest moves rapidly against my own.

I put an inch of space between us, just enough so I can look at her. She's shaking like a leaf and tears pool in her eyes, but she quickly averts them so I can't see. It's too late, and I was never good at watching her cry. I crush her back to me and hold her while her tears stain my shirt. "God, Avi. Shhh, you're okay. I've got you."

I run my hand up and down her back, muscle memory taking over. Touching her feels like it always did. Hugging her… kissing her… everything we ever did felt like home, and I can't deny that even this small moment when she's letting me hold her feels that way.

I wish we could stay here and forget everything else, but as Avi's shuddering slows, I feel her pulling away, even before she physically does.

Bringing her arms between us, she swipes away the tear tracks on her face. She doesn't look at me. Mindful of the curb this time, she eases back and says, "I think I'll finish my walk into town by myself."

And then she turns, leaving me on the curb to wonder what *truth* she doesn't want to tell me.

CHAPTER FIFTEEN

Avonlea - Fourteen Years Ago

We pull up outside Grannie and Papa's farmhouse and I'm pressed against the window. My eyes scan every inch of the Thistle & Tartan property, but he's not here.

Shoulders dropping, I fall back in my seat with a huff.

It's unlike Jamie not to be waiting for me when I arrive, ready to whisk me off and tell me everything about the past year. But today, he's nowhere.

I try to hide my disappointment as I climb out of the car and shuffle up the steps to where Grannie stands, hands on her hips. Her lips tip up in a half smile—that's about as good as it gets with Grannie.

She pulls me into a brief hug and then looks me over in my denim shorts and tank top. I pull it down, feeling self-conscious under her appraising gaze. It fit better a month ago, but Mum says I grew like a weed, because now it shows a sliver of my stomach. Grannie shares a glance with her over my shoulder and shakes her head but says nothing, though I'm sure she'll have something to say to Papa later. I also won't be surprised if this shirt disappears in the washing this week.

Mum says they're *old fashioned*—whatever that means. When she was growing up, they never let her spend too much time with boys or dress too "revealing." Thank goodness they don't mind me spending nearly all my time with Jamie.

Speaking of Jamie... I eye the yard again, but nothing. Why isn't he here? He's not over being my friend, is he? A knot forms in my belly. At fourteen, maybe he'd rather spend the summer with his school friends... not with some city girl.

Before I can go in search of him, my parents and Grannie whisk me inside and I'm trapped in a conversation usually reserved for the adults.

Papa gives me a stiff side hug. "Good drive?" he asks, as if I was the one behind the wheel.

"Too long. I slept most of the time," I say with a shrug, bouncing on my toes with the desire to get back outside.

He nods, releasing me, and turns his attention to my parents.

I see my chance to escape and take it, flying out the back door in search of the person I really want to see.

The opening in the hedge between our two properties is neat and tidy and I take that as a good sign. Jamie's the one who makes sure it's not overgrown, creating our own special portal to each other for the summer. It's like slipping into another world, one that's just for us. I weave my way around puddles because I don't have my wellies on yet, and head for the tire swing.

My heart sinks when I find it empty. I bite my lip and spin in a circle, finding the ladder propped against the side of the inn. Now I'm sure I know where he is, but why is he up there?

I've only been up on the roof once, and Angus chewed us out so thoroughly that we never tried it again. Looks like it's time for another attempt. I make sure no one is watching out the kitchen window and take a breath as I start my climb. One hand over the other, one step at a time.

My head pops over the edge of the tall, slanted roof and I see him sitting with his back against the chimney, eyes closed behind his glasses. He looks peaceful, but my heart tells me he wouldn't be hiding out if something wasn't wrong.

"You know, this isn't the safest spot for a nap," I say, hoping he won't be upset I came looking for him.

His head swivels my way. He looks sad, and as I make my way across the rooftop, I see that his eyes are red behind his lenses, like he's been crying.

"What's wrong?" I ask, moving until I'm right next to him. My thigh presses against his, our arms and shoulders lining up so I can lean into him. I watch his face, waiting for his answer.

"We're moving," he says, refusing to look at me. Instead, he stares out across the trees into the distance.

"What do you mean? Are your grandparents selling the inn? Where's your new house going to be?" I hate the idea of him not being right next door, but Cluaran's not that big. Maybe next summer I'll bring my bike up so I can get to his house more easily.

He shakes his head, and the faraway look on his face makes me uneasy. I hold my breath, a pit opening in my stomach.

"Gran and Grandad are staying here at the inn. But—" He breaks off with a huff and his lip trembles like he's just barely holding it together. "My parents were offered a job building a new distillery from the ground up. In America."

I gasp and cover my mouth with my hand, and his face crumples.

"You can't move to America," I whisper through my fingers, but it's the wrong thing to say.

"It's not like I have a choice, Avi," he snaps back.

This outburst is so out of character for him that I'm stunned silent. Then his shoulders begin to shake and I take a calming breath to rein in how I'm feeling. This isn't about me. Even if my heart is breaking. Will I ever get to see him again if he moves to the States?

"I know. I'm sorry. When—" I stutter over the word. "When do you leave?"

Please say after the summer. Please say after the summer.

"The last week of break..." He blows out a heavy breath and finally looks at me, anguish written all over his face.

I've never seen a boy cry before—unless they were hurt—and decide on the spot that I hate it. It's even more heartbreaking than when my girlfriends cry. Jamie is always so happy and lighthearted. Seeing him like this is horrible.

I need to find a way to make this better, but I have no idea how to do that.

Mustering all the excitement I can, I say, "We're going to make these the best five weeks ever." Then I wrap my arms around him and pull him as close as I can without knocking us both off the roof.

I breathe him in and remember that he needs me to be strong. I can't fall apart about this. Not right now—not in front of him.

"I'll come back," he says. The words are a caress against the top of my head and goose bumps break out down my neck like they touched me there too. "For the summers. I already made Mum and Dad promise I could come back for summer breaks. Like you do. We can still see each other. Nothing changes for us."

His voice is deeper than it was last year—something I'm only just noticing now that it's so close to my ear. I pull back and realize he's waiting for me to say something. Does he really believe anything would keep me away?

"If you'll be here, I'll be here," I say, holding his gaze and breathing easier knowing this won't be our last summer together. "When did they tell you?"

He settles back against the chimney, closing his eyes and tightening the arm he still has looped over my shoulder. "This morning. They said they didn't want to ruin my last few weeks of school. I guess they figured they'd just ruin my summer instead."

"It's not ruined. It's going to be the best yet, even with one less week." I add extra pep to my voice and hope it doesn't sound as false as it feels. I hate all of this for him.

"I don't want to go," he admits.

"Why not? It'll be an adventure. You love adventures." I lean in farther, wanting to feel his warmth and give him my support at the same time.

"I love adventures when they're with *you*. I love adventures in Scotland. What if I hate it there, Avi? What if I can't make friends?" His voice pulls over the words, like it costs him something to ask these questions, like he's afraid to voice them but can't hold them back.

His confidence is shot, and I hate that too.

"You won't have any trouble making friends. You're incredible," I say, and then blush furiously. It's not that it's untrue, but I don't know whether I've said that outright to him before. "I can't imagine anyone not wanting to be friends with you." I clear my throat and move away from the compliments, hoping my flaming face will cool. "Where is it that you're actually moving?"

I want to help him see the positives, if there are any.

"Nevada. But not near Las Vegas." He shrugs. I don't know anything about Nevada, so I'm no help. "They took a trip out there a few months ago. I thought they were just taking a vacation or something. I guess they were meeting the guy who's backing the distillery."

"Are they not happy here? They practically run Cluaran Distillery, don't they?"

"Aye, they do. Dad said this is their chance to have a part in building something from scratch. The guy wants it to be a traditional Scottish distillery, all Scottish techniques... Mum and Dad will basically oversee the whole thing. It's a huge job. They're excited. I just wish I could have been part of the conversation, you know?"

"Could you stay here, with Angus and Aileen?" I ask, not wanting to hope too much. It doesn't make much of a difference for us, since we only see each other during the summers. But him being so far away, even in between, makes me sad. I can't imagine how it must make him feel.

He shakes his head. "I asked. Well, no, I didn't. I told them I wasn't moving, but that didn't go over well. Mum started crying and Dad looked really mad. I don't really want to be separated from them, but I don't want to move either."

His head falls to my shoulder and my breath catches. I hold it for a beat—two, three—before releasing it and resting my own against the top of his. His red waves tickle my cheek, and on my next inhale, I memorize the way he smells, the feel of his warm skin against mine, and the perfect way we fit together like this.

"I'm sorry, Jamie." It's all I can think to say.

He sighs and I feel it in my bones. I reach over and lace my fingers with his. Then we sit there looking out across the back garden in silence and I wonder if he really will come back next summer.

CHAPTER SIXTEEN

Jamie – Fourteen Years Ago

Why does the school year last forever—each day dragging on for what feels like weeks, months feeling like years—yet the summers always go by too fast?

Of course, this one doesn't just feel shorter. It actually *is*, and with only two days left before we leave, the minutes feels like seconds, and I can't slow it down.

At least Mum and Dad have been so busy prepping for our move that I've had free rein to do whatever I want. Avi and I have filled every minute with as many adventures as possible. Where we used to have to imagine most of them because we couldn't leave the garden or the farm, now we venture out for real. Swimming in the loch, hiking on nearby trails, getting chased by highland cows at a neighboring farm... Our imaginations still come into play though, wondering what it must've been like on Skye a hundred years ago, or imagining we're in Middle Earth or somewhere like it where dragons or Hobbits could appear at any moment.

Avi took my little story to heart last year and asked me to keep adding to it so we'll always have things to do when we come back.

I promised her I will.

She promised she'll keep coming back too.

We'll keep having adventures and nothing has to change.

It almost feels like nothing has changed since the beginning of summer. We're on the roof again, sitting side by side with our backs pressed to the chimney. The only difference from that first day to now is that it's warmer outside. Everywhere our skin touches sticks together, but I have no intention of moving even an inch.

Something shifted between us over the past five weeks. She lets me hold her hand more often. Like when we jumped into the loch last week, then afterward when we lay on the grass to dry off. With her in her bathing suit, it was hard not to stare, but she was looking at me too. There's an awareness of each other that wasn't there before.

Her fingers slide over my thigh to intertwine with mine. My breath hitches and my body flushes hot all over. I bite my cheek and squeeze my eyes shut because I can't always control the way I react to her. She's bonny—hot even—and my body knows it. I study her, committing everything to memory. Her blonde hair is braided over one shoulder, and when she turns to look at me, it swishes against her chest. Her lips are a delicate pink, the same color as her cheeks right now, and her freckles stand out more after weeks in the sun.

She pins me with her warm brown gaze when I reach her eyes, and I can't look away. "Can I ask you something?" she says, her voice soft and breathy, and the color in her cheeks darkens.

"Anything."

"And you'll tell me the truth?" she adds before biting her bottom lip between her teeth.

I nod and say, "Always. I'll never lie to you, Avi."

"Have you..." She exhales shakily. "Have you ever kissed anyone before?"

My eyes widen, the question taking me by surprise, and a tingly feeling zips through my bloodstream.

"Uh..." I lick my lips and try to keep my own skin from flushing hotter. "No, I haven't."

I haven't been avoiding it or anything, but I don't hang out with a lot of lasses during the school year, and there hasn't been anyone I wanted to kiss. Or an opportunity.

Until now.

Because right now, I very much want to kiss a lass. I want to kiss *Avi*.

"Have you?" I ask while tamping down the nerves I feel coursing through my veins.

She shakes her head, breaking our eye contact. And I'm not sure if it's that I'm leaving or that I feel invincible up on this roof, but I lift my hand and gently grip her chin. Heat races through my fingertips and they flex against her skin. "Truth?" I ask, and she nods... "Do you want me to kiss you, Avi?"

I hold my breath, waiting for her answer and pleading internally that she'll say yes.

She nods again and I don't think twice.

I dip my head and press my lips against hers in a tentative brush. I pull back and our eyes catch, bright with excitement and the unknown. This is new for both of us.

This time it's her who moves forward to bring her lips against mine. They're soft and taste slightly of sugar from the biscuits we had earlier. I slide my hand back, cradling her face, and let my fingertips slide into the base of her braid. Her lips part on a breath and I get a little bolder, swiping my tongue along them. A zing of pleasure, of excitement, rushes through me. Her tongue meets mine for only a second before she pulls back, a shy smile on her face.

I've never seen this smile before, but it's definitely my favorite.

"Promise you'll come back next summer?" she says, glancing down to our hands.

"I promise," I say, and her gaze sweeps back up to my face. I begin tracing small circles against her smooth skin, and it feels like a lifeline to this place I don't want to let go of. "And the one after that, and the one after that..."

She presses her forehead against mine and says, "I promise I'll come back *every* summer."

CHAPTER SEVENTEEN

AVONLEA - NOW

*T*ruth?

The word hit me like a ton of bricks the second it left Jamie's lips and nearly knocked me off my feet—and to my death. I was attempting to work up the courage to tell him. The words hovered on the tip of my tongue, but I didn't know what to lead with. *Lennox is yours. You have a son. We have a son.* Each version felt like a gut punch, none of them right.

Too much, too soon.

Not enough, too late.

You'd think him asking me for the truth would've been the perfect opening. He was literally asking for what I'm most terrified to give him, yet it only served to remind me that right now there's nothing *true* between us.

I made it that way.

Everything since we parted ways at seventeen comes back to this one truth I couldn't give him then, and still can't now.

Not even the bookstore can hold my attention once I make it into town. Though, the hot cuppa from Freya's Tea Shoppe helps to settle how shaken I feel after the near accident. My body's reaction to being so close to Jamie was just as unsettling.

I can't stop thinking about how good it felt to be held by him. My body melted into his like it remembered, and then it just let go.

How long has it been since I cried like that in front of another person who wasn't my parents? If I'm honest, I haven't been that unguarded with anyone since Jamie.

And how sad is that?

I follow my feet home, watching the uneven cobblestones under my wellies as I spiral deeper into my thoughts.

I never expected an apology from Jamie, and it was so damn sincere too. But he isn't the only one at fault. I played my own part in our friendship—*relationship*... whatever—falling apart.

I'm the one who cut him out of my life and lied when we always promised each other the truth.

Nope, not going to do that.

Beating myself up for decisions I made as a heartbroken and scared seventeen-year-old won't help anything. I had my reasons. And when the sands of time wore those down and I wanted to make a different choice, new reasons presented themselves.

But things have changed, and I need to forge a new path forward.

When I pass a cottage just down from the inn with a *For Rent* placard in the garden, it feels like a sign. My gut tells me it would be perfect for me and Lennox, and the first step on this new path needs to be locking down a place for us to live. Only then can I consider telling Jamie everything.

I wonder—not for the first time—why he's never settled down with anyone. In my years of silently keeping tabs on him through social media, I've never seen a woman make an appearance other than his friend Rory—and she's been around since he first moved to Tahoe. I was irrationally jealous of her as a teen, and as embarrassing as it is to admit it, I still am. It stung to watch him move on with a new friend. Especially another girl.

As a perpetual bachelor, how will he react to finding out he's a dad? Or that he's missed out on ten years of his son's life? I don't even know how I want him to react. Do I want him to want to be part of Lennox's life? The obvious answer is yes, but we have a good thing going. I don't want to completely obliterate our comfortable balance if Jamie isn't even going to be around.

And he won't be.

He has a whole life in America to go back to once everything settles here.

He won't stay. He wouldn't stay for me then, and he won't stay for Lennox now. So, at best, he'd be a part-time "dad" from a world away which will only hurt Lennox... And me.

Or what if he doesn't want anything to do with Lennox? That thought makes my heart ache in my chest. How could he not want him?

Stop, Avi. You're getting ahead of yourself.

I inhale deeply when I reach the loch and look out over the shining waters. There's no use overthinking all the possibilities. I just have to tell him and figure out the rest from there.

I head up the garden path to the kitchen, looking at the bench swing that sits in place of the tire we once played on.

So much has changed.

The kitchen is oddly quiet. The calm before the storm that comes between breakfast and lunch. I set to work chopping onions for tonight's sauce, the scrape of my knife across the cutting board the only sound in the space. I'm thankful for the potent sting the onions elicit—at least if anyone walks in, they'll think my red-rimmed eyes are due to them.

I toss them into a pan with some garlic and herbs and the kitchen is instantly filled with their aromatic scent. Everything inside me relaxes a little. This is where I feel most comfortable, most at peace. In my kitchen.

As I wash my hands, a pair of booted feet pass the window on the way up the ladder to the roof. Jamie's boots.

I guess things haven't changed that much. I wonder if he's headed up there to escape whatever it was that happened between us earlier, or if he just needs to think. Or maybe he wants to write.

I never see him on his computer, like I'd expect if he's working on a new project. Instead, he's always with Aileen or Angus, helping with whatever he can around the inn. Whether it's checking in guests or oiling rusty hinges, cutting back the hedges when they get unruly or tidying up the parlor. I even spotted him turning down beds one evening when they were short-staffed. It's clear he's attempting to lighten their load.

But surely he's still writing?

"Mornin', lass," Hamish says, walking in the kitchen door.

"Mornin', Hamish." I nod in his direction and then dry my hands before checking the onions.

"Everything prepped for lunch?" he asks, looking into the saucepan from the other side of the cooktop.

"Aye, and I got a head start on the sauce for dinner."

Thank goodness Angus already had an incredible team when I got here. It was like walking into a well-oiled machine. I'm sure it would have been rewarding to build a restaurant from the ground up like my mother and father did, but it's been one less stress to have the support of both Angus and Hamish.

"Aye, perfect. I'll take over for a bit if you've got anything you need to do before the lunch rush."

My phone buzzes in the back pocket of my jeans, giving me a timely excuse, and I take him up on his offer. "Okay. Come get me if you need anything," I say, pulling it out and seeing Lennox's name on a banner across the screen.

At that moment, Angus pushes through the door with a smile on his face. "Ah, he's got me now. Go talk to your wee laddie." He points his chin at my phone.

"You're not supposed to be cooking." I level him with a glare before feeling a second buzz in my hand. "Hamish, don't let him lift a finger."

"You're no fun, you know that?" Angus says back. He squeezes my bicep when he passes and then sits heavily in the chair behind his desk. "There, you happy?"

His mock scowl makes me laugh, because not even that look on his face hides the jovial man he is underneath. The bags under his eyes say he's tired, but you'd never know it with the way he acts. But just because he pretends well doesn't mean I don't see it. "Very. Now you better still be right there when I get back or I'll tell Aileen."

"You wouldn't dare," he says, feigning outrage.

"Don't test me." I smile at him and then give Hamish a lift of my eyebrow to let him know I'm not messing around.

Unlocking my screen, I see the texts from Lennox.

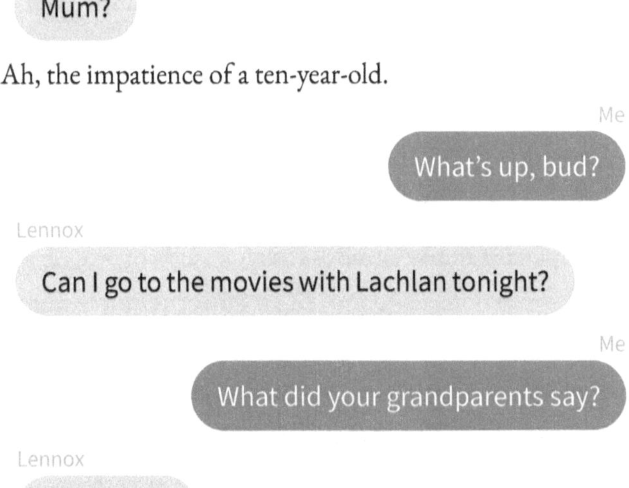

Ah, the impatience of a ten-year-old.

Lennox

(eyeroll emoji) Aye

Me

Okay. Are you busy, or do you want to talk for a few minutes?

Lennox

Sure

And then there's the one-word answers. Parenting at its finest.

My phone rings in my hand and I swipe across the screen and head upstairs with it pressed to my ear.

"Hey, how was school this week?" I ask without preamble, even though I've asked about his day every evening.

"It was fine, Mum." His voice is annoyed... Not my favorite kind of hello. But even with his tone, just hearing my boy on the other end of the line makes my lips lift into a smile.

"Okay, I was just checking. Have anything fun planned with your grandparents this weekend?" I ask.

Letting myself into my room, I sit on the edge of my bed and flop back onto it.

"I think Gran is working, but Pa said he'd take me hiking." There's an uptick in his excitement at this.

My grin widens. Hiking was something I did with my dad on the weekends when Mum had to work. It was where my love for the outdoors started.

An unexpected benefit to having Lennox so young is that my parents get to enjoy all of his active years right along with him. They've only just turned fifty and are still getting out and traveling and taking adventures whenever they can, and now they get to include me and Lennox in them.

"That'll be fun. Is he taking you anywhere cool?" I ask, tucking my arm behind my head and propping myself up.

"Loch Lomond."

"Nice! I can't wait to show you some of the places up here. Since we didn't get a chance to explore last year."

"Gran said you're coming home in a few weeks, but I thought they were going to bring me to Skye."

I stumble over what to tell him.

I can't exactly go with the truth—that his dad is here—so I settle on, "I haven't gotten us a house yet, so I thought it'd be easier for me to come to you for a few days. Once I get our new place figured out, you can come up, okay?"

"Aye, sure, whatever." I can hear the disappointment in his voice.

"So, what's the movie tonight?" I ask.

"I don't know. Whatever Lachlan wants, I guess." I can picture him rolling his green eyes and shrugging his bony shoulders. He's rail-thin after a growth spurt this spring, all knobby knees and elbows.

"Shouldn't you have a say?" I push. I want him to stand up for himself more, and I'm sick of his friends walking all over him.

"They were already planning to go when he said I could come, so I don't think I get much choice."

His "friends" at school have been excluding him more and more lately. I don't know why, but it seems like he's always the afterthought. I'm ready for this school year to be over. Then he can move up here and hopefully find a new group of friends.

One more thing to add to my list: enroll Lennox in the local school. I should ask Jamie about it, considering he actually went to primary school here.

"I hope you have fun at least. You call Gran or Pa if you need to be picked up early or anything."

I miss being the one he could call. This distance between us is so much harder than I anticipated.

"I'll be fine, Mum," he says, like he's exasperated with my overprotectiveness.

"Okay, sorry. I just miss you. You're doing okay?"

"Yeah, Mum, jeeze," he grumbles. Then his voice softens when he adds, "I miss you too."

I close my eyes and soak in those words. Six more weeks. We can make it six more weeks, right?

"Have fun tonight. I love you."

"I love you too."

"Bye—" I start to say, but he's already hung up.

Ten-year-olds, I think with an eye roll. Ten—it's the same age Jamie and I were when we met, and that feels like a lifetime ago now.

CHAPTER EIGHTEEN

JAMIE - NOW

"**G**randad?" I holler into the quiet before closing the door behind me. There's not a squeaky hinge left on this property after I went at them all in my first few weeks here, but I doubt there's any WD-40 left in this whole village either.

"In here," he calls, and I follow his voice toward the parlor where he sits with a cup of tea, a biscuit, and an open book.

"Mind if I join you?" I ask, sliding the wooden box I'm carrying under my arm onto the table.

He motions to the chair next to him. "Of course. What do you have there?" he asks, pulling his glasses down his nose to look at the box. "Ah, I know what that is."

"Yeah?" I ask, and a tingle of anticipation rolls down my spine.

He's got a dreamy smile on his face. "Can you hand it to me?"

I pick it up and place it on his lap before sitting on the edge of my seat, elbows on my knees as I lean toward him. When he lifts the lid, his whole face softens at the sight of the mess of papers inside.

Letters.

It's an entire box of letters. Some in yellowed envelopes. Some loose. Some rolled and tied with a ribbon or twine. Others remind me of the international envelopes you see in war movies with the red and blue striping, covered in intricate stamps.

"You were in the attic, I see." He fingers a few of the letters, lifting one and reading the words with a wistful expression.

The attic was my refuge today when even the roof couldn't help me figure out how to feel after my short-lived outing with Avi earlier. I told Gran I'd help organize some of the old stuff up there—which I did—but then I found this and immediately abandoned my duties to come in search of Grandad.

"I didn't read them," I say, wanting to be clear that I wasn't snooping, per se. "But I am curious."

"Of course you are," he says with a low chuckle. "These are mine and your Gran's letters. All of them... well, almost. We have a new box for the ones we've written since this one filled up."

"You still write each other? Even now?" I ask.

"Not as frequently... but aye, we do."

How did I never know this? That my love for words might not just be mine but was theirs as well. Still is, from the sound of it. "Is that why when I said I was writing a story for Avi all those years ago, you told me to write with my heart?"

"I was pretty wise back then," he says with a cheeky smile. "I'm amazed you remember that."

"You're still pretty wise, and I pretty much live by those words."
I deepen my voice and recite them from memory: "*If you write it with your heart, you'll never go astray.*"

"That's right." He chuckles and holds the box out toward me. "Here, you take these. Give 'em a read. See what you make of them." He taps his nose with a knowing smile. "You might find some more wisdom hidden in there."

"You're sure you don't mind?" I slide my hands around the box like it's treasure, gripping it firmly.

"Och, no. I don't think there's anything in there that would scar you." He laughs, and I do too. But then he sobers and reaches a hand over to cover one of mine. "I can see you're looking for something. I can't guarantee you'll find it in there, but you never know."

Am I looking for something?

Maybe so. I just wish I knew what it was.

"Thanks, Grandad." I stand and hoist the box under my arm again, giving his hand a final squeeze. I'm getting better at reading his good days and bad days—the ones where he doesn't make it into the kitchen or goes to bed before we can all have dinner—but today is a good day.

"Anything for you, Jameson. Anything for you." His grey eyes glitter behind his glasses and he holds my gaze for just a beat too long.

"See you for dinner?" I ask, breaking whatever odd tension there is between us. What I wouldn't give to be able to read his mind.

"Wouldn't miss it. Avi's been working over the meat pies all afternoon, so you know I'll be there."

"Can't pass up a meat pie out of your kitchen," I say, backing away toward the door.

"Avi's kitchen. Hers are better," he says matter-of-factly, unwavering pride resonating in his voice.

"Well, I guess I'll find out tonight."

The anticipation of digging into the letters makes me light on my feet as I head for my room.

I'm staying in the inn's owner suite. Which I appreciate, considering the other option was my old room in the cottage—and my six-foot-two frame was not made for a twin bed. I didn't want to impose on Gran and Grandad's space either, and I like being inside the inn so the night manager can come to me instead of bothering them in their cottage if there's an issue.

In my room, I sit back against the headboard and peer into the box. There must be hundreds of letters inside.

Love letters.

I'm so out of my depth here. I've never so much as written a love letter—unless I count the emails I attempted to send to Avi, but I'm not going to count those. Nope, and I'm not going to think about them either.

I'm leaving all that behind. Time to move forward. No more looking back.

I grab a few of the loose sheets from the top of the pile and am met with two sets of distinct handwriting. My grandmother's is a loopy script, feminine and soft. My grandfather's is more precise and shows his steady hand, thoughtful and exact. I take note of the dates written in the top right-hand corners: *February 1965, March 1970...*

I pull them all from the box and begin arranging them in order. Logically, I should read them that way, right? But it's hard to focus on the dates when the obvious affection pours off the page like water over the falls into the Fairy Pools. It's so clear, so obvious, how much they care for each other with every word written.

Once I finally have them all stacked together—483 letters in total—all I want is to dive into what I'm sure is one of the most beautiful love stories ever written, but there's a knock at my door that pulls me away. Glancing at my watch, I realize it's gone six o'clock—dinnertime. This is going to have to wait.

I'm surprised to find Avonlea standing on the other side of my door.

How is she this stunning in a T&T Pub apron?

"Hi," she says, and ducks her head away from my searching gaze. "Your gran asked me to come get you for dinner."

"Of course she did," I mumble. "You okay, after this morning's scare?"

She nods and I step out of my room, closing the door with a click behind me.

"Aye. Thank you for keeping me from becoming roadkill." She chuckles under her breath and glances up at me from beneath her lashes. I'm glad she can laugh about it, because my heart was riotous the whole walk back to the inn. I think I looked over my shoulder a dozen times to make sure she was okay.

"Happy to be of assistance," I say.

When we reach the dining room, I expect her to go back to the kitchen, but she follows me to the booth in the corner. She hasn't eaten with us since the night she arrived. I think she's been hiding in the kitchen to avoid me. Maybe my apology this morning paved the way for her to feel comfortable eating with us again.

"Aren't you going to take your apron off, dear?" Gran asks.

Avi glances down and laughs. "Oh. I forgot I had it on. Back in a mo'." She saunters into the kitchen, her lithe hips swaying as she goes.

I squeeze my eyes shut and then open them only to see my grandparents watching me with knowing, conspiratorial smiles on their lips.

Well, shit. My propensity toward blushing has never gone away, and I feel the tips of my ears heat. I glance back toward the kitchen where Avi comes out the swinging door a moment later.

My heart stops.

Now I can see what I couldn't before.

She's wearing an Empyreal Mountain Resort sweatshirt. It's faded and worn and looks like it's been washed about a million times. But it's mine—or it *was*. And she still has it.

CHAPTER NINETEEN

AVONLEA – THIRTEEN YEARS AGO

I find Jamie on the roof. How this became our place, I'm not sure, but I've been looking forward to this rooftop reunion for what feels like forever, not just a year.

The ladder to the top is now an affixed, sturdy thing. Angus must've known we'd keep using the rickety old one and were likely to break our necks if he didn't upgrade it.

"Hey, Jamie," I say as my head pops above the roofline to catch him watching for me. He looks... good. Older.

Hotter.

"Hey, Avi," his voice husks, and—wow—that's different too. I can almost feel its deeper timbre like a brush against my senses.

I take my time making my way over to him but stop short and sit with my legs curled under me. Jamie's broad shoulders take up more of the width of the chimney now, so I don't think we can sit there side by side anymore. I take in all of his features and the other ways he's changed.

The most prominent one is his lack of glasses. "Did you get contacts?"

He nods. "Aye, and it's nice not to worry about the glasses all the time." He holds my gaze and, with nothing in the way to block those beautiful green irises, I feel like I'm trapped in them, swimming in a sea of emeralds.

"You cut your hair," he states, scooting away from the chimney so he can reach out and push the lock that's fluttering around my face behind my ear. If I had goose bumps before, it's nothing to the shiver that rolls down my spine now.

"Do you like it?" I duck my chin, effectively pulling away from his hand. The meticulously styled waves fall forward again, brushing my shoulders. All the girls in my class—or the cool ones at least—cut their hair shorter before the end of school, so I did too. But I still don't know that I like it.

"I do." There's a smile in his voice that I want to see, so I look up, letting our eyes lock again. I wonder if he'll kiss me—like the last time we were on this roof—but he doesn't. Instead, he pushes back to sit against the chimney.

I hide the pang of disappointment with a question. "Truth?" I ask, and his smile goes wide.

"Anything you wanna know," he says.

"How do you like it in America?"

His shoulders relax and he looks so cool. Comfortable. There's a confidence to the way he holds himself now that I don't think I noticed before.

"It's pretty great actually. The town we live in, it's near Lake Tahoe." At my mystified expression, he clarifies. "It's a huge loch, but they don't call them that. They say lake. You'd love it. It's so blue and the water is super clear—like, you can see these huge boulders way down beneath the surface. And it's surrounded by massive mountains. The whole area reminds me a lot of Scotland, except it almost never rains."

"What must that be like," I say with a giggle, looking over my shoulder at the darker clouds in the distance that are sure to bring the rain with them.

"Yeah, it's really dry there. But the mountains... It's like being surrounded by a whole range of peaks as big or bigger than Ben Nevis. I even learned how to snowboard last winter, and the hiking is incredible. The people are nice. And there's a lot more of them." He laughs, and I almost miss the one that was more boyish. He's only fifteen, but this is a man's laugh, and it surprises me. "There's two hundred kids in just my year at school."

"Are you making friends?" I can't imagine he isn't; who wouldn't want to be friends with Jamie?

"Aye. I joined the school paper. Can you believe it, they have a school paper? Well, of course your school probably does too, but we didn't have that here. Anyway, it's great. My friend Rory—you'd love her—she and I do that together which is pretty cool. Everyone else is nice too."

I feel red-hot jealousy score through me. He has a new "girl" friend, and she's the only one that he singled out by name. I shouldn't hate that, but a tiny (or not so tiny) part of me does. He didn't call her his *girlfriend* though, so at least there's that.

"That's great, Jamie," I say, forcing a smile. "So you're happy?"

"Yeah, I guess. It's different, but mostly in good ways. I miss Gran and Grandad and my friends here. But I think Mum and Dad were right, and it's been good to get out and experience somewhere new."

"Do you think you'll stay there…?" I ask and then bite my lip. Why did I ask that?

"Like forever?" He scrunches his brows in question.

I shrug. I've thought a lot about his promise to always come back, but what happens when summer breaks become a thing of the past? Will he come back to Scotland or will I lose him to his new home and never see him again?

"I don't know. Mum and Dad really love their new jobs at the distillery. I imagine they'll stay, but who knows what I'll do after I finish school. I mean, I could come back to Scotland for university, but there are great ones there too."

It's his turn to shrug. I open my mouth to tell him about the culinary schools I've been looking at for after I finish secondary school, but he keeps talking, his eyes shifting away from me.

"My girlfriend, Cat, thinks she'll go to UNR—that's the university about an hour from us. It sounds like a good one."

I stutter over the word in my brain. Girlfriend. *Girlfriend*? The stutter carries over to my speech when I say, "You—you have a girlfriend?" My attempt at nonchalance fails miserably. If I thought I was jealous a minute ago when he mentioned Rory, it is nothing to how I feel now.

There's an apology in his eyes. Maybe he can see me turning green with envy.

"Aye, she, uh—she's a cheerleader." He rubs the back of his neck, ears going pink.

I snort a laugh. "A cheerleader, huh? Like with pom-poms?" Turns out my defense mechanism right now is pettiness.

"Aye," he says, sounding defensive. "She asked me out about a month ago."

I never would've pictured him with a cheerleader. That girl Rory, from the paper, sounds more like his type. But what do I know about that anyway? It's not like he ever talked to me about girls before. It's always just been us, in this little bubble on Skye, but now...

"Is she your first? Girlfriend, I mean..." I trail off, feeling so stupid. There I was wondering if he'd lean in and kiss me, and he has a girlfriend. Of course he does, look at him!

"Nah. I've had a couple," he says, and swipes a hand through his hair.

"A couple?" I ask, incredulous.

"I mean, it's high school... well, that's what they call it at least. I think they just like me for my accent."

"Who wouldn't?" I say under my breath, and he smiles like he's pleased by my assessment. He was never cocky, so this is a new side of him that I haven't seen before. If he puts this air on in front of all the girls at school, it's no wonder he's had multiple girlfriends. But I prefer the real Jamie to this one. My Jamie.

"What about you? Any boyfriends?" He waggles his eyebrows at me and my cheeks heat under his stare.

"Maybe..." I say, turning my face away as it flushes deeper. "I don't kiss and tell."

Not that there's much to tell. There was only one boy, and even though the kissing was frequent, it never made me feel the way my first kiss with Jamie did.

His eyes widen like he's surprised… or maybe because he doesn't like to hear I was kissing another boy. I hope it's the latter; jealousy is better than him thinking there aren't any boys who'd want to kiss me.

"Sounds like it was a good year for the both of us." He bumps my shoe with his and I look into the face of my best friend. I nod and force a smile to match his.

But on the inside, my heart sinks as I realize our comfortable contact—the hugs, the hand holding—is a thing of the past for our friendship now. It would be too intimate as just friends, especially now that he has a girlfriend. *Cat.* Ugh, it's such a cheerleader name. She's probably the captain too. I try not to roll my eyes—or cry.

"So, where's our book of adventures then? We've got to make it a great summer as well," I say with all the confidence I can muster, feeling as if our summers will never be the same now.

CHAPTER TWENTY

JAMIE - THIRTEEN YEARS AGO

Why didn't I break up with her before coming to Scotland? I ask myself for the millionth time as I get off the phone with Cat.

I like her—I do—but I don't miss her between our weekly calls, and that tells me something.

We've had three since I arrived. Gran and Grandad only allow me one per week because of the cost, and all she talks about is cheer camp and practice. She never asks me what I'm doing, and though she says she misses me, I'm not sure she really does.

It's probably better that she's not asking, considering all my stories revolve around Avi and I spending time together. Every single one.

If I'd broken up with Cat, I know I would've kissed Avi that first day on the roof... and every day after. That's part of why I didn't. Not because I don't want to kiss Avi—it's the opposite, really. Which definitely makes me a shit boyfriend.

I didn't want to risk ruining what Avi and I have. I love our summers together, and it's not like we can be girlfriend and boyfriend anyway. We don't even live on the same continent anymore. Maybe if I'd stayed in Scotland it could've been possible, but it will only ever be the summers for us. I wouldn't be able to live with myself if she wanted it to be more and our friendship broke.

But I think about that first kiss more often than I should. Even though I've kissed more than my fair share of girls since then, none of them felt as good as that *one* with Avi—and there wasn't even tongue.

So, instead of filling our time with kissing, we've been systematically crossing off adventures from my notebook for the last three weeks. She brought her bike with her, which has given us a lot more freedom. If it's within biking distance, we've done it.

We've gone into town for a couple of shinty matches with my old schoolmates. They all look at her in a way I'd rather they didn't, but she hasn't taken a fancy to any of them—thank god. Not that I could say anything if she did. She can fancy anyone she likes... I just don't want her to.

We've gotten fish and chips in the next town over and popped in and out of every shop in Cluaran at least ten times. The shop owners welcomed me back with open arms and asked how Mum and Dad are, how we like things in the States. And if they didn't know Avi before, they definitely do now.

On the hotter days, we end up down at the loch where someone built a rope swing. I love watching Avi laugh from the shore after

I take a running swing out into the water, but I love it even more when she follows me. Those are the hardest days to keep from kissing her. Her swimsuit isn't all that revealing—I guess her mum knew her grandparents wouldn't allow her to wear a bikini—but the way it fits her is a dream. My dream, at least.

We've done just about every hike in the area too, so today we're sneaking off for a bigger adventure. One we've kept under wraps, because I doubt the grandparents would approve... Hers or mine.

Gran and Grandad have always given me a lot of freedom in the summers, just like my parents did when they were here. I've never been one to get into trouble. My dad's a firm believer in giving me enough rope to hang myself with and hoping that I don't. But Avonlea's grandparents are much stricter, and I feel like we're forever reassuring them that we aren't out causing trouble. They know exactly where we are or where we're going at all times.

So for today's adventure, we might've told a little white lie.

I mean, we *will* be seeing Armadale Castle. It'll just be from the water instead of the grounds.

I hop on my bike that was leaning against the cottage and head for the road.

"You ready?" Avi asks when I get to the end of the drive. She's standing astride her bike in a pair of navy-blue shorts, a T-shirt that shows a sliver of her smooth stomach, and her denim jacket.

I swallow thickly. "Aye, let's go." I shoot her a wink and watch her cheeks go pink before she saddles up and sets off.

The bike ride between Cluaran and the Armadale Ferry Terminal isn't too long, though it's the farthest we've gone this summer. Avi responds to most of my questions with short answers, and when I ride up beside her, she's chewing her lip.

"We don't have to do this, you know," I say, wishing I could give her a reassuring hug—but one, we're on bikes, and two, we haven't really touched at all this summer.

"No, I want to. I just... I don't want to get in trouble." She bites down on her lip again as she glances my way.

"We won't. We'll be back well before dinner and no one will have a clue. But if you want, we really can go tour the castle."

She shakes her head, her shorter hair brushing the tops of her shoulders. I'm still not sure how I feel about this new style. She's bonny—she always is—but I loved the way her hair used to hang down her back in long waves. It was carefree and she never worried about it getting messy, she'd just throw it in a braid and be done with it. Now she spends an hour of her morning—I know because I've had to wait every day—styling it and getting the curls just right. I've noticed the makeup she wears now too. I don't like how it hides the freckles on her cheeks.

"Okay, well good, because the ferry is here and we better get on it." I offer her my cheekiest grin—the one that never fails to garner a blush from the girls back home, and I'm rewarded with one from her as well. Score.

We peddle down to the dock and I buy us tickets with the cash Mum and Dad gave me before I got on the plane to fly here. They weren't able to make the trip with me because of where they are in the process of getting the distillery up and running. It was my first time flying by myself, and while I loved the independence, I did get a little lonely.

We walk our bikes onto the ferry that will take us away from Skye and to the mainland of Scotland, our biggest adventure yet.

We find a couple of seats on the upper deck and watch the water churn behind us. Armadale Castle sits overlooking the water in the distance. "See, we saw the castle." I nudge Avi's shoulder with mine and she pushes back with a smile on her face and a brightness to her brown eyes.

She hasn't looked at me like that since the first day on the roof. I've missed that look.

The wind picks up and her body shivers against my side. I feel warm all over, but that has nothing to do with the temperature. "You cold?" I ask.

She shakes her head, but I don't believe her. Her outfit isn't doing much to ward off the chill. I pull off my hoodie and hand it to her. It's my new one from Empyreal, the ski resort in Tahoe where I learned to snowboard this past winter.

The look she gives me when she runs the fabric through her hands makes my heart inflate in my chest. It's like the moment in a movie when the heroine says *my hero*, and I realize I kind of want to be her hero.

She pulls it on over her denim jacket and it knocks free the small braid she had pinned by her ear. I grasp it between my fingers and set it back, deftly grabbing the pin and fixing it to where it was. I stare into her eyes and watch the golden flecks in their brown depths shimmer in the afternoon sun. She shivers again when my thumb brushes the shell of her ear.

"Thanks." Her voice is quiet, just above a whisper.

"Welcome," I say, and then because I feel like being reckless, I wrap an arm around her shoulder and pull her closer. It's just this side of being too friendly, but I wouldn't have thought twice about it last year, so I tell myself it's fine.

She doesn't pull away. She stays snuggled tight into my side for the entire ferry ride, watching Skye shrink in the distance. She fiddles with the cuffs on my sweatshirt and I want to hold her hand so badly, wrap it in both of mine...

The boat approaches the dock—just in time to keep me from doing something stupid. When Avi stands up, it's clear how big the sweatshirt is on her as it nearly hides her shorts entirely. She moves to take it off, but I stay her hand at the hem, liking the way my fingers accidentally trail over her thigh far too much.

"Keep it. I'm fine, and this way we can sit outside while we eat lunch."

"Alright." Her eyelashes flutter as she looks up at me. "Thanks, Jamie."

We walk our bikes off the ferry, as far from Cluaran as I've ever been without either my parents or grandparents. We didn't often go to the mainland, and I've definitely never done it by myself. But there's a small restaurant called The Bakehouse that sits just on the quay where you can watch the boats come in and out, and that's our destination.

Lunch on the quay with my best friend. Just the two of us. It's not like it's a date... but it feels like one.

We lock up our bikes just outside the old stone exterior and the smell of fresh baked bread wafts around us, mingling with the soft scents of the sea and the flowers spilling out of the baskets that hang on either side of the door. Avi begins bouncing up and down on her toes when we walk inside and see the bakery case. It's overflowing with croissants, danishes, sticky buns...

It's a baker's dream, and I wish I could take a loaf of bread back to Gran and Grandad for us to have with dinner tonight... but that would give away our secret. I should've just told them, but they would've told the Campbells.

"So, which one will it be?" I ask Avi.

She's practically salivating over the selection. "The Baklava danish. Definitely. You?" She turns and we're nearly eye to eye. She grew several inches this year, and while I also grew, I'm only just taller than her at the moment.

"The maple pecan danish... and pizza."

"Well, duh." She knocks me with her shoulder and I restrain myself from wrapping my arm around hers again.

After we've ordered a pizza to share—they make all their dough in-house—and our danishes, we head for a table outside that overlooks the water. Boats putter about in the harbour and people mill around, enjoying the beautiful weather without a cloud in sight... At least for the moment.

"Don't you miss this?" she asks, looking past me to Skye in the distance.

"Aye. Parts of it." I'm only looking at her.

"Which parts?" I feel her gaze like a brand as it lands on me and moves up my torso, finally resting on my face. I definitely don't need a sweatshirt with the heat I feel from just that look.

"My grandparents mostly... and you." I swallow. That was probably too much. "I mean, I know I don't see you during the year anyway, so nothing's really changed, but it feels different. Doesn't it?" I ask, wondering if she feels the distance too.

"It does." She nods. "Do you think we could talk? During the school year? I just mean…" She trails off and bites her lip. Why is it so cute when she does that?

"Aye. I'd like that," I reply, excited by the prospect of having a way to contact her outside of these six weeks each year.

"Okay, cool. Me too. Like, I know phone calls are expensive, but maybe we could email or something. It doesn't have to be all the time, but maybe just to talk about school, or friends, or whatever." She's rambling and it's even cuter than when she bites her lip.

"Email would be good, but I don't want to think about going back yet. I just want to enjoy being here. With you."

My leg brushes hers under the table. She doesn't pull it away and I feel that twinge again—wishing I had broken things off with Cat at the end of the school year—because I'd really like to do more than brush my leg against Avi's, and I know that I can't.

That beautiful weather we were having… Yeah, that disappears in a puff of grey clouds that move in quick and dark.

We're only about halfway back to Armadale on the ferry when they open up in a downpour. We can't even get to the protected interior of the boat before we're soaked through to the bone. We start out laughing, pushing our way to a couple of seats, dripping wet. But as we sit, cold and huddled together for the remainder of the ride, we grow more and more concerned with the time. We caught the last ferry that would get us home by dinner, but we didn't account for the rain continuing to pound the exterior.

And it never lets up, so when we disembark on Skye, we know it's too wet to ride the bikes home—too likely we could lose traction and crash. So, we start walking...

As we approach the inn, I spot Gran standing in the front window watching for us, and I know Avi's grannie will be waiting for her as well. We're late. Now we just have to hope neither of them has any reason to question where we've been.

"We were at the castle all day," I say to Avi, watching a drop of water slip down her nose, "and when the rain started, we thought we'd wait it out at the café there. But it didn't let up, so we decided to walk home in it. Thus the soaking clothes and why we're late. Okay?" I ask her as we get closer and closer to the farmhouse.

"Okay." Her teeth clatter together and her perfectly styled curls hang limply, dripping down over my sweatshirt.

"Get a hot shower and warm up, yeah?" I nod toward her house.

"Y-yeah. I'll come over after dinner if Grannie will let me."

"Okay." I want to hug her. I want to *kiss* her. But I don't think I can even get away with the hug right now, let alone anything more. Not with our grandmothers staring us down from their respective porches.

She rounds the hedge on one side and I go to the other.

"You've got some explaining to do, Jameson," Gran says as I walk up the steps. "You're absolutely soaked. Get yourself to the cottage to clean up and then meet me in the kitchen."

"Yes, ma'am." Her disappointed scowl zaps all the fun out of today in an instant, and I don't even bother arguing.

The rain has died down by the time I'm out of the shower and heading for the kitchen, my mouth watering as I open the door.

"Hey, Grandad," I say, finding him standing over the large island in the middle, a towel thrown over one shoulder and his hands in a pile of dough.

"Jameson." It's just my name, but the way he says it makes me stand a little taller. Oof. Maybe I am in trouble. I glance around the kitchen, at the hustle and bustle of servers and other staff hard at work to get plates out to the patrons in the pub.

"I'm sorry we were late getting back," I say. Might as well jump into the excuses before I forget what they're supposed to be. "The rain—"

"Let me guess," he interrupts me, grey eyes pinning me in place. "The rain hit and you thought you'd wait it out at the castle, but then it was getting late so you walked your bikes back..."

"Aye..." I string the word out, wondering how he knew the exact story I was about to tell.

"Hmph..." It's just a sound under his breath, but it's a distinctly Scottish one, and it tells me in an instant that he doesn't believe me. "I've never taken you for a liar, Jameson."

I startle back like he struck me. "I—" I don't know what to say because I *did* lie to him, but the word "liar" hits me hard.

"Hamish saw you on the ferry," he states.

My face falls. Hamish is the T&T's sous chef. *Shit.*

"I'm sorry. I should've told you." No point continuing the lie now. "Did you... did you tell the Campbells?"

I glance toward the window that faces the farmhouse. I'm not really concerned for my own fate here, but I don't want Avi to get into trouble with her grandparents. This was all my idea and is all my fault.

Gran walks in at that moment and says, "No, we didn't. Thought maybe we should talk to you first."

My shoulders relax and I breathe a sigh of relief. "It was my idea. Avi just went along with it. I don't want her to get into trouble. I shouldn't have lied to you guys. I promise we just rode the ferry over to have lunch and hang around the quay." All the words tumble out of me as I try to convince them to keep this between us.

"Yeah, Hamish saw you two ride your bikes to the Bakehouse," Grandad says.

He must've had the day off if he was going over to the mainland. I want to be mad about him ratting us out, but I know this is my fault, not his.

My shoulders slump forward. "I'm so sorry." A gnawing guilt forms in the pit of my stomach. I hate letting people down—my grandparents most of all. "It won't happen again."

"No. It won't," Gran says, and her tone brooks no argument. "If we can't trust you to be where you say you'll be, Jameson, then you won't be allowed to leave the grounds of the inn. What do you think your parents would think if they knew we let you go galivanting over to the mainland by yourself? They might not let you come back for another summer if they can't trust you to be safe. Anything could've happened and we wouldn't have known where you were."

"You're right. I'm sorry, Gran. I promise it won't happen again. We'll stay in Cluaran, we'll only ever be where we say we are. Promise."

They exchange a glance and I think I have them convinced that I don't have any intention of breaking their trust again.

"You'll be helping with dishes after dinner service each night this week," Grandad says with his stern voice. I've only ever heard it a couple of times and I hate that he's having to use it with me now.

I nod and don't let my disappointment show. I deserve worse and just hope Avi gets off as easy.

I'm elbow-deep in sudsy water when Avi knocks on the kitchen door. She doesn't say anything as she grabs a second pair of gloves and joins me at the sink.

"Did you get into trouble?" I ask, looking sideways at her.

She shrugs. "Grannie was mad I was late, but I think she believed my story. She doesn't want us taking the bikes out of Cluaran anymore." Her face falls but my lips lift. At least that's the worst of it. "What about you?"

"Gran and Grandad know we left the island," I say, shoulders slumping as I press my hands into the counter.

"What?" She whips her head to look at me and drops the plate she was washing into the water with a *plop*.

"Yeah." I blow out a big breath and meet her worried eyes. "Hamish was on the ferry this morning." I grimace at the look on her face. "Don't worry, they're not going to tell your grandparents. But they don't want us riding out of Cluaran anymore either. They're disappointed in me that I lied to them."

My eyes burn and I blink back the wetness that tries to gather there. I will not cry in front of Avi, absolutely not.

"I'm sorry, Jamie."

"No, *I'm* sorry. It was my stupid idea." I keep thinking about how badly I could've screwed up the rest of our summer with this little stunt.

"I didn't put up much of a fight," she adds sheepishly.

I shrug and move back to the dishes in the sink.

She squeezes my hand underneath the soapy water and then grabs for the plate she dropped. "I'll bring you back your sweatshirt tomorrow. Grannie's washing it."

I glance over and take her in for the first time since she came in. Her hair is still damp from her shower, pulled into a messy bun on top of her head, and there's no makeup on her face. I can finally see all the freckles on her cheeks again. She looks like *my Avi*, and I can't help but smile despite the circumstances.

"You can keep it..." I say, when all I want to do is blurt out how much hotter she is like this—relaxed, comfortable, casual. "If you want."

I really liked the way she looked in it anyway, and I love the idea of her having something of mine. Maybe she'll wear it when she gets back home and think of me more often.

"Really?" she says quietly, her cheek lifting on one side as a small smile overtakes her lips.

"Aye." I'm sure Mum will ask what happened to it, but I'll just use some of my allowance to buy another one.

"Thanks, Jamie." She turns back to the sink and so do I. As we finish the dishes, I feel every brush of her shoulder against mine like an electric shock, but I keep leaning in for more.

CHAPTER TWENTY-ONE

Avonlea – Now

After my nightly call with Lennox and one last check of the kitchen to ensure it's gleaming for breakfast service tomorrow, I head for the parlor and the small library of books there. I didn't bring any of mine from home, and though I have my Kindle, I'm craving the feel of a physical book in my hands. I scan the shelves, hoping someone left a book that will grab my interest and keep me from dwelling on the one thing—*person*—that never seems far from my mind these days.

I brush my fingers across the spines and have to stifle a chuckle.

Here I was hoping for a distraction from the man, and instead I see his name on the very spine my fingers are splayed across.

Jameson L. Murray.

Of course they'd have his books in here.

From what I've gathered, Jamie hasn't been back here for years, but that hasn't kept his grandparents from being endlessly proud of his success. I keep my hand on the spine, as if it will connect me to the man himself, but my eyes travel around the shelf where I see several copies of each of his books scattered throughout.

I pull it between my fingers until it slides free and flip it open to the back panel of the dust jacket. Brushing my thumb over his picture, I think of how worn my own copies of these books are back at home. I can't even count the number of times I've read them.

There's history between me and Jamie—plenty of hurt and more than enough secrets—but when I told him I'd be his biggest fan, I meant it. Every first edition, I own. Special editions, they're there on my shelf. The audiobooks, I have those too. The only thing I don't have are signed copies, because though there were stores in Glasgow that carried them, I knew I'd only want his signature if I could get it in person... and that was never going to happen.

"Hey."

The voice behind me makes me jump and drop the book with a thump. Pressing one hand to my heart and the other onto the shelf in front of me, I turn my head and am greeted by green eyes behind wire-rimmed glasses. The skin around them crinkles with his smile. I love that smile, and my heart picks up its pace at the realization that it's the first time he's given it to me since I've been here.

"Hey," I say shakily as he bends down to pick up the book. His book. "I was—"

"Just doing a bit of light reading?" he cuts in, handing it to me. My fingers slip against his and it's like an electric shock to my system, a super charge that makes me weak at the knees.

"Have you seen how many copies of these your grandparents have in here?" I motion with the book toward the shelves.

"Yeah," he says, and rubs the back of his neck, his ears turning pink against his auburn hair. I always loved that he couldn't hide his blushes. I'm glad he still can't.

"It's clear they're proud of you." *I am too*, I think but don't say.

"Not sure I deserve it," he mumbles, gaze shifting around the room.

"You do," I say, clutching the copy of *Journals of Elsewhere* to my chest.

"Maybe." He shrugs. If he feels this guilty about not returning to see them for all these years, why didn't he? He could have come back any time he wanted. "You don't have to read that, you know. Plenty of other books here." His fingers dance along the many spines, touching any but his own.

"There are, but..." I chew my lip and hold the book tighter.

I'm not sure I want him to know how much I love his books. There are a lot of feelings tied up in these for me—about how things might've been different if he'd never published them...

"But what, Avi?" he asks, and I look up into his jewel-bright eyes that are full of questions.

"But yours are my favorite," I whisper, and even though I want so badly to look away, I can't. I can't because his eyes blaze to life with my words, like they lit a fire deep within him that had gone out. It's the most breathtaking sight.

"You've—you've read them?" He steps back and slumps into the corner armchair, like this revelation literally knocked him off his feet. His expression is unreadable as he searches my face.

I nod and say, "They're incredible, Jamie. You did exactly what you always said you would."

That fire burns brighter as my words land.

My words did that.

"And so did you. Or I assume you did, considering you're here—head chef of your very own kitchen. Did you go to culinary school like you planned, or..." He glances away and I wonder what the second part of that question was going to be.

"I did. It was challenging with Lennox, but I managed. I actually did two years at a local school in Glasgow. Mum and Dad helped a lot. Then they hired an au pair to help me with Lennox and he and I moved to Paris for a year so I could go to the school Mum went to. It was a dream."

Lennox was two and it was *not* easy, but I learned so much, and I got to taste independence for the first time in my life. It was after that year that Lennox and I got our own place in Glasgow instead of living with my parents, and I started figuring out the whole single mum thing for myself. They were always there to help, of course, but that year in Paris taught me that I could do it. That I could have my dream, and my son, and the life I always wanted... Even if it was a bit different to how I originally imagined it. Even if it was always missing a piece.

"That's incredible you were able to do that, even with Lennox. He's about ten, right?" Jamie's voice tightens and I avert my gaze because this feels a little too close to the truth of things that I'm still not ready to tell him.

"Yeah, and he's my everything." It's true, he is. I knew he'd change my life, but I had no idea that he would change *me*. I've never loved anything, or anyone, more than I love that not-so-little boy. Which makes this whole situation with Jamie that much harder. I have more to worry about than how Jamie will take this news. I don't know how Lennox will either.

Jamie watches me intently, and I don't know what he sees in my expression, but he nods and his brows pinch together over his frames. "I'm glad you're happy, Avi."

"I'm glad you are too, Jamie." At least I hope he is. I'm about to ask, because my presumption feels like a misstep, but he speaks and drives the question from my mind.

"Do you think—" He clears his throat. "Do you think we could get to know each other again, as adults... maybe as friends?"

I swallow past the lump that's threatening to form and say, "I'd like that."

The idea terrifies me too, but just being around him these past few weeks has shown me how intensely I've missed him.

"Maybe we could go on a hike or something—like old times—or maybe visit Armadale Castle. We never did get to go there together." The corner of his mouth lifts in a half smile. I don't doubt he remembers our excursion to the mainland as clearly as I do.

I play with the hem of my jumper and think about how his eyes grew to the size of saucers last night when I walked out of the kitchen in my Empyreal sweatshirt. Correction, *his* sweatshirt. I'd forgotten I had it on, having grabbed it on my break to cut the chill. Now he knows I kept it, and I can only imagine what he thinks of that.

I wonder what he thinks of *all* of this. Me. Lennox.

"I'm working tomorrow, but I'm taking the morning off on Monday. We could go then?" I want him to say yes, but I also want him to say no. The prospect of that much time alone with Jamie...

"Monday it is. I'll, uh, let you get back to your reading." He nods toward the book I'm still clutching to my chest like a lifeline. Just before he turns the corner, he looks back and says, "You, uh, you know the dedication is for you, right?"

Then he walks away, and I'm frozen to the spot.

What dedication? The one in *this* book? For me?

I sink into the chair he just vacated and flip to the dedication page with fumbling fingers.

To the one who inspired my love of adventure, I couldn't have done this without you.

I cover my mouth with my hand and choke back the sob that nearly tears free.

CHAPTER TWENTY-TWO

JAMIE - NOW

*B*ut yours are my favorite.

She's read my books.

Avi's read my books... and they're her favorite?

I walk into my room rubbing my chest, willing the ache there to dissipate. An ache that started when I saw her holding my book in the parlor. I always wished I could share that accomplishment with her. I used to picture her walking into a bookstore and seeing my books on a display and I'd imagine her smiling and happy for me. But I never once believed she'd read them.

When I dedicated that first book to her, I almost mailed a copy to her parents' pub, but I chickened out. Five years had passed since I'd seen her, six years since we'd spoken, and I just couldn't bring myself to be the one who broke the silence.

Of course, I pictured her living this beautiful life with a husband and child, her parents... She wouldn't need me. But from what she said, it doesn't sound like Lennox's dad has ever really been around.

Did the guy from the pub walk out on them? Or is there more to the story that I'm missing?

Likely. But that's a part of her life I don't deserve to pry into. I broke her heart and she moved on, which in turn broke mine. But she doesn't know that. For all she knows, I left and never looked back... Except the emails I sent. I tried, and she was the one who never gave me that chance to fix things.

I shake my head, willing the confusion to clear.

At least she agreed to find some common ground now. Maybe we can be friends. And maybe it won't be as tragic as it sounds, because no matter how much water is under the bridge with us... I'd happily let the current that is Avi take me wherever it wants to go.

Deep down, I've always known she was *it*. And for ten years, I've been sitting on the bank of my life, watching it stream by, because if I couldn't be in it with her, I didn't want it. One-night stands. Random hookups. No more than two dates with any one woman. That's the pattern I fell into because even in college, with a broken heart, no one lived up to Avi. After college, I told myself I was too busy for something serious. It was easier to keep things casual.

God, I was stupid. Am stupid.

A *buzz buzz* draws my attention to the phone vibrating on my desk. I left it behind when I went down to the kitchen for a snack—Avi's biscuits might rival the ones Grandad makes—before I got distracted by seeing her in the parlor.

On the screen is the name of the only other woman I've allowed a place in my heart. Rory. She's the sister I never had; our relationship so different than mine and Avi's ever was.

Rory

Hey stranger! I miss you.

The eight-hour time difference between Nevada and Scotland has really put a damper on our usual communication. That and I've been avoiding telling her about Avi being here. I don't know why exactly... Probably because I never told Rory what happened that final summer when I came back and saw her with baby Lennox. I never told anyone. But I think it's time I finally stop hiding that piece of the story.

I tap on her contact and she picks up on the first ring.

"Jamie! Hi!" she practically yells into the phone.

"Hey, Roars." I chuckle at her enthusiasm. "How are you?"

"Good. I can't believe you called. I'm this close to saying 'where you been, loca,' but I'll refrain." She giggles, and I imagine her laughing at her own joke.

"Ugh, please, no *Twilight* references." I cringe at the thought and fall flat onto the middle of the bed, staring up at the ceiling.

"Oh come on, you loved it when I made you watch all the movies with me."

"No... It was *you* who loved that. I did it because it made you happy."

"And I loved you for that." I can hear her smile through the phone and I relax instantly, feeling the guard I've had up since Avi arrived finally fall. "So, how're things going? Your grandpa's doing okay?"

"Yeah, he's doing pretty well, all things considered. I'm glad I'm here though. I think Avi taking the stress of the kitchen off his shoulders has helped a lot too—"

She cuts me off and I silently curse, realizing what I've said.

"Wait... Avi is there?" Her voice screeches through the phone and I wrench it back. I can still hear her from a foot away. "Like *Avi*, your friend from the summers Avi?"

I pull my glasses off and press a thumb into the bridge of my nose. "Aye, she is..." I draw it out like it's a question.

"First, listen to you saying 'aye,'" she says in a mimic of my accent, and it's terrible. "You sound so Scottish right now. Second, why didn't you tell me she was there? Weren't you guys kind of a thing during the summers? Oh god, is it so awkward?"

So many questions. I smooth out the space between my eyebrows.

"Rory..." I say, but she doesn't stop.

"She's taken over the kitchen? So, is she there for the long haul? Is she living at the inn? Do we hate her? *Or* do we still like her?"

So, so many questions.

"Rory," I say louder and with a bit more force to get her attention.

"What?" She finally takes a breath.

"Do you want answers or do you want to keep peppering me with incessant questions?"

"I want answers. Zipping my lips now. Sorry." She goes completely silent after making a zipping noise.

I chuckle. "Okay. So, yes, Avi is here. The same Avi I was *friends* with during the summers." I emphasize the word *friends*, but even

Rory knows it's a lie because she harrumphs—though, to her credit, she doesn't interrupt. "We were kind of more than friends one summer... but it all went to shit."

"And by *went to shit*, you mean...?"

"I mean I was an asshole and broke her heart when we were seventeen..." I squeeze my eyes shut and force out the next words. "And in turn she broke mine."

"Wait... What?" Rory says, shock coloring her tone.

I sigh because this is the part I haven't told anyone.

"The summer after senior year when I came back to Scotland, I was hoping she'd keep her promise of spending one more summer together on Skye. That I'd get to apologize, because she'd completely cut off contact after—well, everything. But when I came back, she wasn't here. I went to where she lives in Glasgow and looked for her..."

"And you didn't find her?" Rory asks.

"No... I did. But she wasn't alone and"—I blow out a breath—"she had a baby, Rory. Like, a tiny baby, and this guy... She'd completely moved on. She must have gotten pregnant not long after I left the summer before, so she clearly wasn't as broken up over everything that happened between us as I thought she was."

"Did she... Did she see you?"

"No. I walked out, went to Skye for a couple weeks, and then told my grandparents I was going to change my flight to go home early to get ready for college."

"And you never went back," she says, a sadness filling the space between us. "I'm sorry, Jamie. I always wondered what happened, but I never imagined... Why didn't you ever say anything? I could tell you were hurting, but you wouldn't talk about it."

"I'm sorry. I didn't mean it to be like I was keeping it from you. I just—something about mine and Avi's relationship out here had always been just ours. And I was so ashamed of the way I acted with her that I didn't want to tell anyone what happened. Not you. Not even my parents or grandparents. Then I realized how much I'd messed up, that I loved her, but by that point she wouldn't even return my emails. She just... moved on." I squeeze my eyes shut because that still stings, no matter how mature I'm trying to be or how much I'm trying to let it go. That still fucking stings.

"Jamie..." Rory's voice softens, and I'm glad we aren't on FaceTime because I don't want to see what I'm sure is pity on her face.

"So, anyway," I say, trying to move us back to the present, "she's here now and her son, Lennox, will be here once his school year ends. And she's the new head chef for the restaurant. So, yeah." That's the best I've got.

"Are you okay?"

"Ehhh, depends on the day. She still has my sweatshirt. An Empyreal one I gave her when we were teens. It still looks fucking amazing on her too," I grumble, picturing exactly the way she looked in it last night.

"She can't hate you all that much if she kept it," she says. "Also, you didn't answer my other question. Is it awkward?"

I shrug even though she can't see me. "Kind of, but it's getting better. We've talked a bit, just not about *then*. I think that's best. Maybe we can move on. Be friends... I guess."

"Right..." She drags the word out, clearly having more thoughts on the matter.

"What?" I grump, but it's half-hearted. I can never truly be annoyed with Rory.

"Nothing. Friends is good. So, is the guy coming with her? You mentioned Lennox but not him."

"No, she's single. From what she's said it doesn't sound like he stuck around, which is fucking confusing because I kind of built a whole idea up in my head where she was married and had a kid with this guy... only to find out the guy isn't part of the picture." I want to throw my hands up in frustration. Even though I was an idiot and left Avi once, I came back, and I can't imagine leaving her behind *with a kid* and never looking back.

Rory harrumphs again.

"You sound like my grandad when you make that noise," I clip. "What is it?"

"Nothing... I just... Never mind. Listen, being friends sounds good. Let the rest go and see what happens. You're both there for a while, so that sounds better than being uncomfortable around each other."

I want to force her back a step and make her tell me what she was thinking, but I don't have the energy.

"Yeah, the first couple weeks were brutal."

"I can't believe you waited this long to tell me. I could hit you."

"If only you weren't half a world away."

"True. I wish I was there."

"Me too. You'd like her. I always thought that. Maybe you and Breck and Willow can come visit sometime this year," I say. I'd love to have them come and meet my grandparents... and Avi. "Speaking of, how is everything going with their visas?"

"Good. It looks like they'll actually make it here by the Fourth of July for the fireworks. Now I just need to find somewhere for us to live, which has been tough. As much as I love the little one-bedroom apartment you found me, it's not going to work for the three of us."

I laugh. "No, that place is definitely not a family home." Although... "I have an idea."

"Yeah? I'm all ears, because I am tearing my hair out being dragged around to listing after listing."

I sit up, excited that this is a problem I can actually solve. "Why don't you guys move into my condo?"

"Jamie..." Rory drawls.

"No, hear me out. It has three bedrooms. It's on the mountain, which I know you prefer. This will give you basically a year to find someplace else before I come back." Assuming everything here is settled by then. That thought sticks in my head. Going home would mean Grandad... *No*, I can't go there. I plow on ahead with my idea. "This way I don't have to think about putting it up as a vacation rental and it won't sit empty for a year either."

"I don't know, Jamie. We can't afford what you could make on it as a vacation rental."

"Oh come on, you don't think I'd give you a best friend discount? You cover my mortgage and we'll call it square, yeah?" It's not like I'm paying rent here, and my second book's advance allowed for a sizable down payment, meaning my mortgage isn't heinous.

"Are you sure?" she asks, and I can picture her worrying her thumbnail between her teeth.

"God, woman, just say thank you and ship me a pack of Tim Tams when Breck gets there. I know he'll bring a ton of them with him from Australia." I laugh and it feels good. I've missed this, our easy friendship.

"Fine," she says with sass, and I'd bet my next royalty check she rolled her eyes when she said it. "Thank you, Jamie. Can you get a lease written up? I'd like for it to be legit."

"Aye, if you insist." It's my turn to roll my eyes, but she's probably right. We should at least have a lease.

"Look at you, saving the day once again. What would I do without you?"

"Be homeless," I deadpan.

"Har har. Seriously though, thank you. If there's anything you need, you call me, okay? And I want to talk to you more, I miss you."

"I miss you too."

"How did Brent take the news that you're taking a break? When you emailed me, I was shocked so I'm guessing he wasn't pleased."

"Yeah... He did not take it well, but we've agreed on a six-month sabbatical, and I'll reevaluate at the holidays to see if I'm ready to go back into negotiations with the publisher for a new deal. But I..."

I close my eyes. Am I ready to voice this yet?

"You what?" Rory prods.

"I think I have an idea for a new project," I say quietly, like I'm afraid Brent might hear me and jump into my inbox demanding details.

"Ohhh... do tell!" Rory's enthusiasm is almost more demanding than Brent's, but at least I know hers comes from a selfless place.

"It's different, and I don't know if I can pull it off, but I found this box of my grandparents' old love letters. They're letting me read them and... I think I want to write their love story, or a version of it."

"Hold up. You're going to write a romance? Jameson L. Murray, best-selling adventure fiction author—"

"Oh stop it." I groan and let my head thump back against the headboard, but she just keeps talking.

"—is going to write a romance? Hell yes, I am *so* here for this!"

I bark out a laugh and it loosens everything that's felt strung too tight. "You are ridiculous."

"I know, it's part of my charm." I hear her clap her hands through the phone. "Well, this sounds like the best idea I've heard all day—and you just solved my personal housing crisis. I want to read it, and don't you dare tell me you're keeping this one to yourself like you did with your short story."

"You mean the short story I wrote about me and Avi..." I guess I'm spilling all my secrets tonight.

"Pardon me? Did you. Just say. That story was about *you and Avi*?" Rory yells into the phone, and I have to yank it away. Again.

"Christ, Rory, you just ruptured my eardrum," I say, rubbing the offended ear.

"And *you* keep dropping all these bombs on me. What do you expect me to do?!"

"I don't know... Not scream at me?" When she stays silent, clearly expecting me to keep going, I reluctantly do. "Yes, I wrote that story, and *maybe* someday I'll let you read it, okay... But right now, it's very late here and I should probably get to bed."

"Fine, I'll let you off the hook... *for now*. But I need more details, sir." She huffs, then her voice softens. "Goodnight, Jamie. I love you."

"I love you too. Talk soon."

"Yeah. Bye."

We hang up and I feel lighter than I have in weeks. Both because I got to talk to my best friend and because I finally got some secrets off my chest.

CHAPTER TWENTY-THREE

JAMIE - TWELVE YEARS AGO

She has a boyfriend. *A boyfriend.*

I probably should've seen this coming considering I was the one who came to Skye last year with a girlfriend. But I made a point to be single coming into this summer, and I stupidly assumed she would be too.

I'm jealous... So jealous I'm likely turning green like the leprechauns that are a terrible mockery of my mother's Irish heritage.

"What's his name?" I ask Avi from where we're once again propped on the inn's roof.

She bites her lip and I hate the way it draws my attention to her mouth. A mouth I won't be kissing this summer, even though I've had grand ideas of doing just that for weeks now... maybe months.

This is probably better though. We're friends, always have been, always will be, and kissing all summer would only lead to heartache for one or both of us, so what would be the point?

Yeah, this is definitely better.

"Ian," she finally answers, and her eyes flit across my face like a caress—like she's trying to get a read on me.

"Huh. How long have you guys been going out?"

"Three months." She shrugs like this information means nothing. But three months at sixteen... That's not a small amount of time. It's way longer than any of my past relationships, unless you count the one with Cat last summer... but seeing as we didn't see each other for two-thirds of it, I don't.

"Cool." *That's it, Jamie? The best you can do?* Cool? "How'd you meet?"

"He plays rugby. A mutual friend wanted to go to a match and we all went out for fish and chips after. I started going to all his matches and..." She tucks her chin and averts her gaze before clearing her throat and changing the subject. "What about you? You've probably got a whole gaggle of girls trailing you."

She laughs, but it's weak.

"Nah. I mean"—I swipe a hand through my hair and try to sound more confident than I feel—"yeah, there's girls, but no girlfriend. Not right now at least."

"Oh," she says, and is that disappointment I hear? That I'm single and she isn't? "What about Rory? You always talk about her when you email."

"Gross." I scoff and then backpedal because that came out harsher than I intended. "I just mean that I think of her like a sister.

I can't imagine dating her, that would just be weird. No, we're just friends."

I never even considered keeping the stories about what Rory and I get up to out of my emails. It's the stories with the other girls I never shared. There's never been anything between me and Rory.

"*We're* just friends." Avi's gaze holds mine when she says it, like she's challenging me. Because she's right, we *are* just friends, but Avi has never felt like a sister. Never.

"Yeah... but it's not the same."

She tilts her head. "How so?"

"It just isn't. We've... kissed." The words are out before I can think better of bringing it up and I instantly regret it. Her cheeks turn that perfect shade of pink I love and her eyes bounce away, unable to hold mine any longer with the remembrance of our kiss sitting between us. I scratch my jaw and move us back into safer territory. "So, other than the boyfriend... Isaac? How is school?"

"Ian..." she says, exasperated, and rolls her eyes. Those brown eyes that I think of more often than I should.

"Yeah, right." I don't care what his name is. That probably makes me an ass, but it's true.

"School's good. Not much to tell you beyond what I mentioned in our emails."

Our emails were pretty few and far between, both of us busy with our own lives on different continents, so when we would catch up, it was a lot about school, our friends, and any adventures we'd had... which are never as good as the ones we have together.

"What about the restaurant? Still working with your mum on weekends?"

She brightens at this, her smile growing wide on her face. She doesn't have on all the makeup she was wearing last summer, like maybe she finally realized she doesn't need it... Not here with me, anyway.

"Yeah, when I can. I've started researching culinary programs for when I finish school. The one that Mum did in Paris will likely be accepting applicants, but I don't know if I want to leave Scotland."

"I get that," I say, and then hesitate before continuing. "And if you'd asked me two years ago if I thought I'd leave Scotland for uni, I would've said no. But now—"

"What?" Her eyes bore into mine.

"Now, after having left the bubble of Skye—having seen more of the world, seen other things—I don't know. I love Scotland, but there's so much more out there."

"You don't think you'll come back?" she asks, her face falling.

I reach out and brush her knuckles with my fingers before I pull back, remembering I can't just touch her because I want to.

She's not mine to touch.

"I'm not saying that. I'm just glad I've had the chance to see what else there is. It's opened my eyes to other opportunities." I shrug again, and this time *she* reaches for my hand. I don't stop her when she laces her fingers through mine.

"I guess venturing out isn't so bad. I just think Scotland will always be home for me." She's zoned in on our hands. "It can be for you too."

"I know," I say, dipping my face to her level so our gazes lock. We stay like that, and it's a staring contest I don't want to lose. I could get lost in those eyes.

She breaks first, looking away across the garden. "So, what're you going to study at uni then, wherever you go?"

The change of subject breaks the tension I'd sensed growing between us. "Creative writing, maybe journalism too. Give myself options. But I know I want to write in some capacity."

"Like books?" she asks, her lips parting and then closing again before tilting up in a wide smile. "I can see it now, Jameson Liam Murray, award-winning novelist. What do you want to write about?"

"Adventure mostly."

"Like with the adventures of Jamie and Avi?" she asks, nudging my shoulder with hers.

"Not exactly... Though I might've added a few entries to that one for this summer." I take a breath, searching for the right words. "More like epic adventure. Maybe something like *The Hobbit* or *Treasure Island*. I don't know. That's probably stupid."

"It's not stupid. It's your dream, and I love it!" Her excitement is infectious, building me up and giving me even more confidence in this idea that's been bouncing around in my head lately. "I can't wait to hold your books in my hands. I just know you'll be an amazing success."

My cheeks heat and I know I've gone beet red. Shifting my gaze away, I realize we're still holding hands. I give hers a squeeze and she returns it, and I feel it through my entire body.

"Thanks. For believing in me. I've never told anyone that's what I want to do." I could give Avi all my secrets.

"Well, I feel honored, and just know I'll always be your very biggest fan."

I want to kiss her so badly. I want to crush my lips to hers. I want to feel her warmth against me. I want to feel that approval for my dream soak through from her body into mine and never let it go. But I can't, so I just tighten my grip on her hand and hold her gaze, memorizing the way the sunlight dances in the specks of gold in them.

CHAPTER TWENTY-FOUR

AVONLEA - TWELVE YEARS AGO

I should've broken up with Ian before coming to Skye because it's been a tortuous six weeks trying to keep myself from kissing Jamie. But I didn't want to be the one wishing there could be more with him all summer while he had some girl back in America...

Yet, here I am, still wishing there could be more but not feeling right about ending things with Ian over the phone. Not that we've spoken much, since he's been at rugby camp most of the summer.

I know Jamie wants to kiss me too. It's clear in the way he looks at me. Even Grannie has noticed, considering her warning of putting an end to us spending so much time together if she finds out there's been any *funny business* going on.

Noted.

She does know about Ian, though she disapproves and had words with Mum and Dad when they mentioned it before leaving. She and

Papa have always been old-fashioned, bordering on archaic. Mum told me she never officially dated in secondary school because they forbade it. Not that she didn't sneak off with boys. She just hid it from them.

She and Dad never wanted that for our relationship, so they've always had an open-door policy with me. They want me to feel comfortable telling them anything. And I do.

I told them about Jamie's and my kiss two summers ago. They've known about every boy I've dated since and met them all. They'd rather know what I'm doing than have me hiding it.

But Grannie and Papa... They only tolerate the amount of time Jamie and I spend together each summer because Mum and Dad insist they're okay with it, *and* because they respect Aileen and Angus.

As soon as Jamie told Angus that I was planning on attending culinary school, he took it as a personal challenge to get me ready. He's had me in the kitchen almost as much as Jamie has had me out on adventures—much to poor Jamie's chagrin.

It's been fun to be part of the kitchen and the other staff knows me now and don't seem to mind having me as a sort of apprentice.

Today Angus has me helping with the Scotch Pies and left me to get the dough ready. I'm rolling it out on the worktop when the door behind me squeaks open and Jamie walks in.

My face flushes red hot at the sight of him in a fitted T-shirt and running shorts, and a grin cracks wide across my face. It's an instantaneous reaction, uncontrollable, just like the butterflies I feel in my stomach.

His green eyes sparkle under the fluorescent lights of the kitchen as they take me in, and then he barks out a laugh. I've stopped missing the boyish chuckles—because this manly laugh is something that reverberates through my entire body.

"What?" I ask, hands going to my hips.

His strides are sure as he closes the distance between us, continuing to laugh. He stops just in front of me, making me look up to keep our eye contact, and then lifts both hands to my face.

On the outside, I freeze, but everything inside me goes haywire at his proximity, his touch. His palms frame my face and his thumbs gently brush across my cheekbones in a caress that makes me melt.

His smile is tilted up on just one side now. When he pulls his hands away, there's flour dusted over the pads of both thumbs. I turn the same color of his hair and bite my lip, tasting flour there too. I must really be a mess.

"Did you lose a fight with a bag of flour or did I miss a food fight?" His voice is low and a little rough.

"Har har," I mock-laugh back at him, but I can barely breathe. He's so close. So so close.

"Ah, come on, Avi. I'm just kidding. You look cute."

Tingling warmth floods my system. Cute isn't hot, but it's a compliment from Jamie nonetheless.

"Cute, huh?" I ask, and surreptitiously reach behind me to swipe my hand through the flour on the counter. Before he can react, I smear the white powder across his face and feel a zip of added excitement when my fingers trail lightly over his lips.

They pop open in shock, the white smeared across them. Then he moves. I try to dodge away, but he's too fast, one arm snaking around my waist to restrain me and the other reaching behind me to the same pile of discarded flour. He brings his fingers right in front of my face and I watch them—waiting.

"Don't. You. Dare." I emphasize each word, but even with my impending doom, I can't stop smiling. His smile is wide too, his eyes bright and his excitement all too palpable.

He brings his fingers together and then flicks them. I squeeze my eyes shut as the dusting of flour hits my face. In the fleeting moment while they're closed, I feel his mouth on mine.

The kiss is hot and fierce. The press of his lips and his body are the only things I can feel. I never want it to stop, but he pulls away and it's over as fast as it began.

"I'm sorry—I shouldn't have." His breaths are ragged as he steps away. "Oh god, I'm so sorry, Avi."

I reach for him, but he takes another step back. Puts as much distance between us as the kitchen will allow until he's bracing his hands on the far counter, the skin stretched over his knuckles glowing.

"Jamie..." I don't know what to say. My body is vibrating from just that simple kiss and my mind can't catch up.

"I'm sorry, Avi." He shakes his head, looking down at his shoes before raking both hands through his hair and weaving streaks of flour through it.

"It's... it's okay." My body finally figures out it can move and I take a step toward him only to have his head snap up to look at me and stop me in my tracks.

"It's not okay. You have a boyfriend. God, I shouldn't... I lost my mind there for a second or something. We can just pretend it didn't happen. Just forget it. Aye?"

I should tell him I wanted him to kiss me, take on some of the blame. It's not all his fault when I was flirting first. When I started it. But before I can even get a word in, he walks out of the kitchen.

Under my breath, I finally get the words out: "I don't want to forget it happened."

And I don't. Even when he acts like he has.

For our last three days together, we don't touch and we don't talk about the kiss. He hugs me on the final day before I get in the car to leave, but it's different. It's perfunctory, restrained. Nothing like the hug I want from him. Nothing like the kiss I wish he could give me.

As we drive away, I tell my parents everything, and by the time we get home, I'm ready to break things off with Ian. Never has a single one of his kisses made me feel the way Jamie's did. Even at sixteen, I know I don't want to settle for one thing if what I really want is something else, and it's not fair to Ian either.

I resolve to be single next summer no matter what, and I'll just have to hope Jamie is too... And maybe, just maybe, we can finally have more than one kiss.

CHAPTER TWENTY-FIVE

Avonlea - Now

I can't say how many times I've read and reread the dedication in Jamie's book, seeing it in a brand-new light. Seeing it with me in mind. And every time, I melt for him.

And that's dangerous.

I can't let those old feelings resurface. There's too much history—even without the secret of Lennox between us. And I'm no closer to telling him than I was on day one.

I felt a little bad canceling our hike for today, but the solicitor for the cottage down the street called and I jumped on the opportunity to see it before someone else does. I'm also afraid of being alone with Jamie for that long... I'd probably blurt everything out in the worst possible way. Or I wouldn't say anything at all and that might be worse.

When I push my way into the kitchen, I resolve to banish the thoughts. Angus is poring over a ledger at the desk while the kitchen staff moves with precision through the breakfast rush. He doesn't look up until I put my hand on his shoulder and give it a squeeze.

"Mornin', lass," he says, patting my hand with his. His is cold and I cover it with my other one, wishing I could transfer my warmth into his extremities. I never see him without a sweater and scarf now, even on the warmest days or in the heat of the kitchen.

"Morning. You're sure you don't mind if I take off to go see this house?"

He nearly rolls his eyes. "Lass, this is *your* kitchen and you've already got Hamish set up to be here. Why are you asking me?"

I look at Hamish and he shoots me a wink. He has it under control.

Pinning Angus with my gaze, I slide into the seat opposite him. "Maybe because you're sitting here like a damn mother hen."

He hums at that. "Old habits and all. I'm excited you've found a place for you and Lennox, I hope it works out. Though, we'll be sad to see you leave the inn. Having you around all the time sure brightens up the place."

I tuck my chin into my chest, the sincerity in his words bringing warmth to my heart... and my cheeks. I never received praise or compliments from my own grandfather, not even when we were on good terms, and certainly not after I got pregnant. And now I never will.

"Don't worry, you're stuck with me now, old man. And I'm sure Lennox will be here more often than not once he arrives."

Another reason I really, *really* need to tell Jamie.

That aside, I love the idea of having Lennox grow up here, surrounded by this inn and these people who helped mold me. My dad's parents passed away before I was born, so Lennox doesn't have any biological great-grandparents in his life. Or he didn't, but now he has Angus and Aileen... He just doesn't know it yet. What matters is they do, and after the way they treated me like their own when I was his age, I know they'll do the same for him.

Angus's words encompass that sentiment when he pulls me out of my thoughts: "I can't wait for him to be here. It will be good to have some young blood around all the time again. Might have to install a new tire swing though. You and Jamie used to get into such mischief playing on that thing." He laughs, and it's one of those that comes from deep in his belly.

"I miss that old thing," I say with a wistful smile. I stand and walk to the kitchen window overlooking the garden. "Don't get me wrong, I love the bench swing you built, but that tire swing was—" I break off, not sure exactly what to say. There are no words for the memories I have of that swing.

"Special?" Jamie says from behind me, and I turn to see him standing with a hand on Angus's shoulder. Right where mine was just moments ago.

I swallow, watching him watch me with something tender in his eyes, something I haven't seen in them for a very long time. "Aye, it was special." Dropping my gaze to Angus, I say, "Maybe it is time for a new one."

"I like that idea," Jamie says, moving around Angus under the guise of looking out the window. He stops right beside me so his shoulder brushes mine. "I thought, since we can't go on our hike this morning, I could come with you to see the house. In case you need a second opinion." The pull of his gaze has me looking up to find him peering down at me. He's not exactly asking, and I almost want to tell him I can handle it by myself... but I can't say no to him—not when he's this close.

I let my gaze travel farther down and take in the pair of worn-looking jeans tucked into wellies, his button-down shirt, and his rain jacket. He looks like he'd fit better on the pages of a *Barbour* magazine spread than standing in a pub kitchen. And he looks ready to go.

"You don't have to worry. I'm sure you have better things to do," I say quickly, my first reason for canceling still at the forefront of my mind. Being alone with Jamie is going to be torture, especially when he looks like that.

"Nope, I'm all yours this morning." His eyes glitter a brilliant green in the light from outside and a small piece of hair has fallen out of place over his forehead. I slide my hands down into my pockets to keep from pushing it back.

Why does he have to say things like that to me? All I ever wanted was for him to be all mine, and he never has been. Not even when I thought he might be.

"Okay then." I huff out a drastic breath and put a foot of space between us. Nothing left but to get this over with. "I guess I'll go grab my jacket. Is it supposed to rain?"

"It's always supposed to rain, Avi." He chuckles, glancing down my body. I ignore the way it makes me feel... The heat, the butterflies—I can't feel those things. I can't.

"I'll get my boots too then. I was planning to walk." Fresh air and space. I just need fresh air and space.

"I'll be here when you're ready," he says, and I swear there's added meaning to his words.

Five minutes later, the drizzle is making me very glad for both my rain jacket—which I upgraded when I took this job, knowing it would be both colder and rainier on Skye—and my red wellies. The squelch of the muddy lane under my boots is the only sound between me and Jamie because I've been avoiding saying anything, and he seems content to wait me out until I break and talk first.

The cottage we're headed for is about a half mile down the road from the inn. It's small with two bedrooms and an office that could easily double as a guest room from what the pictures showed. When we arrive, the listing agent Jenny is standing on the porch to keep out of the rain.

"Mornin', Avonlea," she says with a pointed look at Jamie, a question in the rise of her eyebrow. "Mornin'?"

Before I can make introductions, he extends his hand to her with a "Mornin'. I'm Jamie."

She narrows her eyes. "Not the Murrays' Jamie, are ye?" Her accent is much thicker compared to his, but Jamie clearly hasn't lost his ability to decipher even the most broguish of accents.

He ducks his head with a smile and I see a bit of color hint under his freckled cheeks. "Aye, that would be me."

I almost laugh at how his accent thickens just slightly in talking to her, like it wants to fall back into old habits so badly.

"Finally came home then, did ye? Cluaran's grown a good bit since you moved away."

I don't miss the way he stiffens beside me, but his expression doesn't falter. "It has. It's good to be back."

"And with a pretty lady on your arm." She winks in my direction, and now it's me who stiffens.

For one, I am not on his arm—we aren't even touching. Two, that's a notion I better shut down right quick before it becomes the next piece of village gossip.

Jamie beats me to it. "Oh. No, just a friend. Had the morning off and thought I'd keep Avonlea company."

Jenny looks between us, a sharp appraising look in her eye, and then shrugs. "I did think you said it was only you and your son. No handsome young men were mentioned..."

For the love of all that is holy. I blush and shake my head. "Nope. Just me and Lennox. He's ten."

"Well, let's get on then. It's cold and wet out here. If you don't mind leaving your boots at the door. I don't want us tracking mud through the clean house."

We slip our boots off and I attempt to ignore how domestic it feels, mine and Jamie's boots side by side on the foyer mat. Nope, definitely not thinking about that.

The cottage is bright and open. It's not large, but the updated fixtures give it the rustic and homey feel I'm looking for in a home.

Home. A home for me and Lennox.

We've lived in a flat—a nice one, but a flat nonetheless—for his entire life, aside from the first two years when we lived with Mum and Dad. I can't wait to give him a home like this. Somewhere with a garden and space to roam. And a community of people to support him that goes beyond me and his grandparents.

I fall more in love with the space the longer we walk through it. Each room has some small detail that makes me smile and makes this space feel exactly right. I can easily picture my four-poster bed in the master bedroom, and the bathroom has a clawfoot tub *and* a beautiful glass shower. The room that will be Lennox's has a box window with a bench seat built in that looks out into the back garden. I can already picture him reading there. He has a true appreciation of books—something he got from me, but also from Jamie.

"I'll take it," I say to Jenny before she's even finished showing us the kitchen—which, by chefs' standards, is pretty nice. It's not huge, but everything is new and clean and there's enough room for Lennox and me to make a mess of ourselves baking.

"Fantastic!" she says, beaming. "I just need to pop out and make a call. Here's the application. Feel free to look around a bit more if you like." She walks out of the room and toward the porch, phone to her ear.

"It's a great space, Avi," Jamie says, and I watch his hand coast over the kitchen island as he moves around it to stand beside me. I look up into his face and can't decipher what I'm seeing there, too overwhelmed by my own blend of emotions.

"Thank you—" I start, the words coming out breathy, gravelly. I clear my throat. "Thank you for coming with me. You like it then?"

"Not that it really matters," he says with a wide grin, "but yeah, I do. It's precisely the kind of place I can see you living in. You think Lennox will like it?"

God, my heart does a flip every time he says Lennox's name.

Every. Damn. Time.

"Lennox has never had a place like this. I'm sure he'll love it," I say, but Jamie glances away and I tilt my head to follow his gaze. "What?"

"It's still weird for me to wrap my head around you being a mum. Things have changed so much."

He has no idea.

Could I just...

"Jamie," I say, forcing my voice to stay even. He stops avoiding my gaze, and I exhale when I see his eyes are curious, questioning. "Lennox... well, he—"

Jenny resurfaces with a smile and cuts me off. "Do you have that paperwork done, dear?"

Thank god for this woman, because what did I almost just do? It's getting harder and harder not to tell him, but this is *not* the time or the place.

This is something that will not only change Jamie's entire life, but mine and Lennox's as well. And it will forever change the way Jamie looks at me. I don't want that to be my first memory of this kitchen, of this house.

"Oh, no, sorry. Was too taken with the space. Let me finish that up for you."

I grab the stack and furiously riffle through it, signing on the last page.

Lennox and I have a home on Skye, so the last thing keeping me from having him come visit is gone.

Well, the second to last thing. What's left is telling Jamie who Lennox really is.

CHAPTER TWENTY-SIX

JAMIE - NOW

The energy between Avi and me has been oddly charged since we visited the cottage at the beginning of the week. That was the second time I got the sense she wanted to tell me something but couldn't get the words out. There's so much we *could* say about our last summer together, but I haven't wanted to open old wounds for either of us. Maybe that's all it is for her as well—warring desires to talk about it while also wanting to forget.

A light breeze ruffles through my hair and the chains on the garden swing screech like a bird call as it moves. I needed a break from the noise of the pub—where I'd been all morning, mingling with guests and chatting with old acquaintances—and escaped to this place that's always brought me peace. The smell of wild heather fills my nostrils, laced with the scent of mossy rocks and damp earth to create an aroma that is wholly Skye.

It's Scotland.

It's home.

My bound copies of Gran and Grandad's letters sit beside me, untouched for the day. I've sifted through them more times than I can count. Most of them are covered in small notes or questions, thoughts on what I've decided is the most beautiful love story I've ever read. I planned to sit and go through them again while I was out here, but I laid my head back on the cushion about twenty minutes ago and lost myself to the feel of the cool breeze against my skin.

The words from the pages float around behind my eyelids as the story takes shape. I can imagine it. Gran as a teenager, completely ignoring the slightly scrawny boy from the class below hers. That is until one summer when he grew and, having spent his time working in the peat fields, returned to school looking like a much different boy... more like a man.

To hear her tell it, she saw him that first day back at school and decided that, if he'd have her, she'd love him for the rest of her life. Little did Gran know he'd decided she would be his bride the year before, when they met for the very first time.

Their romance started with notes passed in hallways, slid into lockers. Then it progressed through words exchanged in letters when they were separated. My grandmother was the first woman in her family to attend university, and until my grandfather finished secondary school a year after her, their main form of communication was these letters. Ones I've now read and can't believe they held on to all these years.

There is so much love on these pages. Yet, I recognize the folly of young love, having felt it myself. A love based on no experience and not enough knowledge, that sometimes can't withstand the strain. Theirs did though.

Even when they made stupid decisions or said stupid things, they always came back to each other. The apologies are sincere and sweet, heartfelt and laced with a desire to fix whatever was broken between them because in the end they knew the only thing they truly wanted was each other.

The hours I've spent asking each of them questions have felt like catching a glimpse of the Loch Ness monster. It's so rare you can't believe it's real. But I've seen the way they've loved each other my whole life and I can't fathom a world where this kind of love doesn't exist. And I've seen firsthand how their relationship paved the way for my parents'—the way Dad looks at my Mum, the partnership they've built, the mutual respect they show each other.

It's made me take a hard look at the "ladies' man" persona I've worn for most of my adult life. I wish I'd better understood what their example in my childhood was teaching me—that life is better when you get to share it with someone you love, even if it's hard. I've wasted so much time holding my heart back because I was afraid to have it broken. Afraid no one would make me feel the way I did when I was with Avi. Or afraid they would but would leave me behind—abandon me like she had.

"Can I join you?"

My eyes snap open to see Gran standing over my prone position on the swing. Her green eyes glint and the wisps of grey hair flit around her face where they've escaped her low bun.

"Of course," I say, making room for her to sit beside me.

She picks up the bound copies of the letters and a small smile tilts her lips, her fingers trailing over the place where my working title is printed. *With Love, From Skye.*

"Sorry if I interrupted your nap." A cheeky grin lifts her lips and I chuckle.

"Nah, I was just thinking."

"About what?"

I blow out a breath. "My life... Your life... I think I'm tired of being alone. I've never felt particularly lonely, or maybe I just didn't let myself, but now..." I shrug, and she watches me the way she did when I was a kid, like she's attempting to puzzle something out. "I didn't think I was really missing out on anything, staying single. But then I watched Rory fall in love this year. And now being back with you and Grandad, reading your story..."

I pause and look deeper into her eyes. Hers glisten with silver at the edges where tears have begun to form.

"He and I were lucky to find each other when we were so young and we've been blessed to have an entire lifetime to build what we have. I will never regret a minute, not even the hardest minutes we've ever shared, because they're ours. You just need to find the person who makes even the worst moments feel like a blessing because you get to share them."

My gaze tracks over her shoulder to the kitchen window and she follows it. When she turns back, her smile is soft and almost apologetic. She may not *know* what's between Avi and me, but she understands just the same.

"Do you think we all have someone who's meant to be that person for us?" I ask, both hopeful and afraid of her answer.

"I do, and I think that sometimes we have to fight like hell to hold on to them. Other times, we have to let them go and hope they come back to us. And often, we don't get to have them for as long as we wanted. Lord knows I'd do anything to keep your grandfather by my side for another seventy years, but..."

She trails off and I know she's thinking of the unknowns they face, that we all face in life, and what that means for them.

I reach for her hand and squeeze it lightly. "I would do anything to keep him here for you. If I could."

"You're doing it, Jamie, just by being here," she says, and reaches up to cup my cheek. "You being here gives him one more thing to live for, and I'm so grateful for you, my boy."

The earnestness in her voice makes my throat tighten and my eyes sting. "I'm—"

"No. None of that. There will be no more apologies from you for time past. We live only with the here and now in mind, and maybe the future a little bit too."

She glances one more time over her shoulder toward the kitchen and then stands and brushes invisible dirt off her pants just as the door opens and Avi steps out. Her hair is a mess of curls on top of her head where they're falling out of the bun she had them in this morning. "Ah, Aileen, there's a gentleman at the front desk asking for you." She swipes a strand away from her face with the back of her hand.

"Aye, duty calls then," Gran says, looking back and patting my cheek once more with a soft smile and a slight nod of her head. Then she's gone, and I catch Avi watching me from her perch in the doorway—hip leaned against the jamb, arms crossed over her chest.

She's wearing my sweatshirt under her apron again and it makes my heart rate pick up remembering the last time I saw her in it when we were seventeen. Just it and nothing else. I remember that day in vivid clarity; her hair splayed against the pillow, her soft skin against mine, our breath mingling in the small space that was only ours.

"Mind some company?" she asks. "I need a bit of a break from the bustle of the kitchen."

I swallow thickly. "Sure." I scoot farther down the bench so I'm at one end, leaving plenty of space for Avi to take the other.

She does and it's just another reminder of our last summer together. That was the year Grandad replaced the old tire swing. We spent a lot of time on this swing that summer. It was also the place where everything between us shattered. I feel that moment hanging here as we sit, in the same places nearly eleven years later.

"What are you working on?" she asks, holding up the bound letters. "New book?" She arches one perfect eyebrow and flips to the first page without asking.

"Nosy much?" I quip, and slide a few inches toward the middle of the bench, slipping my arm onto the backrest, trying to see which letter she's reading, but I don't reach to take them away.

She glances up with a smile that hits me square in the chest. "Sorry," she says, though she doesn't sound it. "What are these? Love letters?"

"Between Gran and Grandad." Another inch closer and I could graze her shoulder with my fingertips if I wanted—and god I want to.

"Truly?" she asks, rotating so instead of facing me she's facing forward with them in her lap. My bare forearm presses against her back and that small amount of contact is euphoric, like a drug. She doesn't notice it though, or if she does, she doesn't acknowledge it.

Her fingers trail over their words as she flips the pages, but also over mine scrawled in the margins. I can almost feel it like a caress against my own skin.

"I'm thinking of writing a book based on their story. But it's a bit of a different style to what I usually write."

She looks up and leans fully into the backrest where my hand finds her shoulder, my fingers brushing against the worn fabric of her sweatshirt. Her inhale is sharp, brown eyes locking on mine before saying quietly, "Finally going to write that love story I asked for all those years ago?" The tension between us crackles and a buzz begins beneath my skin. Between my inching closer, my arm placement, and her position change, we're closer than we've been in over a decade—if you don't count when I pulled her into my arms on the street last week.

"I don't know that I'm qualified, but I'm sure as hell going to try," I say, my voice thick like the air between us. I can smell her perfume and shampoo, floral and light. It's intoxicating, maddening. Just enough to make me do something stupid.

Something like leaning closer until my shin presses against her thigh, my chest nearly brushing her shoulder.

Her irises blow wide, the dark brown engulfed by her widening pupils, and her cheeks flush crimson. My hand slips more fully onto her shoulder without a second thought and I revel in the feeling of touching her, no matter how minuscule the contact may be.

I want to press my free hand to her cheek so I can feel that warmth beneath my palm. I want to press my lips to hers to see if she tastes the same as I remember. I want what I haven't allowed myself to want for too long. *Her.*

She goes still like she's holding her breath, but there's a fire blazing in the depths of her eyes. A fire I wish only ever burned for me, and when her eyelashes flutter closed, hiding that fire from me, I instantly want it back.

There's no gentle lean in, no questioning, no second-guessing. I close the distance and press my mouth to hers. It's hunger. It's breathing for the first time. It's finding you've been touch-starved for too long because every other touch was never the right one.

Fuck. I've missed her.

My lips move against hers and she melts into me—our chests pressed together as her hand finds my arm that's reaching for her waist. I want to tug her close, but her grip tightens and, instead of pulling me toward her, she pushes it back.

Then... she's gone, ripped away as if by force, leaving my hand stinging and empty. She stumbles toward the inn, eyes downcast and hand reaching for the door at her back. When she finds it, relief washes over her features before she turns and escapes into the safety of her kitchen with only a soft "I'm sorry, Jamie."

I'm left sitting on the bench, entirely alone, and the poetic justice of this moment isn't lost on me.

CHAPTER TWENTY-SEVEN

AVONLEA - NOW

Shit. Bollocks. Fuck. Shit.

Jamie kissed me. *Kissed me.* And I let him. The second he leaned in, my body knew exactly what it wanted.

Him. Always him. Only him.

But that's not possible.

For that moment though, I let myself pretend it was. I sank into the scent of his woodsy soap, or aftershave, or whatever the fuck he uses to make him smell so damn alluring, and the feel of his lips pulled me under.

But then my brain whirred back to life and I fled before I could fall so deep into him I'd never be able to get back out.

He's Lennox's father. I can't get involved with him while a secret like that stands between us. I shouldn't get involved with him period. It's too complicated. Too messy. Too much.

He doesn't live here—not really. And if that kiss is any indication, I'll end up exactly where I was at seventeen: in love with a boy—a man—who won't stay for me.

I press back against the wall inside the kitchen and inhale through my nose, attempting to replace his scent with the smells of braising meat and rising dough. When I blink open my eyes, I see my entire kitchen staff, plus Angus, watching me with looks of confusion on their faces.

"Uh, hi, lads," I splutter, trying to compose myself and failing miserably.

"You alright, Avonlea?" Angus asks, narrowing his eyes in my direction before they flit to the door. Can he sense the shift that just occurred between me and his grandson?

"Aye, yes. All good. Just, uh, need a minute. Be right back." I scurry out of the kitchen, flying up the stairs two at a time until I reach my bedroom.

Flopping onto the bed, I mutter to myself, "Stupid, Avonlea. Stupid, stupid, stupid."

What was I thinking?

That's right... I wasn't.

I just need to tell Jamie. Get this over with. Rid myself of this feeling of being crushed beneath a boulder of lies and deceit.

I walk into the bathroom and throw some water on my face, hoping to cool the mortification over what just happened—both with Jamie and in the kitchen. I can't let this affect my job. I don't just need it. It's all I've ever wanted.

Water droplets drip down my face and onto the sink top. My pupils are still dilated and my skin is pink and warm.

"Get it together, Avi," I whisper to my reflection.

I need a plan to tell Jamie so I can stop living in fear. I'm moving into the cottage tomorrow and then visiting Lennox in Glasgow at the end of next week. After that, there's only a few weeks before he's here full time.

Jamie needs to have time to process before that.

I blow out a breath and swipe a towel across my face before redoing my top knot.

After I get back from Glasgow, I'll tell him. Then we'll figure it out from there.

With a semblance of normalcy and feeling moderately put back together, I'm ready to get back to my day.

This will all be fine.

This is the furthest thing from fine.

I should be on my way to Glasgow right now to see Lennox and my parents, but instead I'm pacing the front porch of my little cottage awaiting *their* arrival.

They're coming here. To Skye. And I still haven't told Jamie.

Bloody hell, what am I going to do?

I walk back into the house to make sure everything is in order. Again.

I moved in on Saturday and have spent every free moment of this week making it into a home. Which made avoiding Jamie a little easier too. A necessity after that kiss last Friday, because whenever we're in the same room, my body screams that it wants to do it again. Avoidance is better, so I've been focused on preparing for when Lennox would be here—in a month. Not today.

I was supposed to go see *him* this weekend. We had plans for just the two of us. Plans with my parents. Plans on plans. And now they've all changed because they're coming here, eviscerating any hope I had of telling Jamie about Lennox before he inevitably sees him.

Crap. Crap. Crap.

Although, my concern over the Jamie-Lennox situation is secondary to the fact that my son got into a fight at school this morning and was suspended. Thus the reason for this lovely change of plans.

My sweet, would-never-hurt-a-fly boy hit someone today. And I wasn't there to pick him up. To talk to the principal. To the parents of the other boy. I wasn't there. Because I was here, and I've had a delightful six hours to wallow in the mum-guilt of it all.

Six hours since my mum called to tell me what happened and that she thought Lennox needed to get out of Glasgow for the week. *The week*. Because he's suspended until next Friday.

So, instead of me driving to them, they're on their way here, and I want nothing more than to hug my kid and comfort him and get to the bottom of whatever is going on at school. *But* there is still the fact that Jamie is right down the road at the Thistle & Tartan, and Lennox is... here.

The rumble of tires over the gravel has me running for the door, ready to get my arms around my favorite person. But the warm and excited welcome my mama heart wants doesn't come. Instead, when the back door of Mum's car swings open and Lennox steps out, I'm greeted by a sullen-faced boy with a shiner blooming around his left eye.

"Lennox," I breathe, crushing him to me. His arms go around my waist and his head rests against my sternum. Has he grown? It's only been a month, but I'm sure he has.

I catch my mother's gaze over his head and she gives me a sad smile, one that's mirrored on Dad's face in the seat beside her.

Running my hand over Lennox's blond hair, I squeeze him a little tighter. "I missed you."

"I missed you too," he says. When he pulls back, he keeps his face angled toward his shoes.

A pair of white trainers—like mother, like son. I'll need to find his wellies because it's set to rain tonight and those shoes will be ruined in no time.

I lift his chin with a finger so I can assess the damage. The purplish bruise under his eye could be worse... but still, this is a first for him.

Their five-hour drive allowed me more than enough time to quiet my simmering rage. Not toward Lennox—though we'll be having words—but for the boys who have been poking and needling him for months until he snapped.

"I think we best get some ice on that," I say, and pull him into my side.

My dad hollers after us. "We'll get the bags and be right in."

"Thank you," I say back over my shoulder, leading Lennox up the front steps and into the house.

He breaks away from me and starts looking around the open living spaces the cottage boasts. "Where's my room?" he asks, and I hear the faintest hint of excitement in the words, so I run with it.

"This way. I've got everything set up, but we can move it all around if you want." I lead him down the hall and the first thing he does is rush over to the large window seat and look out onto the back garden. I knew he'd love that spot.

He spins and gives me a smile, the first one since he arrived, and I soften instantly. He's here, and now this space truly feels like home.

He sits on the bench and I walk over to sit beside him. We look out the window, not at each other, and I ask, "Want to tell me what happened?"

He shrugs and keeps his gaze firmly on the yard.

"Come on, bud, give me something here." I push his hair away from his face and he finally looks at me.

"I'm sorry I got in trouble." His eyes instantly swim with tears and I pull him into me.

"I'm not as worried about that as I am about why you would hit someone. That's not like you, Lennox."

"I know, Mum, but he just made me so mad."

"Lachlan? What did he say?"

He shakes his head and bites his lip. I'm not going to push. Not right now. He's going to be here for a week; plenty of time to get him to open up about everything.

"Okay, we can talk about it later. You hungry?" I ask. He must be, and I'm sure Mum and Dad are too after the long drive.

"Yeah. Can we go to the pub?" he asks, eyebrows lifting.

Of course he wants to go to the T&T, but Jamie is there...

I might have to just hope for the best and pray he doesn't figure it out until after Lennox leaves.

"Why don't we see what Gran and Pa want to do?"

"Aye, okay." He goes in search of them and I follow in his wake.

We find them in the kitchen and Lennox walks over to my dad, who pulls him in for a side hug and whispers something in his ear. Lennox smiles softly and I'm overrun with gratitude that my dad has been willing to be a father figure for Lennox for all these years. He was the best dad I could've asked for and he's been the best possible grandad too.

"Lennox is hungry. Any ideas on dinner for tonight?"

"I wanna go to the pub," Lennox interjects before anyone else can get a word in.

My eyes lock with Mum's and I'm sure she can see the panic in mine, the worry that everything will implode the second we step foot in the inn.

"We could go to Wild Peets. It was always my favorite when we'd come up here," she says, and I relax a little. That is a great idea. We could go into town, which would have the added benefit of giving Mum a little more time before she has to confront her own past. Seeing as she and Dad haven't been here since the summer when I was seventeen. They didn't even come last year when I made the trip with Lennox to settle Grannie and Papa's estate.

"But if we go to the T&T, you can show me your kitchen." He gives me a look—eyebrow raised and head cocked—that says there's no better option than that.

Mum's expression is stoic, and with a shrug, our fate is sealed. I guess we're going to the inn.

CHAPTER TWENTY-EIGHT

JAMIE - NOW

Avi's avoidance of me has made it pretty clear how she feels about our kiss. We haven't so much as spoken a word to each other outside of passing pleasantries when other people are around. So, to keep myself from dwelling on it—because I *really* want to dwell in that moment—I've been channeling everything into writing *With Love, From Skye*.

It's been months since I felt this at ease in my writing, words pouring out of me to move this idea from a jumbled mess into something cohesive. Something people might want to read.

Over the soothing sounds emanating from my headphones, a commotion of voices coming from just down the hall has me pushing my laptop aside, drawing me out of my writing cave.

I hear Avi's voice as soon as I pull the door open, mingling with Gran's and Grandad's, along with several others.

I could've sworn Avi was going down to Glasgow this weekend.

I slide my hands into my pants pockets as I walk down the hall, but the sound of a bellowing laugh from Avi stops me in my tracks.

I haven't heard her laugh like that in—well, years.

She hasn't seen me yet, so I get the chance to watch her for a moment. The smile across her face presses her full cheeks up and the skin around her eyes crinkles. God, she's gorgeous—stop-my-heart gorgeous.

When I sling my arm around Gran's shoulders, she startles but then looks up at me with her shimmering green eyes. The smile she gives me rivals the one on Avi's face. I don't think I've seen that smile since coming back either. She covers it well, but Grandad's health weighs on her—a constant worry, a niggling fear. But this is the lighthearted woman I remember from my youth.

I pull my gaze away and take in the people around me, noting that the entire group has fallen silent. Like, eerily silent. My gaze lands first on Callum and Fiona, Avi's parents—who I haven't seen since I was seventeen—and then on the boy by Avi's side.

The one I can't look away from.

He's tall for a ten-year-old, almost reaching her shoulder, and he looks so much like her with the same blond hair she had at that age, the same nose and chin, and matching freckles too. The most notable difference is their eyes. Lennox's are a vivid green, but before I can wonder what the chances are that the man from the pub had green eyes like mine, I notice a blooming bruise around his left one.

What on earth happened there?

"Hello, Jamie," Avi's mum says, breaking the weird tension that was holding us all in stasis for a moment. She closes the distance between us and wraps me in a warm hug I didn't expect.

"Mrs. Stewart, it's wonderful to see you," I say.

She scoffs. "Goodness, call me Fiona. You're not a boy anymore." She steps back, hands on my shoulders, and looks me over. "Nope, you're most certainly a grown man."

"Mum!" Avi chastises her, and over Fiona's head, I watch her roll her eyes in exasperation. I don't hide my smile.

"What?" Fiona asks defiantly with a pointed look at her daughter.

Her dad is next to step forward, extending his hand toward me. "To keep things simple, why don't you just call me Callum as well."

Am I imagining it or is he squeezing my hand a little too hard for a standard *long time no see* sort of handshake?

"Thank you, sir. It's good to see you as well," I say. I don't remember him being quite so intimidating when I was a teenager.

"Jamie," Avi says, drawing my gaze and all of my attention, "this is Lennox. Lennox, this is Jamie. He's an old friend of mine."

Her voice is even, but there's uncertainty beneath it, like an invisible tremor. Something you'd only be aware of if you could actually feel it, and somehow I think I can.

"Hi," Lennox says with a small smile, a smile that's familiar but not. I can't put my finger on it, but it's not Avi's smile... Yet I feel like I know it.

"Hello. It's nice to finally meet you," I say, extending my hand. He exchanges a look with Avi before he reaches out and shakes it.

This is Avi's son. I knew I'd meet him eventually, but it's surreal. When I slide my gaze to her, there's a softening in her features as she watches him shake my hand, and her shoulders fall away from her ears.

"Did I miss the memo that you were all coming up for the weekend?" I ask. "I thought Avi was making the trip to Glasgow."

The Stewarts trade furtive glances and I wonder what I just stepped into, especially when Lennox drops his chin to look at his shoes. Wellies. Of course she has him in wellies.

"We had a wee change in plans. Lennox has an"—Avi hesitates on a breath before continuing—"unexpected week off school and he wanted to come spend it up here. Right, buddy?" She runs a hand along the back of his head and he looks up with a nod—something passing between them that I don't understand. "Angus, Aileen, I hope you won't mind him hanging around while I'm working."

"Och, no, we're thrilled to have him," Gran pipes in, looking elated at the prospect, and Avi's shoulders drop a little further, her posture softening.

"Dinner?" Grandad asks, clapping his hands together. "You'll all join us, I hope?"

"Oh, we wouldn't want to impose on your family dinner, but if you've got an extra table tonight, we would greatly appreciate it," Fiona says.

"Nonsense, you're all family. Come on." Grandad leans into his cane and motions for the whole group to follow him into the pub.

Dinner is an event of raucous laughter and easy conversation. Lennox keeps mostly quiet, taking in his surroundings and leaning toward Avi most of the night. This past month must've been hard on him, being away from her... And I wonder if the shiner on his eye—that's getting more and more purple as the night progresses—has anything to do with his impromptu week away from school. But it's not really my place to ask.

"Can I see the kitchen, Mum?" Lennox asks when we've all eaten our fill of sticky toffee pudding.

"You don't mind, do you, Angus?" she asks Grandad.

"How many times do I have to tell ye, lass? That's *your* kitchen. Stop asking me for permission to do whatever the hell you want with it."

"Angus," Gran chides with a smile.

"What?" he says, shrugging.

"There's a child present." She nods toward Lennox and offers an apologetic smile to Avi.

"It's alright, Aileen. I'm pretty sure he's heard worse." Avi ruffles Lennox's hair and he rolls his eyes. It reminds me of her at his age. "Okay then, bud, let's go. I can show you the garden too, if it's not too dark."

Who is she kidding? We're so far north and it's nearly the summer solstice; it won't be dark for a few hours yet.

"You coming?" Lennox says.

At first, I'm unsure who he's talking to. His grandparents? But they're looking expectantly at me, and I realize, so is he.

"Oh, I can. If you want me to. But..." Will Avi want me to crash their alone time?

I glance at her, but before she can do or say anything, he says, "Okay."

And that's how I end up on a tour of the kitchen and grounds of a place I called home for half of my life. It's entertaining to hear about it from Avi's perspective, so I mostly hang back, just listening. She introduces Lennox to the staff in the kitchen, showing him around and giving him the location of the secret stash of biscuits she always has on hand. Something I'm personally glad to know as well.

I follow them outside into the garden and, when she sits on the swing, I'm flooded with the memory of our kiss last week and the many many kisses we shared before it. Lennox snuggles down into her side, eyes roving around the space.

"Would you like a picture?" I ask, pulling my phone out. It's a habit I picked up from Rory who, being a photographer, is hardly without her camera. The colors of the garden along with the slowly fading light has Avi and Lennox lit in a perfect golden glow. They should have this memory together.

"Oh. Aye, that would be great," Avi says, so I frame them in—smiling faces, freckled cheeks, bright eyes. There's a familiarity that goes beyond the two of them, but it's gone as quickly as the flicker of the flash. "You know, there used to be a really cool tire swing out here that we played on when we were your age."

"You knew each other that long ago?" Lennox asks, surprise coloring his tone. He makes it sound like it was eons ago that his mum and I were his age... but I guess to a ten-year-old, eighteen years does seem like a long time.

Avi laughs and shakes her head, then pulls him in to ruffle his hair. "Aye, *that* long ago. We spent a lot of time in the gardens around the inn."

"And up on the roof," I say without thinking, and then cringe. Fuck. I shouldn't have said that.

Lennox's eyes track over my shoulder to the ladder bolted to the side of the inn. The curiosity in them is the same I used to carry in my own at the prospect of climbing up there. I guess all ten-year-old boys are the same.

"Oh no. Don't even think about it," Avi says. Her scolding mum-voice is aimed at Lennox, but the reprimanding look in her eyes is all for me.

Sorry, I mouth, my face twisting in a grimace.

She shakes her head, eyes closing and a small smile tilting her lips.

"Ah come on, if you did it, why can't I?" Lennox asks, and I trap my lips between my teeth to stifle a laugh. It's a fair question.

"We were older when we used to go on the roof. And it's not safe. Off-limits. Understood?"

His shoulders sag but he nods. "Fine."

"*Fine*," she mimics, and he bumps her with his shoulder. She chortles before planting a kiss on top of his head.

My heart tugs in my chest with a longing for something I have no part of.

She looks... happy. At ease. This is the most like *her* she's been in the month since she arrived. I thought it was because of my being here that she was different, but maybe she just needed him here. She said he was her everything, and I can see it—he is.

CHAPTER TWENTY-NINE

JAMIE - ELEVEN YEARS AGO

This is the hug I've been waiting for.

Avi feels soft in my arms as I wrap them around her. This year apart felt harder than the rest have. Maybe because I've played that kiss—the one that should never have happened, the one that lasted less than five seconds—on a loop in my head since. Not a single other kiss in the interim has lived up to it. Not a single date with another girl has given me the rush I feel whenever I'm with Avi.

This hug... This hug is exactly what I needed after months of nothing but the occasional email about school, friends, and our everyday lives. Which really aren't that exciting. I know she broke up with Ian not long after she got back to Glasgow last summer, but that was the only mention she's made of anything to do with boyfriends. I don't know if she told me about their breakup to make me feel better or worse about kissing her.

But that all falls away in an instant once she's in my arms. I press my nose into her blonde waves and breathe her in. The floral scent of her shampoo mixed with a new perfume she's never worn before makes me lean in farther, wanting more.

Too soon she pulls back, but her arms that were wound tight around my lower back don't fully pull away. Instead, she rests her hands on my hips and I feel each and every one of her fingers through my T-shirt.

"Hi," she breathes.

"Hi," I say, crushing her to me in another hug.

It's not until a throat clears nearby that I remember we aren't alone. Her parents and grandparents are standing nearby watching our reunion. They all know we're friends and how much we look forward to these summers together, but I think even they realize something is different now. Maybe it's because we're seventeen and nearer to adulthood than childhood. Or maybe it's just a recognition of whatever it is that pulls me and Avi together even after months apart...

We fully separate and I register the deep blush across Avi's cheeks. They're a vibrant red, and if I had to guess, mine match them.

"Hi, Mr. and Mrs. Stewart. Good to see you." I step around Avi to extend my hand to her dad before her mum draws me into a brief hug.

"You too, dear. Your flight over was good then?" she asks.

"Yes, ma'am. Arrived a few days ago."

And a tortuous few days it's been too. It's always harder to be here without Avi, even if just for a little while. Over the last few summers, so much of this place has become tangled up in our friendship that I can't seem to separate the two. I, of course, love being with my grandparents and seeing other friends too—though that's become less frequent with each trip—but it's like Cluaran belongs to me and Avi.

"Good. Well, as usual, I'm sure you'll keep an eye on our Avonlea for us," her dad says.

"Always."

I glance sideways and Avi rolls her eyes, but a smile ghosts her lips. Her grandmother, though, purses hers and gives me a knowing look, like she doesn't appreciate whatever this *difference* is this year at all. Like she knows how badly I wish I could kiss Avi right here, right now. I clear my throat and glance away.

"We'll get your stuff unloaded. Dinner with us tonight, please," Mrs. Stewart says to Avi. They usually only ever stay one night when they drive up to drop off or pick up Avi, so I understand them wanting one more dinner together before they go six weeks without her.

She nods and then squeaks in surprise when I grab her hand and pull her off toward the inn's garden. If I only get her for a few hours today, I'm going to make the most of them. Her laugh rings out behind me as I drag her through the hedge. The one I meticulously trimmed yesterday in preparation for the amount of time we'll spend going back and forth between the T&T and the farm.

"What's the big rush, Jameson?" she says with a lilting giggle that hits me square in the chest. If warmth had a voice, it would be her laugh. That sound lights me up. It makes me melt.

"I want to show you something." I keep tugging her hand, savoring the feel of it in mine, and it reminds me of that first day we met. When I pulled her through the gardens to the same spot I'm leading her to now. Today will hopefully not end in muddy clothes though.

When we're almost to the arch that will take us to the private garden, I turn toward her, blocking her view.

"Close your eyes."

She narrows them at me instead, but with a huff of air, her eyelashes flutter and she complies. I grab both her hands in mine, walking backward until we're right where I want us to be. "Keep them closed," I say, and release her hands to walk around behind her.

Leaning down to close the gap in our heights, which has become even more pronounced this year, I slide my hands onto her waist and let my lips ghost against her ear when I say, "Open."

A tremor runs down her spine and I feel triumphant at the reaction to my touch. But then she gasps and whirls to look at me, eyes alight. Because instead of the old tire swing we loved as kids—that was barely hanging on by its threadbare ropes and was unlikely to hold my weight for one more summer—there's a beautiful wooden bench swing. One that's big enough for two.

"What happened to the tire swing?" she asks, reaching for my hand and pulling me farther into the garden.

"It swung itself into early retirement during a storm, according to Grandad," I say, taking in her reaction, her excitement. I'm glad she's not disappointed in the change.

"It did indeed." Grandad's voice booms from where he stands in the kitchen door, watching us. "And I felt like maybe a more grown-up option that could actually fit you both might be better."

Avi beams and runs over to give him a hug. "It's good to see you, Angus," she says. She tried calling him Mr. Murray once, that very first summer, and he quickly set her straight. "It's a beautiful swing."

"It is, isn't it?" This time it's Gran who's come in behind Grandad, a whole big Murray family reunion, with Avi in the middle. "It's actually become a bit of a favorite spot for me and Angus too, so just know you won't be the only ones vying for time out here."

Avi laughs and envelops Gran. She didn't even hug her own grandparents this enthusiastically when she arrived, but they've never had the same close relationship with Avi as mine have. They're just different.

"We'll let you two have it this afternoon though. I imagine you've got some catching up to do. We'll see you for dinner, Jameson." Grandad nods at me and there's a warning in his eyes. We had a whole talk last night—much to my embarrassment and chagrin—about how Avi and I are getting older and I need to ensure I'm being respectful of her as her friend.

"Aye. See you for dinner." I give him a nod in return. I know they can see out to the swing from the window, just like they've been able to every summer since Avi started coming here, so nothing is going to be happening here... "Should—" I begin, turning to Avi.

Before I can even finish my sentence, Avi rushes for the swing. The soft cushions that Gran made make it almost like a couch, and she curls up on one end, eyes expectant as she watches me move toward her.

I take up the space opposite her, leaving a respectable amount of distance between us. I have ideas of what I'd like to see happen this summer, but it's just that: for the summer. I don't want to do anything that might make Avi uncomfortable or that will ruin our friendship. That's not something I can live with either.

She kicks her shoes off and extends her legs toward me until her feet press against my thigh. My body goes tight with just that small touch.

"Truth?" I ask with a quirk of my lips.

"Anything you wanna know," she says.

"Boyfriend?" I don't need to elaborate beyond that.

She shakes her head, a shy smile and a blush on her face "No. You?"

"No boyfriends for me either," I deadpan.

She giggles and kicks me gently with her foot. I bark out a laugh.

"Stop, you know what I meant." She rolls her eyes, but her grin only widens.

I grab her foot, and instead of letting go, I slide my hand up to rest on the smooth skin of her shin. Her intake of breath makes her chest rise, my eyes falling there for a second too long.

"No, Avi, no girlfriends either."

She nods with approval and bites her bottom lip. She takes in the garden, avoiding my gaze, and I take her in. Her hair is longer, like she hasn't cut it all year. I don't think she's cut it much at all since that summer when we were fifteen. It reaches halfway down her back in waves now—though most of it is pulled over her shoulder to fan across her chest. She's wearing a tight tank top under a flannel with cutoff denim shorts. Shorts that cover very little of her long, shapely legs.

I force my eyes back to her face and find hers on me as well. The freckles that smatter across her pale skin stand out more when she's flushed, and her brown irises dance with interest at my perusal. Her lips are a soft pink and I'm tempted to press mine there to see if they feel as silky as they look, if they taste as good as they did last year.

"Jamie..." she says with barely a whisper.

"Avi..." I husk in return.

She wets her lips. "Truth?"

"Always." I shift closer on the bench seat, bringing her legs across my lap—letting my hands linger on her calves, thumbs moving in gentle circles against her skin.

"Do you want to kiss me again?" she asks, and I've never heard her voice like this. It's like a dream, quiet but perfectly clear.

I don't hesitate, even for a second, before repeating, "Always."

She ducks her head, mouth turned up on one side. When I reach out to lift her chin, she worries her bottom lip with her teeth again and I want to groan at what that look does to me.

"Truth?" I ask, my eyes homed in on that lip, on her teeth pressing into it, on the deepening color. "Do you want me to kiss you?"

God. Please say yes.

There's nothing but brazen confidence in her expression when she says, "Always."

I tighten my hand on her leg and glance toward the window into the kitchen... Anyone could see us from here. I can't kiss her now. No matter how much I may want to.

"Want to go for a walk?" I ask, my meaning clear. When her hand slips into mine, our fingers twining, I feel a zing of anticipation. My heart rate goes haywire, like the organ might actually burst from my chest.

We don't have to walk far, and we don't say anything while we do. The tension between us grows thicker with each passing step, with every flirtatious glance, with every swipe of my thumb over her hand. The loch stretches out before us in no time and the point that juts out into it looms ever closer. It's a secluded spot with trees and rocks obscuring the shoreline from view of the surrounding village. It's a place we've come to swim on particularly hot days, a place where we can just be. Quiet. Private.

Perfect.

This is it. My chance to finally kiss her, to finally have her how I've wanted for years, but my head says we need to set some boundaries. I don't want to ruin what we have.

I slip a hand onto her waist, under the flannel, and her abdominal muscles tighten beneath my fingers.

"Avi... I don't... This is just for the summer. We both know that, right?"

Her gaze blazes a trail across my face, down my chest and back up, and I feel that look like a brand on my skin.

"It's just kissing. We can kiss for the summer," she responds with an emphatic nod.

I catch her chin with my thumb and forefinger and her tongue darts out, swiping across her lips. Jesus, that's hot.

"Just for the summer. Just kissing. We're still best friends at the end," I say in a rush, and then crash my mouth over hers.

Finally, I get a taste of what I've truly been missing with her all these summers.

CHAPTER THIRTY

Avonlea - Eleven Years Ago

Just for the summer. Just kissing. We're still best friends at the end.

Jamie's words from my first day back on Skye run a constant loop in my head, but with every kiss, I still have to remind myself that this is just for the summer. This is just kissing. Nothing changes when the summer ends and I go back to Glasgow and he goes back to Nevada.

It's getting harder to remember that though.

Especially now with him kissing my neck. The hay under us is scratchy, even with the tartan blanket we laid down when we snuck in here. We said it was so we could read in peace and get out of the rain, but that didn't last five minutes.

I'm on my back with Jamie braced over me, his lips seeking out any exposed inch of skin. The line of my sternum is where his attention is at the moment and I can't catch my breath. "Jamie…" I whisper, and he moves his mouth to mine, taking his name off my lips with one soft kiss.

Do we spend too much time kissing? Probably. We've almost been caught several times. On the swing in the dark of night when we thought no one would be around. On Jamie's bed when we were sure Angus and Aileen were busy with the inn. In the field of wildflowers when we were supposed to be having a picnic.

Just for the summer. Just kissing. We're still best friends at the end.

"I have an idea," Jamie says, propping himself on an elbow beside me. I shift onto my side too and grin as I watch him slide his glasses back into place. He's been wearing them more this summer than he has in years. Usually I hardly see him in them at all, but for some reason, he's worn them almost every day. I love it.

"Okay, what's your idea?" I ask, running my pointer finger up his forearm and watching the goose bumps break out against his skin. He pins me with a look and I chuckle. "Sorry, go ahead."

"So far, all our hikes have been within biking distance, but there's one I really want to do with you… We'd have to drive though."

"Alright… Why do you sound so unsure?" I ask, narrowing my eyes.

"Well, I was thinking we could take the campervan. We could camp for the night up by Old Man of Storr, do the hike in the morning, and then drive back? It would be a really long day trip, and I don't want us to have to rush the hike…"

His eyes sparkle with mischief. It's a look I love on him.

But camping for the night? That's a big ask, one that I'm positive my grandparents will say no to.

"I don't know, Jamie." I chew my lip, trying to think of a way I could convince Grannie and Papa to let me go, but... "There's no way they'll let me camp overnight with you."

He nods. "Yeah, I figured. It was a stupid idea."

"No, it was a great idea... I just don't think camping will be feasible. We'll have to make it a day trip." I slip my fingers between his and press forward to feather my lips over his. "They're already suspicious..."

And they're not wrong to be—we'll be picking off every piece of hay when we're done in here so we don't blow our cover.

"Yeah, I think Gran and Grandad are too..." He scooches closer so our bodies press against each other and nuzzles beneath my ear. "I don't know if I could even convince *them* it's a good idea."

"A day trip it is then," I say, breathless. "Do you think they'll let us borrow the car?"

He pulls his lips from my skin to look at me. "Yeah, that much I'm sure they'll allow. If we aren't camping, we can take the Land Rover—easier to park at least."

I roll onto my back and prop my arm behind my head. "I can drive. I know you're used to driving on the other side of the road in the States."

These odd reminders of the different lives we lead always make my heart clench. Reminders that at the end of the summer we'll go our separate ways and not see each other for another ten months.

It's just kissing. Just for the summer. *He's my best friend.*

He's my *best* friend.

Even though I only ever see him for these short periods, even though we only exchange surface-level emails the rest of the year, he's still the best friend I've ever had. I've never been so comfortable with anyone as I am with him. He's also the only one who makes me feel the things I do while kissing him...

Is that a best friend quality?

"We can take turns," he says with a laugh, bringing me back to our conversation. "It's good for me to remember how to do it here. I'll ask tonight and we can go tomorrow if you want."

"What if we wait until Tuesday? It would be a fun last hoorah before you leave on Thursday, and you'd still have Wednesday to pack."

I don't want to think of him leaving. Especially because he'll be flying out two days before I go home. I don't know how I'll get through those last two days without him.

"Okay. Tuesday it is. Are you working with Grandad today?" he asks, and his fingers trace up the outside of my thigh to where my shorts have ridden up.

In between all the kissing, I've been working more with Angus in the kitchen. He's even let me in on a few of his secret recipes, making me feel like a part of their family in a way I've never experienced with my own grandparents.

"That's the plan," I say, rolling back onto my side. His hand doesn't move, but my movement brings his fingers to my inner thigh and our gazes lock, my whole body going hot. I swallow thickly over the rising desire in my body for things I've never experienced before. "Got any other adventures for us in that book of yours?"

His notebook—the one he writes his adventure ideas in, adventures just for us—lies in the hay beside us.

"I can think of a few," he murmurs, but the book stays where it is. Jamie does not. He presses forward, hand notching between my legs, and kisses me. It's both soft and hungry. Familiar and explorative. I never want him to stop.

But it's just kissing. Just for the summer. We're still best friends.

CHAPTER THIRTY-ONE

AVONLEA - NOW

"You can't avoid this forever, sweetheart," Mum says, placing her hand on my cheek. Dad said his goodbyes already and is waiting for her in the car. It's Sunday and they have to head back to Glasgow for the week, leaving Lennox and me to feel out this new living situation on our own before they come back Friday night.

"I know, Mum. I just want to get through these next few days with Lennox and then I'll tell Jamie. If he didn't figure it out by just seeing him…"

Her knowing look cuts me to the quick. She knows me too well—that this confrontation is something I always hoped to avoid and yet here I am with it looming over me like an incoming storm.

But if it's going to be a fight—and I can't imagine another way it could go—I don't want Lennox around to witness it. It's my fault that we're in this state of limbo, that I didn't tell Jamie sooner, but I need this week to go smoothly for Lennox.

"I'll tell him. I will," I insist, lifting my chin and feigning a confidence I don't feel. "After Lennox goes back to Glasgow."

"Alright," she says, admitting defeat. "If you need us earlier for some reason, just call. You're not alone in this, Avonlea."

"Thanks. And thank you for this weekend. I'm really glad you were all able to be here."

"Me too. It was nice to come back—make some new memories to erase some of the hurt… you know?" She pauses to look around us and then glances back at me with a small smile. "Of course you do. You've been doing the same thing. I'm glad your father and I have a reason to come to Skye again. I've missed it."

"I'm glad too." I pull her in for one last hug and then, with a small wave, she joins my father in the car.

I've had weeks to acclimate to being back in Cluaran, to regain some of the positive feelings I used to have for this place before everything happened with my grandparents. But Mum was thrown into this trip with very little warning. And though I worried it would be too much for her, she embraced it. Not that I missed the longing in her eyes when we'd pass the farm—the place she'd grown up and spent so many years of her life.

We're creating a new life here now and we're not going to let the past hold us back.

I skip up the porch steps to find Lennox playing his Nintendo on the couch.

"Hey, bud." I plop down next to him and ruffle his hair. "What would you like to do today?"

He shrugs—focusing wholly on his game—so I use my hand to block his screen. "Hey!" he screeches, attempting to pull it away. I laugh and keep moving my hand to block it until he finally looks up with annoyance.

"Come on, give me five minutes. What do you want to do today?" I ask again.

His gorgeous green eyes bore into me—exactly the way Jamie's used to—and I push back a lock of hair that's fallen into his face so I can see them better.

"Could we just have a chill day?" he asks. "I'm tired after our hike yesterday. Maybe we could go to the inn later or something?"

"I'm tired too," I say with a yawn, then lean my head over to rest on his. "Old Man of Storr was pretty cool though, right?"

It was Dad's idea to pile into the car for a hike and a picnic, and once he got Lennox on board, there was no changing their minds. Even though pulling into that parking lot felt like a gut punch and looking out across the beautiful view tore at a wound in my heart I thought was long healed.

The last time I went on that hike was with Jamie. The time we spent together—barricaded in the back of the campervan to avoid the rain—had been a dream...

I wish we could've stayed in the bubble, lived in that dream, because less than twenty-four hours later everything came crashing down.

Yesterday was emotionally draining as well as physically exhausting. But since no one aside from me and Jamie knows what happened that day, I kept my happy face on, shutting out the memories that bombarded me with each step.

In the quiet of last night though, it flooded back and I remembered it all. Every moment, every detail, every touch... And it felt like my heart broke all over again.

"Aye, it was cool. Can we go again this summer? I want to explore more."

"Of course, bud, we can go on a bunch of hikes this summer. Maybe go out to the Fairy Pools?"

"Oh aye, that'd be cool!" His wide smile stretches his face, a smile that also reminds me of Jamie. I hadn't realized how similar they were until I saw them almost side by side the other night. How he didn't see it I don't know, but I'm glad for it.

"Alright, I'm going to read for a bit and you can play your game. Dinner at the inn sound okay?"

I don't feel like cooking, and as I'll be back to my chef duties tomorrow, I might as well enjoy one last night off for the week.

"Aye, cool."

Aye, cool—the ultimate ten-year-old response. I ruffle his hair one more time and watch him fall back into his game with ease. I settle into a chair across the room and pull my book onto my lap. Jamie's book.

Stepping out of the car at the Thistle & Tartan, the first thing I register is the sound of a drill... I think. My power tool knowledge is not extensive, but I'm pretty sure it's a drill.

Curious, I grab Lennox's hand and relish the fact that he still lets me do this—at least when his friends aren't around—and lead him through the garden toward the side of the inn. The sound gets louder as we approach the arch in the hedge that leads to the swing and side door to the kitchen.

When we walk through, it takes me a minute to understand what I'm seeing. Where the bench swing used to face the front garden, perpendicular to the inn, it's been moved to face the kitchen—sitting closer to the hedge—and next to it is a new structure. And there's a large tire sitting next to it on the grass.

All of that would be enough to make me pause, but the thing that brings me up short is Jamie. Shirtless. Arms lifted above his head as he holds the drill to the piece of wood connecting the side braces to the top. *Holy shit.* His triceps flex, muscles tightening along his torso, his focus solely on the project before him, blissfully unaware of his audience. Of me.

It's a warm day by Scotland standards and a drip of sweat glides down his chest, then lower toward the waistband of his jeans that hang loosely at his hips. I follow its path over the ridges of his abdomen and feel my own stomach tighten in response. This is obscene... And so fucking hot. I should cover Lennox's eyes or something.

Before I can blink out of my stupor, he lowers his arms and uses one hand to push his unruly, sweat-drenched, auburn hair from his face. Then his eyes land firmly on me.

The stare pins me in place, fire blazing underneath my skin. I swallow thickly and so does he, based on the way his Adam's apple bobs in his throat.

Bloody hell, this was *not* what I signed up for today.

"Hey," he says, a smirk quirking up the side of his lips.

"Hey—hi. We, uh, heard the noise," I stammer. "Came to investigate."

"What're you building?" Lennox asks, and I finally pull my eyes away from Jamie's face, only for them to move six inches lower to his bare chest... Again. God, the man is fit. He was in good shape as a teenager even if he was more bookish than he ever was sporty, but this is not the same body I knew all those years ago. No, this is not a boy's body *at all*. This is a man's body, and I want to kick myself for how feral I am at the sight of it.

For god's sake, get a grip, Avi.

I turn my attention to Lennox and hope that my cheeks, hot with embarrassment and lust, will cool. This is what I get for being the equivalent of a nun in the dating department for the past ten years.

"Grandad wanted Lennox to have a tire swing—like we had. He said he couldn't grow up around the inn without one. So..." He shrugs, arms opening as he rotates right and left, indicating exactly what he was doing.

"You're building Lennox a tire swing?" I ask, my heart gravitating to my throat. There's also a sting behind my eyes. I blink rapidly and drop my head back to stem my tears.

"Grandad obviously couldn't do it, and this place really isn't the same without one." His gaze is questioning, one eyebrow raised as he watches me try to keep it together.

"Aye, it isn't." I sniff, still keeping those pesky tears at bay. "Is this what you've been doing all weekend?"

His only answer is a small smile and a nod.

We mostly avoided the inn the last few days. Enjoying the time with my parents, visiting restaurants my mum used to love, going on hikes and adventures. I didn't expect to come back and discover that Jamie spent his weekend building a tire swing for my son.

For his son.

"Mum? Why're you crying?" Lennox asks, an incredulous look on his face.

"I'm not," I say, but I totally am. "I-I'm just feeling a little nostalgic is all." I pull him against me and he offers a chuckle and an eye roll.

"Girls..." Lennox says under his breath, exchanging a look with Jamie, who stifles a laugh behind his hand.

I shoot him a glare, but there's no bite to it. No, there's only softness in me right now for this man... And maybe something else stirring too, but *that* I'm going to ignore. Entirely.

Now I just need him to put on a damn shirt so I can do so.

CHAPTER THIRTY-TWO

JAMIE - ELEVEN YEARS AGO

Turns out Grandad needs the Land Rover today. So, Avi and I pile into the campervan with an absurd amount of snacks, a specially packed picnic lunch courtesy of the T&T Pub (aka Grandad), and strict instructions from both sets of grandparents to be home by dinner at eight.

It's over an hour to Portree and then a bit past that to the Old Man of Storr—a really cool rock formation and hike I've only ever done with my parents.

The old campervan is simple but functional, with captain's chairs in the front for the driver and passenger while the back has been converted into storage and a sleeping space. It's nicer than it sounds with a tartan duvet that Gran made tucked in over soft pillows.

Gran and Grandad don't get away all that often, but this has always been their escape of choice. Camping in the back of this thing while exploring the Scottish countryside. Mum, Dad, and I even took it out for the occasional trip when I was younger. Though the three of us were a bit of a tight squeeze across the bed in the back.

As soon as I asked about camping, I knew it would be a long shot. I just wanted more time with Avi—more time where it could be just us, where we could pretend we aren't going to be on opposite sides of the world in a few days.

Static crackles over the ancient radio and I reach for the knob at the same time Avi does, her fingertips brushing the back of my hand. We've been flipping through stations for an hour to find something worth listening to and we just lost the best one we'd found. I stop on a song set to raging bagpipes and raise an eyebrow at Avi. She laughs from deep in her belly and pushes on my arm.

"This? Really, this is the best we've got?" Her eyes crinkle at the corners and I grab her hand and pull it to brush a kiss against her knuckles.

"What? It's nostalgic... I don't get a lot of bagpipe music back home," I say, but as my smile grows over my joke, hers falls.

"Do you really think of the States as home now?" she asks, and shifts her gaze to look out the window toward the water.

I take a minute to think about my answer. We've only been there for three years, but they've been formative ones, and considering it's where I live, I guess it does feel like home. But this place feels like home to me too.

I swipe my thumb over her hand, but she still doesn't look at me. "I don't know. I guess so, but that doesn't mean this isn't my home too. I think they both can be."

"Sure. Of course," she says, sounding upset. Not that I can tell for sure, because she still won't look at me.

"What is it?" I ask.

"Nothing," she says too quickly. "Have you thought any more about what you'll do next year when you finish school?"

"A little bit. Mum and Dad would like me to stay there, and with the scholarships available I could probably go to university for almost nothing. Coming back here—"

She turns toward me and when she finally lifts her gaze to meet mine, her eyes are misty. I know this isn't what she wanted to hear and I wish I could tell her coming back to Scotland *is* exactly what I want to do. If it meant I could see her more—maybe be with her—I might do it, but I don't know if I'll even get into university here. I can't base a decision like this around someone else.

"Coming back is just more complicated," I say. "I'm happy there. Rory's going to go to the University of Nevada. Their creative writing program is really good and I can get a second degree in journalism. It feels like that might be the best option right now. And what about you? You're still planning on culinary school, right? What about the one your mum went to in France? Didn't she say she could help you get in?"

"I can get in on my own." Her response is sharp, and I wish we could go back to before we started this conversation. I just want to hold her hand and pretend that none of this future stuff matters.

"I know you can, Avi."

"I guess I just hoped you'd at least be considering coming back." Her voice ticks up a notch as she says, "Just think of the fun we could have if we were in the same place for more than six weeks at a time." Her face brightens and I can't deny that I've thought about it, but when I take Avi out of the equation, I know that going to university in the States makes more sense.

Right now, she's here, solidly in the equation, and that makes it harder to stick to that decision though. Especially when she's looking at me with hope and desire mixed up with emotions I don't even know how to place.

"You know... You could come to America for culinary school," I offer.

She scoffs... and then she laughs.

"What? Why's that so funny?" I ask, glancing sideways to look at her before looking back out the window.

"Jamie, why would I move my entire life to America? I have everything I need right here."

Well, that fucking stings. It shouldn't, since it's essentially what I just said to her but in slightly different words.

"I just mean that I have my options laid out for me here. I'm not really looking for something else. But I guess you aren't either... I just thought one of your options would be somewhere in Scotland."

"Avi..." I squeeze her hand, but she doesn't squeeze back.

"No, it's fine, really... It was a stupid question. This is still a whole year away, right? No need to worry about it now." Her face grows serious again and she says, "You'll come back next summer at least, won't you? Even if you're going to be starting uni over there? You'll come back? You promised."

"Of course, Avi. We promised each other every summer. I'll be here, no matter what I choose to do. Will you be here?"

"Aye, I'll be here." Her grip tightens on my hand and I relax and remember that she's here. We're here, and we still have next summer.

The drive is quieter after that, especially once we find a radio station that isn't blaring bagpipe music. We take our time on the drive, stopping off to take pictures with some highland cows. There may be a lot of cows back in Nevada, but none of them are as cool as these furry monstrosities. Their big brown heads, wide-set eyes, and lolling tongues are almost cartoonish, yet they're cute and somehow endearing. Rory will be particularly excited to see these photos when I get home.

Home. There's that word again.

When we get to the base of the hike up to Old Man of Storr, there are grey clouds rolling in that bring a gloom to the otherwise perfect day—just like our conversation did earlier.

The large spire-like rock juts up in the distance and I love watching Avi take it in for the first time. "Ready?" I ask.

"Yeah. Let's do it." She's excited, and that gets me excited. This may be our only chance to enjoy this sight together and I don't want to miss out on it—or another minute of being together—because we're worried about what comes next. I just want to be here, with her, in this moment.

I jog around to her side of the van to open her door, and her cheeks flush scarlet when she slips her hand into mine so I can help her hop down. Not that she needs help with her long legs—on display for me in a pair of tight bike shorts that hit mid-thigh.

Avi saunters toward the trail and I try with everything in me to keep my eyes off her ass, but it's hard when it's right there. She looks back and catches me staring. With a smirk and a wink, she ties her rain jacket around her waist... like that will keep me from looking.

The rest of the hike passes in much the same way. She walks ahead of me and instead of taking in the view, I can't look away from Avi. Her hair in a long ponytail blowing in the wind. Her toned calves.

When we reach Photographer's Knoll, a hill that overlooks the whole area, the tension that's been building between us finally snaps.

"Avi..." I start, wanting to say something, but I don't know what... and instead of my sentence going anywhere, she closes the distance between us and kisses me.

Her arms go around my neck, our bodies melding together in a way I've only ever experienced with her. They fit. It's magic. Her tongue tastes my bottom lip and I groan knowing we aren't the only ones on this hill and that I can't lie down with her in the grass and kiss her the way we were kissing in the barn the other day.

This kiss is different though, almost desperate. I don't know if it's because of earlier or because I'm leaving in two days or because every kiss over the last six weeks has gotten hungrier, more needy...

"Avi," I say again, but this time it's a prayer on my lips. I pull her closer, not caring about the other hikers—not right now. I cup her face with both hands and her arms slide down to band around my waist. Tilting her head back, she parts her lips further and I take advantage by sweeping my tongue in to dance along with hers.

I'm lost in her, like the only air I could possibly breathe in this scenic spot is the same air she's breathing. I want to share air with her, I want to share everything with her when we're together like this. There's nothing that could break me out of the trance I'm in, enveloped in this cocoon with Avi.

Nothing.

At least until thunder rends the air, loud and menacing, charging the space around us with a new kind of energy. Avi and I break apart—my lips feeling slightly swollen and bruised, warm and wet—and I lean my forehead against hers.

Our breathing eases just as the first droplets of rain begin to hit around us. The wind while we've been hiking brought in what looks to be quite a storm. Moving quickly, we pull our jackets on in an attempt to stay somewhat dry, considering we still have a forty-five-minute hike downhill to the van. I reach for Avi's hand and pull her along in my wake down the single-track trail, trying to ensure neither of us ends up in the dirt or sliding down the mountainside.

The rain is falling in earnest by the time the van comes into view. The dirt parking lot resembles a mud pit and most of the cars have already cleared out. The back door creaks when I pull it open and we both jump in, boots and all, to shelter from the deluge. We're drenched and laughing and it reminds me of the day on the ferry. Today though, we don't have a warm house or warm showers to escape into. We only have this van, and there's no one to scold us for staying out too late. We still have hours before we're due back home.

We're bent double at the back of the van, attempting to strip off our dripping jackets and discard our boots without getting the bed and everything else wet. Our shirts are damp from our distracted kiss and from sweat—it was no casual stroll to the top and it was more of a chaotic slog to get down.

"I'll turn the heat on." I climb over the bed to shove the keys into the ignition from behind the captain's chairs and crank the heat as high as it will go. "There. It shouldn't take long to warm up in here."

I look over my shoulder and watch a shiver overtake Avi as she scooches forward on the mattress toward where I'm kneeling.

The only dry clothing in the van is my Empyreal sweatshirt... The one Avi kept two summers ago that she wears more often than not. I've wondered more than I should if she wears it at home in Glasgow too, or if she only does it for me. It would keep her warm, but not over her wet clothes.

I grab it off her seat and toss it to her. "You should put that on."

"It'll just get wet too," she says through chattering teeth, "so what good will that do me?"

"Take the wet stuff off for now. I can put it over the heater vent to help it dry."

She blushes, cheeks turning the perfect shade of pink to match her kissable lips.

"I won't look," I say. "I promise."

We've made out on the shore of the loch in only our bathing suits, so I've seen most of her body—I know how her skin feels against mine—but this is different, and I don't want her to be uncomfortable around me. Ever.

"O-okay." She stammers over the word due to the continued chattering of her teeth.

I turn back toward the front to mess with the vents, hoping to trigger more airflow. There's not much to be done for my clothes.

My shorts are made of a quick dry fabric but they're pretty wet and my shirt is damp and cold against my skin.

"I can get the picnic basket out and we can have lunch back there—" I say, keeping my eyes firmly focused out the windshield, but a hand on my calf cuts off both my sentence and my reach for the basket.

When I turn around, I'm rendered completely speechless. Avi sits with her legs bent under her, the bottom of the sweatshirt skimming her thighs. Her hair is pulled up into a knot on top of her head, and despite the cold, she looks even more flushed than she did a minute ago. A small pile of her wet clothes sits beside her—shorts, T-shirt, sports bra... panties. My mouth goes dry and my body stirs to life, no longer affected by the cold or the wet. It's instantly attuned to her being this close.

She looks perfect in nothing but *my* sweatshirt. Her brown eyes are wide and her hand is still on my bare calf. It shifts slightly higher, just enough for my breath to catch.

I forget about the basket and turn to take her in, until I'm kneeling before her.

"Jamie..." she whispers.

My name on her lips when she looks like this is more than I can handle.

"Yeah..." I husk, unsure if I can form a coherent sentence at this point.

"Truth?" she asks.

I swallow thickly and watch the pulse jump in her neck before I answer, "Always."

"Have you... Have you ever..." She turns her head away and I reach for her chin. I want to see every part of the question in her eyes. "Are you a virgin?" The heat in her cheeks rises, her ears and the skin on her neck, just below where my hand rests, warming as well.

I hold her gaze. Nervousness, excitement, and maybe a little embarrassment all warring with each other for the top spot.

I swallow again so my voice won't crack. "I am." Her eyes widen a little, but she doesn't look away. "Are... Are you?"

Her eyes close, lashes fluttering against her skin just above her freckles, and she attempts to dip her chin, but I still have it in my hand.

"Yes." Those lashes finally open and her brown eyes hold my green ones. "I-I—" she stammers, her voice shaking a little. But it's not from the cold this time. "I think I want it to be you. No, I *know* I want it to be you, Jamie."

My breath whooshes from my lungs and everything in my body goes tight. Hard. Holy hell. Did she... Did she just say...

"Truth?" I ask, that one word coming out rougher than ever before.

"Always, Jamie," she whispers.

I slide my hand from her chin to her neck and feel her pulse race under it. "Are you sure?" I ask.

She nods. "Yes, but do you want..."

Before she can finish her question, I'm slanting my mouth over hers, showing her the answer. Of course I do—want her, need her, want *this* with her. She was my first kiss. It only makes sense for her to be my first for this too.

I lay her down on the bed, and as the rain on the roof of the van gets heavier, it wraps us in a cocoon of white noise that drowns out everything outside.

Inside, it's just us.

CHAPTER THIRTY-THREE

JAMIE - NOW

The hot spray of the shower beats against my skin, washing away both the dirt and the lingering ache from hanging the tire swing this morning. I'd planned to finish it yesterday but was too distracted by Avi's arrival with Lennox—plus they asked Gran, Grandad, and me to join them for dinner, so I had to stop and clean up anyway.

Though, Avi didn't look like she minded the state I was in. I saw the way her eyes trailed over my body. I shouldn't have taken so much pleasure in that fact, but I sure as hell did. She hasn't looked at me that way in a long time and, after everything, I never thought I'd see that kind of desire in her eyes again.

Of course, then she'd cried when she realized I was building a tire swing for Lennox and that sobered me up a bit. It was the reminder I needed that it wasn't just me and Avi having a moment... She's a mum. One who's built a whole life I'm only beginning to glimpse. And our lives are only overlapping for a short time—*again*. Feeling anything more than friendly toward her is a bad idea.

When I joined them all for dinner last night, I settled into the idea of being her friend again. Which means no more kissing on the swing or looking for desire in her eyes. We need to find some semblance of normal—me, her, my grandparents, even Lennox—because we're all going to be here sharing this place for a while. At least I hope we will be.

Grandad's condition is pretty stable, though some days I hardly see him—days when he's too tired to be in the hustle and bustle of the inn or kitchen. I make a concerted effort to seek him out in the cottage on those days, unwilling to let even one day pass without sharing tea or a meal or laughter with him. The doctors say his prognosis is the same. He could still have a year... or he could have only months. We just don't know, so we have to cherish every moment we can.

I step out of the shower to the reverberation of a knock at my door. "Hang on," I call out, and quickly run the towel through my hair and over my body, pulling on jeans and a dark green long-sleeve T-shirt.

Behind the door is Grandad, leaning on his cane, a wide smile on his face.

"Great work on the swing, son," he says, clapping me on the back and stepping into the room without preamble.

"Thanks, I think it turned out pretty well," I say, sidestepping to give him more space to enter.

"It did," he says, turning a jovial grin my way. "Your gran told me she saw *you* on it for a few minutes once it was hung up."

I grin and drop my gaze, chuckling at how it must have looked to her. A grown man standing on a tire swing, pulling against the chains to make it sway. "Well, I figured if it could support me, it was safe enough for Lennox."

"*And* you just wanted to," Grandad says, laughter bubbling up.

"That too. It's been a long time since I was on a tire swing." The feel of it was almost euphoric. I know I was grinning like an idiot the whole time and I guarantee Gran got a good laugh out of watching me. It was the wind in my hair along with the knowledge that I'd built it that made me so gleeful. "I hope Lennox will enjoy it."

Something pinches in Grandad's features for a second before he turns to take in the room. "I'm sure he will. You and Avi always did. So, how's the story coming?"

He walks over to my desk, where my laptop is open next to my copies of their letters.

"Really well. There's a piece of the timeline where I don't have any letters, so I was thinking this week we could sit down and you can help me fill it in a bit."

I've had several sit downs with one or the other, or both of them, to go over details from the letters that needed clarification or to paint the picture in more vivid color, but this period is completely blank.

"Yeah, we can do that." He nods, brow furrowed in a contemplative look. "Maybe this weekend, after Lennox leaves? Your gran and I are going to help Avonlea keep an eye on him while he's here, since she'll be in the kitchen," he explains.

"Of course. I'm here to help too, if she needs it," I offer. I don't have a lot of experience with kids, but Rory's boyfriend has a daughter a little younger than Lennox and I actually really enjoyed hanging out with her this past winter when they were in Tahoe. I wouldn't mind getting to know Lennox a little bit too. He reminds me a lot of how Avi and I were at that age. It's kind of a trip.

"I'm sure that would be appreciated. He might enjoy your company more than ours." Grandad's eyes twinkle in the light, that look he's always had—the one that hides his secrets—showing on his face. "Speaking of, I think he was about to find his way onto that swing when I passed, so I better go check on him."

"Let me go. Why don't you go check on the kitchen? I know you can't stay away for long," I say, wanting to be there to see what Lennox thinks of the swing.

"Aye, you're not wrong... Just don't tell your gran if you see me helping out a wee bit."

I roll my eyes. "Don't overdo it and it can be our secret."

I throw my towel across the back of the chair—I can hang that up later—and slip my shoes on before following him out the door.

The kitchen is pure chaos when we arrive. Apparently a sauce spilled and nearly caused a fire, so everyone is moving a million miles a minute to get everything cleaned up and back on track.

Avi's hair is a frizzy mess piled atop her head, perspiration beaded at her temples. Hamish looks stoic but irritated—it's a quintessential look for this particular Scotsman. Yet, as soon as Grandad enters the fray, the whole tone of the place calms and begins to settle. He's always been good at that. Settling things that feel out of control.

Not wanting to be in the way of an already hectic situation, I head for the garden. I expect to find Lennox on the swing, but he isn't there. It sits empty, swaying gently in the breeze.

Where are you, Lennox?

Did Avi give him permission to roam beyond the garden?

I bite my lip, not wanting to worry her but also not knowing where else he might be. It's fine. I'm sure he's here somewhere. Probably just walking around.

Think, Jamie. Where did you go when you were his age?

That's when it dawns on me and I turn away from the swings to look straight at the ladder to the roof.

Of course.

I've only been up here once since that first night Avi arrived. When I yelled at her and she hit back with the comment about being there for the people who want her. I always wanted her. I just realized it too late, and she didn't want me anymore by that point.

I was too late.

When my head pops up over the roof, I see Lennox, leaning against the far side of the chimney, legs out in front of him as he stares out toward the loch. Avi and I usually sat on the other side, facing away from the street and the farm next door so no one would be able to see us... Also so we'd be able to see anyone coming up the ladder. Lennox hasn't figured that out yet, and he likely doesn't know he's been found.

I purposely make more noise than necessary so he can hear me coming and not get scared. The last thing I need is to explain that I startled him and he fell off the roof.

I scramble closer and he turns, a sheepish expression covering his features.

"If I remember correctly, your mum said you weren't supposed to come up here." Though, if anyone is to blame for this little excursion, it's me, seeing as I gave him the idea.

He shrugs and turns back to look at the loch. "I was careful."

I nod, remembering how invincible I felt as a ten-year-old. "Can I sit with you for a few minutes? Before I force you to come back down."

"Aye." He eyes me where I sit a few feet away with my elbows locked around my knees. "So, you grew up here?"

"Until I was fourteen. Did your mum tell you that we met when we were your age?"

"Yeah, she said she came here every summer to stay with her grandparents. They owned that farm, right?" He points toward the farm that's now owned by a new family. The barn looks better taken care of and they have a bunch of highland cows—including adorable baby ones—munching in the back pasture.

"They did. We used to run around and get into all sorts of mischief... and messes. The day your mum and I met, we fell into a mud puddle under the tire swing. I'm lucky your great-grandparents let her play with me at all after that." I probably shouldn't have told him that... I'm just giving him more bad ideas. "You never met them?"

He shakes his head. "No. They died last year. We never came up to Skye before that, and they never visited us either. Mum doesn't talk about them. But we came up last summer to sell the farm and I met your grandparents. I like them."

"They're pretty great. I think they're excited to have you here. They've missed having kids around. It's been a long time since your mum and I were here." An easy silence falls, but when I look at Lennox, his brows pinch together slightly. "Are you excited to come to Skye?"

"Aye. I wish I could come up now. I'll miss Gran and Pa, but..." He trails off, looking glum.

"But what?" I ask, wondering if the fading bruise around his eye has anything to do with it.

"You moved away, right? Did you like where you went?" I note the change of subject but don't press. It seems Avi's told him a little bit about me.

"I did—to America—when I was fourteen. I love it there. It's been my home now for a long time."

"So, it was good when you left? Going somewhere new?"

"Yeah. I didn't want to go initially, but once I got there and met new people and made new friends, I loved it."

His pinched look relaxes. "I hope I can make new friends here."

"You will. It's a small town, but it was always very welcoming. I'm sure the kids your age will be thrilled to have someone new around." I think of how I was with Avi. "I was so excited the day your mum came to stay with her grandparents—that I'd have someone right next door to spend time with. I pretty much forced her to be my best friend." I shake my head and chuckle, but inside, my heart squeezes.

"She was your best friend?" he asks, cocking his head to assess me.

"Yeah, for a very long time, she was."

"I thought I had a best friend," he states, looking out toward the water, "but he isn't."

"Why not?" I ask, matching his posture and looking at the loch.

"He just…" He pauses, shrugs dramatically, and blows out a breath. "He isn't very nice, I guess. And now I'm suspended."

Those two things don't exactly add up in my mind, but I'm not sure how far to push. "You got suspended?" I ask with as much nonchalance as possible.

"Aye. I hit him. Then he hit me back." I meet his gaze and once again note the greenish bruise under his eye.

"Ouch." I grimace, remembering that feeling. It's been a long time since I got into a fight, but it's not something you easily forget. "Mind me asking why you hit him first?"

"It wasn't my fault. He said—" With a shake of his head, blond hair flopping with the movement, he changes course. "It doesn't matter. He shouldn't have said it, and I just snapped."

I nod. "I get that. I got suspended once for fighting."

His eyes blow wide with interest and I can't help but smile. "You did?"

"Yeah." I chuckle. "My parents were not pleased."

"Did you get into trouble?" He scoots a little closer to where I'm sitting.

"They lectured me about how fighting isn't the answer, and I had to do a lot more chores that week because I wasn't in school."

"Are you going to tell me the same thing—that fighting isn't the answer?"

"It usually isn't, but it's not really my place to tell you that. What did your mum say?"

He shrugs. "I told her what happened and she got really mad, but not at me. So I kind of thought maybe it was okay that I hit him."

I narrow my eyes, wondering. What did this kid say that even Avi would feel justified in Lennox hitting him?

"Look, if you can avoid a fight, it's better to do so. But there are some that are worth having."

Lennox studies me like I'm under a microscope, but I don't know what he's looking for. Then, in a rush, he says, "Lachlan said Mum left me behind and wasn't going to come back. Just like my dad. That I was an orphan."

I draw back, the words hitting like a physical blow. Fuck, *I* want to hit this kid. Yes, I know that sounds bad, and no, I'd never actually do it—but damn, that's just fucking cruel.

"Lennox, I—" I don't know what to say. No wonder Avi was pissed.

"I know it's not true. She loves me." He just shrugs again.

"She does. She's missed you so much in the time she's been up here." He trusted me by sharing this; the least I can do is ensure he knows just how much Avi loves him.

His eyes brighten, a silver sheen coating them and making the green shade spark. I think about the second part of his friend's taunt and wonder for the millionth time who his dad is, this man who supposedly left him—if his friend is to be believed, which is a long shot, but still. I don't think Avi would appreciate me asking him. It's clearly a touchy subject for Lennox and not one I have any right to dig into.

"And because she loves you so much, we should probably get off the roof before she kills us both," I say to lighten the mood.

His boyish laugh is light and unencumbered, and I give myself a mental pat on the back for helping bring him out of whatever funk he was in.

I make my way down the ladder first, feeling suddenly protective over him and needing to see him safely to the ground. When he reaches the final rung and hops off, lifting his hand for a high five, the kitchen door opens and we're met with Avi's wide eyes and a scowl.

Oops.

CHAPTER THIRTY-FOUR

Avonlea - Now

"The roof, Jamie? Really?" I scold the man in front of me, but I can barely hold in the smile that wants to take over my whole face.

Seeing him come down the ladder, followed by Lennox, made my heart skip a beat... and not out of fear. No, it was because I know, even if Jamie doesn't, that he just shared something that he loved as a kid with his own kid and... damn. Just damn.

"It was my fault, Mum," Lennox explains, eyes downcast. The smile that was on his face when I stepped outside fades to a frown.

"Nah, it's on me, Nox. If I hadn't told you about the roof, you wouldn't have been up there," Jamie says matter-of-factly with an apology in his eyes. Then his brow furrows, likely at whatever face I'm making.

He called Lennox "Nox"—just gave him a nickname like it was the easiest, simplest, most inconsequential thing in the world—and I felt everything in me shift with that single word. I can see Lennox's wheels turning too, like he's mulling over the name and deciding if he likes it.

Nox.

His lips pull up at the corners, eyes sparking in the afternoon sun... I guess he does.

"Nox?" he asks, testing it out for himself.

Jamie startles. We'd been locked in some kind of stare-down, so when he looks at Lennox, he must realize what he said. "Oh, yeah... Sorry, I have a tendency toward nicknames or shortened names... I can call you Lennox. I don't know where that came from."

"No, I like it," he says, glee emphasizing every word. "Nox is cool."

"Well, then Nox it is," Jamie proclaims, and with them standing side by side, I see every similarity they share. Physically it's mostly their eyes and their smiles that stand out, but even just the way Nox said *cool* reminded me of Jamie when he was ten.

"Buddy, why don't you go grab your book and hang out for a few minutes in the tire swing. I'd like to talk to Jamie."

"I'm going to go read in the parlor instead, is that okay?" Lennox asks, running off through the door behind me before I can answer.

"Sure," I mumble under my breath, only to catch a small chuckle from Jamie.

I shoot him a playful glare and he instantly stops. "I'm sorry if I overstepped with the nickname..."

"No, it's okay. He likes it. I can't blame him—it is cool." I chuckle and lean against the frame of the door, looking over my shoulder to see a few of the kitchen staff watching us. "Can we talk for a minute?"

I close the door and walk toward the bench swing, sitting at the far corner. This is such a dangerous place for us to be, the place we kissed...

"Of course. I promise I didn't take him up there. I was looking for him, and there he was." Jamie sits opposite me, crossing his booted foot over his knee. The picture of casual confidence. I always loved that look on him, but it's even better now as an adult.

"I know. He wouldn't have been able to resist the allure of such a thing once he knew it existed." I raised an adventurer, what can I say.

"That's also my fault though," Jamie says with a sheepish smile.

He has no idea, because as much as I *raised* an adventurer, Lennox's shared blood with Jamie *made* him one.

I shrug and reach back to loosen my apron straps. "He would've found his way up there eventually. You did. We did. More often than not." I look up toward the roof. So many memories carried on the breeze of that space. They permeate into the shingles, the rocks of the chimney, the smoke on the wind. "I appreciate you going up after him. I'm sure you have other things you could be doing. I'm sure Angus and Aileen do too." I press my fingertips into the bridge of my nose to alleviate a growing headache. "I wasn't prepared for him to be here this week. I just—"

"Hey." Jamie closes the distance between us on the bench—only by a few inches, but I feel them disappear one by one like barriers falling between us. "It's fine that he's here. None of us mind. This is—" He stops and swallows hard. "It's your home too. It always has been. Gran and Grandad have always loved you like a granddaughter, and I know they're thrilled to have Nox here. You should have seen how excited Grandad was when I told him I'd make the swing happen for him. He lit up like a Christmas tree."

I *can* imagine it... But if I had to guess, the reason Angus was so excited was because he knew it was a father building a swing for his son. Something Jamie still doesn't know.

This is so hard.

"Jamie," I say at the same time he says, "Avi..."

"Sorry," he continues when I stop.

"No, it's okay, you go." I lean back against the bench seat, willing the courage to build up so I can just say what I need to say. He can talk first, I can talk second. I'll just tell him. Waiting for this weekend be damned.

"I'm really glad you're here. I know I wasn't in the beginning. I know I let my own stuff get in the way of telling you that." He reaches across the space and gently lays his hand over the one I have resting on the back of the cushion. "But I am."

He squeezes my fingers in his and my breath catches in my throat as tingles race up my arm. His words fill me with warmth, the same way a hot cup of tea would, and I let my hand turn in his until our fingers interlace. They still fit together perfectly—like they did when we were children, like they did when we were teenagers, like they did when he made love to me in the back of that campervan.

I tuck my chin to hide my blush at the thought. God. That is the last thing I need to be thinking about right now.

I swallow over the lump rising in my throat and look up into the eyes of the boy—the man—I have always loved. Even if I didn't want to. "Thank you, Jamie. I'm glad you're here too."

We sit like that for what feels like hours, but it's likely only minutes before the back door flies open and Hamish looks out at us with a raised brow and a smirk. "Chef, we need you."

I jump up, putting space between us and brushing my hands down my slacks. "Right, sorry, Hamish. I'm coming." My steps take me closer to the building, but I can already feel the tug back toward the swing. The tug of the piece of my heart that I thought was long lost but may still be there, attached to the heart of a man I didn't know I still wanted.

I look over my shoulder one last time before going inside and the soft expression on Jamie's face is what I'll see every time I close my eyes for the rest of the day and the last thing I'll see when I close my eyes tonight.

It's the same one he used to give me when we were young. It's the one that made me love him so damn much.

"Mum." Lennox drags out my name, exasperated because I just flicked flour into his face.

I'm obviously a very mature parent.

"*Len*-nox." I enunciate the two syllables with the same irritated tone, a smile on my lips.

It's late… Probably too late for a ten-year-old to be up making biscuits, but I had to wait for the kitchen to close. This might not have been my most *responsible* mum move, but Lennox asked… and I couldn't disappoint him. Especially as I've been pretty busy with work the last few days.

He shakes out his blond waves and the flour that dusts his skin like white freckles complement the brown ones.

"You wanted to make late-night cookies, so you have to deal with my shenanigans," I say, ruffling his hair and knocking the remaining flour from it.

He huffs out a sigh but looks pleased as he rolls out more dough on the floured surface of the butcher block. "Well, just don't expect me to clean it up."

I bark a laugh because his attitude is all me, and I can't even fault him for it.

Angus and Aileen went to bed hours ago, and I haven't seen Jamie much today—I haven't seen him much since our little chat on the swing two days ago. I'm not sure whether he's working on his book, avoiding me, or if he's just trying to give me space.

"Ready to put those ones in?" I ask, reaching for the tray Lennox has been placing the rolled dough onto.

"Yeah." He slides it toward me.

"Thanks, bud. And thank you for how good you've been about my work schedule this week. I'm sure it's not a lot of fun for you."

He shrugs. He's had schoolwork to do and I've seen him a couple times with either Angus or Aileen looking over his shoulder while he worked. He even had Jamie looking at something yesterday in the parlor when I went out to check on him.

I spent five minutes creepily watching them from afar and wondering... Wondering how they'll both feel once they know who the other is. Wondering just how angry they'll be with me for keeping it from them. But I wanted to protect them—I did it *for* them... or at least that's what I've spent the entirety of Lennox's life telling myself.

"It hasn't been that bad. Aileen offered to walk with me into town tomorrow and show me around a little. That's okay, right? I can go?"

"Of course, Lennox. If anyone knows the fun places in Cluaran to show you, it's Aileen... well, and Angus, but I'm guessing a walk might be a bit much for him."

He sticks pretty close to the desk in the kitchen or the cottage, and even small trips between them tend to leave him out of breath. I should offer to take him into town next week on my day off, to spend a little one-on-one time with him.

The idea of losing him feels like a physical weight in my soul, and I don't want to miss out on this time now that I have him in my life again. My heart is even heavier for Lennox, who is just getting to know Angus—his great-grandfather—and the idea of that loss for him makes my eyes prick with tears.

"Aileen said we could bring him back a treat." Lennox moves around the kitchen, looking in the drawers and cabinets, curiosity his constant companion.

"That sounds like a good idea. So, you're enjoying being here?" I ask, hoping he really is excited for this move and will be happy here. Happier than he is in Glasgow.

"I wish I didn't have to go back this weekend," he says, deflating against the counter. "Couldn't I just stay?"

I sling an arm around his shoulders and pull him into my side. Goodness, I feel like he's grown another inch somehow. "I wish you could, but you've got to go and finish the school year. It's only a few more weeks."

He sags against me with a frail nod. I press my lips to the top of his head and squeeze him tighter. "I miss you, Mum."

"I miss you too," I whisper.

The buzzer of the oven pulls us apart and I have to nearly restrain Lennox to stop him from grabbing a melty, gooey chocolate biscuit straight from the tray. "Give it a second to cool, will you?" I roll my eyes with a laugh and he pouts, long lashes framing his emerald irises.

"I'll clean up and we can put these on a plate to take home, aye?"

"I hope you don't plan to take them all home with you." Jamie's voice comes from the door and I whirl to see him standing there in a pair of light grey joggers and a navy hoodie. It has a white willow tree printed on the front with a branch drawn down one sleeve. His hair is damp, framing his face like he ran his fingers through it moments before pushing into the kitchen, and his wire-rimmed glasses are perched against the bridge of his nose.

"We can share, right?" Lennox asks, and all of the sadness about school and going home are gone in a flash.

"Of course, bud." I turn to Jamie. "Want one now?"

The look Lennox gives me could make a bear cower. "Mum! You said I had to wait for them to cool." He's incredulous, and I release a bark of a laugh. Jamie chuckles from across the kitchen too. Then

Lennox joins in and there's a symphony in the sound, the three of us laughing together. It feels easy, normal, domestic... The way a family would sound laughing together in the kitchen over late-night biscuits.

The heaviness in my chest now creates a different kind of ache. A longing for something I've never let myself imagine.

"I'll wait for them to cool. Nox, you want to help me give the lobby a quick once-over to make sure everything is squared away for the night while your mum cleans up her mess?" Jamie gives me a pointed look, one eyebrow raised and a smirk on his lips, then flicks his gaze to the flour spread around the prep station. I probably have a good bit on myself as well.

"Aye, okay." And in a flash, Lennox is on his way out the door past Jamie, who follows behind him.

He turns at the last second, his gaze raking down my body then back up to my face. Every part of me warms under that look, especially when it settles on my mouth. "You've got a little something... right there—" He swipes his thumb along his bottom lip, then he walks out in pursuit of my son... his son.

My tongue darts out and tastes the flour there, part of me wishing it could have been Jamie's tongue to swipe it away.

CHAPTER THIRTY-FIVE

JAMIE - NOW

I have a shadow. I mean, obviously I always have a shadow, but today I have an extra one in the shape of Nox.

It turns out when kids don't have a lot to distract them—like other kids and school drama—they can get a lot of work done in just a few days. Meaning Nox has completed all the work his teachers gave him and he still has today and tomorrow before his grandparents arrive to take him home to Glasgow. So, he's been hanging out at the front desk with me most of this morning.

When the receptionist called in sick, I set aside my work on *With Love, From Skye* to help out. Gran is supposed to walk with him into town later, so I can work on the book then.

"Welcome to the Thistle & Tartan Inn," Nox says from beside me to the couple approaching the desk. Their faces light up with warm smiles, the woman's eyes going all soft at the sight of him.

"Thank you," she says, delighted. "We were hoping to get an early lunch."

"Of course," I say, but before I can continue, Nox jumps in to help.

"I can show you to the pub, if you'd like." His enthusiasm is contagious, and I remember being that excited about helping Gran when I was his age. Excited to be part of something like this. It was my home and I loved it, even when it meant I was left to my own devices a lot.

"Thank you," the woman says, and he turns to lead them to the dining room. Then, to me, she adds quietly, "Your son is so sweet." The look that goes with her words feels like a pat on the back for something I didn't do.

"Oh, um..." I don't really know how to respond to that. It feels awkward to say that he isn't mine, but it's like she's congratulating me on how great Nox is when I can't claim any of that. He's all Avi. She's raised him to be a great kid all on her own. It kills me that she had to do that.

"He looks so much like you, too. Those eyes..." she states, and then follows after her husband who's already down the hall chatting with Nox at the hostess stand.

She's so far off base though... Having the same color eyes doesn't mean anything. Green eyes are much more common in Scotland than in most parts of the world. It's just because she saw us together and assumed... And we know what they say when you assume.

But it is odd to watch him here in the inn. It's almost like watching a blond version of ten-year-old me walking and talking and living a life just like the one I did.

I hope that means he'll get to have the kind of childhood I had. One filled with love and friends and happiness. That is what this place was to me for a long time.

Until I let my own feelings and heartbreak taint it.

I never should've done that. I should've put my love for this place, for my grandparents, above it all.

I can't change the past, but I will do my damnedest to ensure I prioritize the important things going forward.

"Jameson..." Gran's voice comes to me through a fog and I shift to see her standing next to me, finding a quizzical look on her face.

"Hi, Gran. Sorry." I pull her in and lean down to kiss the top of her head.

"Jameson?" It's Nox this time who says my name. When I face him, a look of open curiosity lights his features. "Your name is Jameson? Not Jamie?"

"That's me. Told you I like shortened names... *Nox*." I shoot him a wink. "Gran and Grandad are the only people who really call me that anymore. And my best friend when she wants to get a rise out of me." I chuckle and feel a soft pang at the thought of Rory.

"My middle name is Jameson!" Nox exclaims, like this is the best thing he's heard all day. "How cool is that? We have the same name."

He's looking at me expectantly, ready for me to respond with a high five or some similar celebratory gesture, but a prickling sensation is creeping down my neck.

His middle name is Jameson... Lennox Jameson.

Lennox. *Jameson.*

Jameson?

Jameson. Jameson. Jameson.

The name hits like a snare drum in my brain in time with the beating of my heart in my chest.

She named her son after... me? Why?

My brain stutters over the word again and again, trying to make it make sense. She named him Jameson. But we were done by then. We weren't talking. I'd walked away. She wouldn't even respond to my attempts to contact her. She never came back. She moved on. She was with someone else.

She *was* with someone else, right?

The words from moments before come back in a rush. *Your son is so sweet. He looks so much like you. Those eyes...* But she was wrong.

He can't be...

I glance at Gran and her face is frozen, just like her frame is against my side, but there's an apology in her gaze. An understanding of things I had no idea were even possible hits and my gaze flies back to Nox...

His eyes are wide with confusion. His *green* eyes. Maybe that particular color isn't as common as I thought.

I clear my throat and push down the panic—*is that what this feeling is?*—then force a smile. "That is cool, Nox. I-uh, just need a minute. Can you hang here with Gran for a bit?" I ask, pulling away from her. With one last glance, the look on her face tells me everything, and the only world I've ever known crashes down around me.

I bolt for my room, and the second I'm through the door, I sprint for the toilet. I hit my knees, the hard tiles unforgiving against them, and my meager breakfast from this morning makes a reappearance, along with the tea I was drinking at the desk.

It can't be true. There's no way. It's not possible. We were only together once—well... twice—but we used protection.

She would've told me.

Someone would've told me. My grandparents... hers.

If Gran had known, she would have said something. We're family. You don't keep secrets like this in a family.

My brain decides to lay on some guilt and remind me that I kept secrets from them for years about why I never came back too. Maybe if I'd just told them what I saw in Glasgow that day they would've encouraged me to ask some damn questions. Maybe I wouldn't be heaving my guts up right now.

The wracking clench of my stomach stops and I slowly push to my feet. The mirror shows me a man who's white as a sheet. Even my freckles look paler than usual. My eyes glisten behind my lenses and I'm going to blame that on the vomiting instead of the emotional roller coaster taking place inside my body.

There's a knock on the door, gentle but firm.

"Jameson." Grandad's voice permeates through the wood and I flinch at my own name.

Jameson. Jameson. Jameson.

Lennox Jameson.

Lennox Jameson with the green eyes.

Holy. Fucking. Hell.

I can't hold the words in any longer so I swing the door open, coming face-to-face with a man I have admired my entire life. "Did you know?"

He squeezes his eyes shut and shakes his head, but I don't take it to mean no.

"Take a breath, son. It's not what you think." His voice has always been a balm—something calming in times of stress or turmoil—but right now, even it can't reach me through my dismay.

"It's not? I can see on your face that it's exactly what I think." I spit the words, unable to hold in the pain searing through my soul. I have never once yelled at my grandfather, but right now I have zero ability to regulate my emotions, and he's taking the brunt of it.

"When I saw him last year, I wondered. His age. His eyes... They're like yours, like your grandmother's. We've only known since then." He looks like he wants to touch me, hug me, do *something*, but I feel like a caged animal and begin to pace around the room.

A year. They've known about this for a year.

A year where their contact with me has grown ever more persistent. A year where they kept asking me to finally come visit. Was this why?

"Why didn't you tell me? Why did you never say anything? Does she know that you know?" Dammit, this is making my head hurt. "Avi. Does she know?"

My stomach threatens to revolt again and I swipe my hand across my forehead, feeling cold sweat.

"Yes," he says with a sad, apologetic look in his eyes.

"God dammit." I push my hands into my hair and down to my neck, pressing my fingertips into the base of my skull.

My chest feels tight, like I'm stuck in a vice, and I can't breathe properly. The last breath I took is stuck somewhere in my lungs and can't escape. I can't move. I can't see. My vision blurs as my eyes fill with tears and I'm afraid I might pass out.

"Jameson. You have to breathe."

The comforting hand on my back brings me just barely back to myself, enough that the exhale shakes free and I'm able to suck fresh air into my lungs again.

"Fuck," I say on the next exhale.

"Look at me, Jamie." Grandad never calls me Jamie; it's always *always* been Jameson, so this is enough to catch my attention and make me lift my head. "It's going to be okay."

"H-how can this possibly be okay? That's my son out there? I have a—" I squeeze my eyes shut and will the queasy feeling to dissipate. Shaking my head, I don't say another word. I stare straight ahead. I can't look at my grandfather, but he doesn't stop looking at me, though he stays silent. If only I could keep my thoughts quiet...

But they are riotous.

I saw her with that guy. I saw them together. It made sense. I hurt her and she moved on. I never thought of the possibility that the baby I saw in her arms could be mine...

I never would've believed she'd keep something like this from me.

Honesty. Truth. We promised each other that, hadn't we? *Always.*

Round and round the questions—the implications—spin through my mind like a tornado, and it's wreaking irreparable damage on everything it touches.

I thought we were friends? I thought we were rebuilding something here. I thought... Hell, I don't know what I thought because clearly everything since the second she set foot in the inn a few weeks ago was a complete and total lie.

I clench my jaw and worry my teeth might crack with the strain. I need to get out of here. It feels like I'm suffocating. I need air. Though, I'm not sure there's enough air in all of Scotland to help me catch my breath at this point.

I rip my messenger bag off the back of the chair and snatch the keys to the Land Rover, pushing past my grandfather—unable to look at him—but he grabs my arm. It's gentle but firm and my eyes narrow in on it.

"Jameson," he says with sorrow laced underneath.

"Don't. Please. I need to... I need space."

He nods and squeezes my arm firmly. "Don't do anything you'll regret."

My laugh is humorless. "It's too fucking late for that."

"Jamie."

"Just. Don't," I bite out. With a shake of my head, I walk away.

"I love you, son," he says softly behind me, and it lands like a blow to my already crumbling emotional state.

Son.

He's called me that for years, but the meaning is suddenly very different. It's just a placeholder for grandson, a shorter endearment, but now with the possibility of my own son in my head, it grates against sore nerves. It's salt in a fresh wound and it hurts.

It hurts so damn much.

I should go out the back door, to the cottage or the car, or make my way around the inn to the street to take a walk, anything to get away from everything... everyone.

Space is a good idea.

Not making assumptions is a good idea.

Not making a scene is a good idea.

Fuck. Good. Ideas.

I avoid the front desk, not wanting Nox—Lennox, my *son*—to see me like this, and head straight for the kitchen. I stand in front of the door, my hands shaking, before I clench them into fists at my sides and push it open.

"Jamie?" Avi's head pops up. She's got on my Empyreal sweatshirt and another piece inside me breaks. She dries her hands on a towel thrown over her shoulder, concern shifting across her face. I can only imagine what I look like to her right now. "What's going on? Is it Angus? Lennox?" Her voice rises with each question, a fear taking over that someone might not be alright.

If only she knew... It's me who's not alright.

"They're fine," I clip, ignoring the looks of everyone else in the kitchen, feeling them all watching me.

"Oh, well..." She draws out the words, confusion replacing the concern that was marring her beautiful features. "What's going on? Are you okay?"

I shake my head and clench my fists tighter, feeling my fingernails bite into my palms. I incline my head toward the door and stalk past her, hearing the slap of my shoes against the tiles. Her brow furrows, but she follows me out.

The moment the door closes I whirl on her. "Is he mine?" I exhale the words with a lethal calm I'm definitely not feeling.

She stumbles back and her mouth goes slack. "What?"

"Is. He. Mine?" I know he is from what Grandad said, but I need to hear it from her. I need to know for sure.

She holds my stare and I swear I can see it all right there, in the eyes I've always loved so much. The truth.

"Oh my god. He is." I rake my hands through my hair again, wanting to tear it out at the roots. My hands come away wet. I didn't even realize it was raining. I can't feel it. I can't feel anything outside my body at the moment.

"Jamie, I—" Avi says with a step toward me, but I throw up a hand.

"No. You—" I wheeze, unable to pull in a full breath. "You don't get—" I rub my hand across my chest, pressing hard like it will hold together the pieces of my heart that are splintering apart as I speak.

"Come sit, Jamie, you need to calm down. You're—" She moves toward the swing. The swing that's been both a place of love and a place of heartbreak over the years.

"I need... to calm down?" Everything comes out stilted, chopped and short because I can't breathe. "Are you"—I suck in a short inhale—"fucking kidding me, Avonlea?"

"Jamie..." She glances at the kitchen, clearly afraid of who might be watching or listening.

Fuck.

"I need to go," I say, stepping back. One step and then another until I bump into the tire swing. Then I turn for the cottage and the car waiting there.

"You can't drive like this." Avi's voice is laced with concern—with regret and heartbreak and fear.

"I can't fucking stay here," I yell, eliminating the distance between me and the car while she runs behind me. I reach for the door and yank it open.

"Jamie, please, let me explain..." she begs, and I know tears are mixing with the droplets of rain on her face.

"Explain? Explain!" I shout back at her. Then I lower my voice to a forced whisper. "Explain to me that I have a ten-year-old son? Avonlea, you kept him from me... How do you explain that? My god, ten years. Ten fucking years. How? How could you do this?"

"Jamie, I—"

"No, I can't do this right now."

I slide into the seat and slam the door, throwing my bag onto the floor. Before she can do more than take two steps forward, I've wrenched the key in the ignition and shifted into reverse. I focus on the rearview mirror until I reach the alley that will take me to the street, turning the wheel and shifting into first. Before I step on the gas, I look out the window in time to watch Avi fall to her knees in the gravel with her head in her hands.

CHAPTER THIRTY-SIX

Avonlea – Eleven Years Ago

"I love you, Jamie," I say, and then shake my head, looking at myself in the mirror. I feel ridiculous talking to myself, but I want to tell him and it has to be right.

How do you tell your best friend that you love them? Especially when they live half a world away.

"Jamie, you're my best friend and I love you. As more than a friend. Ugh," I groan. I can't say that. But he leaves tomorrow morning and I have to tell him something. If I don't tell him now, I won't have a chance to tell him again until next summer and then it'll be too late. He won't choose to come back to Scotland, but maybe if he knows how I feel it will make a difference in his decision. If I wait, he'll already have made his decision and there's no chance we can ever be together. He'll never come home. I can feel it.

But I know he feels the same way. He has to. After what we shared yesterday—making love in the van—that alone was enough to tell me he loves me the way I love him.

My face grows hot just thinking about it. It was perfect. A little awkward, a little uncomfortable, but also it felt right that it was with him. To share yet another first with him, to give him that part of me. It was always meant to be him.

I draw my fingers across my lips and remember how swollen they felt by the time we got back on the road to drive home. There's still an ache of soreness between my legs, but only enough to make me blush every time I think of it. He was sweet and gentle, exactly like I expected, and it didn't last all that long either... Also like I expected. At least not the first time...

The second time was more... Just *more*.

It wasn't like I went into yesterday planning for us to have sex. Had I been thinking about it all summer? Had our makeouts been moving us in that direction? Sure, but as we got closer and closer to his leaving, I assumed there'd never be a right time. But cocooned in a van, with the rain falling heavily around us, I couldn't stop myself from asking.

It was something he'd obviously been thinking about too, considering we both had condoms in our bags. God, what would Grannie have done if she found them? If Mum had known this was even a possibility, she would've gotten me on the pill before my trip, but even I didn't know this was going to happen.

"Avonlea," Grannie calls from outside the bathroom. "Jameson is at the door for you."

I nearly jump out of my skin at the sound of her voice while I'm in here thinking about sex. My cheeks heat even further.

Get it together, Avi.

"Coming," I say, and finish brushing my hair. I curled it and put on more makeup than I have all summer. Usually when I'm here I don't wear much. Jamie never seemed to care, and it's easier when I don't have to think about it getting messed up if it rains. I spin once in the flowery sundress I pulled on—the only one I brought with me—excited for one more day with Jamie before he leaves early in the morning for the airport. I picture us sneaking into his room to make out one last time or finding our secluded spot down by the loch...

I flounce down the stairs, floating like a butterfly on the wind to get the door. He's standing on the porch in a pair of shorts and a T-shirt fitted across his chest and arms. He's not wearing his glasses, so the brightness of his eyes is on full display for me. Much like they were yesterday when he moved above me, having taken them off because they kept sliding down his nose or bumping against my face when we kissed.

"Hi," I say, a little breathless.

"Wow," he says, and his gaze tracks over the spaghetti straps of my dress, across my shoulders and collarbone, then lower, and I can almost feel the heat in them as I watch them widen. The sweetheart neckline does nothing to hide my cleavage; if anything, it accentuates it. His Adam's apple bobs in his throat.

"You like?" I ask and lift an eyebrow. Stepping out onto the porch, I close the door behind me and he takes my hand like it's the most natural thing in the world. And I think it just might be.

"Yeah, I really do." He twirls me, the skirt flying out around my legs, and I giggle uncontrollably.

Happiness bubbles in my stomach while my heart beats a rapid rhythm in my chest that is only for him. Jamie. The boy I love.

We walk, without talking, to the bench swing in the garden. He looks over his shoulder to the window into the kitchen and when he doesn't see anyone, pulls me across his lap, causing a little yelp of surprise to escape me. But he quickly swallows it up with a kiss that makes my toes curl.

"How are you today? Okay?" he asks against my lips, and I know he's not simply asking about my general wellbeing.

"I'm fine." I dip my chin and blush again... Can I not control that one thing? "A little sore."

"I didn't hurt you, did I?" He lifts my chin with his thumb and forefinger and looks deep into my eyes.

"N-no, I think it's normal soreness." Not that I'd know for sure.

"Alright. And you're okay about it, that we..."

I silence him with another kiss.

"Yes, I'm glad it was you. I—"

"I'm glad it was you too," he cuts in, and I don't know if it's a good or bad thing, because I almost just said *it*. That I love him.

His thumb trails over my lips, and when he kisses the corner of my mouth, I feel my heart trip in my chest.

"I wish we had more time," I blurt, and then duck my head into his shoulder.

He rubs his hand up my back. "Me too. These summers are always too short. But we have today." He kisses below my ear and then moves his lips to my shoulder. "And we have next summer, and then—then I guess we'll see. I don't know if my parents will keep paying for me to fly back every summer and who knows if I'll be able to afford to fly here myself, but I—"

"I love you, Jamie," I say, cutting him off this time. If he's going to talk about what the future could look like, then we should probably have it all out there.

He goes completely still beneath me, his lips freezing on my collarbone.

"Jamie?" I ask, leaning back and dipping my head so I can look into his eyes.

"I-I just wasn't..." he stutters. "I wasn't expecting you to say that. I mean, you know you're my best friend, and I care about you so much, but I—"

"You're my best friend too." I smile and brace my hands on his cheeks. "I guess I just thought that, after yesterday..."

He rears back, his eyebrows drawn down. I don't understand his reaction...

"That what, Avi? I'd somehow stay? I can't. I leave tomorrow, and I won't be back for another year. How is this supposed to work?" He sounds flustered, almost mad. I shift off his lap, every word landing like a blow, and I feel the sudden urge to protect myself.

"I-I don't know. I guess I thought we could talk about it. People have long-distance relationships all the time." I bite my lip and hope it will keep the tears welling in my eyes to stay where they are. This isn't going at all like I hoped it would.

"Not across oceans... I mean, I'm sure some do, but Avi... we're seventeen! We—we can't do this. Not now at least."

"Then when, Jamie? When you come back next summer? Will you stay then?"

"No, I... I don't know. I told you yesterday I don't think I'll be coming back for uni. I care about you, of course I care about you, but I just don't see how this can work, Avi."

"How can you say you care about me and then just, what, not want anything with me?" My voice rises, frantic and desperate to make him understand. "You were fine with having sex with me, but we can't be together?"

"That's not fair. We both wanted that. We... It..." He stumbles over the words and his face is twisted into an expression I've never seen before. Like he's in pain. Like this is hurting him, but it can't be. Not like it's hurting me.

I stand up, needing even more space. I told myself when I got ready today that telling him might not change anything, but I believed it would.

Everything feels cold inside me now, the heat from just moments ago completely gone. Jamie stands too and the distance between us feels insurmountable—like a chasm has opened and there's no closing that gap now.

"I'm sorry, Avi. Maybe yesterday was a mistake. I didn't know you were feeling like this. We shouldn't have... It's only confused things. You're my best friend, I'm yours... That's all this can ever be. We don't live in the same place. We don't live the same lives. It could never work. I'm sorry, I—"

"But we could talk more. I can use the money I make helping Mum at the pub to pay for phone calls. I could save up so I can come visit you too. We could—" I watch him shake his head, anguish crumpling his features.

"I'd love to talk to you more, to see you even. But, Avi, your life is here. What if you end up in France for culinary school next year? I can't follow you there, not when I really want to go to uni in the States. It wouldn't be fair to either of us. I won't ask you to give up your dreams."

What he doesn't say is that he doesn't want me to ask him to give up his either. He steps forward and presses his lips to my forehead. I close my eyes, the heat of his lips is nothing compared to the hot tears that track down my cheeks. Then he pulls away, and with the precision of the sharpest knife, takes a piece of my heart with him when he says, "I'm sorry, Avi."

He backs away before turning around and walking into the inn.

I bolt through the hedge, my stupid dress catching around my knees, and head straight to my room where I bury my face in my pillow and sob.

I refuse to go down to dinner. I refuse to talk to anyone. And when Grannie tells me in the morning that she saw Jamie drive away with his grandparents an hour earlier, I know he's gone.

Will he ever come back? Or did I really see my best friend for the last time and not even get to say goodbye?

Six Weeks Later

Everything about the last six weeks has been *the worst*.

I tell my mum everything, but I haven't been able to bring myself to tell her about me and Jamie. That we had sex. That I told him I love him. That he didn't say it back. That he walked away and didn't even say goodbye.

She knows something is up, but I'm trying to keep everything as normal as I can, because nothing she says will change anything. School started right after I got home, and I picked back up with all my friends, throwing myself even more into those friendships than ever. Jamie and I may have only been a summer thing, but I feel his loss so acutely that I need to fill the void with more urgency than usual.

He hasn't emailed, and neither have I. I've thought about it. Thought maybe we could talk it out now that our emotions aren't so high.

But now...

Now I can't just email him and fix this. Nothing can fix this. Everything has changed and there's no going back to the way it was before... But it also feels like there's no true way forward.

I swipe away the tears tracking down my cheeks using the sleeves of my sweatshirt—his sweatshirt. How do I still have more tears to cry? It's been hours and they're still coming—hot and wet and making everything about my face feel swollen.

This can't be happening.

"Avonlea?" Dad's voice follows his knock on my bedroom door. He tries the knob but it's locked. I never lock it. "Are you okay?"

I sniffle and try to pull myself together, but I can't quite get there and my attempt at saying "I'm fine" comes out more as a sob.

"We need you to open the door, love," Mum says.

Oh good, she's here too. Probably better to get this over with now. I'll have to tell them both eventually anyway.

I swipe the tears from my face, only to have them replaced with fresh ones, and stand on wobbly legs. I unlock the door with a crisp click and it pops open.

"Hey," Mum says, her voice soft and soothing. "Can we come in?"

I nod and turn away from them, wrapping my arms around myself as I walk back to my bed. I pull my pillow into my lap, like having something to squeeze will make this easier. It doesn't, but at least I can bury my face in it.

"What's going on, mo nighean?" Dad asks, concern clear on his face as he sits on one side of the bed while Mum takes the other. Surrounding but not touching me, like they aren't sure if I need comfort or space.

When I look up, their gazes are set on me, full of questions, and I know they'll only have more in a minute. I blow out a breath and with it the words I've been avoiding saying aloud pour out. "I'm pregnant."

Stunned silence.

Nothing but stunned silence.

"But... How?" Dad asks, and then backtracks, horrified by his own question. "No, don't answer that. I just mean, are you sure? I didn't..." He looks at my mum, who appears just as bewildered.

She continues his thought. "We didn't know you were having sex. When did this happen?"

I meet her eyes and they widen at whatever she sees in mine. "Jamie?" she asks.

I nod and then start to cry again in earnest because how can I not? I told him I loved him and he didn't reciprocate it... How can I tell him I'm pregnant? He doesn't even live on this continent. This won't change that.

"I don't want to tell him," I choke out.

"Avi, you have to tell him. He's a good boy—" she starts, softening her voice and reaching to push a piece of hair behind my ear.

"Man," Dad cuts in. "If he can get my daughter pregnant, he's a man, and he should take responsibility like one."

"What good will it do to tell him?" I ask, looking imploringly at my dad. "He's not here. He's... He's not coming back." My voice breaks on the last word.

"What do you mean?" he asks, softer now as he slides a hand onto my knee.

"When he finishes school, he's staying in the States for uni. He's not coming back to Scotland." It's not entirely true. He did say he'd come back next summer, but even if he does, I can't see him. Not if I don't tell him. "I don't want to be the reason he feels like he has to. Not if he doesn't want to be here, if he doesn't want me."

"Are you sure he doesn't?" Mum asks.

I shake my head. "He doesn't."

Dad stiffens, and if I know him at all, he has something to say about Jamie not wanting me, but Mum puts her hand on his thigh and he relaxes and holds his tongue—something I appreciate.

"What do *you* want?" she asks instead, reaching for my hand. It forces me to let the pillow drop to my lap.

The question surprises me because all I've thought about since I peed on the stick after school was Jamie and whether or not to tell him I was pregnant, that I was having a baby… I never paused to even think about the options.

"I don't know. I didn't think—we were careful, I promise. I don't know what happened."

"I believe you," she says. "Jamie aside, what do *you* want to do, Avonlea?"

I run my free hand across my stomach, and though I know it will be months before there's anything there to feel, I know I won't pass on the chance to do so.

"I want to keep it."

They both nod, exchanging a look I can't read.

"And you're sure you don't want to tell Jamie?" she asks.

"Yes." And with that one word, everything changes.

CHAPTER THIRTY-SEVEN

JAMIE - NOW

G od dammit!

I hit the steering wheel and yell into the quiet. The car absorbs the sound and it's almost as if it was never there. The dull thrum of the rain on the exterior drowns out everything else.

Without even knowing where I'm headed, I end up at the ferry terminal, and within fifteen minutes, my car is the last on the boat and I'm moving away from Skye—away from everything that just changed in my life.

Maybe if I can get far enough away from it, closer to home, I'll feel some semblance of normalcy... But I know I won't. There's no going back. No changing what just transpired. No changing the fact that I have a son—that I'm a father.

I yank on the handle to recline my seat until I'm staring up at the roof of the car. Getting out and being around a single person on this boat isn't an option. My emotional state would likely have them worried I'd jump off at any moment. I close my eyes and just breathe as I attempt to reconcile what I have believed for the last ten years with this new truth.

I can't process this alone right now—I need my best friend. So, reaching for my phone, I type out a quick text before dropping it onto my chest.

The phone buzzes against my sternum and I lift my head enough to answer and turn on speakerphone. I knew she'd call.

"Jamie? Are you okay? Is it your grandad?" Rory's voice is frantic, though I can hear the sleep-addled undertone as well. It's still the wee hours of the morning there. I can't bring myself to apologize for waking her.

"No, he's fine," I answer. My voice comes out rough, like it's been scraped raw and dragged through gravel.

"What is it, Jamie?" Rory's voice pitches high. "You're scaring me. Are you alright?"

"No. I'm not. I'm..." The words feel like glue on my tongue. "I have a son, Rory." Silence. Absolute dumbstruck silence meets me from the other end of the line. "Are you still there?"

"Yes. Yeah, I'm here. I'm going to need you to repeat that though." I hear her swallow and envision her attempting to compartmentalize what she's feeling so she can be whatever I need her to be. That's just the kind of person she is.

"I have a son. Lennox is my son."

Lennox is my son. Will those words ever feel like less of a blow? I can't imagine it.

"Alright, that's what I thought you said," she says, and I can hear clicking in the background like she's on her computer. "I'm looking for flights to Scotland."

"What? No, you don't have to do that," I say, sitting up so fast the blood rushes away from my brain and makes my head spin... And now I feel queasy again.

"I'll wait to hit purchase until we finish this conversation, but I won't hesitate if I think you need me there."

Everything inside me loosens slightly at her words. I know she would jump on a plane, cancel any elopements she's supposed to photograph, and be here tomorrow if I so much as asked.

"Thank you." I resume my prone position, staring through the sunroof.

"Ready to fill in some details for me? I have a lot of questions," she says calmly.

"You and me both," I say with a choked chuckle. I pull off my glasses and squeeze the bridge of my nose. "His middle name is Jameson."

"Okay..." she says. I'm guessing him sharing a name with me doesn't seem like enough of a clue to have set this all in motion.

"His middle name is Jameson and he has my eyes and, god, all the things I thought felt familiar but brushed off because I was once a ten-year-old boy at the inn..." I know none of this makes sense, it hardly makes sense to me the way it all just clicked together. "But it was Gran's reaction. You should've seen her face, the apology written there, as the truth dawned on me."

"She knew?" Rory's shocked proclamation fills the cab of the Land Rover.

"Yeah, they both knew. I talked to Grandad after I got violently ill in my washroom." The betrayal stings anew. Theirs, Avi's... I feel betrayed by everyone right now. "Why the hell didn't they say anything, Rory?"

"I don't know. I'm so sorry." She takes a breath and then very calmly and carefully asks, "Have you talked to Avi, confirmed this?"

"Yeah. He's mine." I blow out a breath and snap my eyes shut. I leave out the part about how I yelled at her. "Ten years, Rory. I've had a son for ten years and had no idea."

"So, ten years means..." She trails off, and I know what it is she wants to ask but isn't sure how to.

"She got pregnant when we were seventeen." I answer her unspoken question.

"Right. Okay, and then she just never thought to tell you?" She's doing her best to stay subjective, but I can hear her indignance under the surface.

"Pretty much. I didn't really give her a chance to explain before I left. I'm so mad, Rory, but I'm also sad, and... scared? I have a kid. What am I supposed to do with that knowledge?"

"Where are you now?" she asks.

I listen to the raindrops on the sunroof for a minute before answering. "On the ferry."

"And then what?"

"I don't know... I can't actually leave." I might want to. My instinct for self-preservation is kicking in and I know I could go straight to the airport, get on an airplane, and never look back. But doing that at seventeen didn't do me any favors and it won't fix this. I can't do that to Gran and Grandad either. As mad as I might be, I can't.

"Does he know who you are?"

"Lennox?" I ask. Christ, I hadn't even thought about that.

Does he know who I am? No, I don't think so.

"Yeah, Lennox." Rory's voice goes soft around his name like it's something precious.

"I'm not sure, but I don't think so based on our interactions over the past few days. He was surprised to find out my name was Jameson, like his middle name. That's how this all got started. And god, I just bolted. Left him standing there with Gran. He's probably so confused."

Fuck. Well, that makes two of us.

"Do you want to tell him?" Rory's gentle voice is back.

I shake my head, then nod, and then remember she can't see me. "Yes. No. I don't know. He has this whole life with Avi and her parents and now there's me, on the outside. I don't even live here, not really. I never planned to stay forever. I don't know what Avi wants—"

"I'm not asking what she wants," she snaps, cutting me off. "Sorry. But I'm asking what *you* want. This is your life, your son. You should have been part of the decision years ago, you deserve a say in how this goes now."

"I don't know how to be a dad, Rory. I don't have siblings. Other than spending time around Willow last winter, I've hardly been around kids since *I* was one. And being cool Uncle Jamie is very different to being a dad."

"I don't know anything about being a mom either, but I'm going to figure it out when Willow and Breck get here next month. No one knows how to be a parent until they are one. It's all trial and error."

"But you're amazing with her, a total natural. And you also have a partner who actually wants you to fill that role and be part of their family. Avi and I are practically strangers at this point. Doesn't sound like a recipe for successful co-parenting to me." I inhale sharply. "Fuck. Co-parenting... That sounds daunting. Do I even have a right to try and parent a kid I don't know?"

The overwhelming feeling of panic begins to build again as my breathing shallows and my eyes blur.

"Jamie, take a breath, okay. You don't have to have all the answers right now. It sounds like you and Avi have a lot to talk about still. But if you want this—a relationship with your son—I can promise you right now that he'll be lucky to have you. He'll be the luckiest kid in the world to know you, because you're an amazing man."

"Thanks, Roars. I needed to hear that. I'm just really freaking out."

"That's understandable. Now, do you want me to click buy on these tickets? I can be there tomorrow if you need me to be."

I smile for the first time in what feels like years. "You're the best, you know that? Let's wait on pushing the button. Let me get my bearings and I'll keep you posted."

"Okay. And for what it's worth, I think you'll be a great dad if you want to be. The rest of it can be figured out as you go. I love you."

"You too."

The call disconnects and I give myself a few more minutes to just lie there in the car, wondering what I should do now. Get off this ferry and drive—where to, I have no idea—or turn around at the other end, get right back on, and go home to figure this out?

Home.

I think that's my answer. America has been my home for a long time—it still is in so many ways—but Skye has always been home. The Thistle & Tartan, Gran and Grandad, Avi… they've always been home. Nox. He's part of that now too.

I don't know what that means, how it will work, or what it'll look like, but right now I wish I could turn this ferry around myself and head straight back to where I just left. If nothing else, I think that's a good sign.

I spend the rest of the crossing to the Mallaig terminal getting lost in my thoughts—in the what-ifs and the what-the-hells. After I drive off and pull a U-turn, I decide to get out and take in the fresh air on the upper deck. The rain has stopped and with it comes the clarity of a sunny, blue-sky day. Maybe I can find that same clarity if I sit up here and soak it in.

CHAPTER THIRTY-EIGHT

Avonlea - Now

The gravel bites into my knees through my leggings, but I don't care. Rain falls in sheets around me and I don't care about that either. I'm wet and cold, but it's nothing to the icy feeling in my gut.

What have I done?

"Avonlea?" Angus's voice comes from behind me, and the next thing I see is his cane laid next to me so he can bend to wrap me in his arms. "Come now, m'eudail, up you come."

He slowly helps me stand, bending cautiously for his cane before wrapping an arm around my waist and guiding me into their cottage. He shouldn't be in the rain. He shouldn't be overexerting himself to help me. Yet here he is—the strength I don't have for myself right now.

I slip onto a stool by the kitchen island and blow out a breath, heavy and stilted, then wipe at my face that's streaked with rain and tears. "Jamie knows about Lennox. I don't know how he figured it out. He didn't say. He just asked if Lennox was his. I've never seen him so upset." I look at the man who has been more than a friend to me. He's been a grandfather, a mentor, and I beg him with my soul to give me an answer to my next question. I need his wisdom more than anything. "What do I do now?"

He shakes his head, the corners of his mouth turning down, and I know he won't have the answers I need. "I don't know, love. Besides talking to him, getting everything out in the open, there isn't much you can do. He's had a shock, and I don't know how he'll react. It may take him a while to figure that out for himself."

"But Lennox... What about him? Does he know?" Oh god, I should've asked more questions about how Jamie figured it out. Is Lennox somewhere in the inn just as upset and confused as Jamie is right now? I spring to my feet, ready to run to him, but Angus's hand on my arm steadies me.

"I don't think he does. He's with Aileen. He's a little confused about why Jamie took off like he did, but he's okay. Aileen will stay with him. I think she's got him playing a board game at the moment."

I relax back onto the stool and drop my head onto my arms, resting them on the counter.

"Give yourself some time to think, lass. Don't get ahead of yourself. First you should probably talk to Jamie—when he gets back from wherever he went."

A terrible thought hits me and I lift my head to look at Angus. "What if he doesn't come back?"

"He will." Angus is so sure of his grandson. I want to have that same level of faith, but I've been on the receiving end of Jamie walking away before. "He's not the same boy he was," he says, and I'm reminded of the fact that Jamie walked away from them too. "Talk to him. Tell him everything. Then you figure out how to tell Lennox. And we'll be here, Aileen and me. We're here, okay?"

My face falls, the gratitude and the hurt and all of it mixing together into a mess of emotions I'll never be able to figure out. "I shouldn't have put you in the middle. I'm so sorry. What if—"

"Avonlea," he says in his gentle voice, one that instantly helps me feel calmer. "We're here for you *all*. Jamie, you, *and* Lennox. Yes, that might be a bit tricky for a while, but you are *all* family. It will work out, you'll see."

God, I wish I had his confidence.

I nod and attempt to steady my breathing. "Okay. Thanks, Angus."

He embraces me then, wrapping me in his arms like I'm a child, and lets me cry into his shoulder until the tears run out and I have nothing left.

"You keep a change of clothes in the kitchen, don't ye? In the drawer of the desk?" Angus asks, and I sniffle, looking at him through what I'm sure are very puffy eyes.

"Aye?" I ask.

"I'll go get them. Why don't you stay here, take a shower, get changed. When Jamie gets back, you two can talk here where it's private."

"What about the lunch service... And Lennox?"

"I'll tag Hamish in and help if they need it," he states, and I open my mouth to protest but he pushes a finger against my lips. "I can help plate or something easy. Relax, lass. And Aileen can keep Lennox company. It'll be fine. Stay, take some time to think. Talk to Jamie. I promise he'll be back before you know it."

I nod and can only hope that he's right.

After what I'm pretty sure was the longest shower I've ever taken—letting the scalding hot water careen over my body, warming every last millimeter of skin—I got restless just sitting in Aileen and Angus's cottage kitchen waiting for Jamie to come back.

So, I started baking. It's what I've always done when I'm upset or restless. God, I hope they won't mind. There's a mess of bowls and ingredients all over the counter and the smell of Scottish shortbread fills the space. I loved seeing that there were all the necessary implements and ingredients here. It tells me Angus loves to cook at home as much as he does for the pub. It tells me he's like me—or maybe I'm like him. Like my mum. She's the same way.

Cooking for the people in my life is how I show them I love them. I figure it can't hurt my chances at this conversation with Jamie going well if I have his favorite dessert waiting for him.

I'm lifting the final tray out of the oven when I hear a car outside. My heart jumps to my throat, beating a fast and anxious rhythm.

Will he come in here immediately? Go in search of his grandparents? To his room? What if he doesn't want to talk to me? What if my waiting here is exactly what he doesn't want?

I don't have time to continue down the interrogatory spiral I'm in because the door opens and he's there.

He really did come back.

Jamie came back.

There's something in that alone that feels instantly soothing—almost healing.

He closes the door behind him and I take him in. His jeans still look slightly damp from our time in the rain, but his hair has dried, though it's a disheveled mess. He looks weary, like the weight of this revelation—of this whole world he didn't know existed—is bearing down on him. A weight that comes from the knowledge that you're a parent or going to be one.

I've held that weight before.

This is the loudest silence I've ever experienced. It goes on for what feels like forever, neither of us speaking. I plead with him with my eyes to let me explain, my gaze never leaving his, and it's like a standoff between us for who will break first.

I'm aware it needs to be me.

"I'm sorry, Jamie," I say, knowing those words will never encompass everything, but it's the only place I can think to start.

His face crumples and he looks away, swiping at his cheeks. My feet move and I'm halfway around the kitchen island when his head snaps up and I stop in my tracks. I might want to offer comfort but that's clearly not what he needs from me right now. I don't know what he needs.

"Can we sit?" I ask gently, indicating to the couch in the parlor.

His solemn nod is all the answer I get. He sits at the far end, kicking an ankle across his knee and leaning back with one arm on the back. It's an easygoing pose, but even after all these years, I know there's nothing easy happening with him right now.

I sit on the other end, clasp my hands in my lap, and stare at them. The silence stretches again until he finally breaks it, and with his words, my heart shatters too.

"You lied to me, Avonlea." His voice is calmer than it was in the driveway earlier, but the hurt underneath is palpable.

I look at him and wish I could say anything but "I'm sorry." My brain isn't providing anything else at the moment though.

"You're sorry?" He shakes his head, disappointment clear in every line of his face. His auburn hair bounces with the movement, falling across his eyes. "We promised each other truth—honesty—always. This... How you could..." He stumbles over each attempt to share his thoughts.

"I was hurting, Jamie. I was broken-hearted and I was hurting, and I made the decision that made sense to me at the time." I know I'll never be able to make him understand—his stunned face is enough to tell me that—but this is a decision that has plagued me for years. "You left me. You walked away. You didn't even say goodbye. I thought we were done, Jamie. You had the life you wanted in the States. Nothing about that was going to change. You didn't want me, and I wasn't going to force you into something, no matter how much I might have wanted to."

He rears back. "So this is my fault?" He looks even more hurt now. "Because I was an idiot seventeen-year-old boy who hurt you, I didn't deserve to know I had a *child*?"

"No, that's not what I'm saying. I'm just trying to tell you how I felt as an idiot seventeen-year-old girl who was scared and didn't know what to do."

"But I tried, Avonlea... I tried to get in touch with you. I tried to apologize. I wanted to fix it and you—you..."

"I blocked you," I whisper, knowing that knowledge will hurt him all over again. I always wondered if he tried to get in contact, but I never gathered the courage to look—to unblock his email and see. Maybe I should've, but it's too late for maybes.

The pain in his eyes only intensifies. I've never seen him so broken, but now... "You—"

"Blocked you, yes. I'm—"

"Don't say you're sorry," he spits, and the anger that he deserves to feel seems to overpower the rest of his emotions.

"But I *am* sorry. Please let me explain. Please, Jamie," I beg, searching his face.

His jaw is set tight, clenched as he struggles against what looks like the urge to scream at me. I deserve it, his anger. He stretches his neck, eyes closed, inhaling deeply, and I'm braced for the blow... But when he opens his eyes and they lock with mine, he gives me the smallest of nods. Relief floods me and my hands tremble against the hem of my shirt.

"When you left, I was a mess. You were my best friend and I loved you." My chest tightens with those words because the last time I told him I loved him, he left me. I want to cry for the heartbroken girl

I was then and for the heartbreak we're both enduring right now. "We'd had sex and I was vulnerable, and all I heard when you walked away was that you didn't want me."

Jamie shifts, lips twitching like he might say something, but I keep going, needing to get this all out. "When I found out I was pregnant, that was the only thing I could think of—that you didn't want me, and I had no reason to believe my being pregnant would change that. And what were you going to do? Move back just because I was pregnant…? No, I wasn't going to force you into being with me. So, I made the choice. I decided to keep the baby and not tell you." I let out a deep sigh. "My parents weren't particularly thrilled with the decision."

Jamie goes rigid, his expression hardening into something livid.

"Not about Lennox," I say, knowing he misunderstood my words. My parents were never anything but supportive about Lennox, unlike my grandparents. "About you. They wanted me to tell you. But they respected my decision once it was made."

"But your grandparents?" he asks, confusion crinkling his brow. "They had to have known. Why didn't they tell—"

"They disowned me, Jamie," I say quietly, interrupting him. "They disowned Mum and Dad too, actually. They were so ashamed of me." My face falls and I watch my hands in my lap where I twine and release my fingers just for something to do with them. "They didn't want anyone here to know, and when Mum and Dad stood by me, by my decisions, they told them never to come back to Skye to see them either. And we didn't. I didn't set foot on this island until they died last year and I came up to settle their estate. Last weekend was the first time my parents have been here since they picked me up when I was seventeen."

"But... your grandparents were the ones who told me you'd moved on, that it was your choice not to come back to Skye."

My head snaps up. "When?" I ask, and squeeze my eyes shut because—what?

"When I came back," he says evenly, like this news isn't enough to rock me to my core.

When did he come back?

"When, Jamie?" I ask again, more firmly.

"That last summer. Before uni. You weren't here."

He came back?

I choke on a sob, covering my mouth with my hands, eyes squeezing shut. He came back and I— "I didn't know you came back that summer," I say, lowering my hands and lifting my head so I can face him.

He scoffs—a mean sound from deep in his throat. "You would if you hadn't blocked me. Why the fuck would you do that?"

I deserve his ire, but it stings to be on the receiving end of it.

"I... It was a mistake. I knew I couldn't just be your friend anymore, and I knew it would break me if you ever emailed me and tried to pick things up where we'd left off, and then with the baby... I knew I wouldn't be able to keep from telling you—"

"You *should* have told me, Avonlea. You should've at least respected me enough to let me be part of the decision."

Ouch. He's right. I know he's right, but...

"What would it have changed?" I say with a plea in my voice.

"*Everything.*" The sincerity in his voice breaks me. "It would have changed everything."

"Exactly, and you would've resented me for it!" I yell, because *I know this.* That's part of why I didn't tell him. "Look at the life you have, Jamie. You wouldn't have any of it. You didn't want to come back to Scotland. You didn't want me. You would have resented me... resented him." I jab a finger in the direction of the inn. "I couldn't have that."

He shakes his head like he doesn't believe the words coming out of my mouth, but I know they're true.

"I loved you too much to do that to you, and I loved myself too much to do it to me, or to Lennox." Tears spill over because that is the crux of it all. "In the beginning, I didn't tell you because I was hurt and afraid you wouldn't come. Then later, I didn't tell you because I feared you would and you'd end up hating me for it."

His posture sags as he rests his elbows on his knees, head bowed. "But I loved you too, Avi."

He hasn't called me Avi since he found out and I'm almost too focused on that to pick up on his other words. But then they click, along with the shattered look on his face when he lifts it to look at me.

"You—you what?" I stutter out the question.

"I loved you too, and I knew I'd screwed up. I knew it as soon as I got on that plane home, but by the time I worked up the courage to reach out to you, to apologize, you didn't respond. I sent you so many emails that year. Then I came back for you, and you weren't here." He inhales, his eyes closing tight behind his glasses, like he's bracing for what he wants to say next. "So I went to Glasgow."

"You came to Glasgow?" Confusion rages beneath my skin, questions ricocheting through my brain: how, when, why? I'm basically a walking English lesson now.

"Yeah." He nods, eyes downcast. "And I saw you."

"What do you mean you saw me? I never saw you, why didn't you say something?"

"Because you had a baby, Avi. You were holding Lennox—not that I knew him as such at the time—and there was this guy with you." His voice hardens with his next words. "I watched him kiss you both. What the hell was I supposed to think?"

I shake my head, mind reeling. A guy? What guy? Kissing us? It's not possible, because there was *never* another guy, no matter what my grandparents might've said to him. There was no moving on—no other guys. There never has been.

"There was no other guy, Jamie." I need him to look at me, but when he does, there's only suspicion behind his green eyes as they narrow behind his glasses.

"I didn't imagine him, Avonlea. He was there, and I swear you looked at him like you used to look at me." His voice breaks slightly and he clears his throat, trying to regain his composure.

This conversation feels like a roller coaster. With every new revelation, my stomach lurches, my emotions get tangled and confused, and my nervous system can't keep up with all the changes.

"Where was this?" I can't think of who he could be talking about.

"The pub. Green Gables. I figured, if I was going to find you, that was the best place to start. You were sitting at a table with this guy, you had Lennox in your arms, and then he got up, kissed Lennox's head and then yours, and you smiled at him." That seems like a trivial thing, but watching his face change when he says it... I can almost picture eighteen-year-old Jamie and the devastation he felt in that moment.

All this time, he knew I had a baby and believed it was with someone else. God, what a mess.

Ten years is a long time and a lot of memories to sift through, but I can only think of one time when Lennox was a baby that I was at the pub with a guy.

"Bloody hell." I furrow my brow, pulling my phone out of my back pocket. I scroll in search of a social media profile for someone I haven't talked to in years. "Is this him?" I flip the phone to face Jamie.

He slides closer on the couch to look at it and his eyes are steely behind his lenses.

"Yeah, I think that's him." He's curt and short in his answer, jaw clenching.

I want to scream and rage because he had to have been so close that day. He was right there, and *this* is what kept us from reuniting?

"Jamie, this is Colin," I say with as much calm as I can muster. "His dad was my mum's sous chef. He was only visiting for the weekend because his boyfriend was the guy playing music that day in the pub. They were both in college in Edinburgh. I practically grew up in the kitchen with Colin. If he kissed me, it was purely platonic. I don't even remember him doing that. I haven't spoken to him in years. His dad launched his own restaurant just before I came back from Paris, which opened up the sous chef role for me to fill."

Jamie shakes his head. "It doesn't matter who he is, Avi. None of that matters. Not really. What matters is that you kept this from me all these years. A son, Avi... You kept my son from me for ten years of his life."

I wish he could understand, but I know he never will. "You left, Jamie. You—"

"I came back!" he yells, pushing the phone back into my hand.

"But I didn't know that!" I shout back, unable to stop everything wound tight inside me from flowing out in a way that will make things worse.

"You would have if you hadn't blocked me. You would have known everything. You would have known how much I regretted it all. But you didn't because—"

I interrupt him. "I was stupid, okay? Jesus, don't you see that I know that? I made the wrong choice. I've known that for years, but then it was too late!"

He stands and begins pacing like a caged lion in front of the couch.

"Too late? You could've come for me, called me, something. *Anything*. But you never tried to fix it, did you? I wouldn't have been hard to find if you'd wanted to. But you didn't. Why?"

"I did it for you, Jamie." He narrows his eyes on me, mid-prowl, and I adjust my wording. "I *thought* I was doing it for you. Every time over the years when I've thought about finding you, telling you..." I shake my head. He doesn't need my excuses.

He needs the truth. All of it.

"I almost flew to the States once, to tell you," I admit, and that stops him in his tracks.

"When?" he demands, eyes blazing.

"Right after you graduated from college. I was about to board the plane, but then I just"—I huff a breath out—"didn't."

"Why?" His gaze searches mine but I look away, my own heartbreak from that moment rising again as if I'm still sitting in the airport.

"Because I knew I was about to ruin your entire life and I-I couldn't do that to you." The words are a whisper between us, but I know he hears me because he drops to his knees in front of me, wrecked by them.

"What are you talking about, Avi?" His words are just as quiet as mine. A whisper. A prayer. A plea for me to explain. I feel the pressure of his hands on either side of me on the couch, caging me in... almost offering support but without actually touching me.

"The day I almost got on that plane?" I look up into his beautiful eyes and wish I didn't have to say these words. "It was the day you announced your book deal."

CHAPTER THIRTY-NINE

Avonlea – Six Years Ago

Why are airport seats so uncomfortable? You'd think with the amount of time people spend sitting in them they'd put more effort into making them suck a little less. The metal armrest digs into my side because I've got my legs pulled up and my arms wrapped around them. I've tried every imaginable position to get comfortable, but it's proving impossible.

I haven't been away from Lennox for more than a day or two since he was born and the separation from him feels like I left a piece of my own heart behind. But an international flight with a four-year-old, by myself, sounded worse. And considering what I'm flying to America to do, I thought it might be best if I left him with my parents.

I figure it'll be less of a shock for Jamie if I tell him on my own rather than showing up with Lennox in tow and saying "hey, here's your son I didn't tell you about."

This is going to be a disaster.

But if four years with Lennox has taught me anything, it's that he's amazing and worth knowing. Jamie deserves that chance. He always has, but he was in college, he was living his best life... Something I only know because I follow him from a dummy account and have watched it all play out from the shadows.

Now, he's graduated, and somehow that feels like a turning point.

My flight is set to board in fifteen minutes and considering I can't get comfortable enough to let my brain rest, I pull my phone out and decide to torture myself a little. Why not go ahead and immerse myself in Jamie's world now that I'm one step closer to seeing him for the first time in five years.

I don't even have to type his name in on the search bar when I click on the app. His most recent post is front and center on my feed the second it opens.

It's a blue background with a white square full of text in the middle.

Words stand out but my brain can't seem to link them all together. *Publisher's Marketplace. Deal Report.* Journals of Elsewhere *by Jameson L. Murray. Major deal. Multi-book deal. For publication.*

I feel myself smiling even though I don't fully understand what all the words mean or who all these people listed at the bottom are.

He got a book deal.

I tap on his caption and read his words:

> *The adventure begins. I had no idea when I started writing this book that it would bring me here. I dreamt of it but never believed it would happen. Yet here we are, and I still feel like I need to pinch myself to prove that it's real. But it is. The adventure fiction novel I've been lovingly pouring my heart into for the past few years is going to be published, along with two additional books to complete the series. Is this my life?*

Yes, Jamie, it is your life. A tear tracks down my cheek and rolls across my still-smiling upper lip into the corner where I can taste it with my tongue. I click on the new profile handle he tagged after the caption, @authorjamesonlmurray, and take in his profile pic. A brand-new headshot I haven't seen before. His hair is tousled slightly on top—it's a true auburn now, less fiery than ever—and his glasses are perched on his nose, framing his beautiful green eyes. The ones he gave his son.

My heart sinks.

I'm still smiling for the boy who was my best friend, but hot tears begin to fall in earnest because I know now I won't be seeing him tomorrow like I planned. I won't be seeing him at all.

He has everything he always wanted and I refuse to be the one who rips that away from him. For years I kept this secret for my sake—too afraid to tell him and have him reject me again. I wasn't strong enough to take that on. But now...

Now I'll keep this secret for his sake. So he can have that life and not be faced with a decision he has no idea even exists.

It's been nearly five years, but I still love him, even if I might wish I didn't, and I won't take away his dream when he's only just had it handed to him.

The gate agent's voice comes over the intercom with a boarding announcement and I barely register the words. I continue to stare at the boy who's become a man while tears roll down my cheeks. I ignore the stares from those milling around me as they line up to board a plane I will never set foot on. The space around me clears and a gate agent finally approaches me with a wary look.

"Ma'am?" the man asks, his discomfort over my tear-streaked face and watery eyes palpable. "Are you on this flight? I'm about to close the door."

"No. You can close the door."

As far as I'm concerned, that door closed the second I saw his deal announcement.

The man nods and walks back to his podium, and I find the will to stand and scrub the tears from my face. I steel my spine and take a steadying breath, and then I walk out of the airport with my head held high.

CHAPTER FORTY

JAMIE - NOW

Avi's words slice through me like a knife made of ice, leaving me frozen in place—fingers digging into the couch on either side of her.

My mind races.

She almost came for me. The day I announced my book deal.

That day feels light-years away now. So much has happened in the six years since then, but I remember that day in vivid clarity just the same. I'd finally gotten the official Publisher's Marketplace announcement and was so excited to share the news. I'd created my new author profile and was feeling like I was on top of the world. Exactly as I should've been, yet I had no idea that thousands of miles away my success in one area of my life all but solidified the failure of another...

"I-I think I need a minute." I push to my feet, away from her, away from the sadness in her eyes. "I need some time. Can you, um, can you go? Please?" The words are getting harder to force through my throat and I really don't want to lose it in front of her again. "Please, Avonlea."

She stands and the grief in her eyes is something I never wanted to see. But at the same time, my heart is shattering as all the implications of this bombshell begin to take shape in my mind.

"I know you don't want to hear it, but I *am* sorry, Jamie. I'm sorry for all of it, but I'm especially sorry you found out this way. I've been wanting to tell you for weeks but couldn't find the words. *This* was never what I wanted." She walks past me, and when we come shoulder to shoulder, she squeezes my bicep and looks up to meet my gaze.

I flinch away from her touch—not because I don't want it but because my entire body feels like an exposed nerve. Raw and painful. Her face falls and she drops her hand—along with her gaze—and walks out of the cottage.

I don't even bother to go to the couch. I just slump down onto the floor and drop my head into my hands.

What the fuck do I do now?

CHAPTER FORTY-ONE

Avonlea - Now

I'm not sure whether that went well or not. What would be the definition of "well" for this scenario anyway? If there's a manual for how to tell your estranged best friend—whom you loved as a teenager and maybe still do—that he's been a father for more than a third of his life, I sure as hell wasn't given a copy.

I make my way to the garden, and though I'm headed for the bench swing, I end up stopping at the tire. I wonder if it will hold me. If I sit here long enough, could it take me back in time?

I should go inside, search out Lennox, begin untangling this mess I've made. But a little bit of quiet might be prudent right now. To get my head on straight and my feelings sorted out so they don't overwhelm him the way they are me.

Lennox. My heart aches for him in the same way it aches for Jamie.

For years I've justified my choices to myself. But in light of today, there's some pretty dark shadows cast on all those reasons and they feel less and less valid with each passing second. I kept Lennox from Jamie, and Jamie has every right to be angry at me for that. But I also kept Jamie from Lennox, and that might hurt even worse.

I've worked so hard to give Lennox everything he could possibly need. He has had a loving family to grow up in and wanted for very little, yet the increase in his questions about his dad over the past few years just shows that he was missing something. Something I couldn't give him on my own, and fuck, that stings.

He's been my everything for so long, and to know that deep down I couldn't be everything to him hurts a little. I know it's unfair; his desire to explore the other half of himself is natural, and instead of telling him the truth, I always put it off.

I had planned to tell him about Jamie eventually... I did. But it was never the right time, and now I'm out of time because there's no way forward but through, and we'll have to figure out what that looks like together. The way it should've been since the beginning.

"Mum?" Lennox's voice is quiet and unsure. I look up and see him standing in the kitchen door, Angus and Aileen at his back with sad but encouraging smiles on their faces. "Are you okay?"

"Yeah, bud. Want to take a walk with me?" I ask, thinking fresh air will lighten the blow of what I need to tell him.

"Okay." He looks up at Aileen. "We can finish our game later?"

She nods. "Of course. Why don't you two take the rest of the day off, head home. We've got everything covered here."

I'm about to protest when Angus pipes in. "It's okay, lass. We've got this. You two take the evening. We'll see you tomorrow."

There's no arguing with him and I know it. "Alright. Go grab your bag, Lennox, and we can walk home. We'll get the car tomorrow."

He takes off like a shot. I hold my tongue, and with it the reminder that running through the kitchen is dangerous and not allowed, and walk over to Angus and Aileen.

"He's in the cottage. He said he needs space, but that might just mean from me. I'm sorry to leave you guys to deal with the pub and everything…" I trail off and wave my hand toward the cottage and the man I left there.

"It's alright. You focus on Lennox tonight. We'll see to Jameson," Angus says with more kindness than I deserve.

A thought occurs to me and I grimace. "I, uh, left a mess in your kitchen. I made shortbread, but then Jamie got back and I didn't have a chance to clean up. I'm so sorry, I—"

"I'll take care of it," Aileen says. "It's good for me to have something to busy my hands with in the evening anyway so I'm not just sitting around twiddling my thumbs." She chuckles.

"Thank you," I say, pulling her into a hug. "I don't deserve you. Either of you." I swap out Aileen for Angus and hug him as well.

"We're family, lass, you don't have to deserve us or earn our love. It's just there. And it always will be," he says, and I let myself believe him.

Goodness, why are they so good to me?

"Ready, Mum?" Lennox says from behind them, backpack on his shoulder, wellies on his feet.

"Aye. Let's go," I say with as much normalcy as I can manage.

Tugging him in against my side, we wave back to Angus and Aileen, and with one last glance toward the cottage, I think I catch a flash of auburn hair in the window. My lips tug up at the corners and I turn to my son, ready to finally tell him about the man I loved all those years ago.

We get to the street and Lennox pulls away, looking down at his feet.

How much did he pick up on today in all the chaos? Did he hear more than he let on?

He startles me when he blurts, "I think I made Jamie mad, but I don't know what I did."

His eyes go wide when he looks up after his little exclamation and then he bites his lip, something I tend to do when I'm upset too.

"You didn't make him mad, bud." My chest constricts. He's got such a good heart.

"Are you sure? We were having fun at the desk and then... well, I found out his name is Jameson—did you know that?—and I told him that was my middle name and then he just kind of stormed off... Did I do something wrong?"

Ah, so that was the catalyst for the implosion of my carefully laid lies.

I shake my head and stop Lennox, squatting down in front of him so we can look each other in the eyes. "You didn't do anything wrong. I did. And Jamie isn't mad at you, buddy. He's mad at me."

"Why?" His blond brows draw down on his face as he looks at me, confused.

"Because I lied to him... about something really important." I have to swallow the lump growing in my throat before it chokes me.

Damn, this is hard.

"I thought we weren't supposed to lie," Lennox says with so much innocence and sweetness it makes me want to cry.

"We aren't. And this is why. It only ever hurts people in the end. In this case, it hurt Jamie and—" I blow out a breath. "It hurt you too."

"What do you mean?" Lennox's gaze bounces around my face.

"I lied to you too, in a way."

"You did? About what?"

I stand and grab his hand, wondering if he'll still let me hold it after I tell him. I start walking again and he follows, looking up at me with so many questions in his eyes.

"About who Jamie is. To me. To you."

I lead Lennox up the front steps of our cottage and sit us down on the porch swing so he's tucked against my side.

"Jamie is your dad, Lennox."

CHAPTER FORTY-TWO

JAMIE - NOW

It wasn't five minutes after I watched Avi walk away with Lennox yesterday before my grandparents were in the cottage with me. But everything from my conversation with her was still too raw, so I asked for space from them as well—wanting the opportunity to sift through some of this on my own.

I don't know how to feel about them knowing this whole time—for the last year at least. At some point we'll have that conversation, but yesterday wasn't the day for it... I don't know if today is that day either.

I still need to call my parents. We've talked at least once a week since I got here—mostly to give Dad updates about how Grandad is doing. I can't even begin to imagine how they'll react to the news that I'm a father, that they have a grandson who's ten years old.

How can I have a ten-year-old son?

Did Avi tell him last night? What does he think of all this?

My stomach grumbles violently. I haven't eaten since breakfast yesterday, and considering it made its reappearance not long after, I'm starving. Even the shortbread Avi made wasn't able to tempt me into eating, and I skipped dinner too—not wanting to sit and make small talk with my grandparents but not ready to talk about the important stuff either.

The dining room is quiet when I reach it, with only a few people still sipping their tea or picking at their meals. I'm tempted to sit and order a full Scottish breakfast thanks to the scents of bacon and sausage lingering in the air, but a bowl of porridge is probably a safer option.

I rarely sit in the dining room for meals except dinner, ordering instead with the kitchen staff and taking my meals wherever I want... But chances are Avi is in the kitchen and I'm feeling a bit like a chickenshit at the moment. Unsure if I'm ready to face her.

There's a small window in the door, so I peek through and do my best to get a good look around. An instant sense of relief overtakes me when I don't see her. Popping my head inside, I find Grandad sitting at his desk, bent over a ledger of some kind.

"Mornin'," I say, and he glances up, a cautious smile forming around his lips, eyes crinkling slightly beneath his readers.

"Mornin', Jameson." He hefts himself out of his chair to give me a hug and I sink into it, wrapping my arms around him the same way he does with me.

All might not be forgotten, but forgiven? I think I can do that, even if I still don't understand.

"Can we get you something to eat?" he asks, pulling back and looking me up and down.

"Porridge would be great," I say, looking over my shoulder at Hamish, who gives me a nod. "Is Avi... Is she here?"

"She's on her way. Has a few things to check in on this morning and then she'll be taking Lennox back down to Glasgow."

"I thought her parents were coming to get him?" I wonder aloud.

My brain conjures every negative scenario in an instant. Her deciding to go back to Glasgow for good. Lennox being angry about me—being angry *at* me. Lennox being angry with Avi.

"They were, aye. Plans changed," he says, giving nothing else away.

Everything changed yesterday.

A moment later, a steaming bowl of porridge slides across the desk and I tuck into it with abandon. God, I was hungry. I'll have to ask Gran if she saved the shortbread from yesterday, because now that I don't feel so unsettled, I really want some.

"I think I'm going to take my computer into the garden to work for a bit," I say once I've finished my breakfast. What I don't say is that I want to get out of the kitchen so I'm not sitting here when Avi walks in. I made things awkward enough amongst the staff when I burst in here yesterday.

And I don't know what to do when I see her. I'm not sure I'm ready to continue our conversation. I don't have any idea what to think about any of this.

"Sounds like a fine idea. Soak up the sunshine out there before it inevitably rains again." Grandad nods toward the window where dust particles play in the bright rays shining through.

I sling my messenger bag over my shoulder and head out of the kitchen. The warmth of the sun outside hits me and I turn my face up to greet it, eyes closed, and just breathe. Heather and the damp, earthy smells from the loch waft my way on the breeze, ruffling my hair lightly.

When I open my eyes, it's to find I'm not alone in the garden.

Nox sits on the tire swing in a pair of jeans tucked into wellies and a wrinkled T-shirt. His rain jacket lies discarded on the bench swing with a book wrapped inside it.

He watches me from his perch, assessing me.

"Hi," I say in a reserved tone. I'm not entirely sure what the protocol is for talking to my son for the first time. We've talked plenty in the past several days, but this is different and we both know it.

"Hi." He tucks his chin, making his blond hair fall across his face. When he flips his head back to get it out of his eyes, I can't help but smile because that exact hair flip is a maneuver I've perfected over the years and he looked just like me doing it.

It's this that gives me the confidence to approach him. "Can I sit? Maybe we could, um, talk?" I ask, closing the distance between us and taking up my standard seat on the far end of the bench.

He nods and hops off the tire swing, feet landing with a splat in the small puddle beneath it. That makes my smile grow slightly wider. He moves his jacket and book to the center of the swing, like a barrier of protection between us. He has his hands in his lap, fingers splaying and contracting against his legs.

"So," he says, looking up and biting his bottom lip. Now, *that* is a look he got from Avi, through and through. "You're really my dad?"

He studies me, taking in every inch of my appearance like he wants to prove it to himself one way or another. If anything tells the tale, it's the green of our irises. I think he knows it because he has yet to fully look me in the eye.

"Yeah... I am." I try for a neutral tone, wanting to keep the ever-changing range of emotions I'm grappling with from making their way to him. I'm sure he has enough of them on his own.

He nods again, eyes downcast. "Are you mad?" he asks, and my brows draw down in confusion.

Mad? At him?

"Nox," I say, and he finally—*finally*—looks at me, our eyes clashing for the first time. I hold that stare, feeling woefully unprepared for any of this but knowing it's important. "I'm not mad—not about you—okay?"

He nods, eyes shifting away before they're drawn right back to mine. "Aye, okay. But you are mad at Mum?" he asks, and I want to squirm under his gaze.

"I don't know exactly." Honesty seems like the best policy right now, considering. "I'm feeling a lot of things."

"Yeah, me too. I don't know if I'm mad at her or just... I don't know, sad?" His eyes plead with me, as if I hold the answers. And god, I wish I did, but I'm right there with him.

"You can be both. I think I'm both too."

"You really didn't know?" The wetness along his bottom lashes hits me in the gut.

"I promise, Nox, I had no idea. I—" I don't know what to say because the *I would have* sentences in my head are just sentiments at this point, and not ones I can even say with any semblance of truth. I have no idea what I would have done had I known. I'll never be able to answer that question, because I wasn't given the chance.

A flare of anger rises in my gut. *I guess I am mad.* But not at Nox. Not at this boy who's looking at me with so much hope in his eyes.

The anger deflates and I shift toward him, moving his jacket. The book inside slides out and my brow furrows when I see it's a copy of *Journals of Elsewhere.*

"Mum told me that's your book. It's been her favorite ever since I can remember."

I ghost my fingers across the worn dust jacket. Evidence that the book's been read repeatedly, that it's been well-loved. Now it's my eyes that have gone misty and I blink rapidly to clear them. I guess she wasn't lying when she told me my books were her favorite.

"I always kind of thought maybe she named me after the author." He taps my first name on the book. "I guess she did."

"Yeah, I guess so. Have you read them with her?" I ask, wondering if my own son has escaped into the adventures I've written. They're not written for children, but I know a lot of readers have read them with theirs.

"Not yet. She told me we could read this one together this summer though."

My heart clenches, a deep ache that hurts but also feels good—like pride wrapped in sadness tied up with something else I'm afraid to name.

"That sounds like a great idea," I say, trying for an even voice.

"You'll still be here when I get back, right?" he asks, clasping the book to his chest now like it's a lifeline.

And this is where it all gets complicated. Yes, I'll be here when he gets back… but for how long? My being here was never meant to be permanent. It was tied to Grandad, and Gran, and how long they needed me here. But that was before—well, all of this.

"Yeah," I say carefully, "I'll still be here when you get back. Only a few more weeks of school, right?"

He shrugs. "Aye, I wish I could skip them and stay here."

"I'm sure your grandparents are looking forward to a few more weeks of having you all to themselves before you move. I bet they're going to really miss you."

"I think they'll come to visit a lot. Wait…" His gaze bounces over to the inn, then to me, and back to the inn… His mind is whirring and I wonder what it is he's—

"Angus and Aileen are your grandparents?" he finishes.

"Aye, they are." I can see where this is going.

"So, does that make them my great-grandparents?" he asks with a smile—it's small but it's there.

"It does."

His grin widens and I match it with one of my own. I don't know how I didn't see it before, that his toothy grin is exactly like mine was at his age.

I might have no idea what I'm going to do or what happens next, but I do know that this is a moment I'll never forget.

"Lennox," Avi says tentatively from the door, drawing our attention. Her eyes are cautious when they meet mine, but they soften as she takes us in—both of us smiling. "Can you come in and help Aileen gather your things from about the inn? Don't want you to forget anything."

"Okay." His tone cools significantly from the excitement over his new great-grandparents and I see Avi register the change as well, her features pinching.

"Hey, Nox," I call after him as he reaches the door. Avi's hand finds his shoulder and he shrugs it off. The crestfallen look on her face is like a dagger to the heart. "Try not to get into any more fights, aye?"

He smirks and, with a nod, walks inside, leaving me and Avi in a tense silence.

She closes the door behind her and takes a few steps over to the swing but doesn't sit. "You two talked?" She bites down on her lip and fiddles with the hem of her open flannel shirt.

"We did. I hope that's okay," I say, still not clear on what my place is here.

She nods and laces her hands in front of her. "Of course it's okay. I just—" She squeezes her eyes shut and shakes her head. "Is he really mad?"

I cock my head and watch her. "I don't think so. Not really."

She arches an eyebrow.

"Okay, yeah, he's mad... but I think it's more that he doesn't know how to feel."

"Are you?" she whispers, and lifts her head to look at me "Mad?"

"I don't think so. Not really," I repeat, surprised to feel my lips tip up a little. And with that, there's a small shift in her features. Relief maybe. "It's a lot. I don't really know how to feel right now either."

"That's understandable. For you both." She puffs out a breath. "I'm getting ready to take Lennox back to my parents. I think he and I could use a little more time to talk about things. He wasn't super receptive to hearing me out last night and he's been pretty quiet this morning." Her fingers continue to fiddle with her shirt and her words get more frantic and clipped. "But I know you and I have a lot to talk about too. I'm sorry that I'm leaving with things still so—"

"It's okay, Avi, this is how it should be. He needs you. We can talk when you get back. I'll be here."

Those three little words seem to calm her, lift the edge of panic that was pressing down on her.

"I'm only staying tonight, so I'll be back tomorrow afternoon. I've missed too much work already. Your grandad should probably fire me—or just give Hamish the job. He's a lot less trouble."

And the panic is back, the concern for her job creating an undercurrent of anxiety beneath everything else.

"Avi," I say, moving forward on my seat but not moving to reach for her. "Hamish is used to taking over, he did it with Grandad too. And he'd never fire you for needing to be there for Lennox. Things will calm down once he's up here full-time."

She exhales and her shoulders sag, relaxing away from her ears. "Aye, you're right. I don't know how we ended up with you comforting me, but I just—thank you, Jamie." She shifts toward me—the pull between us too much to stay apart—and on instinct I stand and pull her into a hug.

I don't know if she needed it or if I did, or if it's just the natural way of things between us. Everything feels less daunting with her in my arms. I turn my head just enough to bury my nose in her glowing blonde waves and inhale the floral scent that has always been hers. Just Avi.

I may have no idea what happens now, but I do know that this has always felt right.

With one last tightening of her arms, she releases me and steps back, a glimmer of a tear on her cheek that she swipes away with the back of her hand. "I'll see you tomorrow then?"

"Tomorrow," I say with a nod.

After she leaves, the scent of her lingers around me like a memory.

I can't touch it, but I know it's there.

CHAPTER FORTY-THREE

JAMIE - NOW

I groan as I flop onto the bed, perpendicular to the mattress, legs hanging off the side. I toe off my shoes, listening to the soft thud they make as they hit the floor.

Today was busy. The beginning of the summer tourist season is upon us and there were more new arrivals than any other day since I've been here. But I savored the busyness, as it worked to keep my mind off Avi... and Lennox.

Grandad oversaw things in the kitchen while Hamish filled in for Avi... but we all know the "Angus version" is much more hands-on than the doctor would prefer.

Gran had her hands full ensuring all the rooms got turned over with the housekeeping staff, that everything was clean and tidy around the inn, and doing the other millions of things she does on a daily basis to keep this place running smoothly.

I was even relieved when the night manager called to say she was running late so I could offer to cover the front desk while Gran and Grandad ate dinner together.

I know the conversation about what comes next, what they've known about Lennox and when they learned it, will have to happen eventually, but I'd like one more night to think about all of this—or not—before we have to have it.

A knock at the door pulls me away from staring blankly at the ceiling and I roll toward the pillows with a groan. The crinkle of paper against my face brings me up short and I pull back, seeing a cream-colored envelope beside a small bundle tied together with red-and-white string.

Another knock. "Coming," I say, narrowing my eyes on the envelope.

I grab it and head for the door, pulling it open to reveal Hector from the kitchen with a tray laden with food.

"Angus asked me to deliver this to you," he says with a flat smile.

Of course he did. "Thank you," I say, taking the tray. The comforting smell of shepherd's pie engulfs me as I set it on my small table. Crunchy bread accompanies it and I rip off a piece and pop it into my mouth, its warmth spreading through me.

Damn, that's good.

I sit down and contemplate the envelope in my hands.

At first I thought it might be from Avi, but we were never the letter writers. Tipping my forefinger under the upper corner, I slide it across, tearing it open and pulling out the singular piece of paper within.

My lips tilt up when I see the writing.

I settle the letter on the table, smoothing it out, and reach for another piece of bread. Then I begin to read.

Jameson,

I'm sure you noticed that there are no letters between your Gran and I from 1967 to 1968. I've known the time for this part of the story was coming—the broken part—and I'm sure you're wondering why I'm writing to you about this now. I promise there's a reason.

The bundle of letters are the ones I wrote to your gran during that time, but I never sent them. She's never read them. Never wanted to. She knows I'm giving them to you now though, and she approves.

This is part of our story. A story I think you've romanticized into this perfect thing in your head. But love is never perfect. It's always messy. It's always hard. It's always work.

Even ours.

You've seen the 'other side' of our story, but you haven't seen the middle—the mess, the hard...

That's what's in these letters.

My wish for what you'll find in them is hope.

Hope that even in a situation that feels as impossible and messy and hard as yours does right now, that there is beauty on the other side. Hope that there is healing and reconciliation on the other side. Hope that there is love on the other side.

Your gran and I will never be able to change the part we played in keeping Lennox from you for this past year. There will never be a reasonable explanation for it in your eyes, and we understand that too. The choice to either respect Avi's wishes where Lennox was concerned or to tell you was never an easy one, and with the past couple months, it only became more complicated.

Perhaps we made the wrong one but second-guessing it now won't change anything. We can only apologize for the hurt we caused, and hope for your forgiveness.

We love you so much, Jameson. Having you home is the greatest gift you could have ever given us—given me.

We are here if you need to yell and be angry. We are here if you need comfort. We are here. You can ask us anything you want. You can give us the silent treatment. You can choose to leave—though we hope you will not.

But remember that in whatever you need to do or feel right now, we will be here on the other side because we love you. And for what it's worth, if you'll let her, I think that Avi will be here on the other side as well, because she does too.

All our love,

Grandad & Gran

I wake with a start, my glasses askew on my face and with what I'm pretty sure is drool on my cheek. I pull my glasses off and scrub a hand over my eyes, blinking the world into a semi-blurry reality.

Letters are scattered around me on the bedspread. My legal pad of notes and questions sits on the bedside table. I wipe my glasses clean on my wrinkled T-shirt and slide them back into place.

My dishes from dinner still sit on the table because once I ripped into the first letter last night, there was nothing that could pull me away. What looked like a modest stack of letters actually contained twenty-four—and with them the piece I didn't even know I was missing was found. I tap my mousepad on my laptop—also still on the bed—and find that it's dead. Of course it is, because I was up writing half the night before I passed out fully clothed.

The sunlight streaming through my window tells me I slept past breakfast. That's what happens when you stay up until three a.m. lost in a story, an idea. The new manuscript on my computer may be bare bones, but there's something that tugs me toward the words, even now after a full night of working on it.

It's the same way I felt when I was writing *Journals of Elsewhere* and it's something I haven't felt since I turned in the final manuscript for book three. There hasn't been a story to captivate me like this and there's something even deeper in this one. More than I ever expected when I picked up that box of letters in the attic.

I got lost in Gran and Grandad's story last night, pushing my own aside. But in the light of today, I realize how much I learned about myself, my life, my story at the same time. I don't have all the answers, but maybe I'm learning I don't always have to.

They didn't, yet here they are on the *other side* as they said in their letter to me, and better for all the things they went through together.

Is that what I want? Someone on the other side? Is that what I've been searching for all these years and never found, despite the fact that it was right where I left it?

An ache I've always had—like a piece of myself is missing—thrums dully in my chest. I guess a piece *has* been missing for a long time, I just didn't know it. But now that I do, I want to fill it—I want to find it.

Within an hour, my disaster writing session is set to rights—all the letters neatly stacked, my computer charging, notes where they should be on my desk—and I'm showered and dressed in a pair of jeans and a fresh T-shirt. I slip on my wellies, aware of the fact that it poured rain all night while I was working and it'll be a mess outside.

I've got a single-track mind, but I allow it to take a small detour...

I find Gran leaning against Grandad's desk in the kitchen. He sits in the chair and their knees are pressed together, hands laced on top of her thigh. It's funny to see them this way, almost eye to eye. Grandad is an imposing Scotsman through and through—even with dark circles under his eyes and a cane by his side—and Gran is this petite little thing, a dichotomy I've always loved. They're opposites in so many ways, but perfectly compatible, or at least as perfect as two imperfect people can be.

"Afternoon," I say, drawing their attention and hesitant smiles.

I walk over and draw Gran into a hug. She seems to melt into it, wrapping her arms around my waist. Then I reach back and grip Grandad's hand until he also stands on shaky legs and engulfs me.

We're here, together, on the other side of all of this, and I don't even need more explanations or apologies. This is family, and it's all I need.

The chirping of birdsong and the crunch of my boots over the gravel while I walk alongside the loch isn't enough to distract me from the ringing in my ear as I wait for my dad to answer his phone.

It's no use putting off the inevitable, and after the clarity of last night, I don't want to wait. I can't run from this, nor do I want to.

"Jamie?" Dad's voice is laced with concern, groggy with sleep. "Are you okay?"

Shit. I once again didn't consider the time difference.

"Everything's fine. I'm sorry to call so early."

"It's okay," he says, and I can hear him shifting in the bed. "You're sure you're alright? Is Dad okay?"

"Grandad's good. I just had lunch with him and Gran a bit ago. I'm sorry if I scared you."

Through the phone, I hear Mum too—though she's muffled and I can't make out what she's saying.

"Good morning, sweetheart." Her voice rings through clearer now.

"Hey. I'm sorry I woke you." I scrub a hand across my bearded jaw and let my feet carry me up the porch steps.

Avi's porch steps.

I want to be close to her when I tell my parents about Lennox—even if she's not here.

"Oh stop apologizing," she chides lovingly, bringing a smile to my face and a pang to my heart. I miss her. I miss them. "Was there a reason for this particular wake-up call? Not that you ever need a reason to call us."

I sink down on the top step and stretch my legs out long in front of me.

Here we go. This is about to become a lot more real.

"I have some news." I work to keep my voice even, but as the words begin to bubble up toward the surface, I can feel it waver. How do I say this? "I—god, I don't even know where to begin."

"Jamie..." Mum's voice rises an octave, and I know I'm making it worse by dragging it out.

Rip it off like a bandage, she always said, so that's what I do.

"Lennox, Avi's son, is... well, he's mine. He's my son." I say the words so fast I'm afraid they might not have caught them. "And I know that's not what you were expecting and you're going to have a lot of questions but—"

Dad cuts me off. "Jamie, stop worrying about us. Are *you* okay?"

I move my feet to the bottom step so I can rest my elbows on my knees. "Still kind of in shock. But I'm alright."

"How long have you known?" Mum asks, her voice still too high.

"A couple days," I say with a wince. I'm sure they'll be mad I didn't tell them immediately.

"Bloody hell, that's quite the news. Did you tell your grandparents?" Dad asks.

I don't want to throw Gran and Grandad under the bus, but with all the lies and deception going around, I don't want to perpetuate that habit. "They've known for a while—but before you get mad, just know they had their reasons and—"

"They knew?!" Mum shouts, incredulous.

"Maeve…" Dad says at the same time I say, "Mum, please…"

"And Avi, she obviously knew all this time. Isn't Lennox ten years old?" she continues, not heeding our warning tones for even a moment.

"Yes, he's ten. And, yes, they all knew. Though Gran and Grandad have only known for about a year," I explain, and Mum harrumphs in her throat. I almost laugh because it's such a Scottish noise and it's one I haven't heard from her in a long time. "I understand you being upset. I was too, but none of us can change what happened in the past. She had her reasons as well… It's all very complicated."

"It sounds like it," Dad says, and I can't read his reactions over the phone like I can when I'm with him in person. He's always been a pretty stoic man. "And Lennox… Does he know?"

I blow out a breath and lift my eyes to look out at the loch across the way from Avi's cottage. "He does now. He's—" I don't know what to say. How do you explain to your parents how it felt to meet your son for the first time? "He's a great kid. Avi's done an amazing job with him. He—he actually reminds me a lot of myself at that age."

My throat stings, and there's a pinching pain behind my eyes and in my nose. Gah, I don't want to cry on the phone with my parents about this. I don't want to cry about it at all. But god, I have a son, and I've missed so much, and now that I know some things about him, I just want *more*.

"You're truly doing okay, Jamie?" Mum's voice has gentled, all her concern for me laced into each and every word.

"It's a lot, but I'm wrapping my head around it."

"You have a son," she says, like she's testing the words and finding them just as foreign as I did the first time I said them.

"I do," I respond, relaxing further into that truth the more I hear it and say it myself. "You guys have a grandson."

She laughs, but it's watery—she's definitely crying.

"Och, mo chridhe," Dad lovingly admonishes her. "A grandson." There's a different kind of wonder in his voice. "So, what happens now, Jameson?" he asks, and it brings me up short.

"That's a great question. Any advice?"

He barks a laugh. "Unfortunately, this isn't a scenario I've ever been through. But you've loved that girl for most of your life, maybe it's time you stopped running from that and try embracing it instead."

Wait... what? "What are you talking about?" I ask in disbelief.

"Jamie, you might not have told us what happened between you two all those years ago, but we've watched you pursue nothing but casual relationships ever since... It wasn't hard to put it together."

"We're your parents. You didn't have to tell us for us to know," Mum tacks on.

"But..." I want to ask for more about what they knew, *how* they knew, but this isn't the time. "Never mind. I still don't know how we move forward."

"With one step at a time," she says, and her voice sounds watery again, though I think it's with a different kind of tears.

"One step at a time," I repeat. "Yeah, I think I can do that."

CHAPTER FORTY-FOUR

Avonlea - Now

The five-hour drive back to Skye wasn't enough to figure out how to make all of this okay.

I think Lennox and I are alright now, considering we had the same hours-long drive yesterday to hash things out. There was yelling on his part, tears from us both, and finally some level of acceptance.

The biggest question at the end of the day, whispered across his pillow while I tucked him in last night, was whether or not Jamie is going back to America or if he'll stay in Scotland. It's a question I don't know the answer to. His time here was supposed to be temporary—a year at most. Two of those twelve months have already passed... So what happens at the end?

This was part of how I justified my decision to keep this to myself. I know what it feels like to be left by Jameson Murray, and I don't want that for Lennox. I don't want it for me again either.

I don't want to hope he'll stay for us—for me.

But I think I'm already lost to that hope.

And seeing him on my front porch when I pull up to the cottage only raises them. Even if it's just as likely he's here to dash them instead.

He's sitting on the top step. Green boots planted a few steps below, a cake of mud around the soles. His dark jeans are tucked into the boots and his classic white tee hugs his shoulders and chest. His forearms are propped on his knees and his hair is tousled, eyes hiding behind his glasses.

I park and swallow a breath that feels too thick before pushing the door open. Before I step out, I reach to the passenger seat and grab my red wellies, sliding them on because there was no driving in them.

The gravel crunches under my feet, taking me closer to the man who holds so much of my future in his hands.

His chin dips, perusing me as I walk. From my boots to my bare legs. The denim shorts and my white flowy top that's tucked into them. It was warm in Glasgow this morning, but there's a bit of a chill here, and goose bumps break out across my exposed thighs.

When his gaze finally meets mine, there's a warmth—a heat—in his eyes that makes me blush. Those green eyes. I swear I've always been able to feel them when they're on me. I feared I'd never feel their focus on me the same way again.

"How long have you been waiting here?" I ask, my voice high thanks to my nerves.

"A little while." He holds his hand out to the side, silently asking me to sit. So I do, keeping a few inches between us. Afraid if we touch, the conversation might not happen. "I wanted to be here when you got home."

Why does that make my heart beat erratically in my chest?

"Do you want to go inside to talk?" I ask him, squeezing my hands in my lap to keep them from shaking.

"I thought maybe we could take a walk, if you want." He nods toward the lane.

"I've been sitting in that car for hours. A walk sounds good."

He pushes off the step to stand, his fingers brushing against mine, and it's enough to electrify my entire body. How he manages to have such an effect on me after all this time, I'll never understand.

"Avi?" he asks, and I glance up to find that same hand extended toward me, a grin around his lips that brightens his irises to match the greenery around us.

I slip my fingers into his and he trails his thumb over the top of my hand before he pulls me up. There's something about this casual Jamie that reminds me so much of the boy I knew.

Is he still in there—that boy I fell in love with? I've glimpsed him under this new manly exterior, but he's so different. I know I'm different too.

With a light tug, we start walking and I gently shake my hand free, under the guise of pulling my hair into a braid over my shoulder. The constant state of touching is more than I can bear right now. My body, my heart, and my brain don't know how to take it.

"Nox doing okay?" Jamie asks, glancing sidelong at me before looking ahead to wherever he's leading us.

I love that he's thinking of Lennox—of how he's doing. Concern for his well-being is a good sign... And that hope blooms again.

"I think so. We had a lot of time to talk. He had questions, many of which I can't answer for him..." I watch my feet, afraid to ask those very questions myself. At least Lennox was brave enough to voice them, unlike me. "And he's not particularly thrilled about being in Glasgow for another few weeks. He wants to be here, but Mum and Dad are determined to make it as special for him as possible."

"And how are your parents? You told them—that I know—I assume?" he asks, voice low and cautious.

"Yeah, I got to be on the receiving end of one of my mother's 'I told you so' looks." I glance up and catch his puzzled expression. "She told me that if I didn't tell you, you'd figure it out, and she was right. Dad was—well, Dad. He's worried about all of it."

"I think I understand a little better now why his handshake that first night was a little intense." He shakes his head, lines forming between his brows.

I chuckle and say, "I think my dad got over the fact that you got me pregnant a long time ago." My attempt at humor falls short and I see Jamie flinch slightly. "Shit, I'm sorry."

Too soon for jokes about this, I guess. It's a deflection method I've gotten good at, but it's not always the most helpful.

"It's okay. I just—I still can't believe it, you know." His eyes find mine, and they're sincere and full of emotions I can't begin to understand. "That wasn't a reality I lived through like you did. It's a shock is all. You were *pregnant*. And I missed it." He shakes his head like he truly can't fathom this, and the sadness in his voice makes it sound like he wishes more than anything he could've been there, seen it, been part of it.

"I—" I begin, but he cuts me off.

"Please don't apologize again." He holds a hand up and offers me a kind smile—one I'm not sure I deserve. "We're past the apologies I think at this point."

"Are we?" My voice cracks. I feel like there must be more apologies I owe him. I'm not sure I'll ever believe it's been enough.

"We are," he states matter-of-factly, and then he grabs my hand and pulls me toward the loch. Toward the small cove we used to come to. The one where we kissed for the first time our last summer together, where we agreed to a summer of only kissing and staying friends in the end.

How very stupid we were.

"Jamie." I'm breathless and a little nervous about why he'd bring us here of all places.

"I haven't been back here. Not since that summer." He walks a little ways away before turning around to face me. "I couldn't bring myself to come alone. I knew it had to be with you, or not at all."

"Why now?" I ask, tentatively taking a step, and then another.

He shrugs and closes the distance between us with one large bootstep. We're close enough that just leaning in would bring us together, bodies brushing.

"Truth?" Jamie asks.

My swallow is heavy—thick with nerves—and my stomach clenches. "Always," I whisper, because going forward, he deserves to always have the truth from me. He always did.

"Would you like to go on a date with me?"

"A date?" I say, shocked, but my lips tug up involuntarily, eyebrows meeting my hairline.

"A date, a real one. We never got that chance. Instead, we agreed to a summer of just kissing, where we'd stay friends in the end. None of that worked out the way we planned. Maybe we need a new plan." He pushes a wayward strand of hair behind my ear.

Butterflies zip to life in my stomach and my heart flutters in rhythm with their wings. The fear of the unknown from earlier gnaws at me too, and I don't know what to say.

"I don't know, Jamie." His face falls so I hurry on, pressing my hand lightly to his chest. "It's not that I don't want to. But your time here is temporary, and I already don't know what that means for Lennox. I—"

"Avi," he interrupts me, and the way he says my name, though gentle, leaves no room for argument. "I'm just asking for one date. A chance—to talk, to listen, to see..."

"But..." I bite my lip and watch him from under my lashes.

"Please, Avi. Let me take you on a real date. Something I never got the opportunity to do, and maybe we can find some answers to the questions we both have about what happens next. We take it one step at a time, yeah?"

His sincerity mixed with the smell of him, earthy and masculine, weakens my resolve. As if it wasn't already putty around this man.

"Okay." I breathe the word and with it feel something inside me shift slightly. "One date."

His lips lift into the first true smile I've seen on his face today. That smile used to be the thing that brought me more joy than anything else. I would've traded every smile from every other person in the world if I could just have one more of them. The only smile that rivals it is Lennox's, and as I think about it now, it's because it's always reminded me of Jamie.

CHAPTER FORTY-FIVE

JAMIE - NOW

Deciding I wanted to take Avi on a date was the easy part...

The challenging part? Actually making the date happen.

She's been hard at work all week—refusing to take a night off because of her unexpected trip down to Glasgow last weekend. Her fear of failing my grandfather, or the kitchen, has had her nose to the grindstone from breakfast through dinner for eight straight days.

We've sought out quiet moments together—sitting on the garden swing when she takes her breaks mainly—but it's not enough. We've had more than enough time to think about things, now we just need the time to discuss them. I'm ready to put into words the many thoughts I have in my head... and tonight I finally get to.

Not that this week's been a complete loss. While Avi has been busy in the kitchen, I've been immersed in *With Love, From Skye.* It's taking shape in a way I've never experienced with my writing before, the storyline and characters filling the pages with thousands of words I didn't know were possible for me to write. It's nothing like I expected it to be—writing a love story—but I wonder if I should've listened to Avi all those years ago and given it a shot. I might be in a very different place right now—professionally and personally.

Even after learning of the role they played in it all, I can't regret my other books. Those stories were the escape I needed during a time of my life when I felt dangerously unsettled. They're a part of my soul in a different way than this book will be. Assuming I can get my agent on board to pitch it to the publisher.

But none of that could be further from my mind as I check my collar in the mirror. Tonight I get to take Avi out on a real date—something I stopped imagining would happen a long time ago. Even the downpour outside can't dampen my spirits, but it is going to put a literal damper on my plan to walk to the high street for dinner.

In the lobby, I see Gran at the front desk talking with Freya, the town's caffeine slinger. I swing around the front desk and plant a kiss on the side of Gran's head. Her answering smile is bright and only grows wider as she takes me in. I'm in a pair of dark jeans, cuffed at the hems above my brown leather Chelsea boots, and a dark green button-down.

"That shirt brings out your eyes," she says. "Doesn't it, Freya?"

Freya does a long perusal of my body that would make me blush if she wasn't nearly eighty. "Aye, it does, and it definitely brings out your muscles too," she says with a wink in my direction. "Hot date?"

Okay... well, now I'm definitely blushing.

"Matter of fact, yes," I say just as Avi walks in the front door, making my heart stop.

Sweet Jesus.

Her head is braced against the rain when she steps inside and she's focused on brushing the wet from her boots on the mat, giving me a glorious minute to absorb every inch of her.

The navy-blue dress she's wearing fits her body like a glove from her exposed collarbone—due to the off-the-shoulder cut—to where it dips in at her waist then flares out again over her hips.

I've never wanted my hands on those hips more than I do right now. Gone is her teenage-girl physique, and I don't miss it even a little bit. This is a woman's body, and there has never been a body I've been more drawn to. The dress hits her mid-thigh and her over-the-knee boots make my own knees want to buckle.

Fucking hell, is she trying to kill me?

She turns from the coat rack and catches me gawking, mouth open, eyes wide.

"Hi," she says on a breathy sigh.

"Good evening, Avonlea," Gran says, covering for my inability to speak. Her eyes twinkle and she exchanges a knowing look with Freya.

"Looks like I was indeed correct," Freya says. "You're smokin' hot in those boots."

Avi's cheeks flush scarlet, and when she ducks her head in embarrassment, her hair falls forward to hide them.

"Alright, I think that's enough of that," I say, walking around the desk to greet her. With my hand on her elbow, I lean in to brush my lips against her cheek. The rush of having them against her skin is euphoric. "You ready?" I husk into her ear.

She shivers and looks up at me with those wide brown eyes I love so much. Our lips are only inches apart. "Yeah, I'm ready."

Reaching behind her for her jacket, my fingers brush her back and she steps just slightly closer.

"Goodnight, Gran. Freya." I shoot them a glance and Gran's smug expression makes me want to roll my eyes.

"Goodnight, Jameson. Avonlea. Have fun." She winks and I turn away, not needing to see the looks she's exchanging with Freya right now or hear the words they'll be speaking as soon as we walk out the door. I slide Avi's jacket into place, letting my hands linger a moment too long on the nape of her neck under her hair where she holds it aside. Then I grab my own and slip it on.

The rain has relented some, but not so much that we aren't hustling to get to the car. I'm glad I thought ahead and brought the Land Rover around to the front of the inn so there's no need to run through the garden to the cottage.

I jog to the passenger side—pleased with myself that I went to the correct one on instinct—and open the door for Avi. She gets in quickly and I close the door before hastily making my way behind the wheel.

As soon as the doors are closed and the sound of the rain on the roof encloses us in the space, an awareness blooms between us. She's looking at me. I'm looking at her. The air in the car feels thin as I attempt to pull it into my lungs.

"You know, Freya was right," I say with a wicked smile, "you are *smokin' hot* in those boots." I deepen my accent to match that of the older woman.

The girlish giggle that leaves Avi is the sweetest sound, and with it I turn the key in the ignition and drive us into town.

Soul Mio is the one little Italian restaurant on this part of the island. I figured it would be a nice change from the pub food we've both become accustomed to. My runs around the village have become much more frequent than my routine in Tahoe ever was, all to burn off the fried fish and chips, heavy meat pies, and stews.

It's delicious, but damn.

"How's Nox doing?" I ask from across the table, ripping a piece of bread from the chunk in the middle and dipping it into a mix of balsamic and olive oil. I ask about him in some capacity every day, but I don't know how much is too much. I never know if I'm overstepping.

"I talked to him before I left and he said school was okay this week. He—well, he told his friends about you." She glances up and the look on her face is... wary?

"Okay..." I say, unsure what the problem is. Honestly, I'm kind of flattered he'd want to tell his friends about me after only knowing me a week. But then I remember what he said about getting suspended. "Oh right, the fight. It was about you... and me."

Avi's mouth pops open. "He told you about that?" she asks.

"He did, that day on the roof." I scrub my hand against the back of my neck. "He told me some kid said he was an orphan because you'd left him… like his dad." I swallow against the bad taste the words leave in my mouth. "I just didn't know at the time that *I* was the dad in question. God, I hate that for him." I say the last sentence under my breath, but Avi catches it and reaches across the table to lace her fingers through mine. I hate it for me too.

"You didn't leave him, Jamie." Her eyes blaze and emotions war on her face. "You aren't to blame for not being there. That's all on me. I should have told him sooner. I should—" She squeezes her eyes shut and drops her chin.

"We don't have to keep doing that," I say, clutching her hand in mine, a reassurance for us both. "The 'shoulds.' They don't help us move forward."

She blows out a breath and shakes her head slightly. "I guess you're right, they don't."

We order and eat our meals with easy conversation. We talk more about her time in Paris, my books, Tahoe, even Rory. She seems a bit sensitive to that particular subject, and though I'm glad she cares enough to be jealous, I realize I'm going to have to clarify just how much Rory is like a sister to me—that she is very happily taken by a strapping Australian. I don't ever want Avi to feel insecure about my friendship with Rory. That's a conversation for later though, as we sink further into the opportunity to catch each other up on the lives we've missed these last ten years.

Our fingers are interlaced once again on the drive back, resting on her thigh—her very bare thigh, which makes focusing on the road very hard for me. It makes other things hard too. I breathe through my nose to stop my body from reacting to her, but instead, her scent fills my nostrils and it only makes it worse. *Fuck.*

"To the inn, or I can drop you at home and you can get your car in the morning?" I ask, wanting the opportunity to drop her off. To maybe kiss her goodnight—without the prying eyes of my grandparents or the inn's visitors.

"Home, I think," she says with a squeeze of her fingers in mine.

Watching her long legs stretch for the ground as I open her door, skirt hitching ever so slightly higher on her thighs, is a sweet torture. When her hand slides into mine, I clench my jaw to keep from taking what should be a wholesome kiss to end our first date to something nearly feral.

We reach the door and the glow of the porch light illuminates her hair, tumbling over her bare shoulders, her back... her breasts. *Dammit.* Oh, and the freckles across her face as well. She's...

"Beautiful," I say, pushing her hair behind one ear with my fingers, letting them brush the arch just enough to make her shiver and step into me. Her body brushes mine and every nerve ending ignites.

Her eyes drift closed, lashes fluttering against the skin that's dappled by her freckles, and her breath quickens. Her hand comes between us and presses into my sternum, and the warmth over my heart makes me lean in, but she pushes ever so slightly.

I pause. "What is it?" I ask, searching her face.

Her eyes open and I wish I could read her mind. She takes my other hand that's still in hers and places it over *her* heart. I can feel the rapid beat against my palm. "I'm scared, Jamie."

The bravery in that statement—to tell me this—knocks the breath out of me.

She softens her voice and as she speaks I understand why. "I've been here before. I've been on this side of things." She's softening the blow. The blow to my heart as she lays bare the hurt I caused her. "The side where I'm not going anywhere, but you are, and I don't know if I can do it again. I—"

"Avi." I push her hand tighter against my chest so she can feel just how hard my own heart is beating. I hate that I hurt her—that she has lived for eleven years believing I didn't want her. "I'm scared too. But walking away from you is the biggest regret of my life. It is not a mistake I plan on repeating. Not now, not ever."

Her eyes search mine for a moment—two—the silence between us filling with my desperate need for her to find truth in my words.

Please believe me, Avi.

Sometime in the last week I came to the conclusion that if she wanted me here, if she made space for me in her life—in her heart—I would fill it and there'd never be another place I'd rather be.

"Truth?" she asks, using our game for reassurance.

"Always," I say, and in the next moment, her lips are on mine.

CHAPTER FORTY-SIX

AVONLEA - NOW

*A*lways.

That word from his lips is my undoing and I launch myself into his arms. Our lips find each other like magnets. His are soft and warm, a perfect contrast to the delicious scratch of his beard against my skin. My hands are trapped between us, along with one of his, where they're pressed over our respective hearts. I swear I feel them trip in unison as the kiss deepens.

His free hand dips further back along my neck and into my hair at the base of my skull, inviting me closer. My breath leaves me in a rush, lips parting so his tongue can slide against mine. The flavor of whisky from dinner still lingers and it is intoxicating. I might be drunk off just the taste of him. Jameson and whisky. His parents certainly got his name right.

I press up on my toes, molding my body to his, and a low moan rips from his throat. Our arms break free at the same time and he wraps his around my waist, drawing me flush against him, highlighting every muscular inch of his body and the hard ridge pressed against my belly. He wants me—really wants me. My hands run through his hair to his nape and I pull him down to me, wanting more.

This kiss is so much more than the one in the garden. This kiss is eleven years in the making. Eleven years of longing and want. Eleven years of desire. Eleven years of heartbreak being healed by just the simplest act of lips on lips, tongues tangled with tongues, hands moving over bodies. Each movement is a prayer, an apology, a question, an answer...

There are words that need to be spoken, things to be discussed, yet with this one kiss, the fear of moments ago subsides. This kiss is a homecoming—our homecoming.

"Jamie," I breathe against his lips, the inch of space between us closing for another silky brush of his against mine. Then he presses our foreheads together and we share the same air for a moment.

"Avi." Reverence and something else—something I won't let myself consider or even voice inside my own head—fill that one word.

He drags his fingers up and down my arms, leaving goose bumps in their wake, while I continue to tangle and untangle mine in his hair.

"That was..." I release my breath and it shakes on the way out.

"Yes, it was." He puffs out a chuckle and then his lips are ghosting my forehead, my cheek, my nose, and finally, with the most delicate brush, they cross my lips again. "I should probably say goodnight here."

Ever the gentleman, but I can hear the restraint in his voice—like leaving right now is the last thing he wants. It's the last thing I want too, and I have something for him that I've been holding on to all week. Waiting for tonight.

"If you think you can behave," I say, raising an eyebrow and smirking, "I have something for you."

"For me?" he questions, curiosity sparking in his gaze.

I turn to unlock the door and take his hand, leading him inside.

It's the first time he's been here since we came to view it, when it was empty and lifeless. Now it's filled with my furniture, my things, Lennox's things. Pictures are hung on the wall—thank goodness for my dad's visit and skill with a hammer—and it feels like a home. Our home, mine and Lennox's.

I've never invited a man into our home before, not once, and though it's Jamie, it still feels vulnerable.

His eyes rove over the space, taking in every inch, every decoration. "It looks amazing, Avi."

"Thank you," I say with a blush, the praise lighting me up inside. "Would you like a dram?"

"Sure," he says, eyes continuing to take in the space around him. "How did Nox like it? The house."

I pull the bottle of Cluaran's finest from the shelf above the fridge along with two short glasses. "He really likes it. He's excited to make his room more his own. We couldn't paint in our flat, but we can here, so he wants to do that this summer." I turn around, a whisky in each hand, to find Jamie on the couch, looking at my tattered copy of *Journals of Elsewhere*. His fingers brush the broken spine and fraying dust cover.

"Part of me still can't believe you've read this..." He trails off, awe in his voice.

I blush scarlet and my eyes flick to the shelf behind him that carries all the copies and special editions I have. My first editions though, the copies I bought the day the books were released and read a million times, are my favorites. Like the one in his hands.

He follows my line of sight and his eyes widen. He hops over the back of the couch with the grace of a gazelle to stand in front of the shelf. Then his eyes cut quickly to me. They're wet.

"Avi..." he says, and I hear nothing but affection.

I shrug, feeling embarrassed. "I told you I was your biggest fan." I set our glasses onto the table and round the couch to stand beside him.

He thumbs through the book in his hands and then goes back to the title page... like he's looking for something.

"None of them are signed," I say, answering the question I can feel coming. "I didn't want it if it wasn't there specifically for me."

I hang my head. *God, that sounded stupid.*

His fingers find my chin and tip it up, forcing me to hold his gaze—to get lost in it like I used to.

"Do you want them signed?"

My eyes fill with tears and I nod. The next thing I know, he's crushing me to him in a fierce embrace, his lips finding mine for a kiss that makes my entire body blaze to life in a way I haven't felt in a *very* long time.

He finally slows the kiss and pulls back to kiss my forehead. "Sorry, I... I had no idea that you having my books would..." His words taper off with a low laugh and he rests his mouth at my temple. "Do you have a Sharpie?"

"I can grab one. And you can just sign these three," I murmur as I reach for the shelf and grab my well-read copies of his other two books—*Expedition to Elsewhere* and *Beyond Elsewhere*—and place them in his arms with the first. Then I blush furiously and walk away in search of the Sharpie.

When I come back, he's sitting on the couch again, the books stacked on the table, while he flips through a photo album I had on the coffee table. It's the one from our summer vacation to Ireland last year.

You'd think it held the answers to world hunger, the cure to cancer, and the ability to broker world peace with the way he's looking through it. His eyes move voraciously over each page—taking in every last detail—while his fingers linger over different images before flipping to the next so he can do it all over again.

"If you like that, I think you'll really like this," I say, nudging a box that's also sitting on the table a little closer. I set the marker beside his books, but his focus is on the box.

"What is it?" he asks with boyish excitement.

"Open it up and see." I try to hide my nerves behind a smile, but he must see them because instead of opening the box he takes my hand in one of his and lifts it to brush against his lips.

When he returns his attention to the box, I release the breath from my lungs. The flaps open and he pulls it closer, his legs splaying open on either side so he can get a better look. On top is Lennox's baby book and underneath are photos, albums, keepsakes from those early years with him.

"You can take it with you, if you'd rather look through it on your own. I just thought—"

He interrupts me with another kiss that steals my breath and shoots a zing of desire down my spine. It's a heated kiss, but the underlying meaning is clear. It's a thank-you.

He leans back and settles into the couch, his hands moving to the baby book on top, and I can see a tremble in them. He places it on his lap. "Will you look at it with me? You can tell me everything."

"Everything?"

He smiles. "Everything."

"I'd love to," I say, and for the next several hours, I do just that. I tell him everything.

CHAPTER FORTY-SEVEN

JAMIE - NOW

Avi and I are dating.

And it's exhilarating.

Since my schedule's flexible compared to hers, we fit our dates in whenever she doesn't have to work... which hasn't been often. She still feels guilty for the amount of time she's taken away from the kitchen since she arrived, even if no one else is holding it against her.

If she can escape for a morning hike, we do that and talk about her pregnancy and those early years with Nox. If she has the afternoon off, we grab the ferry and go to lunch at The Bakehouse like we did when we were teenagers—then we kiss on the top deck like we still are. If she only gets a short break, we sit on the swing under the sunshine and I tell her about college, about my parents and how excited they are—now that they've gotten over the shock—to meet Nox. We eat dinner with Gran and Grandad each night—or I do. And on nights when Avi can join us, they watch us, sitting close on our side of the booth, with stars in their eyes.

The almost two weeks since our first date have been a blur of writing for me, cooking for Avi, and stolen kisses for us both. After eleven years of not kissing her, of telling myself I never would again, of filling my life with women and kisses that didn't compare in the slightest, I want to get lost in the feel of her skin and the taste of her lips.

Tonight is her first full night off since Soul Mio and she's cooking me dinner—not from the T&T kitchen but from her own, and there's something infinitely more intimate about that.

I press a shaky finger to the doorbell outside her cottage then swipe my palms down my thighs.

Get it together, Jamie. It's just dinner.

But it feels like more than that.

She swings the door open and I'm struck by her natural beauty. Damn, she's a vision. Her smile lifts her freckled cheeks, setting off the cutest crinkles at the corners of her eyes. Her hair is pulled up in a casual top knot and several tendrils have broken free to frame her face.

"Going to come in?" she quips, then bites at her bottom lip.

"Aye. Of course. Thanks." I step through the doorway and watch the way her jeans hug her curves when she turns to shut it. She has a basic white tee tucked into them that accents her waist and does nothing to hide her cleavage with the low V-neckline. Her feet are bare, toenails painted a crisp green to match her fingers.

Fingers that brush my arm and catch my attention as they slide up to grip my bicep. "It's just dinner, Jamie."

But it's never *just* anything when it comes to Avi, not now. Every minute, experience, and touch with her feels like a gift.

I toe my shoes off and line them up next to hers by the door, then watch her ass sway as she walks back down the hall. "I've never actually had a woman cook me dinner before..."

"Never?" she asks, and I follow her voice to the kitchen. She laughs, but at the look on my face, she says, "You're serious?"

"Aye. I really never dated—like this." I wave my arms around us like it can encompass the way she and I are dating in comparison to the way I dated women back in Tahoe.

"Like this?" she asks, eyebrow cocked in question.

I splay my hands on the counter and hang my head. "I never really did the relationship thing, or saw anyone for more than a couple dates. I never wanted anything serious." I lift my head and her eyes are locked on me.

"And that's different because... we're serious?" There's genuine curiosity in her question.

"I am." I've never been more serious about anything in my life.

She nods and looks away to hide her smile. "I guess that explains why I never saw you with anyone."

Why she...? "Yeah, you're going to have to explain," I say, my brow furrowing.

She goes beet red and hinges at the waist to check something in the oven. "I've followed you on socials for a long time. I never saw a consistent woman in your life—other than Rory."

She did? "I would've noticed if you followed me—"

"It's not an account with my name." She looks at me now, her blush spreading down the V of her shirt. "I'm sorry... I know I shouldn't have done that. It's actually how I found out about your publishing deal. I saw it that day at the airport."

Remorse crashes over her features, a look of sadness and raw emotion so strong it pulls me toward her like an undercurrent. I wrap my arms around her and press my forehead against hers. "Avi, don't go back there. Not while I'm right here. It's in the past. Yeah?"

She nods and her forehead slides against mine.

"I'm sor—" she begins, and I silence her with a kiss. One that lights my blood on fire and makes me come alive for her... Only her.

I back her into the counter, caging her in with my arms... but the buzzer on the oven interrupts us before I can lift her onto it. Damn. She pulls away, her gaze heavy with want.

She opens the oven, speaking over her shoulder. "So there was never a girl who caught your eye? Rory never..."

I hate that this is still a concern for her.

"Never. I love her, but it's never been like that for us. And in case you need a little more confirmation of that, the day I flew here, she was flying back from Australia where she followed the love of her life. Now he's moving to Tahoe with his daughter next month to be with her. And I couldn't be happier for them both."

"Oh. Okay."

She seems stunned that I gave her that much information, but I don't ever want her to feel inferior.

I walk over and tug the oven mitt off her hand so I can place it over my heart. "There is no competition. No one has ever come close to making me feel this way."

She blinks, quiet tears forming while pink blooms in her cheeks. "Well, that conversation took a turn I wasn't expecting." She chuckles and swipes at her eyes. "Come on, let's eat."

I finally allow myself a moment to appreciate the smells wafting around the kitchen. "Did you make—"

"Steak and ale pie? I did. Mum's secret recipe. I've never made it outside her pub kitchen before."

"Well, I'm honored that you chose to make it for me. I promise not to ask for the recipe..." I joke, and she laughs, slipping her hands back into the oven mitts and carrying the pie to the table where there's already a basket of crusty bread and an open bottle of red wine.

She sets it down and I move to her side, slipping my arm around her waist and leaning in to kiss her gently. "Thank you for cooking for me."

"Thank you for giving me someone to cook for." She brushes her lips once more against mine before we both sit.

"So," I start, not sure I really want to know but figuring I probably should, "what about you? Was there ever anyone..." I take a swig of my wine. "Serious?"

I still haven't fully wrapped my head around the fact there was never this other guy like I always imagined. And seeing as I never let myself so much as look her up online, I had no idea there wasn't.

She shakes her head and starts to nervously fill our bowls without answering.

"Avi?"

She lifts her head and her eyebrows are pulled down, bottom lip between her teeth again. "I—" She clears her throat and passes me a bowl. "Dating wasn't something I concerned myself with for a long time after Lennox was born. I had him, I had school, then I had him and school in Paris, which was insanely busy..."

"No Frenchman ever caught your eye?" I say with a chuckle, but she shakes her head, not laughing.

"I went on a few dates once we moved back, mostly to get my parents off my back. But there was never..." She swallows thickly, eyes avoiding mine. "There was never anyone else."

Does she—no, there's no way she means what I think she does. She can't mean there's never been *anyone* else, as in she's never *been* with anyone else... in all this time.

I'm speechless, my spoonful of pie halfway to my mouth. The tension grows thicker as that admission sits between us. Fragile and precious.

"Say something... Please," she whispers.

I do the only thing that seems right and that's to slip off my chair and kneel at her feet; this woman who has, by some miracle, only ever been mine.

"I don't deserve you. I don't deserve to be your only, but I'm sure as hell going to try to be worthy of it." Her eyes fill with tears and I watch one fall, knowing dinner is going to have to wait.

I wrap my arms around her torso and stand, bringing her with me until she circles her long, strong legs around my waist. I groan at the way it settles her right where I want her, right where I've dreamt of being for so long.

I remember where the bedroom is from our tour, which is good because with the first step in that direction, Avi seals her mouth over mine in a kiss that would make even the strongest man weak in the knees.

"M'eudail, if you kiss me like that, I won't make it to the bedroom," I husk between shaky breaths.

She nips at my bottom lip and I growl at the intense shock of pleasure that shoots down my spine.

Thank god this cottage isn't very big. The hallway that splits off toward the two bedrooms is short and I'm through the doorway and laying her onto the bed, hovering over her, before she can unman me any further. The room is dark, only the light of the moon shining in through the window, and that won't do. I need to see her for this. So I can appreciate her. Worship her. *Love* her.

She whimpers when I pull back and stand, walking over to flip on the bedside lamp and then the other, basking the room in a soft glow.

"W-we don't need the lights. We can just—"

I stop her with a finger on her lips, leaning over her where she's propped on her elbows. "I want to see you."

She tucks her chin, eyes fluttering closed, and turns her face away from me.

"Avi?" I question, guiding my finger under her chin to bring her face back to me, but her eyes are still pointed away.

"I-I had a baby, Jamie," she says in a shy whisper that trips on my name.

My lip tips up in a smirk. "Yes, I'm aware. It may be a new fact for me, but I haven't forgotten."

She pushes lightly at my chest, forcing me away. In that space she slides herself up the bed, bringing her knees with her and wrapping her arms around them.

"Don't be cute," she says, and it only makes me smile wider as I crawl up the bed to kneel before her. "Look, the last time you saw me I was... I was seventeen and ran for fun and hadn't had a baby. I don't—" She blows her breath out and a silver tear drips down her cheek, instantly wiping the grin off my face. "I don't have the same body I did then, but you... you look like a freaking supermodel under that button-down and I just don't—I don't want you to be disappointed."

Disappointed?

She said she hasn't been with anyone else, so I know it wasn't some asshole who put that thought in her head, but nonetheless it's there and I sure as hell won't stand for it.

I banish the tear with a tender swipe of my thumb, and the way she leans into it tells me she's here, even if she's self-conscious.

"Avi, tha thu bòidheach," I say, dusting off my Gaelic and hoping I got it right. Her lip tips up just slightly, so I must have, but I repeat it in English just to drive the point home. "You are beautiful. I've never seen a more beautiful woman in my life. God, I can't take my eyes off of you when you're around. And I can't keep from picturing you when you aren't. There isn't a curve, or scar, or mark on your body that could change that."

I run my free hand up her ankle, over her calf until I reach her thigh, letting my long fingers span the space from her outer thigh to her inner thigh. Her breath catches when I slip my hand a few inches higher and she straightens her legs so I'm now straddling them on the bed, my thumb impossibly close to the apex of her thighs. My other hand skims down to her waist, rucking up the fabric of her shirt just an inch so she can feel the heat of my palm against her skin.

"Can I show you?" I slip my hand an inch higher and she tenses just the slightest amount beneath my fingers. "Can I show you how beautiful you are? Will you let me see you?" I lean forward and press a kiss to the corner of her mouth, watching her eyelids flutter closed in surrender.

"Y-yes," she stammers. It's so quiet I barely hear it, and her eyes are shut tight.

"Look at me, mo leannan. I want you to see how badly I want you, exactly like this."

Her eyes meet mine, the lights making the gold flecks in them shine, and she nods. I offer her one in return, and then with the reverence she deserves, I slowly bring both hands to the hem of her shirt and begin to slide it up her torso.

It's agonizingly slow, but I won't rush this. Not with her. Not ever.

As the shirt coasts up past her rib cage, I can see the silvery lines that show the miracle of what she did. Carrying our son—fuck, that thought hits me like a freight train. I gently kiss each one, letting my lips linger over them. The badges of honor she carries for what she did. I sit back up and pull the shirt over her head, take in the quick rise and fall of her chest, the soft white of her bra against her skin, the softness of every inch of her that I can see.

It's not enough. I need more.

She's never been with a man who could make her feel every bit as gorgeous as she is. The seventeen-year-old version of me did my best with all my own nerves and insecurities, but I didn't know what a woman needed then. Now though... The man I am now plans to worship this woman's body so she never feels the need to hide it from me again.

CHAPTER FORTY-EIGHT

AVONLEA - NOW

Oh god. Ohgodohgodohgod.

Jamie's lips are feather-light as they travel from hip bone to hip bone, showing extra care to every stretch mark, not fazed in the slightest by the differences in my body.

He sits back on his heels, taking my shirt with him, and I let the rest of my insecurity go at the look in his eyes. He can't fake that look. The desire, the uninhibited longing. Like he's been waiting for this moment for as long as I have.

He coasts his fingertips from my hands, up the inside of my arms, to my collarbone, where they slip just barely underneath the straps of my bra. My breath catches, the feel of his fingers leaving a branding fire in their wake, just like his kisses did along my belly. I release a rough exhale, and his fingers follow the movement over the cups of my bra as my chest lowers. There is a zing of anticipation as they pass over where my nipples are peaked under the fabric.

"Jamie," I breathe, eyes squeezing shut. The sensations, the fact that it's him with me right now… It's overwhelming.

"Is this okay? We can slow down. We don't have to—"

"No," I pant, opening my eyes and mustering every ounce of confidence within me. "I don't want slow, not with you."

That fire in his eyes burns brighter and the smile that goes with it reduces me to my basest instincts. It's the smile I've always loved, the smile I've missed more than air these past eleven years. It's my smile. I press up into a sitting position and pull my legs in so I'm on my knees before him. We're eye to eye now, only inches separating us, and I'm ready to close that gap, but I want to see *him* first.

The green paint of my fingernails stands out against the white of his button-down, making their trembling that much more obvious. I curl them under the hem and, with painful slowness, move to undo the bottom button, and then another, exposing the skin I've dreamt of for years. Seeing him in the garden with his shirt off was nothing compared to having him this close. He's intoxicating. The masculine scent of him overtakes my senses as I move higher. My fingers trail ever so gently against the smooth skin on his sides and he shivers.

I reach his chest and feel his heart beating frantically beneath my hands. He shifts his shoulders back so I can slide the shirt off and finish what I started. I throw it to the floor where it lands with a soft thud and my hands are on him, hungry to memorize every inch of exposed skin. But what I want more is his skin on mine, so I surge forward, moving my hands into his hair as our bodies collide. My softness against his hard lines and muscle, a perfect dichotomy. A perfect fit.

The give and take of our lips, tongues, teeth, all show how desperate we are. The rest of the world always disappeared when we got our mouths on each other, and that hasn't changed. But this kiss... this one is world-ending, devastating, the kiss to beat out all other kisses. Because this kiss isn't two teenagers fumbling with feelings and nerves, nor is it laced with the unknown like those of the last two weeks. It's knowing and being known. It is a revelation, a promise. This kiss is everything.

We don't slow—our mouths fused, hands roaming, breathing ragged—but we do shift, moving until we're lying on the bed with Jamie firmly propped between my thighs. I can feel him hard against me, and when he shifts his body forward an inch, I gasp, fireflies dancing behind my eyelids.

He trails his lips to my ear with another roll of his hips. Another gasp escapes. "We can do this all night, Avi. I can get you there and I can come in my pants like a teenager and we can think about doing more another time, or..."

"Or. I definitely want whatever comes after that *or*. Please." I'm a whimpering mess, but I don't even care because this is Jamie, and he's pressed against me in a way that has my entire body built up like a volcano. I'm sure I *could* actually come like this, but that's not how I want it. Not tonight.

He chuckles against my ear, and with one more shift of his hips that makes me groan, he pulls back enough to rake his eyes over me again. I follow suit. Fair's fair. There are scars I've never seen before, stories we will have time for later, but I'm not worried about those as he reaches for the button on his jeans and slides down the zipper.

When he climbs off the bed to shuck them off, leaving them in a heap by his shirt, I take the opportunity to say farewell to mine as well. I shimmy them down my legs until Jamie's hands meet mine to give them their final tug, discarding them with the rest.

He lies down beside me, on his side, fingers tracing my hip and down my thigh. "Did I tell you that you're beautiful yet?"

He knows he has, but I nod anyway, feeling my already flushed skin warm more under his perusal. I'm not in sexy lingerie but he devours me with his gaze as if I were. "Did I tell *you* that you're beautiful?" I parrot his words back to him. They're true; he's stunning. He shakes his head with a smile and a chuckle. "Well, you are."

I roll onto my side and our bodies press together again, hotter, more insistent as my mouth finds his and our hands begin to move more freely.

He moans and I gasp. He nips and I suck. He pinches and I squeeze. Each movement is a puzzle piece fitting together to form the whole picture. The picture of who we are now and who we're meant to be.

We take our time. The dinner on the table forgotten, other needs taking priority over things like hunger for food. No, the only hunger that matters is the one we have for each other, and we're voracious.

The only moment of hesitation comes just before Jamie brings us fully together, when he leans down to press the sweetest kiss to my lips and whispers, "Tha gaol agam ort."

I love you.

And then he shows me it's true.

We sit with bowls of reheated steak and ale pie in our laps on the couch. I'm dressed in only Jamie's button-down shirt, and the messy bun I was sporting earlier is long gone, my hair cascading around my shoulders in chaotic waves.

"What will I have to do to earn the secret recipe for this? It's incredible." Jamie moans around another mouthful before tearing off a chunk of bread to dip into the thick gravy at the bottom of his bowl.

"Hmmm." I hum and tip my head side to side. "I don't know. It's a closely guarded secret. I can't go around giving it to just anybody."

"But I'm not just anybody," he jokes, waggling his eyebrows, "now am I?"

I laugh and set my bowl aside. He anticipates my next move and sets his down too so he can grab my waist when I settle over him, straddling his hips on the couch. I've never eaten dinner in such a state of undress, but I don't mind it with him, because considering he's in only a pair of dark boxer briefs, there's little between us. And even though it's been less than an hour, I want him again.

"I guess not." I press a kiss to his bare chest, just above his heart. I lean back, moving my hand to replace my lips over the thumping rhythm in his chest. "Truth?" I ask, holding his gaze.

"Always," he whispers with a kiss against my jaw.

"Did you mean it? What you said?"

The whispered Gaelic wasn't a one-time thing while he made love to me, worshiped me, made me feel things I never imagined, but it's still hard to believe it's true.

"Yes." He punctuates the word with another kiss, light and soft against my lips. "I know it's soon, but it doesn't feel that way at all... I've never not loved you. I made myself forget that I did for a while, but it was always here. It *will* always be here. *I* will always be here."

I study him, not sure if I should let myself believe those words either. "What are you saying, Jamie?"

"I told you after our first date that I wouldn't walk away from you again... And I won't. I can't. I want you, I want us... I want a relationship with Nox. I can't have those things from Tahoe."

"But your whole life is there... I—"

"But my whole heart is here. What good is a life without it?" he asks, tipping forward to kiss me again, and I melt against him. Letting everything he's said fuse together the parts of my heart I never thought would heal.

And this time it's me moving above him when the words slip from between my lips. "Tha gaol agam ort."

I love you.

CHAPTER FORTY-NINE

JAMIE - NOW

L ennox is arriving today. I'm nervous, and excited, and unsure of how we'll all fit together now that I've decided on a move to Scotland.

I thought voicing that decision, making it official, would be scary—that I'd have all sorts of second thoughts, but that hasn't been the case. I'm at peace over the idea.

This is my home, it always has been. Tahoe is home too, but not in the same way. Avi is home. Nox will be my home. I hope. If he'll let me, I'll be part of his home too.

A vibration in my pocket stops me just short of the kitchen door. When I pull my phone out, I find an unexpected name on the screen.

Breck

> Rory filled me in on everything happening there. If you ever want to talk about dad stuff, I'm here mate.

> Or moving across the world for the woman of your dreams stuff… I have a pretty good grasp on that too.

I push through the door with my shoulder, grinning down at the message.

"What's got you smiling?" Avi asks, and when I look up, I see she's got her hands splayed in a ball of dough on the counter.

"A text from Breck... Rory's fiancé." That thought makes me smile even wider. She called me last week to tell me they'd gotten engaged under the Fourth of July fireworks and I couldn't be more thrilled for them. What started as a casual, friends-with-benefits situation quickly became something else, and as much as I told Rory to protect her heart, she didn't. But it all worked out in the end.

"Everything okay there?" Avi asks, and I appreciate her asking, caring about my friends back in Tahoe.

"Oh, yeah. They're fine—great, actually. He was just offering to talk. I told you about his daughter, Willow? She's probably the only reason I wasn't completely lost hanging out with Nox when he was here. I'd never spent much time around a kid before her. Anyway, Breck's a great dad, and I guess he figured I could use some pointers." I laugh but it's somewhat humorless. I honestly could probably use some pointers. I have no idea what I'm doing when it comes to Nox.

"Jamie." Avi lets my name sit between us until I lift my head to look at her.

"Yeah?"

"You know none of us really know what we're doing, right? Parents? We just do the best we can. And Lennox, he wants to get to know you. You guys will figure it out. But... extra pointers from someone who's been there never hurt either." She smiles and nods toward the phone in my hand.

"Right, yeah." I nod and open the thread with Breck.

Me

> Thank you for the offer. Might be a good idea.

> I have no idea what I'm doing.

That feels a little more vulnerable than I want to be with my best friend's partner, but it's already sent... and delivered, so here we are.

Breck

> None of us do.

Me

> That's what Avi said. Actually, Rory said that too when I first told her.

Breck

> We've got ourselves some smart women.

I laugh and catch Avi's eye. She smiles back, and I feel warm knowing she's mine.

Breck

If you love him enough, them enough, the rest will all fall into place. Worked for me and Rory.

Me

Is she doing okay? She was really calm when I told her I wasn't coming back…

Breck

She's sad. She's going to miss you. But she wants you to be happy and she knows you need to be there for that to happen. She also wants us to plan a visit to see you soon.

Me

I'm glad you're there for her.

Breck

I always will be. We'll both always be here for you too.

Me

Thanks, Breck. Hug your girls for me.

Breck

I will. Call me anytime.

Me

Will do.

"Well..." Avi questions.

"He said the same as you, nobody knows what they're doing... Not sure if that makes me feel better or more terrified." I chuckle. "He did say they want to come visit soon."

"I know someplace they can stay." She shrugs her shoulders to indicate the space around her, unable to do much with her hands that are still kneading the dough.

"Yeah. I think we may have a lot of visitors here. My parents mentioned wanting to come out soon too. They want to see Grandad, but they also want to meet Nox... Do you think he's up for that?"

"Am I up for what?"

Both Avi and I snap our heads around to the door.

"Lennox!" Avi shouts and sprints the twenty feet between them, wrapping her arms around him while trying to keep the sticky mess on her hands from transferring.

"Mum..." He drags out the word like he's annoyed, but his face doesn't hide his excitement, nor does the way he grips her around the middle.

Grandad, Gran, and Avi's parents all arrive in the doorway a moment later.

"Sorry," Avi's mum says, "we couldn't hold him back another minute."

Avi pulls back from him, holding her hands up in front of her like some sort of odd mannequin. "Just a sec," she says, and walks briskly to the sink to rinse them off.

In her absence, the rest of us stand in quiet awkwardness. I don't quite know how to act with Nox. Avi's parents are looking at me in a way I can't interpret. And my grandparents are watching it all unfold like spectators at a movie—all they need is the popcorn.

"Hey, Nox," I say with a hopeful smile.

To my surprise, he walks over and gives me a hug. I must look as shocked as I feel because the adults all hide smiles behind their hands and choke back laughs. I bring my arms around him and return the hug.

"Hey, Jamie," he says, stepping back, and we both swipe a hand through our hair. It would appear I passed on my nervous tic to the boy.

"Okay," Avi says, rejoining the group. "Who's hungry?" She pulls Nox into her side and ruffles his hair.

"I'm starving," he says.

"As if you didn't eat every snack in the car on the way here," Fiona says. "And a whole pizza when we stopped for lunch."

"Thank goodness your mum's a chef, aye?" Grandad jokes, and Nox beams at him.

"I'll take over from here, boss," Hamish says to Avi, ushering her out of the kitchen. "Now y'all get out of here."

Grandad must've assumed we'd all be eating dinner together, because when we get to the dining room, the long table from that first time I met Nox is waiting for us. But this time I have him and Avi beside me and my heart inflates in my chest, putting pressure on my sternum.

The table quiets when Grandad pushes laboriously to his feet, glass in his hand. He may be sick, but at this moment, he's the man I've always looked up to. The patriarch of our family.

"I think a night like this deserves a toast. Our two families have been long connected by proximity as well as friendship, but those are the least of the things tying us together now. As far as I'm concerned, every person at this table is family, and I'm grateful to have gotten to see us come together in this way. This is my home. It has always been my home. And it's yours now too, all of you. Slainte!"

He lifts his glass and we all follow suit with our own shouts of "slainte." Under the table, Avi slides her foot across to caress my leg, and I catch her eye. They're glistening as she nods. Then I look at Nox, his gaze bouncing between me and his mum, and the smile on his face matches my own.

CHAPTER FIFTY

Avonlea - Now

When Angus asked me to accelerate our move up to Skye, everything was such a whirlwind that the actual prospect of leaving my parents, the Green Gables, and our life in Glasgow behind was almost an afterthought. Especially with Lennox still there, tying us to that place.

But Mum and Dad headed back this morning, leaving Lennox and me here. That chapter of our lives is closing and, though I'm excited for this next one, I'm a little sad to let it go. I miss them already.

"You in your head?" Jamie asks from his spot on the bench swing. He's relaxed, with a book in one hand and his other on my feet that are propped in his lap.

I lift my head from the cushion. I'm fully laid out, enjoying the quiet of the garden and the sun and breeze on my face while I take a short break from the kitchen. "I'm just thinking about my parents."

"They're not too far away. We can go visit and you know they'll come up here too."

"I know. It's just that their unwavering support has been my constant. They've been my rock, my solid place to stand, for so long. Even when I was away in Paris, they were the foundation. Does that make sense? This feels different, like I'm really standing on my own for the first time, and the ground beneath me feels foreign."

"I thought I was the writer here." He chuckles and squeezes my foot. "But seriously, it's understandable to feel that way. Although, these legs look pretty damn strong to me," he offers with a wink, then slides his hand from my foot, up my calf, until it rests against my thigh, his fingertips trailing lightly toward the inseam of my shorts.

"Jamie," I hiss, looking around. But Lennox is with Aileen on a walk to the loch, Angus is resting in the cottage, and the kitchen staff are all busy—or they should be—since I'm on my break.

"What? They are strong." He kneads the flesh of my thigh and his hand slides just slightly higher. "And, not that you need someone to support you—because you don't. You've proven just how capable you are of supporting yourself and Lennox. But I'm here now too. And my grandparents. Now that we've covered that, back to these legs..."

He reaches with both hands so they skim up my legs until he has both hands on my waist, almost bent over me, and with a lift of his eyebrow, he yanks me toward him. I squeal and then begin to giggle as he uses his fingers at my waist to tickle and tease. I sit up—which is clearly what he wanted, because he can now leverage me onto his lap so I'm straddling him on the seat.

"Jamie..." I say again, but it's a soft exhale of a word.

He plants a soft kiss to the hollow of my throat before he works his way up my neck to my ear. "I love these legs," he whispers, and his fingertips press into my flesh, my denim shorts riding up indecently high. "And these hips. God, these hips drive me crazy." He grips them now, pulling me down against him until I drop my forehead to his shoulder at the feelings that course through my body. Next, he skims his thumbs up, just under my shirt so they slip across my stomach above the waistband of my shorts.

Every time he touches me, there's a reverence to it, like he can't believe he gets to. Like he can't believe I'm his to touch. Like there isn't an inch of my skin he doesn't love.

"Have I told you today how beautiful you are?" he asks, dipping close to my ear again before lightly nipping at the earlobe.

I gasp against his shirt, glad I'm hiding my face because lord knows it must be as red as his hair. "Jameson..." I warn, because it's unfair for him to get me all worked up when I have to go back to work in a few minutes.

He doesn't seem to care. He threads a hand into my hair, making me lift my head, and then he pulls my lips against his. They're warm and soft and taste like black tea and sunshine.

It's our first unbridled kiss since Lennox arrived. We aren't keeping any secrets from him—I learned my lesson—so he knows Jamie and I aren't just friends anymore. He also knows Jamie's staying in Scotland. But he's only ten and doesn't need to see us making out, so we've kept things pretty tame the last two days.

But Lennox isn't here right now and goodness I've missed these lips—these hands.

"How much longer is your break?" Jamie says against my lips, unwilling to allow even the smallest amount of space between us.

"Ten minutes max," I say, and then squeak in surprise when he stands from the bench, hands under my ass. I wrap my legs around his waist with a tight squeeze and he grunts at the friction between our bodies. I giggle, loving that I can affect him this way.

"I can work with that," he husks, then he carries me around to the inn's back door, one that avoids any prying eyes and leads directly to his room.

CHAPTER FIFTY-ONE

Jamie – One Month Later

When Grandad told me all those years ago that if I wrote with my heart I'd never go astray, he had no idea how on the nose he would be. For many years my heart led me down a path of epic adventure and I loved every minute of it. In coming to Scotland though, I had no clue the turn my writing would take would be toward an epic love story... His love story, no less.

It's been two and a half months since I first found the letters, and I now have a solid first draft of *With Love, From Skye*. With the way my agent's been hounding me for updates, despite my still being on the sabbatical we agreed on, I've decided to go ahead and send him the first ten chapters. I warned him it's nothing like what I've written before and that if he's not willing to represent it to publishers, I'll publish it myself.

I've never believed in a story more than I do this one and I'm determined to see it on shelves around the world—a testament to the love of two people, the struggles they overcome, and the way a simple life can be the most epic adventure of all.

With the whoosh of that email sending, I stand up and stretch. I woke up early this morning to get that sent off so I could focus on the much more important parts of today.

I'm dressed in a pair of grey exercise pants, a green athletic tee, and my hiking boots. Grabbing my rain jacket, I head for the front of the inn and find Avi and Nox talking with my grandparents. Gran is standing behind the desk while Grandad sits in the chair that we brought in so he can sit with her anytime she's up here—or when I'm up here.

His stamina has declined over the past month, but the brightness that comes with his laugh never fades.

"You two ready?" I ask, looking them over from their own hiking boots up to the rain jackets they carry. Avi's fitted leggings make me want to haul her back to my room, but there's no time for that... At least not at the moment.

"Aye, let's go," Nox says, excitement for our adventure scrawled all over his face.

Avi ruffles his hair and says, "I'm ready too."

He rolls his eyes before meticulously pushing his fingers through it so it sits just the way he had it.

"Alright then."

I press a kiss to the top of Gran's head and squeeze Grandad's shoulder. He gives me a wink, and the sparkle in his eyes that says he's got a secret is there in full force. But this time, I'm in on it.

We pile into the Land Rover and I reach across the front seat to lace my fingers through Avi's. Today is going to be a good fucking day.

Honestly, every day feels like a good one lately.

At first, I wasn't sure how I'd fit into the dynamic between Avi and Nox, and I wasn't looking to force my way in and change everything. But I couldn't deny that I wanted to be a part of it.

As soon as I wrapped my head around the concept of Nox as my son, I wanted to know everything about him. Avi filled me in on so much of those younger years in the weeks before he arrived, but I haven't wasted a day of the last month connecting with him.

It worked out that since Avi had to work and I could wake up early or stay up late to write—the two times I'm most productive anyway—I've spent most of my days hanging out with my son. Sometimes it was just sitting on the roof at the inn—something Avi allows so long as I'm up there with him. Others we'd ride bikes into town or down to the loch or go on a hike. When Grandad needed to get away from the inn for a bit, we'd take a drive and he'd tell all sorts of stories about me at Nox's age.

With each passing day, we feel a little more connected—a little more like family. I hope that today will only solidify that further. Because there's nothing I want more than this. Avi. Nox. Skye. I had no idea coming here would lead to this, but I'm incredibly grateful that it did.

For the first half of the drive, Avi pulls out *Journals of Elsewhere* and reads it aloud. It's bizarre to hear my words in her voice, to watch Nox's reactions as the story unfolds, but I love it too. Sharing this piece of myself with them. We're already nearly done with this one and Nox says he wants to jump straight into *Expedition to Elsewhere* once we are.

As the road gets windy the farther north we drive, Avi has to put the book away. We fill the remaining time talking about the upcoming school year for Nox, which starts in two weeks; his teacher assignments; and the small group of local boys he's met over the past few weeks.

The constant chatter has kept me from having the chance to feel nervous. But pulling into the car park at the base of Old Man of Storr, the first hint of anxious excitement hits my stomach.

It's been eleven years since I was here—very nearly to the day, which is crazy to think about. As is the way with most natural landmarks, it hasn't changed, but it feels completely different somehow.

Nox jumps out of the car and finds the sign that talks about the hike and the mountain, while Avi and I sit for a moment in silence looking up at the large spire before we look at each other. There's something wistful in her eyes, a remembrance of that day so long ago when we gave ourselves to each other and had no idea that it would change both of our lives the way it did.

"I love you," I whisper, picking up her hand that's clutched in mine and pressing a kiss to her palm.

"I love you too."

An hour and a half later, we stand at the top of Photographer's Knoll, taking in the vast views of the sea and mountains, all greens and greys and blues. It's a stunning sight to behold, and one that reminds me just how majestic this country is; my homeland, my home.

Nox is an excellent hiker for his age. Something he picked up from all his time hiking with Callum. He sprinted a couple sections and was scrambling over rocks as well or better than any mountain goat I've ever seen. He has so much energy and I wish sometimes I could siphon a little bit of it off for myself.

He's standing with Avi when I walk up and wrap my arms around her waist. "At least it's not raining today," I say into her ear, and she settles more fully into me, letting me take her weight as she leans her head against my shoulder.

"Well, now that you've put it out there, it probably will," she says with a sarcastic bite, and I chuckle against her.

"Probably." I kiss her hair and she sighs, crossing her arms over mine where they rest around her.

I glance down at Nox and he raises an eyebrow in question, then nods toward his mum. I chuckle again. Ten-year-olds are so impatient. But we are here for a reason, so with one more kiss to Avi's hair, I unwind myself from her and take a step back, and then another. Enough space for her to miss my presence and turn around.

But instead of us coming eye to eye, she finds me on one knee. The damp earth is already seeping into my pants, but I couldn't care less because I'd do anything to keep the look of delighted shock on her face.

Nox looks almost as excited as she does, bouncing from foot to foot with a wide grin on his face.

"Avonlea Lorna Stewart." I reach up and grab her hand and she grips me so tightly I'm afraid she'll cut off the circulation. "I've loved you for most of my life, and now that I have you, I never want to let you go. Will you marry me?"

Her eyes fill with tears and she squeezes them shut on a laugh. A joyful laugh, like the ones she used to gift me when we were young, one that is accompanied by a smile that takes my breath away.

When she opens her eyes, they're filled with so much love, and with a soft nod, she says, "Yes." Then she falls to her knees in front of me and throws her arms around my neck to kiss me senseless.

"Oh, come on," Lennox mutters under his breath.

Avi and I separate, both of us laughing as we look up at *our* son. He offers an unapologetic shrug, but he's smiling too.

"Were you in on this?" she asks, standing and pulling him into a hug.

He just shrugs again, like he hasn't been keeping this under wraps for two weeks. I asked him for permission to marry his mum the same day I called her dad to ask for his. Lennox tried to play it cool with a casual "Aye, I guess that'd be cool." Whereas Callum and Fiona both cried.

"You're forgetting the best part..." I say, holding out a ring box and swiveling it side to side.

"I thought *you* were the best part," she quips, reaching for the box, but I pull it out of her reach.

"So, you don't want this then...?" I joke, and she jumps for it, colliding with my body. I wrap my free arm around her and pull her close.

"I want you," she whispers, "but I also want to see what's in that box."

I kiss her forehead and lower it just enough so she can snatch it from my fingers.

The click of the lid is accompanied by a short gasp before her eyes fly to mine. This was one of the other things Nox helped me with: picking out the ring. And I'm going to guess I got it right.

The center stone is a large oval. The soft bluish-green tint makes it stand out against the gold filigree that surrounds it, accented with small diamonds and pearls.

"Jamie, this is—"

"Perfect, right, Mum?" Nox says, and her soft look of love shifts to him.

"Perfect," she says with watery eyes and a quivering lip.

Pulling the ring from the box, I slip it onto her finger. Then I lift her hand like I did in the car, but this time I place my kiss right over her ring—the one that says she's mine.

"So, when's the wedding?" Nox asks.

"That's a great question, bud," Avi says, looking at me. I swallow hard. "Soon, I think."

There's an understanding in her eyes, a hint of sadness.

"Soon," I echo, and wonder if we've learned to communicate the way my grandparents do, without words. There's no reason to wait, but there is a very big reason to do it sooner than later.

For Angus, because there's no way either of us wants to do this without him, and time is not on our side.

On the car ride home, I pull up Rory's contact and punch the call button. It rings a few times before she answers, a little breathless.

"Jamie!" Her enthusiasm fills the car.

"Hey, Roars," I say, and she chuckles.

"Gah, you're worse than my brother these days. Can't you just call me Rory like a normal person?"

"Nope, I like to bug you too much."

"Whatever," she says.

"I'm calling because I have a wedding for you to add to your calendar."

Rory and Breck run an elopements business where she's the photographer and he acts as the officiant. I used to fill the officiant role back when I was in Tahoe, before Breck came into the picture, but they're the perfect team.

"Okay, I'll have to check the schedule. Whose wedding is it?" she asks, completely oblivious, which only makes this more fun.

I squeeze Avi's hand and she beams. "Mine."

CHAPTER FIFTY-TWO

Avonlea - One Month Later

Jamie asked me what I wanted for the wedding and I only had two requirements: our families all together at the inn, and him in a kilt.

He promised to deliver on both counts.

The past month has been a dichotomy of time moving much too slowly and way too fast. The required month-long waiting period to get a marriage license in Scotland gave Rory's fiancé Breck just enough time to get registered to officiate the ceremony. But it's been stressful watching Angus's health slowly decline and praying daily that we'd get to share this day with him. That he'd get to see what his subtle matchmaking did. That he'd get to see another happy ending unfold because he loved us all so much.

I peek out the window of the cottage—where I've been getting ready—and smile as I watch him make his way slowly to his seat in the front row. He looks positively dapper in his kilt. The blue and greens of the Murray tartan match perfectly with Aileen's dark green dress. She's got a firm grip on his arm. For such a tiny woman, she may be the strongest one I've ever met—both inside and out. Before they reach the front row, Jamie's dad, Craig—in a matching kilt—comes to Angus's other side to help him to his seat.

Angus refused to sit in the wheelchair today, wanting nothing more than to walk down the aisle to watch his grandson get married.

Not a single one of us argued with him.

Maeve, Jamie's mum, pulls Aileen into a hug once they've gotten Angus settled and then reaches to squeeze his hand. The four of them take up the single row of seats on one side. Craig and Maeve have been here for two weeks, and it's solidified the knowledge that our time together is fleeting and precious.

Mum stands at the archway we erected in the garden, fiddling with the flowers and tartan that adorn it. There are only two seats on my side, one for her and one for Dad. I have one moment of wistful wishing that my grandparents would have supported me, that they could have lived long enough to see our families become one, but then I push that thought aside. This isn't a day for thoughts that are anything but uplifting.

From the kitchen door, Breck emerges. I know Jamie and Lennox will come next and the thought has anticipation rising in my blood. It's almost time.

We told Breck he didn't have to wear a kilt, but Rory insisted there was no way she was going to miss out on the opportunity to see him in one. He strides confidently toward the arch, the fabric swishing around his knees. He opted for Murray tartan as well and the dark blue sweater he's wearing fits him like a glove. Rory whistles as she pops up beside me at the window, my little spying spot, making me laugh.

"Who knew an Aussie could wear the hell out of a kilt?" She giggles and bumps my shoulder with her own.

She's not wrong. His blond waves frame his face and every detail down to the dark brown boots and matching sporran hanging around his hips make it look natural as anything.

"It's a good look for him. You bought the kilt, right? At least you can make him wear it whenever you want now." I shoot her a wink and her giggle turns into a cackle of laughter.

I was nervous to meet Rory—to meet this woman who had so much of Jamie's time over the years. A woman who was given the title of his best friend. I was afraid I wouldn't measure up, or that there might be more under the surface than Jamie let on. But when she exited the airport in Glasgow—Jamie, Lennox, and I had driven down to get them—she hugged *me* first, even before Jamie. And the sincerity of her hello, of her excitement for us, of her embrace for Lennox and then finally Jamie, erased all my fears. She's his family in the most platonic form of the word. So, I guess she's my family now too.

We turn our attention back to the garden and watch Lennox emerge. He holds his head high, golden blond hair gelled and styled exactly the way Jamie does his. They're so much more alike than I ever allowed myself to recognize, especially on the inside.

The day we went to the kilt shop to have everyone fitted, Lennox came to me wringing his hands, eyes misty because he didn't know if he should wear Stewart tartan—like my dad, for the name he's always carried—or Murray tartan. I told him he had the choice of two strong names from two men I love dearly, that the tartan he chooses doesn't make him who he is. He is a Stewart, but he is also a Murray.

I won't pretend I didn't see Jamie pull his glasses off and swipe at his eyes when he watched Lennox walk out of the dressing room in his family's tartan. Even Dad nodded his approval, looking a little choked up. Who knew buying kilts would be so emotional.

"Lennox sure cleans up nice," Dad says in my ear, sidling into the open space on my other side to watch out the window.

"He does—" My voice cracks a little and I have to inhale sharply to keep tears at bay.

Mum pulls Lennox into a hug and then steps back to assess him—moving a stray hair, fiddling with his sporran, picking something from his off-white sweater. When she finishes with him, he moves to stand to the right of the arch.

He's the only one standing with us today.

My breath catches when Jamie walks out, strides sure and strong, shoulders back in a sweater that matches Lennox's. Only the difference in their hair color sets the two apart today—and Jamie's meticulously trimmed beard, of course. The blue-and-green Murray tartan, struck through with lines of red, brown boots, and sporrans to match.

I can't believe they're mine.

I'm glad we opted for more casual kilt attire, with sweaters and boots, over the more formal suit-like jackets and vests, shined shoes, and kilt hose. It feels right. All of this does.

Trailing behind Jamie comes Willow, Breck's daughter, with a camera slung around her neck, clicking pictures of Jamie walking toward the arch. For an eight-year-old, she's pretty damn good with that thing. Rory told me she assists with all their elopements back home and sometimes ends up with the best shot of the day when they go through all the images.

I wonder with a smile what the best shot from today will be.

Jamie finds his place between Breck and Lennox, and I blow out a breath. It's almost time.

"Are you ready?" Rory asks, her hand squeezing my lace-adorned shoulder.

Her fitted seafoam-green dress hits mid-calf over tall boots and she has a tartan blanket scarf wrapped around her shoulders. For mid-September, it's a bit cooler than usual, but at least it's not raining... yet. Her strawberry-blonde hair hangs over one shoulder in an elaborate braid, and she wears a smile that tells me there's nowhere she'd rather be.

"Aye, I am." I turn away from the window and walk over to the long mirror hanging on the entryway wall. My cheeks are pink, my freckles standing out against them, and my blonde hair falls in simple waves down my back, the sides pulled back and weaved together to hold it away from my face. I'm wearing my mum's dress—my something borrowed—and have never felt more beautiful.

It's all delicate cream lace over a champagne satin that slides against my skin. The A-line skirt falls over my hips and down to a short train, the bodice is cut in a deep V in both the front and back, and fluttering lace sleeves drape over my upper arms. It's feminine and romantic in the most effortless way.

Dad wraps a Murray tartan blanket scarf around my shoulders, squeezing them gently. "You look stunning, m'eudail," he says, and kisses my cheek.

He slides my hand into the crook of his arm and we walk to the door of the cottage. He's the only one in Stewart tartan today, the bolder red standing out against my off-white dress.

Rory opens the door for us and steps back a few feet, the click of the shutter going as she captures every movement. I reach for my bouquet of cream roses and purple-blue thistles, accented with greenery and white heather, off the sideboard with my free hand and we step out into the warm sunlight. My train swishes along the ground and I pull my tartan blanket scarf tighter around my shoulders.

Dad walks me with careful precision toward the arch and everyone stands, even Angus—holding firmly on to Aileen's hand. His body may be frail but there is nothing that could dampen the joy radiating off him. His smile is wide, reaching his eyes and making their grey color dance with barely concealed silver tears.

My gaze slides to Jamie and the whole world stands still. Our eyes lock and I almost falter a step at the look of blissful elation on his face. His delight makes a buzz break out over my skin, my heart rate beating a gleeful rhythm in my chest.

I love this man. I have loved him for as long as I've known him. And now I get to have him. My feet pick up their pace, carrying me toward him across the garden. The garden where our story began eighteen years ago; the garden where we broke; the garden where we found healing; the garden where we now get to choose each other for the rest of our lives.

My dad presses another kiss to my cheek when we come to stand before Jamie and Breck. There's no formal "giving me away"—just this kiss and a hug for Jamie where Dad whispers something in his ear that I can't hear. When they part, Jamie nods and says, "Always."

I melt at that word, at its implication, at its meaning for us.

Jamie takes both my hands in his, bringing them to his lips and making goose bumps break out across my skin.

Dad joins my mum and everyone sits. I hardly notice the click of the cameras or the way Rory and Willow move around us to capture the ceremony. I have eyes only for Jamie.

We opted to combine our vows with a traditional Scottish handfasting ceremony, and the overwhelming sense of belonging, of home, I feel with our hands clasped together, wrapped in a swath of Jamie's family tartan, has me feeling warm all over.

"Avonlea," Jamie begins but has to stop to clear his throat, his voice thick with emotion. "In this very garden, eighteen years ago, I met my soulmate, my true home. I might not have known it then, but I know it now. I love you. I have always loved you. And now I get to love you as my wife, as the mother of my son"—he glances over his shoulder to where Lennox stands, and their matching grins widen—"as my best friend. Tha gaol agam ort. Always."

Tears well in my eyes, brimming over as one slides down my cheek. The pad of his thumb moves across my skin to wipe it away and I take one shaky inhale, then another, preparing myself to speak my own vows over our hands.

"Jameson." I look up into his eyes and their green depths hold me there, entranced. "Our love has always been something more than I could understand. It spanned oceans and years where it had to bide its time for us to find each other again, but it was always there. Quiet and unimposing, patient. It's a love that lasts and the only kind of love I could ever want. Because it's yours. You are my family, our family, and we love you. Tha gaol agam ort. Always."

We're supposed to wait for Breck to say "you may kiss the bride," but we don't. Our love is no longer patient, it is wanting and insatiable as our mouths meet and the small crowd of our families hoots in celebration. The sound is a dull roar compared to the rushing of blood in my ears as I kiss my husband, the man I've always wanted and thought I would never have, the father of my son, the love of my life.

And what a life we're going to live now that we can finally be together.

EPILOGUE

Jamie – Three Months Later

I wind my arms around Avi's waist and press my nose into her waves, inhaling her floral scent and relishing the fact that she's here—in this place—with me. She melts against my chest with a sigh and I tighten my grip.

"What do you think?" I ask before pressing a kiss below her ear.

"It's beautiful, Jamie. I can see why you love it here so much." She winds her fingers through mine where they rest across her abdomen, keeping her gaze locked on the snowy expanse of trees and Tahoe's tall mountains in the distance outside the window.

"I do love it here, but do you know what I love more?" I ask, trailing my lips down her neck.

"What?" I can hear her smile as she snuggles in against me.

"You. And Nox. And our life on Skye." I punctuate each of these things with a kiss to her bare shoulder where her sweater has slipped down.

She turns in my arms, looping her own around my neck, and pins me with her brown eyes—full and bright but soft with the love we have for each other. Just as she presses her lips to mine, we're interrupted by a melodic voice with an Australian accent.

"So it's not just my parents who are all over each other all the time."

We pull apart to see Willow, Breck's daughter, standing beside Nox in the kitchen and staring with looks of disgust on their faces. It only makes me want to kiss Avi more.

"Yeah, they're insufferable," Nox scoffs.

I snort a laugh. "Big word there, bud," I say. "We're not that bad... Or we usually aren't, but now? Now I think I'll be truly insufferable about my affection for your mum."

And with that I tighten my grip around Avi's waist, slide a hand into her hair, and dip her low to kiss her senseless. I let it go on just long enough to draw out low groans from both kids before I stand Avi back up.

Nox's displeased "Ugh, gross, Dad" is the first thing I hear when we separate.

Dad.

It still brings me a rush of pure joy every time I hear the word. The first time he used it with me was the day Avi and I got married. I don't know if it was a conscious choice or just his way of protecting himself, waiting until he knew I wasn't going anywhere, to let me all the way in. I didn't want to pressure him, had told myself I'd be okay if he called me Jamie forever, but deep down I wanted that acknowledgment of who we are to each other more than anything.

Even now, as he chastises me, it makes me feel more than a single word should.

I turn and ruffle his hair. "Sorry, Nox, I just can't stop myself."

This earns me another eyeroll from him and a giggle from Willow.

"Stop yourself from what?" Breck asks, joining us in the open kitchen and dining space with Rory in tow.

"This," I say, and kiss Avi heartily again to a cacophony of renewed groans from the kids and laughs from the adults.

"Oy, yeah," Breck says with mirth. "I can't stop myself either."

And with that, he's pulling Rory into his arms for an equally passionate—if theatrical—kiss. The kids fall to the floor in exasperation, though I'm pretty sure they're laughing as well.

"Hey now, it looks like we're missing all the fun," Rory's brother Wes says, pulling his wife Joss into the fray from where they've just walked in the front door.

Willow shoots up from the floor, screams, "Uncle Wes!" and runs full tilt, slamming into him and knocking him backward.

"Hey, kiddo," he says, picking her up and running a hand down her curtain of dark hair. "It's good to see you."

"It's been ages!" Willow says, eliciting chuckles from the adults in the room. It's been less than six months since she and Breck moved to the States from Australia to be with Rory, but an eight-year-old's perspective on time is a bit different than ours.

When Wes releases her, it becomes a flurry of movement as hugs and hellos are exchanged, with Breck and Rory taking their turns to welcome the newcomers.

"Big day coming up. You feeling good?" Wes asks Rory, and then lowers his voice to a whisper we can all still hear. "You know if you want to back out, I'll drive the getaway car." He shoots a furtive glance at his best friend and nudges his sister playfully.

This leads to Breck tackling him to the carpet in the living room as raucous laughter ensues from all of us watching.

I think for the millionth time that it's a beautiful thing the way all this worked out. That Wes went to his best friend in Sydney for solace in a time when he needed escape and found the love of his life in the process. Then, in turn, Wes put Breck on a plane with Willow to escape to Tahoe in order to heal from his own heartbreak, only for him to fall in love with Wes's sister.

Turning away from the wrestling match, Joss faces me with a soft smile. "So glad you could make it home for the wedding, Jamie."

"Wouldn't have missed it. Who else is supposed to officiate seeing as Breck is the groom?" I say with a glance at Rory, who's watching her brother and her fiancé tumble around the floor with a wistful, and vexed, smile on her lips. Bringing my attention back, I pull Avi into my side. "Joss, this is Avonlea, my bride."

I plant a kiss to the top of her head, and that closeness helps relieve the pang in my chest as I say the words. Words I love to utter as often as I can, but they're words I learned from a man who's no longer here to say them to his own bride, and that hurts.

"I've heard so much about you," Avi says, pulling out from my arm so she can hug Joss.

"What about me?" Wes interrupts, finally having extricated himself from the headlock Breck had him in. "Haven't you heard about me? All good things, I'm sure."

Avi's melodic laugh breaks out as he pulls her from Joss and hugs her just as fiercely as he did his sister.

"I have—" She continues to laugh. "Mostly good things at least."

Wes's bark of laughter echoes off the high ceilings of the living room. He steps back only to have his gaze land on Nox, who looks a little unsure of the dynamics of this group, and then it jumps to me. Taking the two of us in.

"Damn, that is uncanny," Wes says.

"Wes," Rory chides at the same time Willow yells, "Swear jar!"

He instantly reaches for his wallet and hands her a twenty.

"Keep the change, I'm sure I'll owe you at least that much by the end of the night. Seriously though, who's going to introduce me to the best-looking guy here... And no, I don't mean you, Jamie."

I can see Joss restraining herself from rolling her eyes and I think Rory wants to hit him upside the head.

"This is our son, Lennox—or Nox," I say, my chest overflowing with the pride I feel to be able to call him such. To be able to claim this amazing kid in front of my best friend and her family, a family I've considered my own for a long time. Avi and Nox are just the newest and most important—at least to me—members of it.

"Well, it's nice to meet you, Nox. I'm Wes, or Uncle Wes, if you'd like."

Nox extends his hand and nods. "Willow told me I should call you Wessy." He doesn't even crack a smile when he says this, totally deadpan, and the whole group erupts into hysterics around him.

Wes most of all, having to forego the handshake to brace himself on his knees and catch his breath.

When he glances up, it's with a glare at Willow. "You," he says.

She points at herself with a look of innocence. "Me?"

He shakes his head and finally stands as the rest of us pull ourselves together. Rory offers Willow a high five, wiping tears of mirth from below her eyes. "That was amazing, oh my god." Wessy is Rory's nickname of choice for her brother—much to his chagrin.

"Yeah, yeah, everyone make jokes at my expense," he says, then turns his attention back to Nox. "I like you." Then, without preamble, he pulls him into a side hug and ruffles his blond hair, like they're best buds.

Nox's smile is infectious, growing wide just like mine, his green eyes alight... just like mine.

I watch my two families collide, and instead of any friction or dissonance, they meld perfectly, with ease.

A little while later, with food in our bellies and drinks in our hands, we sit around the large sectional in the middle of the living room while the sounds of Willow and Nox playing foosball from the next room over carry toward us. That was a new addition to the condo when Breck and Rory moved in, though most of the decor is the same as when I left it.

Because this is my house. Technically. At least for a few more weeks.

We have a week until Breck and Rory's wedding. Then while they go on their honeymoon to Canada, Avi, Nox, and I will stay here with Willow. In that time, I'll go through everything I left behind and figure out what I want to take home to Skye with me and what

I want to part with, and when they get back, we sign the papers that will make this condo theirs.

"How did your meetings go with your agent and publisher?" Rory asks, drawing me back to the group around me. "Was Aileen beside herself with pride?"

My grin widens. "They went great. It was good to meet with them in person to go over everything seeing as that won't be easy to do going forward. And Gran... well, she won them over with all her charms."

"If they had even an ounce of doubt about this story, she would've been the one to seal the deal, but they don't," Avi says, winding her arms around me on the couch as she snuggles closer. "You should've seen how excited they were about this new direction." She lowers her voice and attempts an American accent that I think is supposed to sound like Brent. "'The great Jameson L. Murray—from epic adventure to epic love stories—he can do it all.'" She laughs good-naturedly and returns to her normal voice. "I mean, he *can* do it all, but it's funny to see the way they fawn over him."

"I can't blame them, I'm dying to get my hands on this book myself," Rory says, giving me a very pointed look.

"Yeah, yeah, I know. Don't ruin your wedding present for yourself..."

"Wait, seriously? Do I get to read it on my honeymoon?" She's so excited, and I love the way she's always supported me in my career.

"Thanks a lot, mate," Breck says on a sigh. "Now I'll be competing with your book for her attention the whole time."

Rory gives him a playful shove and he grabs her hand and brings it to his lips.

"We're *not* talking about what you'll be getting up to on your honeymoon, thank you very much," Wes says from where he's sitting on the floor, propped up against the chair Joss is occupying.

"Where is your Gran?" Joss asks. "I thought she'd be here."

"She's staying with my parents, but she'll be at the wedding. So you can meet her then, if not before. She's excited to take in all the sights while she's here."

We arrived in the States a few days ago, flying into San Francisco so I could meet with my publishing team for *With Love, From Skye*. It felt monumental to have Gran with me while I signed my contracts and to meet the people who will be helping me bring her and Grandad's story to life.

I just wish he were here to see it happen. That he were here for this whole trip. I hate that he and Gran never had the chance to come visit Mum and Dad and see the distillery they helped build. But Gran's doing it now. We closed the Thistle & Tartan for a few weeks so we could all come out for Christmas and the wedding—we all needed a little step back, a little space.

Like she can sense the direction of my thoughts, Avi presses her lips to the side of my throat, which bobs as I try to rein in my emotions. Even after two months, it's still as raw as it was the day he passed. One day he was with us—laughing in the kitchen, sitting in the garden with Nox, eating dinner as a family—and the next he wasn't. Gran says it wasn't that his heart gave out on him while he was sleeping but that it had been waiting for the moment it was so full of love it couldn't fit any more. I like to believe that's true.

"We were sorry to hear about Angus," Breck says, and the room feels quiet and solemn now. "I'm glad we got to meet him at your wedding. I think I learned more about what I want my marriage to look like in those two weeks than I had in my entire life up to that point." He looks at Rory, and her turquoise eyes soften and go misty.

I clear my throat and try to keep my own from filling with tears. "Yeah, he had a lot of wisdom for me over the years. I wouldn't be where I am today without him." I glance around to find everyone watching me, and it leaves me feeling too exposed, vulnerable. "Speaking of marriage... y'all ready for the big day?"

I catch Rory's gaze and silently plead with her to take the conversation in a safer direction.

"Yes!" she says excitedly, taking the hint. "Everything is done and ready. I didn't want to be racing around the whole week leading up while you guys are here. I want to enjoy my time while I've got you all in one place." It's unlikely we'll be together again like this for a while. That's the only thing I wish could be different, that we didn't all live on different continents. "And you're sure you and Avi don't mind staying here with Willow while we go on our honeymoon?"

I bark a laugh. "A little too late to ask that, isn't it? What the hell else would you do with her if we said no?" She knows I won't be saying no.

"Fine, okay, I was just asking." She shoves at my arm from where she's perched on the loveseat next to Breck.

"I mean, we could have stayed here with her," Wes pipes in.

"You have your first anniversary to celebrate. Your cake is in my freezer by the way, if you want it..." Rory says.

"You've been carting that cake around from freezer to freezer for a year? Rory, seriously?"

"What? It's tradition!" she states.

"For fuck's sake," he mumbles under his breath... but not quiet enough.

"Swear jar!" Willow's shout comes from the other room and he groans.

"I owe her another twenty already, don't I?" He turns to look at Joss and she just shakes her head.

"You're ridiculous," she sighs out.

"You love me," he counters.

"I do." She presses a kiss to his lips.

"You know," Rory says, pulling all our attention to her, "if someone had told me last year that we'd all be married by the end of this one, I would've said they were crazy. But look at us now... happier than ever."

And she's right. I am happier than I've ever been. And I can see that's true for her and her brother as well.

"It's been a bit of an adventure, hasn't it?" I ask, taking everyone in. "But what an incredible gift that we all found love along the way."

Avonlea – Eighteen Months Later

"Mum!" Lennox comes running through the door to the kitchen, a frantic look in his eyes and a wide smile plastered to his face. "It's here! Where's Dad?"

His gaze flies around the kitchen, as if this is the most common place for him to be.

"Calm down, lad." Aileen stands from where she was sitting at the desk—Angus's old desk... My desk now. "What's here?"

He holds out the package that was tucked under his arm and, though she takes it, she falters a step to sit back in her chair, her other hand covering her heart. It can only be one thing.

"Did I hear Lennox call me?" Jamie asks, walking through the back door. He'd been reading on the swing, waiting for me to take my break... which I guess is now, considering the whole family has descended on my kitchen and completely distracted me—and everyone else.

"Dad! It's here!" Lennox shouts again, pointing at the box in Aileen's hands.

She lifts her bespectacled gaze to Jamie's and there's tears in her eyes and the softest, emotion-filled smile on her lips.

"The book?" he inquires quietly, awe and grief and anticipation warring on his features.

She nods and he moves toward her to perch on the desk in front of her. A place I watched Angus sit a million times over the years. It feels like the exact right spot for this.

With trembling hands, he takes the box from her and lifts his gaze to meet mine. Tears already streak my cheeks, and I'm not prepared for the overwhelming look of uncertainty I see behind his glasses. I move to stand beside him while Lennox does the same by Aileen, our family closing ranks for a moment we've been waiting so long for.

"You should open it," Jamie says to her. "It's your story after all."

Aileen has always been the strongest woman I know, but watching her steel her spine and reach for a pair of scissors to open the box that contains not only parts of herself but of the man she's loved her whole life, helps me to understand better just how strong she truly is.

She slides the hardcover book free of the box and its wrapping with a stunned expression. The watercolor and pencil sketch of Skye, the inn, letters and stamps, all combine to showcase everything about this book that makes it unique.

With Love, From Skye is emblazoned in gold foiling across the top.

Aileen's fingers trail over the letters, stopping on each one and giving particular reverence when she slides them across Jamie's name at the bottom.

"It's beautiful, Jameson," she whispers, flipping the cover open and finding the first page...

He reaches for my hand and watches her with bated breath, waiting for her reaction.

One tear slips free, followed by another and another as she reads the dedication silently to herself. Lennox's hand is braced on her shoulder and she grabs it in hers as she squeezes her eyes shut. When she opens them again, they're only for Jamie, and the smile on her lips is one that reminds me of how the pain love sometimes causes is worth it because it's better than not having loved at all.

"He would be so very proud of you, Jameson," she says to him. "He *is* so very proud of you."

Jamie's shoulders begin to shake beside me, and I squeeze his hand between both of mine. It's not until she stands to envelop him in a hug that I let go. This is a moment just for them and I can feel the love between them like a physical presence—almost like the love of another has engulfed them both.

I reach for the book Aileen set on the desk and Lennox moves to stand beside me as I flip it open, finding the same page she was just reading.

With one arm around my son and the other pressing a hand to my mouth, I read the dedication and feel everything inside me break and heal all at once.

There's something in finding love young.
Nurturing and protecting it, and holding it dear for a lifetime.
There's something else in seeing love break and choosing to forge ahead
on the harder road of mending it, watching it reform into something
entirely new.
I learned the value of both from one man.
My grandad.
He showed me both in how he loved my gran—but also in how he loved
me.

Acknowledgements

I may never live in Scotland, but there's something about it that feels like home to me, nonetheless. It's a place I feel drawn to and in awe of, and I feel honored to have had the chance to capture that on the page. I'm so grateful for the writers before me that showcased its beauty in such a way that I knew I had to write about it as well. I look forward to my next visit more than anything.

I had some incredible grandparents/grandparent figures in my life who inspired much of the way I portrayed Angus and Aileen. One in particular, my great-uncle Phil who called my grant-aunt Joanie his 'bride' often and with such love, inspired that aspect of Angus. It always stuck with me and I'm glad to be able to immortalize that little piece of him in this book.

I have grown so much as a writer in the past two years, through writing this series, and I am proud of where I am and of how far I have come. It breaks my heart a little to say goodbye to these characters, to this world I created all on my own and lived in for so long, but I am also so incredibly excited to see where I will go next. To see what story I will get to tell you next. I hope that you have loved the Love Along the Way crew as much as I have.

Now, for all the thank-yous that come with writing and publishing a book, because there are many!

I want to thank God, my light, my savior; without whom I would not be able to do what I do.

I want to thank my family. Traver, you've been my adventure partner for twenty-one years and with countless love letters passed back and forth, across oceans and continents, thank you for always being my favorite pen pal and my biggest supporter! To my kiddos, who are avid supporters of what I do, I'm so glad to have you both in my corner. Mom and Dad, thank you for always being willing to help, and even trying to make a Scotland research trip happen for this book (spoiler: flights are freaking expensive), I don't know what I'd do without you.

Now for the long list of people who support and encourage me daily. If I forgot someone, I'm sorry, know that I didn't do it on purpose...

Stefanie, this book wouldn't be what it is without you. When I was most insecure about making Jamie a dad and moving forward with the secret child plotline, you bolstered my courage and didn't let me back down from the challenge. Thank you for always being there for me!

Hannah, you've been a solid friend and sister for my entire writing career, and I look forward to many more years of us leaning on each other in the lightest and darkest of times, because we know they will come, but also know that Jesus will always carry us through them.

To my writing group girls: Stefanie, Grayson, India, Cindy, and MJ... I'm so glad to be part of our little group and I'm eternally grateful for the way we huddle together to lift each other up and support each other through every aspect of this crazy writing life we've signed up for.

To my beta readers: Stefanie, India, Brittany, Lulu, Christina, Megan, and Kayla... Your feedback means the world to me, and I appreciate the time you took out of your own lives to help make this book the best it could be.

To my editors, Britt and Brooke, thank you for the time and effort you put into not only editing my words to ensure that this book is the best version of itself for my readers but for taking the time to help me learn and grow as an author as well. I know I'm a better writer for having worked with you.

To Sam, my cover designer, for always finding a way to capture exactly what it is that I want with your art. I do not have the skills to create the beauty that you do, and I am so glad to have you in my corner (and somehow in my head) to create the covers you do.

To my street team, wow you guys really know how to make a girl feel loved and supported. You have amazed me with your constant praise and encouragement. I am blessed to have you all on my team!

To the bookstores, authors, friends, and followers who have bought my books, talked about my books, answered my questions, dropped into my DMs with your excitement and praise... I am grateful for every single one of you.

To ALL my readers, this book's success is greatly influenced by your choice to read it and share it with others. I know there are so many books out there and your choice to pick up mine is not something I take lightly. I appreciate you so much. I hope that you loved it!

About the Author

J.A. Forde is a romance writer, Navy wife, and full-time mom to two crazy kids (and a furry pup). She currently resides wherever the Navy has most recently told her to live. You'll likely find her with her nose stuck in a book... or more realistically chasing her two kids with an audiobook in her earbuds.

She loves to travel and go on adventures which is why her Love Along the Way series takes you to some of her favorite destinations. She hopes to write more books set in fun locales both as an escape for herself in writing, and for you as the reader!

instagram.com/the.sah.authormom

facebook.com/groups/5399737321294418

amazon.com/stores/J.A.-Forde/author/B0D8XR17Q5?ref

goodreads.com/author/show/50002193.J_A_Forde

pinterest.com/jafordeauthor/